Juliette Mead is an English-American dual national born in London in 1960. After graduating from Oxford with an English degree in 1981, she pursued a career in finance, working in Dallas, New York and London for various investment banks, as well as taking a year out to complete an MBA at INSEAD. She left finance to work as a headhunter in the City. She now lives in Wiltshire with her husband and two young children. *The Headhunter* is her first novel, and she is currently at work on a second.

The Headhunter

Juliette Mead

POCKET BOOKS

New York London Toronto Sydney Tokyo Singapore

First published in Great Britain by Pocket Books, 1994
An imprint of Simon & Schuster Ltd
A Paramount Communications Company

Simon & Schuster Ltd
West Garden Place
Kendal Street
London W2 2AQ

Simon & Schuster of Australia Pty Ltd
Sydney

A CIP catalogue record for this book is available from the
British Library.

ISBN 0–671–85231–0

Song on page 195 'Je ne sais pas où tu commences' written by
Georges Moustaki and Hubert Rostaing is quoted from the album
Georges Moustaki – Here's To You arranged and conducted by Hubert
Rostaing (Polydor)

Dictionary quotations reproduced by kind permission of:
Thomas Nelson English Teaching
Oxford University Press
Longman Group UK

Typeset in Sabon by
Hewer Text Composition Services, Edinburgh
Printed in Great Britain by
HarperCollinsManufacturing, Glasgow

ACKNOWLEDGEMENTS

My sincere thanks to Julia Kreitman and Ginny Iliffe, without whose encouragement I would never have attempted to write a book at all.

My equally sincere thanks to Jane Bradish-Ellames of Curtis Brown and Jo Frank of Simon & Schuster, without whose help, support and confidence I would certainly have never written this one.

I have a great list of friends to thank for reading various stages of the book: Tina Jenkins, Lea Noudelman, Beate von der Seipen, Anette Falkner, Elise Ballantyne, Simon Gillis, Ilene Hersher, Georgina Brown, James Del Favero, Christine Mead, John Mackay and Laura Jenkinson. Their comments, corrections and enthusiasm were invaluable.

I would also like to thank two people whose friendship and example have taught me a great deal about the art of headhunting: Susie Cummings and Philippa Rose.

A great and continuing debt of gratitude is owed to my husband, my parents, Tom and Eleanor Mead, and my two sisters; I would also like to acknowledge the contribution of my two sons, without whom this book would have been finished far more quickly . . .

For Guy

headhunter, a company or a person, that tries to find suitable managers, or people for certain jobs, by approaching the managers direct. Usually this contact is made without the manager's present company knowing about it. Often the offer of a job by a headhunter is accompanied by an offer of increased salary, etc.
(*Collins Business English Dictionary*)

head-hunter, savage who collects heads of his enemies as trophies
(*Oxford English Dictionary*)

headhunter – see killer.
killer: slaughterer, butcher, huntsman; lynch mob; homicidal maniac, psychopath; headhunter, cannibal; predator, bird of prey, beast of prey, man-eater.
(*Roget's Thesaurus*)

PROLOGUE

FRIDAY, OCTOBER 4TH, 1991

Glory hated London. She hated the fact that people couldn't understand her accent; that people didn't know where Oklahoma City was; that you couldn't buy an edible hotdog in the whole of the United Kingdom let alone London; that you couldn't get a decent Bloody Caesar – not even at Harry's Bar; that the so-called dealmakers took two weeks even to arrange a meeting; that everyone she met seemed to have gone either to Oxford or Cambridge, and seemed to know everyone else she'd ever met; that the traffic was terrible, that her flat was squalid, that nobody cleaned up when their dogs crapped on the street, that people stopped working at seven o'clock at night, that everyone then went to the *the-ah-ter* or the *op-a-rah*. She hated London; hated it with a vengeance. She was determined to go back to New York – back home – but she had only been here for a month so far and was damned if she was going to go back before she'd proved her point.

Glory's sense of outrage and injustice at being dumped into the anachronistic City of London was so great that she was blind to the beauty of the place. She didn't even see how brightly the sun shone, how the trees fluttered in the lightest of breezes. All she could see was the queue of cars held up by an oversized truck trying to turn at the end of Charlotte Street. She crashed the gears of her Mercedes sports car, and then reversed the wrong way down a one way street to turn left into Oxford Street, ignoring the large sign that said 'Buses and taxis only. Private vehicles prohibited'. She was already fifteen minutes late for work, and would have missed the morning meeting, thanks to the traffic. If the cops stopped her, she could always flash her biggest smile and wave her American passport through the window. Damn traffic. Damn London. Damn the Brits, the whole goddamn lot of them.

Candida Redmayne reclined in her chair, stretching her extravagant black-stockinged legs out so that her feet protruded from beneath her desk, and slowly lit a cigarette. She luxuriated in the sense of her own power before picking up the telephone line that flashed impatiently at her.

'Malcolm? I'm so sorry to keep you waiting,' she drawled lazily, inwardly delighted to have left a director of Hayes Goldsmith on hold for at least three minutes. 'How can I help you?'

Her manner was unctuous, but her tone of voice made it clear who she believed was really serving whom. As she talked, her eyes strayed around her office, taking in the understated elegance that she herself had created, all the trappings of power and influence, with none of the tat that one found so frequently in City offices. None of the second-rate prints of English hunting scenes, none of the green leather library chairs that sought to be antique and cracked, none of the highly polished mahogany that reeked of beeswax. Candida's office was, like Candida herself, beyond definition: somewhere between an art nouveau salon and an intimate sitting room, furnished in cool greys, leather and rubbed silk, and ornamented by one calm, Piper print on one wall, and on the other a silver-framed, free form painting by her three-year-old niece. Early Georgian armchairs were scattered amongst Eileen Gray leather and steel originals, and the soft colours and contours of the room were thrown into stark contrast by an enormous display of rather lurid purple delphiniums slap bang in the middle of the low coffee table. Opposite her desk was a Regency mirror, and as she listened to Malcolm, she regarded her own reflection with a considerable degree of satisfaction.

Candida Redmayne was not in the first flush of youth, but other than the look of experience in her eye, and the faint curl of cynicism in her lips, there was nothing to betray the fact that she was nearly thirty-seven. There are women whose faces, at the age of thirty-six, promise a mature beauty yet to come, and there are others whose faces bear witness to a lost girlish prettiness. Candida had always worn her age perfectly; at seventeen, she had been radiantly pretty, at twenty-six, she had been considered a great beauty, and now, ten years later, she had developed into an arrestingly lovely woman. Her legs were seen by many as her best feature, impossibly long, slim, endless legs, with a delicate knee, a shapely calf, and a fragile ankle. Not for her the severe, box-like suits adopted by so many women in the City. Candida wore her skirts short – very short. She liked the impact of a severe appearance from the waist up, the tailored navy blazer, the brilliant white shirt, so that when she stood up to greet a visitor, their eyes plummeted immediately to her flirty skirt, undeniably sexy legs, and ridiculously high heels. It threw people – even women – off their guard, and Candida loved throwing people off their guard. Her large eyes were a clear, limpid blue, a shade most commonly seen in flawless aquamarines, fringed by dark, feathery lashes and eyebrows with a – not entirely unartificial – quirk. Her nose was perhaps a little too sharp to allow her qualification as a true classic beauty. Her glorious auburn hair had been marshalled into a strict, uncompromising chignon, but a few tendrils had escaped to cling around the nape of her neck. She rarely wore make-up, taking pride in her even-toned, alabaster complexion, and never wore perfume. Candida smelt of — Candida.

At the age of sixteen, whilst captain of lacrosse at a famous girls' public school, she had been approached by one of the leading modelling agencies. Two things had set her against a modelling career: first, the fact that her height of five foot seven inches would prevent her from working on a catwalk, the key to any model's success in the eighties, and second — and more important — her mind was too fierce, too independent, and all too dominant for her to end up using her body alone. Candida wanted to rule the world — and in her own eyes, she had come pretty damn close to doing so.

Still gazing at her own reflection, she interrupted Malcolm Fairchild. 'Malcolm, let me make something perfectly clear. I can't represent you. I have told you a thousand times that I only work for five clients, and if and when I choose to lose one of them, you will be the first person I contact. Until then, there's nothing I can do.'

'Candida, I'm not even asking you to take us on as a client — of course I want you to — but I understand your position. I'm asking you to take our people off limits; stop poaching them. Bill Burrage was really the last straw. Have you seen what *The Times* City Diary wrote about it? Doesn't our relationship mean anything to you? Can't you for once put your personal feelings above your professional ones?'

'My feelings don't enter into this,' Candida replied calmly, as she looked at the column in *The Times* which reported the defection of Bill Burrage from Hayes Gold-smith to Morgan Stanley, 'personal or otherwise. This is a question of judgement — and my personal and professional judgement is no, we can't take your people off limits. You are not a client, and therefore your people are not off limits. Do I make myself clear?' She ringed the Diary article with a thick red marker.

There was no answer from the other end of the phone.

'Do I make myself clear, Malcolm?' she repeated, a sharp edge entering her tone of voice.

'Yes; abundantly, painfully and characteristically clear, Candida. You always make yourself clear. It's just that it's very hard for me – people knowing about us, the Board talking and everything – they don't understand why I can't persuade you to lay off our people, that's all. It's almost as though you're carrying out some sort of a vendetta, for Christ's sake. You've taken six of our best people off the desk since February. It's very embarrassing, I don't know what to tell them . . .'

'Tell them the truth. Tell them you don't own me. Tell them that all I do is find their staff better jobs. Tell them it's time they thought about why their employees were so easy to move. Tell them to stuff it. Tell them whatever you like – I really don't care – but stop telling me your problems. You get on with your job, and I'll get on with mine.' Candida hung up the telephone. A thin smile played across her lips as she dialled the number of Joanna French, lead columnist for *The Times* City Diary. Joanna was out, but Candida had a bottle of champagne sent round with a thank-you note so that Joanna would find it on her desk on her return. Candida always, but always, paid her debts.

There had been a time, years ago, when she first started her headhunting business, when Candida would have died rather than hang up on a director of Hayes Goldsmith. But times had changed. She now ran the most successful, the most exclusive, the most sought after headhunting firm in the City of London. She was fiercely proud of her achievement, and rightly so.

The fact that she had been sleeping with Malcolm Fairchild for a little more than a year was neither here nor there. Business was business.

*   *   *

The dealing room of Steinberg Roth and Partners rang with the shouts of frenzied traders, desperately trying to cover their positions after hearing the announcement from the US Department of Labor of unemployment figures for the previous month. Unemployment was up 4.6 per cent, when the whole market had bought the dollar, in expectation of an improvement. The last thing a trader who was long the dollar, in layman's terms holding a large position in the currency, needed was bad news. The whole market was in uproar. The whole market except Mike Miccinelli, that is. Mike leaned well back in his chair, put his feet up on the desk, and lit a large cigar, smiling at the frantic activity going on around him. The dealing floor of Steinberg Roth in London was a caricature of City dealing rooms, a cross between a battery chicken coop and a space-age technology centre. The salesmen and traders were packed into one long narrow desk, barely a foot between each person, huddled behind their dealing screens which blinked like the life support systems in an ICU. The air, even at this time in the morning, was already acrid with cigarette smoke. The shouts rang across the room, virtually bouncing off the walls.

'Jeeeeee-sas Christ! Jeeeeee-sas fucking Christ!'
'Done! I'll sell you twenty dollars – yours at a quarter!'
'Don't pick up twenty-two, for fuck's sake! It's Merrill – don't touch that fucking line – '
'Jeeeeee-sas H Christ!'

Mike held a special position at Steinberg's. He was a proprietary trader, which meant that he invested the firm's capital in foreign currencies for short or long term positions. This enabled him to stand back from the crowd of traders forced to quote buy and sell, or 'bid' and 'offer', prices to the competition day in and day out. He simply surveyed the market, noted the sentiment of his less exalted colleagues, decided his strategy, placed his bets, and sat back to await the result. He was normally right, although the size of his bets had regularly scared his department manager half to death. In the two years since he had returned from Steinberg's head office in New York, Mike had established such a glowing reputation that department managers across the firm were told to bite their tongues and sweat, but not to get in the way of Mike's trades. People on the desk said that Mike could smell money being made or lost, and if he didn't like the way the market was going, he made it change direction. Mike would say that the mark was crapping out, and sell 250 million. The mark would rise, and Mike would turn around and sell a billion. When the mark then really did begin to crap out, he'd turn to his boss, and say, 'See? What did I tell you?' Nerves like Mike Miccinelli's made steel look like plywood.

Spig Hall, one of the junior traders, stopped by his desk and raised an eyebrow inquiringly. 'How did you do, Mike?'

Mike leant forward to peer more closely at the screen blinking provocatively in front of him. 'Okay,' he shrugged.

'What's okay?'

'I scored. Up seventeen and a half million so far,' he drawled.

Spig prostrated himself on the carpet at Mike's feet. '*Il Duce!*' he said, with veneration.

'Mike! Pick up line twenty-eight!' A disembodied voice shouted from the mêlée.

'Yo!'

'Is that Mike Miccinelli?'

'Sure is.'

'Michael, my name is Candida Redmayne, of ARC. I'm a headhunter, and I would like to meet you. Is this a bad time to call?'

'No time like the present, as I always say.' Mike flipped

open the diary on his desk. 'I'll be with you this afternoon. Say five thirty?'

'That will be fine. Nineteen Finsbury Square, five thirty. I'll look forward to it.'

'You and me both.'

On the other side of London, in a leafy garden in Notting Hill Gate, a pretty young woman wearing cut off jeans and a sloppy sweatshirt lay on the grass, idly turning the pages of a magazine. She felt too mellow even to read. England was enjoying a rare Indian summer, and the sunshine filtered lazily through the trees, licking the woman's bare arms and legs with delicious warmth and lulling her to sleep. On the other side of Stanley Gardens, she could hear the normal sounds of London, children playing, traffic, the muffled thump of rock music coming from an open window, the worried voice of one of her neighbours calling for a dog . . .

Teddy made an effort to stir herself. It was nearly noon, and high time she did something productive. Sitting up suddenly, as if she had just decided on a course of positive action, she reached out for a bottle of suntan oil, applied it to her bare legs – liberally, as directed – and lay back down, wallowing in a sense of contentment. On the point of falling asleep, she was jolted back to consciousness by the mobile phone, buzzing impatiently beside her.

'Hello? Oh, Charlie, darling! I'm *so* glad its you! I couldn't bear to talk to anybody else. I'm lying in the garden and feeling so lazy and indulgent, and it's such a lovely day,' she prattled on, before finally asking, 'Why have you called? What's up?'

'Teddy, you goose, you called me. You left a message for me to call you urgently.'

Her deliciously throaty laughter rippled down the telephone line. 'I think the sun must have got to my brain!

Of course I called you! I wanted to ask you to dinner. Tomorrow. Mike's invited a friend of his from the States, and she sounds terrific, and I thought maybe just the four of us would have dinner – you know I can't really cook, but I'll do something simple – and she sounds right up your street – racy, American, unattached – I haven't met her though, and you never know, it might just be the start of something wonderful, for you – and her, of course, though she might not be good enough for you, nobody could be, darling – '

He interrupted her mid-stream, knowing from long experience that Teddy could talk without a pause for hours.

'I'd love to come. Shall we say about eight o'clock?'

'Oh, try to come earlier so that I can have you all to myself for a little bit – '

'I'll do my best. I've got to go, Ted – the market's really moving. See you tomorrow.'

Charles hung up, the smile still lingering on his lips as he thought about Teddy Winnington.

In a small hotel on the Left Bank of Paris, Jack Delavigne put his suitcase on the bed and started to unpack. He always stayed at the Saint Simon when he came to Paris, partly for sentimental reasons, and partly because he detested the large luxury hotels favoured by his peers; the characterless George V, the Bristol, even the Meurice had become little more than conference centres for jetsetting executives. At least at the Saint Simon he was safe from bumping into colleagues and clients, and could have the privacy to think his own thoughts. He unpacked the few shirts and ties necessary for a three day trip. He still had an hour before his lunch appointment with the investment director of Paribas. At the bottom of the suitcase was a small, silver-framed photograph. On examination, the photograph looked very old and worn; it was in black and white, and was heavily creased, with a tear across one corner, but the frame shone brightly. It was regularly and lovingly polished. Jack took it out and sat down heavily on the bed, gazing intently at the snapshot, lost in thought. Finally, he put the little frame on his bedside table, and by putting his head in his hands and pressing his fingers against his eyes, saw only a dull red darkness, and was able to blot out the image that so obsessed him.

Alex Fitzgerald put the fear of God into most people. In fact, many people who met him secretly suspected that he *was* God. And if he wasn't God, the next most likely option was the devil. There were those of his staff who couldn't resist sneaking a look at his feet whenever Alex went out in the snow . . . it was truly amazing how quickly it melted. As one of the senior partners of Steinberg Roth in Europe he held almost unrivalled power in the business and financial worlds, and was intent that people shouldn't forget it.

This Friday morning he was like a bear with a sore head, roaring around his office and growling at his long suffering secretary, Louise. Most people felt sorry for Louise, wondering how she put up with his boundless energy and exacting standards. Louise, however, had spent the past six years of her life working for Fitz, and knew that this sort of display of bad temper was not threatening. She feared Alex most when he was cold and silent. Alex Fitzgerald's bite was far, far worse than his bark.

'Louise! Where the hell is that itinerary? I asked you to have it ready first thing!'

'It's on top of your in-tray, Mr Fitzgerald.'

'And where the hell is Nat Kovitch?'

'He's on his way up now, Mr Fitzgerald.'

'And coffee . . . Where's my coffee?'

'On the tray by the window, Mr Fitzgerald.'

'God damn it, Louise! What do I have to do to get some fresh coffee – brew it myself? Roast the fuckin' beans? Can't anybody do anything right round here?'

'I'll get some more right away, Mr Fitzgerald. Is there anything else you require?'

Alex only grunted. It was not distinguishable as an apology, but it was as good as one in Louise's book. He flipped open *The Times* to the City Diary page, to check that Steinberg was not mentioned in a derogatory fashion. Alex Fitzgerald was a man who had an unhealthy concern for image – both his own, and that of the firm. His eyes fell on a small item at the bottom of Joanna French's daily column:

'Oh, dear, what can the matter be at Hayes Goldsmith? In the good old days the only way people left Hayes was to be carried out in a coffin, but ARC, the headhunters led by the redoubtable Candida Redmayne, appear to have launched a virtual exodus, culminating with yesterday's desertion by Bill Burrage to the fixed income desk of Morgan Stanley. Are there any more rats to come, we wonder? Better ask Ms Redmayne – she seems to be in better control than some we could mention . . .'

A slow smile spread across Alex's face.

'Forget about the coffee, Louise; this pot is just dandy. Get me Candida Redmayne on the phone, could you?'

Christian de Clement-Grandcourt picked up his Patek Philippe from the bedside table, and saw that it was a quarter to one. He would be a little late for lunch. He sighed, snapped it on to his tanned wrist, and levered himself out of bed gently, so as not to wake the luscious blonde who lay tumbled in a pile of sheets next to him. He dressed quickly, as a man who is accustomed to having to dress quickly, then sat down at the escritoire to pen a short note on the paper provided by the hotel:

'It was, as it always is, a sublime interlude in an otherwise brutal world. I leave tomorrow for an extended trip to New York, but will call you on my return. Amuse yourself whilst I am away. I will count the hours. Devotedly.'

He was not about to leave for the States, but Christian hated goodbyes, and he had never 'ended' a relationship. It seemed so unchivalrous, such an unkind way to repay a woman after a few months, or even weeks, of intimacy. Far better to leave things on a note of hope. And anyway, he didn't rule out the possibility that he might find himself missing Helene's warm, full body in a few weeks' time. Surely it would be a mistake to make any abrupt decisions at this point. He extracted a large wad of franc bills from his wallet, and slipped the money and the note into an envelope which he tossed on to the bed.

He checked that the requisite roses and champagne had been left chilling in ice in the basin, and shut the door behind him, taking the stairs two at a time. With a wink at the receptionist, who had the discretion not to wink back, Christian de Clement-Grandcourt slipped out of the front door of the Hotel Saint Simon, and into the back seat of the discreet black car waiting outside.

In an apartment on Seventy-Eighth street, on New York's Upper East side, Esther Levenson was woken up by what sounded like a cab screaming down the street. She opened one eye. It was two a.m. She still had three hours sleep left before she had to get ready for work. She turned over, and was rapidly snoring.

CHAPTER ONE

The CV, though brief, told a story of glowing academic and professional success:

CURRICULUM VITAE

Michael Miccinelli

Age: 32
Nationality: British
Marital status: Single

Education: Caius College, Cambridge BA/MA
                    Economics, First Class Honours
                    Harvard Business School MBA; Baker
                    Scholar.
                    Thesis on Business Psychotheory

Employment: 1990–present Steinberg Roth and
                    Partners, London
                    Manager, Proprietary Trading
                    1986–1990 Steinberg Roth, New York
                    Principal Foreign Exchange Trader
                    1981–1984 Shearson Lehman Brothers,
                    London
                    Foreign Exchange Trader

Interests: Sport (rowing, squash to competitive
                      standard)
                      Economics
                      Wine

Candida tapped these brief details into the computer
database and rose from her desk as the receptionist showed
Mike Miccinelli into her office.

Hollywood had shaped the image of the 'young Turk', but
in many ways Mike Miccinelli had perfected it. Candida
knew a lot more about Mike than his CV revealed. She
knew that he commanded the respect of his male peers,
inspired the desire of his female peers, and provoked the
trepidation of his counterparties in the market. She knew
he was no good at conforming; if Mike Miccinelli didn't
like a rule, he simply had it changed. He had an ego the
size of a house, but he didn't need to have it stroked; she
suspected he did all the necessary stroking himself. Mike
was a self-made man, and considered himself a blueprint.
Before deciding to interview Miccinelli, Candida had made
a series of discreet checks in the market, phoning former
and present colleagues to see how they evaluated the man.
It was clear that he was not universally popular, but he
was respected, and no one had questioned his professional
abilities. She rarely interviewed traders; by and large, she
found them to be arrogant, self-obsessed, and intrinsically
boring. But Mike Miccinelli seemed to be playing in another
league. Candida was used to making rapid assessments, and
as soon as he entered the room, her trained gaze took in the
confident challenge in his nearly black eyes, the aggressive
tilt of his chin and the consummate ease with which he
took possession, uninvited, of her sofa. This was the aspect
of headhunting that Candida really loved – the strange
intimacy that could spring up between two people meeting

for the first time; the knowledge that she had the chance – no, the right – to ask the most personal question, and have it answered.

'Do sit down,' Candida said coolly as she walked from behind the seclusion of her desk, but as she had anticipated, she failed to disconcert him. To the contrary, he ignored her sarcasm, and emitted a low whistle.

'I've heard a lot about you, but nobody told me you were so good-looking.'

'I've heard a lot about you, too, but that's not the description that leaps to most people's lips.'

He laughed easily and leant forward, relishing a bout with this extraordinary woman, in order to have a better look at her legs. A long and leisurely look.

'Have you quite finished? Perhaps we can return to the purpose of this meeting . . .'

Candida was keen to assume control of the interview, and sensed that Mike wasn't going to be an easy subject. None the less, she was able to steer him adeptly into a discussion of his past career, his current position at Steinberg Roth, and his aspirations for the future, taking careful notes. Mike talked openly and expansively. He believed in talking to headhunters – you never knew when they might come in handy, and he was a born opportunist – and anyway, he loved talking about himself. Candida deftly steered the dialogue into less tangible areas, trying to build a thumbnail portrait of Mike's personality.

'What motivates you, Mike? What makes you get up in the morning? What drives you?'

He returned her stare unblinkingly. 'Winning. Sex. Money. Power. All the standard drives. I'm a pretty ordinary guy, I guess.'

'No, I don't think so, and I don't believe you do. Who do you trade with?

'Anyone who'll pick up the phone.'

'And why do you like trading?'

'I'm good at it. It's a buzz.'

'Is that why you like sex?' Candida asked in an innocent tone of voice.

'Yes. But trading lasts longer. It's better than sex, most of the time. Aren't you going to ask me who I have sex with?'

'No, because it would be a waste of time; I suspect I know your answer: "Anyone who'll pick up the phone . . ."'

'My, oh, my . . . You can read me like a book!'

'What frustrations do you have at the moment?' Candida resumed her questioning.

'I have one very large, growing frustration,' Mike drawled suggestively.

Candida's eyes turned steely. 'What's that?'

'Why don't you try to find out?'

'I will, but on one condition.'

'What's that?'

'That you stop talking like a script for a new *Carry On* film; *Carry On Trading*, perhaps,' Candida snapped, and was rewarded by a burst of laughter.

'Okay, you're on. I'll come clean and make a general confession, but I have one condition, too.'

Candida raised one eyebrow.

'Come to dinner with me tomorrow night.' She frowned, and he continued, 'Not just with me – don't worry – my fiancée and I are having a little party. I'd like you to join us . . . with your husband, if you like . . .'

Candida inclined her head graciously. 'I'd like that. But I'm not married, I'll come alone. Who is your fiancée?'

'Teddy. Theodora Winnington. Do you know her?' Candida made a note, and searched her memory. 'It rings a bell, but I don't think I've met her. No, I don't think so. Doesn't she work at Steinberg's too?'

'She used to, but they don't approve of husbands

and wives both working for the firm ... You know, Chinese walls, conflicts of interest, all that crap. She's looking for a job. She's the one you should talk to, not me. She's a real class act, if I say so myself.' He looked smug. 'I'll put in a good word for you ... You scratch my back – maybe I'll get the chance to scratch yours ...'

Candida's smile vanished.

'So, tell me what's wrong, or what's so right, about Steinberg Roth ...' she said briskly.

After Mike Miccinelli had left, Candida returned to the computer to record the interview. She rated him an 'A', meaning that professionally he was top calibre, and entered her initials after it, so that her colleagues would know which consultant had scored him. Mike had left her in no doubt that he was content at Steinberg's and therefore not mobile. She moved the cursor down to the entry labelled 'Relationship:' and added 'E: T Winnington'. This would explain to anyone who was familiar with ARC's internal coding that Mike was engaged to T Winnington. Recording these little personal details was an important part of her database, and could avoid substantial embarrassment. In the space left for a personal summary conclusion, she typed: 'Cocky, self-centred bastard. A bit of rough who has polished up well. Poor boy made good. Will continue to go far.'

Then she tapped in 'WINNINGTON' and hit the search key. There were three Winningtons listed. She selected T Winnington, and read the following entry:

'Theodora Winnington (aka Teddy). Age 28. British. New College, Oxford. Left Steinberg Roth Corporate Finance dept August '91. Good track record. Worked under Pitt-Rivers. Said to be charming and competent to boot. Intelligent, disciplined, hardworking, well-connected. A looker. A real catch.'

Candida took great care to keep her files updated and cross-referenced. Nothing was more valuable to her business than her database, and nothing was more valuable to Candida than her business. She methodically moved the cursor to the 'Relationship' field and added 'E: M Miccinelli'.

A real catch. Lucky old Mike Miccinelli.

Mike had finally agreed to have the party at Teddy's house, rather than his own more spacious flat. One of the perks of working for Steinberg Roth was that the company provided him with an apartment in a prestigious Kensington mansion block. Mike loved the flat. It was about as far removed from his parents' little terraced house in North Shields as a house could be. He loved the large rooms, made more spacious by the virtual absence of furniture. He loved the white walls, the white silk curtains, and the nearly white wall-to-wall carpets. His parents' home was full of colour and clutter, dreadful reproductions of famous paintings and vases full of plastic tulips dumped permanently on the enormous television. He loved the hi-tech kitchen, although he rarely touched anything in it other than the fridge and the microwave. Most of all, he loved the marble-clad shower, which was not only equipped with a high-pressure power-shower, with a full range of massage, needle and champagne jets, but also with a state-of-the-art, pre-programmed telephone which had its own niche within the shower cubicle, just in case Mike felt the urge to trade with Tokyo or Helsinki, and couldn't be bothered to walk to the bedroom phone. Teddy's hatred of his flat centred on that telephone. She had once tried to sabotage it by holding it directly under the full force of the massage jet, but she had not succeeded, much to her chagrin and Mike's relief.

Teddy lived not far from Mike in a little house – almost a cottage, tucked on to the end of Stanley Gardens, a tree-lined street off Ladroke Grove. The house had been a present from Teddy's grandmother, who had used it as a *pied-à-terre* until she had become too old to make regular trips to London. Out of loyalty to her grandmother, Teddy had not removed a single item of furniture, nor a single painting from the house in the seven years that she had lived there. She wanted Matty to feel perfectly at home on the few occasions a year when the old lady came to stay in Teddy's guest bedroom, and besides, Teddy liked the house to be filled with little treasures, lovingly collected by her grandmother over a lifetime of travel. It gave her a sense of continuity, a sense of belonging. Looking round her at the drawing room piled high with old Sunday papers, worn tapestry cushions, bridal magazines, discarded clothes, cosmetics, silk scarves tossed carelessly over the backs of chairs, and all the other detritus of a single-but-about-to-be-married woman's life, Teddy was forced to admit that one could take the spirit of continuity a bit too far. The house *was* a little small, and would require a major clean-up before tonight's party.

Pushing up her sleeves, she set to work. She heaved all the debris that littered the room into one enormous pile and stuffed it under the sofa. She had always found this the most effective method of clearing up; first, the room was left spotless, and second, those things that she didn't retrieve within a week could be safely left there undisturbed. She reasoned that anything she wasn't forced to dig out, she probably didn't need. She scampered around the little house, plumping a cushion here, arranging a bowl of full-blown roses there.

It was going to be hard work persuading Mike to move in with her after they had finally tied the knot, but she was determined that this should be their marital home. At the moment Mike was hung up on his Kensington flat — particularly as it was rent free — but Teddy felt confident that she could bring him round in time, and persuade him that in this day and age, money was no longer everything. She felt sorry for Mike, was deeply sensitive to his feelings, and knew how much the trappings of success meant to him. He had hated his childhood, and still disliked his parents because they evoked too many memories of the poverty and deprivation of his youth. Although Teddy admired how far Mike had been able to come, with all the odds against him and only his innate talent to rely on, she was secretly embarrassed by his materialism, and believed that she could change him with gentle coaxing.

She turned her attentions to the kitchen. It was a bomb site. There are some people who do the washing up after they have eaten, and there are some people who are only forced to do the washing up when they are about to eat. Teddy Winnington definitely belonged to the latter category. Satisfied with the state of the house, Teddy thought about the provisions for the party, and bolted to the shops, or rather, to one shop.

If you had to pick one place *not* to be late on a Saturday afternoon, one place in the whole of London, it would be Harrods Food Hall, Teddy thought as she battled and pushed her way through the crowds of tourists and impatient shoppers. And yet, it was Harrods Food Hall where she found herself most Saturday afternoons. Teddy was an impulsive and generous hostess. She frequently felt the urge to entertain on a Friday, arranged last-minute dinner parties for Saturday night, and then spent a couple of hours lying in bed with her cookery books on Saturday morning, leafing through page after page of tantalising photographs before accepting that her culinary skills simply weren't up to a terrine of langoustine and tomato aspic, or a galantine of pheasant. Reluctant to serve her guests the one meal she had absolutely mastered — *les oeufs brouillés sur ses lits de toast* — she resorted time and time again to the trusted banks of pre-cooked food deep in the cavernous belly of Harrods. Fortunately, nobody ever seemed to mind, and she and Mike were easily able to afford the steep prices that Harrods levied on lazy, or hopeless, cooks. She paused at the fresh vegetable counter, surveying the immense variety of continental lettuces, thinking to compensate for buying a prepared Mexican feast by making her own salad, but after careful thought, and a glance at her watch, Teddy decided it was too much effort, and loaded up on ready-bagged mixed salad.

Her plans for an intimate dinner for four, a bid to matchmake Charles with Mike's friend Glory, had exploded into a buffet dinner for sixteen – no, seventeen, she remembered. Mike had mentioned that he had asked another woman, a headhunter, at the last minute. Teddy and Mike seemed, to an outsider, to have little in common except their good looks and shared penchant for doing things at the last minute. It must be something to do with working in the City, Teddy mused. She was always under such pressure to race from one deadline to the next; to be efficient, to be accurate, to be punctual, if not early, to be ahead of the game, so that when the office doors closed behind her, everything else in her life seemed to erupt into chaos. She was on the point of leaving Harrods, weighed down with carrier bags, when she remembered that she hadn't picked up the month's load of clothes left at the dry cleaner, and they would now be closed for the weekend. Bolting back through the huge swing doors, she raced to the first floor to find something to wear.

By nine o'clock that night, the party was in full swing; the French doors on to the garden were flung open, the Margaritas were flowing, and the guests vied with the jazz tape to be heard.

'Hey, Miccinelli! What about the dollar? I say it's time

to go long dollar, short the mark – the charts say we're set for a dead cat bounce – '

'– so I went down the road to that little auction house on Lots Road, and they had *three* Georgian fireplaces for a fraction of the price – '

'Where did you get that suit, Stevie? Is it St Laurent?'

'Well, I'm still going to put my money on Bush. The Midwest is never going to give a draft-dodging adulterer the keys to the White House.'

'You're dreaming. The dollar's going to hell in a hand basket. How many times have I told you that the point about a dead cat is that it only bounces when it hits the bottom! Also, that it means it's dead. Any trader worth his braces knows the dollar hasn't begun to find its floor yet – '

'Teddy, we've taken a simply wonderful villa in Umbria for next May; seven bedrooms, a pool, a tennis court, a cook. What about you and Mike coming for a week or two – '

'Lamont said – '

'Versace. I got it on the last trip to Milan. I get everything in Milan, now, Paris is finished for men – '

'– Don't give me Lamont! Lamont's dead in the water! The idea of Norman Lamont caring about unemployment is like Hitler sitting down to a plate of gefilte fish – '

'Sounds great, Pippa, but I'll have to talk to Mike. You know he'll never make a commitment that far in advance, but I'd love to come – '

'Salomon's? I wouldn't work for Solly's if it was the last job on earth. You know what they're saying . . . It's a great place to be *from* – '

'– yeah, but they're the guys paying the big bucks this year . . .'

Whilst listening with one ear to Pippa gabble on about the luxury villa she and her husband had rented for the spring,

Teddy couldn't help but notice the elegant woman who shared the sofa with Charles Bartholomew. They seemed to know each other well. Their heads were bent close together, and they spoke quietly, detached from the hubbub around them. The stranger looked up, and meeting Teddy's eyes over Pippa's shoulder, gave her a dazzling smile. Teddy excused herself to Pippa, who simply made a quarter turn, cranked her voice up a notch or two and directed her speech on the glories of Umbria to someone else, allowing Teddy to make her way over to the corner of the room.

'Teddy, darling, I was just telling Candida all about you.' Charles rose to embrace her.

The auburn-haired woman also rose, and shook Teddy's hand. 'I'm Candida Redmayne. I would have introduced myself earlier, but you seemed frantically busy with your other guests. I met your fiancé yesterday and rather cheekily accepted what I'm sure was a half-hearted invitation to your party.'

'I'm delighted you came,' Teddy said warmly. 'Mike wasn't half-hearted at all. He was very impressed by you.'

'I simply can't believe that you two have never met before. Candida knows virtually everybody in London — she certainly knows most of the people in this room . . .' Charles drawled.

'Charles, you know very well that as a headhunter I have two separate ways of knowing people. There are plenty of people in this room who would be highly embarrassed if I showed signs of recognising them before they acknowledged me. It's a little bit like being a VD specialist,' she explained to Teddy with a smile, 'everyone uses a headhunter at one time or another, but nobody likes to admit it, particularly in company. You'd be amazed how many people spend a couple of hours with me, and cut me dead in a restaurant the next day if they are in the company of a colleague, or a boss . . . I think it's better to protect their insecurities and pretend I don't know them.'

'What a ghastly way to live!' Teddy exclaimed.

'Not really, it can be quite amusing at times. I like walking into a room and seeing the look of terror that comes over people's faces . . . You can seeing them asking themselves, "If I pretend I don't know her, everyone will think I'm too unimportant for her to have contacted me, and if I admit I do know her, they'll all think I'm looking for a job . . ." It tells you a lot about somebody, whether they come right up, as Charles does, or whether they hide ín the room to see who else admits to knowing me.'

'What does it tell you about Charlie?' Teddy said curiously, taking Charles's arm.

'It tells me that he's not afraid of what people think. Perhaps that he doesn't even care what people think. It tells me that he wouldn't be afraid of greeting a VD specialist if he knew one.'

Charles choked on his whisky and soda.

'Oh, I could have told you that!' Teddy responded warmly. 'Which reminds me, Charles, without wanting to cast aspersions on your physical health or personal habits, the whole point of this little shindig was to introduce you to Glory.' Teddy pointed discreetly to a tall blonde clad in a shimmering scarlet sheath who appeared to be in the middle of a violent altercation with Mike. Charlie's jaw dropped. Teddy led him across the room, with one last word of advice. 'I suggest you wipe the drool off your chin before you meet her, you old lecher.'

Teddy returned to Candida, and continued her train of thought. 'I think I promised to tell you everything about Charlie.'

'I'm sure you could. But right now, I'd far rather hear everything about you.' Candida patted the sofa, and Teddy accepted her invitation.

Within a week of the dinner party, Teddy had had four meetings with Candida, and was surprised to find herself in receipt of a job offer – not from one of Candida's clients, but from Candida herself. Teddy had initially rejected the idea of becoming a headhunter, but Candida had intrigued her, and subtly manoeuvred her into a position where, much to her own surprise, she was now seriously considering joining ARC. She had promised Candida that before making any final decision she would meet Candida's partner, David Aston-Stewart, and discuss the business with him, and this morning she was off to the City to keep her appointment.

David Aston-Stewart looked down at the CV on his desk. He had not been actively involved in headhunting itself for some years now, preferring to act as the company manager and strategist of the business, but Candida always involved him in the selection of new staff for ARC. He made a significant contribution, in that he knew Candida very well, and was perhaps better able to judge who might fit in with the company, and who might not. Candida had asked him to give Teddy a straight interview, and see how he thought she'd get on.

Her résumé was unusually brief. It told David that Teddy had sailed smoothly – almost too smoothly – through an academic career, and had then gone on to work for two of the classiest acts in the City, Morgan Mitchell Bankers and Steinberg Roth and Partners. But it said nothing else, nothing about what this woman was like, what she enjoyed doing, what her interests and values were. Candida had told him very little, wanting him to make his own appraisal. David passed the CV over to Jamie Ferguson, who was sitting in on the interview, and raised his eyes to look at Teddy Winnington-Smythe.

He saw a woman of considerable beauty, who yet failed to fit any of the conventional descriptions of 'beautiful women'. She wasn't a raven-haired temptress, or an English

Rose, nor a flaxen-haired, blue-eyed Viking goddess, nor a red-haired firecracker. Her hair was an indeterminate colour, somewhere between blonde and chestnut, and was worn pulled severely back from her face in a simple pony tail, which made her look older than her twenty-eight years. Her eyes were large, oval in shape, and very green, accentuated by unusually dark and thick eyebrows, that gave her gaze an intensity which was hard to meet. Her cheekbones were high, again focusing attention on her eyes. Her mouth and nose were in proportion, and were not features that David Aston-Stewart found of particular interest, but nor did they detract from a face of grace, intelligence and depth, held together by those bewitching emerald eyes which promised all manner of things.

Her body formed a stark contrast to the maturity and severity of her expression, and gave David and Jamie a clue as to the two sides of Teddy Winnington-Smythe. Looking at her restrained hair style, lack of make-up and calm deportment, David had rather expected to see her clothed in a little grey suit – possibly Chanel, definitely French – a white shirt with a floppy bow tied under her chin, a string of unostentatious pearls, and smart, but sensible low-heeled shoes – something from Russell and Bromley, perhaps. Reality was far from expectations. Teddy *was* wearing grey, but the garment she wore seemed to cling and flow at the same time, caressing her full, high bosom and the curve of her hip, and ending suddenly half way up her thigh exposing an outrageous length of leg. He knew instinctively that she and Candida would make a daunting team. His wife would know what fabric her dress was made of – some sort of fine wool, cashmere or jersey – it didn't matter. What did matter, mattered a great deal, was the way it flattered her, stroking her body in a way that was absolutely feminine, and yet absolutely elegant. She wore no jewellery, other than a single immense square cut emerald on her engagement finger. She gazed back at him, calmly and quietly, and David Aston-Stewart felt a little afraid of her. He felt nervous for the first time in over fifteen years of interviewing.

'Well, Theodora. Uhhh, Teddy. Candida has asked me to give you our standard interview, although I know that you and she have talked at great length about the possibility of your joining us here at ARC. I hope this won't bore you too much, but Jamie and I would like to hear all the details of your career to date, why you chose to leave Steinberg Roth, and how you feel about the future. Then perhaps we'll have time to answer any questions you may have outstanding. At ARC, we believe in placing people where there will be a good fit, and that applies to our own staff as much as it does to those we recruit for clients. I hope it's all right with you if we begin on that basis?'

Teddy smiled, and David felt as if the sun had come out after a month of rain.

'Fire away.'

'First of all, tell me why you have dropped the Smythe from your name. I know your father, slightly, and of course I have heard of your grandparents, but I notice from your CV that you have chosen to call yourself Winnington.'

'I simply think it's too much of a mouthful. Can you imagine being called Theodora Winnington-Smythe? I suppose I should just be grateful that my parents didn't come up with anything worse – it could have been Gladys Winnington-Smythe after all. It's far too pompous. I don't really hold with that. I went through years at school with it hanging round my neck like an albatross, so when I went to Oxford, I decided to drop it. I haven't missed it.'

'I'm sure not. Now let's talk about your work ... You were on the marketing end of corporate finance at Steinberg, is that right?'

'Yes, I worked under Tom Pitt-Rivers; he's now moved

over to head up equity syndicate. I enjoyed it. I like a close client relationship, and at Steinberg we were really given the time to build close ties with our clients, and focus on particular industries. I specialised in media related companies.'

'How did you get on with Tom Pitt-Rivers?'

'He was perfectly fair to me. He does his job very well; I know nothing bad of him, and if I did, I wouldn't say it,' Teddy answered diplomatically.

'What would *he* say about you? What would he say were your greatest faults?'

'As a colleague?' Teddy looked very serious and took her time to answer. 'He would probably say that I was too feminine. Tom doesn't really like the idea of women working in corporate finance. He pretends he does, but he doesn't. It's not that he's against women in the City, but he thinks we should stick to "girly" jobs, like sales. Not "serious men's" jobs, like corporate finance.' She mimed a caricature of a butch man, swaggering her shoulders. They laughed. 'He thinks we're all too dependent on feminine intuition, and not sufficiently rational. He would probably say that I jump to conclusions too quickly, and that I'm too proud, not really prepared to toe the line.'

'Is that a fair criticism? Not being able to toe the line?'

'Perhaps; it depends who's drawn the line. I don't consider it a major fault. If I'm really honest, I think that pride is a fault I'm rather fond of; false humility, and even honest-to-God genuine humility, can do just as much harm as pride. There are other faults I could mention, such as intolerance, selfishness, and prejudice, that I like less. But I guess we all have a touch of wickedness.'

Jamie spoke for the first time, quoting softly from the other side of the room,

'They say best men are moulded out of faults,
And, for the most, become much more the better
For being a little bad.'

Teddy laughed outright, surprised to find a Shakespeare scholar in a headhunting office, and then immediately apologised for her prejudice. This time, they all three laughed. The interview gathered pace, and the two men admired Teddy increasingly as she demonstrated time and time again her intelligence, integrity and charm. After an hour's chat, David decided to broach the subject of joining ARC.

'Teddy, what was your first reaction when Candida suggested that you might become a headhunter?'

'Well, frankly, I was a little appalled. I didn't know much about it then, and I'm sorry to say I thought it was a rather silly job.' She blushed. 'All you seem to do is talk to people, introduce one set of people to another set and take a fat fee for it. It seems, well, frankly, parasitic. I think of it as a fledgling industry that just grew up on the back of the Big Bang, and the whole City boom through the Eighties. Somebody once gave me some good advice about headhunters; he said never get too excited about the advances of a headhunter: the most they can give you is a job, and you've already got one of those.'

David Aston-Stewart and Jamie Ferguson smiled in unison. They were used to this reaction to their profession. Many people thought of headhunters as flesh peddlers, pimps, bloodsuckers; even the name of the business was derogatory, and yet so much more descriptive than their formal title, 'executive search consultants'.

'Teddy, forgive me, but isn't that really what you do marketing corporate finance products? Just talk to people, and introduce one lot to another, for a fat fee? Isn't that the relationship building function that you were so enthusiastic about?'

'I suppose so, but I talked to people about their expansion plans, capital requirements, stock purchasing plans – rather more important things. Corporate financiers play a very influential role in a company's growth . . .'

'I see,' David picked up the conversation thoughtfully. 'Wouldn't you find it equally satisfying to play a major influence in people's lives, in an individual's growth? You see, Teddy, in this business, there are three real areas of job satisfaction, ones that I think you would identify with. The first is the thrill of the chase; it is a hunt, after all. The second is the thrill of a deal; just like when you close a major equity financing, and your client's very happy, and you've made 1.50 per cent, or maybe even a massive 2.5 per cent. The only difference for us is that we make 33 per cent. Same thrill, bigger pay-off. And third, we occasionally have something that I suspect you don't often find in the corporate finance department: sometimes, and I admit it's not every time, but sometimes, we can actually feel that we've changed somebody's life for the good. Maybe a person whose light has been hidden under a bushel for a few years, and we can see the glow, and persuade somebody to give him a chance. Maybe we can help somebody who feels he's reached a dead end. Don't you think that that could be more satisfying than lead managing yet another convertible bond issue for Royal Dutch?'

Teddy had listened intently to David's speech, leaning well forward in her chair.

'You may well be right. You're certainly convincing enough to make me want to go away and think about it a little. There are a few more practical questions I would like to ask you.'

Having satisfied her remaining concerns, Teddy stood up. Jamie prided himself on being both a connoisseur of beautiful women, and a 'new man' who was vehemently anti ogling women – particularly those women he might end up working with. The two forces battled within him as he was now in a position to admire her from glistening top to well-heeled toe.

'Could you tell Candida that I will call her before the weekend?'

She shook hands warmly with David. Jamie stumbled in his haste to open the door for her, and received a special smile for his pains, one that lacked any coyness, and yet made him feel like a spaniel having his tummy rubbed. When Teddy was safely out of earshot, he let out a low whistle through his teeth, and turned back to David Aston-Stewart.

Teddy, meanwhile, was on her way to meet Charlie Bartholomew for lunch. She had told him on the phone that she had an urgent matter to discuss with him, and Charlie had agreed to meet at their habitual watering hole, although he had sounded far from his normal happy self. When she arrived at Corney and Barrow, Charlie was already waiting for her, swilling a tomato juice around in his glass and wearing an expression of utter wretchedness. He kissed Teddy on the cheek, and before she could open her mouth, poured out his heart.

'It's no good, Ted. I just can't do it any longer. Never let it be said that Charles B Bartholomew would shrink from the call of duty, but this is simply insupportable. Giving up one vice is bad enough, but giving up two at the same time would break a better man than me.'

Charles, a heavy drinker and a heavy smoker, had rashly bet a fellow trader at Bergdorff Weintraub that he could do without smoking and drinking for a month. Two weeks had passed, and the strain was beginning to take its toll.

'It's not that I *can't* do it, you understand, Ted, it's just that life doesn't seem worth living anymore. I can't work, I can't trade – I've already lost two million this month and it's only the eighth – I'm a wreck. Buy me one little glass of wine, a little Mâcon-Prissé, a little snifter of Puligny-Montrachet, a tiny, tiny verre de Gevrey-Chambertin. At least get one yourself and let me sip it – no, just smell it – and don't tell that bastard Dave!' He glanced quickly around the full bar, looking for spies.

'Charlie, are you really prepared to pay a grand for a glass of wine?'

That was the bet; a thousand pounds to Dave if Charles failed to keep the bet, or a thousand to Charles if he succeeded. Teddy couldn't bring herself to disapprove of Charlie's betting habit. He made ever more outrageous bets with Dave. The whole business had started one day when Charlie bet Dave a fiver that Lulu, their sales assistant, would be wearing a pink bra. The two men had gone through extraordinary contortions to try to verify the colour of her bra without Lulu realising, dropping bits of paper for her to pick up, asking her to change a light bulb, whatever they could think of that would give them the best view. Charlie had won that day, and had won most of their subsequent bets where the outcome was a matter of judgement. But now that the stakes were rising, Dave had become crafty, and more and more of their bets depended on Charlie's self-discipline, not a characteristic in which he held a long suit.

'Charlie, I'll buy you a glass, but only on condition that you promise to tell Dave as soon as you get back. I won't be party to any deception. In fact, I'll call him myself this afternoon and check.'

'Excellent!' Charles swung round to the bar and called in a loud voice, 'A bottle of Chambolle-Musigny 85, De Vogue, my good man, and twenty of your finest Marlboro. Might as well be hung for a sheep as a lamb.'

After he had sung the praises of the blushful Hippocrene, holding up his glass to the light to admire the fine colour of the wine, Charles turned his full attention to Teddy.

'Now that we have taken care of urgent matters, tell me all. Has the wretched Miccinelli done a bunk, I ask in hope?'

Teddy feigned irritation. Charlie had always rejected Teddy's boyfriends as unworthy of her, and Mike was no exception. Although the two men had established a rapport, Charlie continued to feel that Teddy was making a mistake, and took every opportunity to point it out. Teddy was not in the mood to discuss her romantic life, and quickly told Charles the saga of her meetings with Candida and David Aston-Stewart.

'They're a good firm,' Charles mused. 'Probably the best. Real specialists. There are a lot of spivs in the market who do nothing except punt CVs across people's desks. I even met one headhunter who rented his office by the hour. I had to go back after our meeting to pick up my umbrella, and the name on the door had changed! But ARC plays in the first division. I've known Candida for a long time, since she started the business. She tried to get me to leave Bergdorff and move to Warburgs. But she's a really tough cookie, Ted. I've heard stories about her that would make your blood run cold. Talk about being driven; she doesn't stop at anything. I think it's not a bad idea for you, but headhunting is a strange affair, it can be very absorbing, like having a whole series of lovers, one after the other, all of whom you feel passionately about. In some ways I think that the arrival of headhunters has had more to do with the explosion of jobs in the City, the increase in prestige, and undoubtedly the increase in salaries than any kind of deregulation has done. But for God's sake don't think you're getting into a nice, ladylike little business. Candida Redmayne is about as ladylike as Attila the Hun, and twice as determined. Did I ever tell you about the offer she made me?' Charlie shuddered at the memory. 'It was whilst I was considering going to Warburgs. She never came right out and said it, but she implied that she'd go to bed with me if I signed with Warburgs. What scared me most about it is that I very nearly agreed . . . I can't think now what stopped me, quite out of character . . .'

Teddy laughed. 'She sounds rather good. Maybe that's why she's become so successful. She says she moves about four people a month – that's forty-eight to fifty a year, over eight years . . . Getting on for four hundred bonks . . . That would even beat your record, Charlie . . .'

'Ah, yes, but your calculations are wrong. First, you're assuming that all candidates take up Candida's offer, second, you're suggesting that all Candida's candidates are male, and third, you're implying that I never have a return match, whereas you know perfectly well that once is never enough for me . . .' Charlie placed his hand on Teddy's knee, and received an immediate slap.

'Charlie, I'm a married lady – nearly.' Besides, once for her was enough. Once had been plenty.

Teddy and Charlie, firm friends since university days, had once, in a carefree and champagne-enhanced mood, stretched their friendship over the platonic line and fallen in to bed. It had been mildly embarrassing for Teddy the next morning, but otherwise unmemorable. Charles had never quite given up the hope that a second try would meet with more success, but had not been given the opportunity to test his theory.

'There's many a slip 'twixt the cup and the lip,' Charlie muttered darkly.

'Also, Bartholomew, I am not implying that all Candida's candidates are male. If she is as dedicated and unscrupulous as you think, why on earth shouldn't she sleep with her female candidates as well as the men?'

'Interesting theory,' Charles mused. 'Anyway, Ted, you know my policy: live dangerously. Take the job – but watch out for Candida, and don't get on her wrong side. And don't start sleeping with your candidates, male or female, or I will be extremely cross.'

'Talking of which, Charlie, you never told me how you got on with Glory McWhirter.'

Charles looked faintly — but only faintly — embarrassed. 'I'll tell you about it another time, Teddy. She's a strange girl — not exactly my type, I suspect.' He drained his glass, and gave Teddy a peck on the cheek.

'I'll call you later . . . After I've spoken to Dave.'

Teddy's threat was unnecessary. Not only was Charles Bartholomew honourable in all betting matters, but the contented glow on his face would give the game away before he had had a chance to utter a word. In any event, he was in sufficiently mellow mood to absorb criticism, recrimination and even debt, without experiencing any pain.

When the postman slipped her letters through her open kitchen window the next morning, Matilda Winnington-Smythe was delighted to find amongst them one addressed in her granddaughter's flamboyant script. Taking her coffee into the conservatory which overlooked her gardens, she sat down to read the news from London.

Wednesday

Dearest Granny,

I haven't forgotten that you're coming to stay next weekend, but I couldn't wait till then to talk to you. I have to ask your advice about A Major Decision. (Sounds ominous, doesn't it?)

Last week I met a woman called Candida Redmayne who runs a headhunting business in the City. She's extremely impressive, very charming, and successful to boot, which isn't that common a combination these days, and surprise, surprise, she wants *me* to come and work with her. Do you know what headhunting is? I'm sure you do, Granny darling, you always know everything. So should I accept? I'm very tempted, I must say, and Mike is dying for me to accept, so long as I don't try to poach any of his colleagues from Steinberg Roth. It's a very profitable business, so I'd probably make just as much money as I did at Steinberg, but I think it would be a lot more fun – and somehow it sounds rather more satisfying – trying to find exactly the right job for someone, meeting lots of interesting people, than sitting on a phone trying to persuade people to issue stocks all day. It sounds a rather *noble* career, don't you think? I rather fancy myself as a wonderfully wise, perceptive woman bringing happiness and job fulfilment to all sorts of poor, unhappy people. Charles says it isn't noble at all – he says it's incredibly cut-throat and can be deeply unethical – but you know what Charlie's like. He thinks everything's unethical, including himself. And even he says that Candida is the best in the business.

I tried to talk to Mummy and Daddy about it, but you know what they think. Mummy just wants me to break off my engagement to Mike and marry some titled bigwig (! – the idea!) and anyway, she doesn't think that women should work after they're married, and Daddy just says, 'Whatever makes you happy, darling,' and carries on reading his book. (He did say that David Aston-Stewart, who is Candida's partner, was a good sort – he's probably a member of Daddy's club or something.) So I make that two for (Mike and Daddy) and one against (Mummy) and Charlie appears to have abstained. I thought you should have the casting vote.

No more time to write. I'm scribbling this so fast it probably doesn't make any sense at all, but darling

Grandmother, what am I to do? I have to make up my mind quickly. Candida has found somebody else she wants to hire if I say no, and I promised I wouldn't keep her waiting.

What would you like to see next weekend? Charlie says he can get hold of four tickets for *The Merchant of Venice* at the Barbican, and he wants to be your date. I suppose I'll have to drag Mike to it kicking and screaming as he's not exactly a fan of W Shakespeare. Can't wait to see you – your room is all ready – but will you write back by return and give me Your Considered Opinion about my future?

All my love, as ever,

Teddy

For half an hour, Matilda gazed out at her level lawns and thought about her granddaughter. Teddy had always been an impulsive child, and she felt that she would have benefited from a slightly firmer hand in her upbringing. Not for the first time she felt irritated by the behaviour of her son and daughter-in-law. She happened to agree with Laura that Mike Miccinelli wasn't exactly the most suitable husband for Teddy, but then she wasn't at all sure that Teddy was ready for marriage in the first place. She still had an enormous amount to learn about life. Her son Nathaniel and his wife had met every problem in Teddy's childhood by saying, 'Whatever makes you happy, darling,' and Teddy had grown up with the idea that happiness was her due, and not the result of careful decisions and sound judgement. Matilda had always rather regretted that Teddy had inherited her mother's beauty. She had regretted it in Laura herself when Nat had first brought his girlfriend to meet them, convinced that such good looks brought nothing but misery, but she regretted it even more in

Teddy's case. Laura had never had anything except her beauty, but Teddy had so many assets that should prove to be more loyal and long-lasting friends. There was no doubt that all that had saved Teddy from becoming a horribly spoilt child, and a horribly spoilt young woman, was the girl's innate strength of character. And possibly, Matilda acknowledged, the example set by her grandmother.

Matilda had never really forgiven Laura for putting her foot down and refusing to have another baby; it wasn't good for a child to grow up in a wholly adult environment, and however hard a time Laura had had during her pregnancy and delivery, she should have thought about her daughter and been a little less selfish. Matilda herself had given birth to six children in wholly unsatisfactory conditions in India, and prided herself that she had never uttered a word of complaint; well, almost never. She was now highly tempted to pick up the phone and give Nat and Laura a piece of her mind, but Nat was too old to be told what to do by his mother, and Laura was too flighty to help her daughter, and, she was forced to admit, Teddy was too old to continue to make other people responsible for her own choices. Moving to her writing desk, she picked up pen and paper, and sat down to reply to her favourite grandchild.

The Manor
Great Wishford
Wiltshire

October 24th, 1991

My dear Teddy,

What a treat to receive your letter, and what an
honour that you should ask my advice on such an
Important Matter.

I must say first of all that I know absolutely nothing
about the business of headhunting, and I try not
to give uninformed advice. In matters of City life, I
always feel like a newborn infant, and need words
of one syllable to understand what people are talking
about – there seems to be so much jargon. Your
grandfather was certainly never 'headhunted' (*can* it
be used as a verb?) from the Indian Civil Service – he
would have been absolutely horrified by the very idea.

Teddy, it's probably rather naughty of me to say
this, given that I am your grandmother, but I rather
feel that at this stage, and on this issue, you should
disregard your parents' advice. I also feel that you
should disregard mine, which is why I'm not going
to give you any. The people you should listen to are
those who know what headhunting is about, and
those who know Candida Redmayne. Don't disregard
Charles, I think he is far better equipped to judge
the situation than I am, and certainly don't disregard
Michael. These are the people who know what
you are talking about, and both of them know you
extremely well, and should be able to judge whether
or not this is a career that would suit you.

One word of advice – I can never resist just one,
even if you do disregard it – do look before you leap.

There's no reason why you should be rushed into a sudden decision. I'm sure that if this woman is as intelligent as you think she is, she would be prepared to give you the time to think carefully. This is An Important Decision; I know it's very unfashionable now, and clearly goes against the grain of any 'headhunter', but I was brought up to believe that a career choice was a lifelong decision, and that a commitment to an employer should be a long term one. In some ways, it's nearly as important a decision as whom you choose to marry.

Theodora, you are not a little girl any longer; you haven't been for quite some time. I am quite confident that you are well on the road to becoming a 'wonderfully wise and perceptive woman'. I am also confident that you have all the skills required to be a good headhunter; whether or not it would be a 'noble' profession isn't for me to say. But I think that now is the time to *exercise* your wisdom and perception, and Make Up Your Own Mind. You have a very good head on your shoulders, and it's high time you used it.

I would be delighted to see *The Merchant*; how dear of Charles to suggest it, though why on earth he wants to spend his Saturday night escorting a seventy-five – horrors! Seventy-six! – year old woman to the theatre baffles me. If there is any Shakespeare play that could work a conversion on Michael, I should think it is *The Merchant of Venice*, so I hope there won't be too much of a struggle when you drag him to the Barbican gates.

I shall arrive on the six thirty from Salisbury. You are *not* to meet me; I see it as rather an adventure taking the train, and finding my own taxi. I may even treat myself to a whisky and water in the buffet car. Barton is simply appalled. He considers it frightfully fast of me.

With my love, dearest Teddy, and I hope you don't
find my tone too stern,
Matty

She addressed the envelope carefully, and rang the bell.
Barton, who had been with Sir Nathaniel and Lady
Winnington-Smythe for over forty years, was instructed
to take the letter to the village immediately, so that Teddy
would indeed receive her answer by return of post.

And so she did. Teddy was not surprised by the firm
tone of her grandmother's letter, but it amused her that
Matty persisted in affecting surprise that Charlie, and
other of Teddy's old friends, should enjoy her company.
Lady Winnington-Smythe was one of strongest characters
Teddy had ever come across, and was broadly admired
for the sharpness of her mind, and the courage of her
heart. After thirty years' service in India, she had returned
to England owing to her husband's ill health, and had
worked tirelessly nursing him and raising funds for the
Chohumadu Irrigation Project in Maharashtra. She always
spoke sensibly, and Teddy generally took her advice. She
hadn't waited for Matty's advice this time, however. She
had followed her own instincts, and phoned Candida that
morning to accept her offer to join ARC; she had agreed
to start work immediately after Christmas. She *had* looked
before she leapt; she *had* thought about it carefully. She
had thought about it for a whole day.

CHAPTER TWO

Teddy slipped into life at ARC like Cinderella into her slipper. By the end of January she had mastered the database that stored the details of thirty thousand candidates that Candida and her colleagues had built up over the years, and marvelled at the efficiency and professionalism of her boss's business. The phones at ARC never stopped ringing. Candida juggled candidates and clients with ease, arranging interviews, soothing ruffled feathers, negotiating contracts, rewriting CVs, conducting interviews, making introductions – and that was just a morning's work. She never seemed to forget a name, her memory storing even more details than her beloved computer. There was no doubt that Candida loved her work, and fulfilled her own theory that if somebody enjoyed their work, they tended to do it well. The other consultants at ARC also seemed to love their work, so much so that although Louise Davies and Philip Gottlieb, two of her new colleagues, welcomed Teddy warmly, they hardly had a chance to say hello before flying off on a search.

Candida also believed in learning by doing, and had thrown Teddy in at the deep end. In early February ARC had been given an assignment to fill a director level post at FRG Barnekov, a specialist investment banking boutique, and Candida had handed over the brief to Teddy, with Jamie Ferguson to hold her hand. 'I'm not going to babysit you, Teddy,' she had said, 'Jamie will show you the ropes, and you two get on with it. I have every confidence in you.' Teddy had thrown herself into the job with gusto, and the only problem so far had been that Mike was increasingly irritated by the long hours she worked. Teddy and Jamie had reached the point where they could now begin to compile a list of potential candidates for the job, and start the laborious task of sifting through them.

Teddy fed the requirements for the position into the computer:

Age range:	35–45
Sex:	M/F
Nationality:	Brit/Fre/Ger/Spa/Ita
Languages:	Eng/Fre/Ger
Location:	UK/Fra/Ger
Prof Stat:	1–3
LOB:	CorpFin/InvBank
Product:	Equity/All

The search specifications would mean nothing to anyone not versed in ARC's coding, but to Teddy and Jamie it was as clear as day. The computer had been instructed to search the database for candidates aged thirty-five to forty-five, of either sex, of any major European nationality, who spoke English, French and German, who were currently based in England, France or Germany, whose professional status was between managing director and senior vice president, who operated in the corporate finance or investment banking line of business, and whose primary product experience lay in equities of any description. Teddy studied the requirements again, and nervously hit the search button. The computer whirred, and completed its task. Teddy looked up at Jamie in horror.

'There are over three hundred names that fit the description!'

'Then you must have left something out; I'd expect there to be about five hundred,' Jamie said smugly. He looked over her shoulder and nodded. 'Add Scot and Yank and Scandi to the nationality field. What was it FRG said? They are looking for a 'citizen of the world'. Take the minimum age down to thirty-two, there might be some young hot shot you're missing. And add BusDev to the LOB field.'

'BusDev?'

'Business Development,' Jamie explained patiently.

Teddy did as she was told, and the computer re-sorted its files.

'Shit. Four hundred and eighty-two.'

'That's more like it,' Jamie said with satisfaction. 'Well, my darling, I'm off. I'm meeting a most gorgeous leggy blonde for dinner, and I'm sure you wouldn't want me to keep a lady waiting . . .' He stood up and stretched. 'Ah, Teddy, one little favour . . . You wouldn't have a spare fiver on hand, would you? I couldn't get to the bank today, and I'll have to pick her up in a taxi . . .'

Teddy pointed him in the direction of her handbag, her eyes remaining glued to the computer screen as she began to plough through the names the search function had generated.

Jamie extracted a twenty pound note from her wallet, and with a jaunty, 'Sorry, no change! Happy hunting!' he beat a retreat.

The office was silent. Candida was in Paris for a couple of days, and both the secretaries and the two research assistants had left at five thirty. The two other consultants that ARC employed were conducting an interview. Teddy ploughed through the names on the screen methodically, storing those that should be considered, and eliminating those candidates who had moved too recently or were otherwise unsuitable.

James Abercrombie, Lawrence Able, Antonio Acciari, Susannah Acland, Stephen Adler, Philippe Albert, Anstruther, Appleby, Arbuthnot, Armitage, Armand-Delille . . . For each entry, Teddy examined the candidate profile screen, noting their professional experience and potential mobility. She felt a little like a peeping Tom as she pried into their histories, and read the comments that others had made, unbeknownst to the individual concerned. By the time she reached the Bs, it was nearly eight o'clock. She looked at one more entry before calling it a night:

Name:	von Budingen, Konrad
DOB:	12/7/49
Sex:	M
Nationality:	German
Languages:	Ger, Eng, Fre, Dutch
Current employer:	Delius-Zech gmBh
Previous employer:	Deutsche Bank
Prof status:	Managing Director, dept. manager
LOB:	Equity New Issues and Mergers
Product:	European Equity/M & A
Mobility:	Possible
Last salary:	DM 420,000 + bonus
Last interview:	7th October 1990 (see records)
Rating:	A+ (CR)
Relationship:	
Comments:	Hi-powered, hi-profile kraut. Formal. Heel-clicker. Tough. Wary. Professional. Great reput. with corp. clients. Gets things done.

Teddy moved Konrad von Budingen's name to the shortlist file, and logged out of the computer. She called Mike's private number at Steinberg, and a woman answered.

'Mike Miccinelli's line?'

'This is Teddy. Is Mike around?'

'Hi, Teddy, it's Glory. Mike left about half an hour

ago. Pretty mad at you. You were meant to meet him here at seven.'

'Oh, Christ, I totally forgot . . .'

'Oh, don't worry about it, you know what he's like . . . He's just used to having everyone at his beck and call. Tell you what, why don't you swing by here, and I'll give you a lift back to Notting Hill – we could have a drink or something. I haven't had a chance to talk to you since your party, and I'm dying to hear about the new job. Mike says he's never going to tell you the name of one of his colleagues ever again in case you try to headhunt them . . . I'm just dying for you to headhunt me – I'd take any job, *any*, so long as it was back on the other side of the Atlantic . . .'

'Okay, Glory, that sounds fun. I'll be with you in about ten minutes.'

Teddy was a little uneasy with Glory McWhirter. She had met her for the first time at the Mexican party last October, and found Glory a little too loud for comfort, but she felt that she owed Mike the effort of trying to get on with his friends and colleagues. She also felt a little sorry for Glory being friendless in London. Teddy had a habit of adopting waifs and strays, and although from what Teddy had seen of her Glory didn't really fit into the category, she had made the decision to look after her.

Arriving at the front entrance of Steinberg's huge new office development, Teddy found Glory parked in front, the engine of her silver Mercedes sports car purring like a large tiger. Teddy reluctantly agreed to having a drink at Jules Bar in Jermyn Street, once Glory had assured her that Mike had not gone home, but had stomped off for a night out with the lads.

'He won't be home for hours, Teddy. You've got to beat him at his own game. Get liberated! If he goes off for a drink with the boys, why the hell shouldn't we tie one on, huh?'

Glory swung the car into the heavy traffic round Trafalgar Square, only avoiding a collision by sheer bravado. She slipped a CD into the player and turned the volume up. Teddy listened to the frenetic thump of what sounded like an early Talking Heads album, and wished she hadn't agreed to meeting with Glory. She was too tired to keep up with the American woman's incessant chatter, and longed to soak in a hot bath, preferably with Mike.

Glory was in the middle of badmouthing every one of her fellow traders at Steinberg with the exception of Mike.

'Have you met Spig Hall, Teddy? What a jerk – I mean, really. He's the kind of guy who gives abortion a good name. His mother could have done the world a real favour. Brain dead. I nicknamed him Spig Hall, MD, and the idiot actually thinks that it stands for managing director. All the guys on the floor know it stands for mental defective. Then there's Big Bill Desmond, who thinks with his prick. Yesterday, he fucked up a trade so bad he should have been shown the door. Then there's Hal – he's totally off the wall; must spend a fortune on shrinks and valium. None of these guys would last a week in New York, I'm telling you – ' she glanced sideways at Teddy, and cut in front of an irate taxi driver, her middle finger raised, '– except Mike, of course. He's my only real buddy on the whole floor. We go back a long way, me and Mike. He's the best, Teddy. You really ought to let him go back to New York, that's where he should be, and that's where the power is. He's wasted in this shit hole.'

'It wasn't my decision that Mike came to London. We hadn't even met when he moved back, and he's never said anything to me about wanting to go back to the States.' Teddy allowed a defensive edge to creep into her voice.

'No?' Glory sounded surprised. 'Well, I guess he feels you wouldn't really like it, and doesn't want to put you in a difficult position. He's all heart. I mean, really.'

'Really.' Teddy echoed tonelessly. She feared it was going to be a difficult evening.

By the time Teddy got to Mike's flat, it was well after eleven. The flat was in darkness, and Mike had gone to bed. Teddy crawled in next to him, and arched her body around his, placing feathery kisses on the back of his neck, aching for his touch and for some sign of affection. Mike grunted, and pulled away from her, rolling to the far edge of the bed. Teddy, her head pounding with Glory's voice, retreated miserably to her side, and fell into a light and restless sleep.

When the alarm went off, Teddy groaned and reached out to touch Mike. He normally rose first, and she had a cup of coffee in bed whilst he showered. But the bed was empty, and there was no smell of freshly brewed coffee wafting from the kitchen. She struggled out of bed and found a note on the hall table.

'You can reach me at the office. If you can possibly manage it, we might have dinner tonight. I have to go to Tokyo for two or three weeks tomorrow. If you're not going to turn up, call me so that I can make other plans.'

Teddy felt hurt. She had never, in the course of their relationship, stood Mike up deliberately, although he had frequently been late and occasionally not come home. She was bright enough, and honest enough to admit that she would have felt less aggrieved had she actually enjoyed the evening, but she hadn't. She had only gone out with Glory under the misguided impression that it would please Mike if she befriended his 'buddy'. Although she was prepared to admit that she had been in error for forgetting their arrangement the night before, it annoyed her that Mike was still nursing a grievance the morning after. There was something badly brought up, she thought crossly, about getting out of bed on the wrong side. It showed a lack of stamina. After dressing, she called through to Mike, and was given the cold shoulder. He clearly had no idea that she had been out with Glory the previous night.

'But didn't she tell you? She told me you'd gone off for an evening with the boys! She suggested we went out. I really didn't want to go . . .' Teddy pleaded.

'I suppose she just pulled out a gun and forced you to go, right? For Christ's sake, Teddy, you can do what the hell you like. It would just be a courtesy to inform me of your plans in future, okay? You're the one who's always so hung up on courtesy and manners, for God's sake.'

'But Mike, I really thought you'd be pleased if I got to know Glory – you've been saying what a character she is . . .'

'Stop whining, will you? Anyway, as you like Glory so much you'll be glad to hear that I've asked her to come out to dinner with us tonight. So if you're going to be late, let us know so we don't have to hang around twiddling our thumbs whilst you piss around with people's CVs . . .'

'Mike! You wanted me to take this job! Anyway, I thought we were going to be alone tonight. If you're going away . . .'

'Can't be done. Glory's coming to Tokyo too, and we need to talk through some things before we go. We don't get a chance in the office. You'll probably be bored, so don't bother to come if you're otherwise engaged. If you are coming, bring my car into the City. I took a cab this morning.'

'I'll be there at seven,' Teddy said flatly. His injustice stung, but it wasn't worth fighting about at this stage.

It was an absolutely loathsome way to start the day. Teddy decided to get into the office early, as she would have to leave by six thirty, and managed a wan smile at the security guard as she pulled Mike's Ferrari out of the private car park. Not up to listening to the *Today* programme, she pushed in the cassette that Mike had been playing, and recognised the same music that she had heard last night in Glory's car. It made her feel uneasy. Mike and Glory had so much in common; their work, their time in the States, their taste in music. She would have to try harder to make Mike comfortable, and enjoy the things he enjoyed, that was all. Maybe it was a blessing that he was going to Japan for a while. It would give things time to settle down. He was probably just preoccupied about the trip, which had clearly come up very suddenly – and when he got back she would make a real effort to pay more attention to him.

Teddy scolded herself that she *had* been preoccupied for the past few weeks, what with the new job, learning the systems and the search. It wasn't fair on Mike to expect him to put up with her being so distracted when he had grown used to her being at home all day for the past six months. On the other hand, it was time he grew up a little and realised that her career was as important as his. Teddy had been working at Steinberg's when they met, so Mike had originally known her as a career woman, but ever since they had become engaged and she had resigned from the bank Mike had increasingly taken it for granted that she would be at home when he wanted her to be, and that he came first on her list of priorities. Even when he encouraged her to take the job at ARC he hadn't taken it very seriously, and seemed to regard it as a way of amusing her. The problem was that Teddy had always taken her work seriously, and expected Mike to do the same. It was clearly going to take Mike longer to readjust than she had thought. She resolved to act as if nothing had happened that night, and was determined to make it a happy evening. The thought did little to lift her spirits.

Dinner was not a success by any account. Mike, Glory and Teddy went to Harvey's, on the edge of Wandsworth Common, a restaurant that Teddy found hideously pretentious and overpriced, but one which Mike loved. It was apparent that Teddy had not been forgiven. Mike ignored her attempts to ask questions about the forthcoming trip to Tokyo, and concentrated on talking to Glory. In contrast, Glory bent over backwards to involve Teddy in the conversation, and when Mike slipped away from the table, took Teddy's hand and said, 'Don't worry, honey, he's being a bad boy because he's a little stressed out. I'll look after him in Tokyo for you – make sure he fits in a real good shiatsu massage – have you ever heard about the bars they have in Tokyo? Apparently, there are even places where the hookers have had all their teeth removed so they can crawl around on the floor giving *real* satisfying blow jobs . . . kinky, huh?'

Teddy couldn't manage even the ghost of a smile, and spent the rest of the meal in virtual silence, toying with her food. When she and Mike returned to Kensington, she poured him a brandy, which he ignored, and suggested that she moved some of her things into his flat.

'I'm going to miss you so much, I thought I'd rather sleep here.'

'It's ironic that when I'm here you are always fighting to stay in your own place, and now I'm going away, you want to stay here . . . do whatever you like. I don't own you,' he replied brusquely.

'Oh, please, Mike, I'm really trying to say sorry. Don't go away leaving things like this, tell me what's wrong . . .' She wrapped her arms around his neck and clung to him, as if she could somehow fold herself into him and become part of him again.

Mike gently, but firmly, removed her arms from his neck. 'Nothing's wrong, Teddy. I'm tired, and I need to get some sleep. It's a good idea to move some stuff over here. It's a hell of a lot safer than your place. You can keep an eye on my car, too.'

He gave her a kiss on the top of the head and a light pat on the rump, but once again rejected Teddy's advances for the second night in a row. Mike and Teddy had enjoyed a passionate and fulfilling sexual relationship from the start, and knowing Mike's almost insatiable sexual appetite, Teddy knew that his apparent lack of interest was intended to be a very hard punishment indeed.

It was quiet whilst Mike was away. The first night Teddy moved a suitcase into the Kensington flat and slept in Mike's bathrobe, surrounding herself in the very essence of him as she wept herself to sleep, but after a few days she felt calmer, and even found it restful being alone again at night. Mike phoned every day, though briefly, and said he missed her, and even asked how the search was progressing. After two weeks of research, and burying her nose in the database, Teddy felt ready to go through a shortlist of twenty names with Candida. She had barely seen Candida since she had started work, as her boss had been flying in and out of the country almost non-stop. When they had met, Candida had been very encouraging, and never failed to tell Teddy how well she was doing. Now, Teddy felt, she was going to show Candida the fruits of her labours for the first time; and the proof of the pudding was in the eating.

Jamie was late, as usual, which left Candida and Teddy a little time to talk. Candida inquired after Mike, and told Teddy that she had heard through the grapevine that Mike was up for promotion. Teddy was delighted. As the two women relaxed over coffee, Jamie burst into the room.

'I'm sorry, I'm sorry, I'm sorry – you wouldn't believe what's happening on the tube . . .'

Candida, as ever, reacted directly. 'If that's a preamble to saying I don't pay you enough for you to afford a car, you can forget it. Now get some coffee and sit down. Teddy is about to go through your preliminary list of candidates to see if I can give you any additional input.'

Teddy started. As she read out each name, Candida either nodded or commented.

'Stephen Adler?' Nod. 'Bill Anstruther?' 'Yes, but he's a tricky personality – you'll have to handle him carefully.' 'Olivier Beaumont?' 'Pass.' 'Konrad von Budingen?' 'Brilliant – he could be your man. Go on.' 'Ramon de Carranza Guell?' 'Pass.' 'Christian de Clement-Grandcourt?' 'Hmm, interesting; he's unbelievably smooth, and unbelievably French.' 'Jonathan Davies?' 'Which Jonathan Davies?' 'The Warburg's one.' 'Yes; I've heard good things about him.' 'Steve Davis, Morgan Grenfell?' 'No, he's off limits unfortunately; they used to be a client, and their staff are barred for another twelve months. Shame; he's a good guy. Go on.' 'Jack Delavigne, at Hayes Goldsmith?'

There was silence, and Teddy looked up from her list. Jamie shifted uncomfortably in his chair.

'Jack Delavigne? Do you know him?' Teddy repeated.

'Yes. He's not appropriate. Take him off the shortlist. Who's next?'

'But Candida, he sounds perfect! He was my favourite of the whole lot of them!'

Candida sat staring out of the window, her jaw clenched and her pen snapping against the pad on her knee.

Teddy continued, 'We don't have much about him on the database, but his background is perfect, exactly the right experience, and you said that Hayes has been going through such a tough time, I thought maybe he'd be mobile – we've never interviewed him – '

'Take him off the list, Teddy. I know him. He isn't suitable.'

'But why isn't he? I'm sure it's worth a try, Candida. When I was doing the sourcing calls, he was the person that most people recommended. Really, he sounds great. Let me read you the comments, I've got them here, somewhere – ' she shuffled through the papers in the folder.

'No, Teddy, I said take him off! We are never going to approach Jack Delavigne, d'you understand? Not for this job, not for any job. I would be grateful if you could accept that I have a little more experience in this business than you do, and simply trust my judgement.' Candida was standing, her body rigid with tension, and her normally cool eyes flashing in anger. She had not raised her voice, but Teddy felt the fury coursing through her, and looked to Jamie for assistance.

'Candida's right, Teddy. Delavigne simply isn't the right man for the job.'

'Not the right man for any job,' Candida concluded bitterly.

Teddy sat in silence. The room seemed oppressive. Candida was clearly furious, and not prepared to say why, and Jamie was embarrassed. She cleared her throat and went on to the next name, her voice trembling. 'Dusserre; Pierre-Marie?'

To every name that followed, Candida gave a curt nod, and Teddy raced through the list, anxious to get out of Candida's office and interrogate Jamie. At last, it was over. Candida told Teddy that it looked like a decent list, and instructed them to get on with approaching candidates. She seemed to have recovered her sang-froid, although her manner was detached, and as they left she closed her office door behind them, radically against her policy of always leaving her door open unless she was conducting an interview.

Jamie looked at Teddy's ashen face, and said, 'Buck up.

Let me buy you lunch. I'll fill you in on all the gossip, but I'd rather do it out of the office.'

Teddy struggled to get on with the job until lunchtime, when she and Jamie could slip out.

'It's a very long story, Teddy, and I certainly haven't heard it from Candida. And you certainly haven't heard it from me.' Jamie lifted a glass of wine to his lips, and paused for effect, relishing Teddy's baited breath.

'Jack Delavigne is Candida's ex-husband.'

'Oh my God! Why didn't you tell me!'

'I didn't realise he'd come up on the list. I did the same thing myself maybe four years ago; Candida put me on a search, and I went through the database and came up with Delavigne. I trotted off to her, wagging my tail, and said I'd found the perfect guy. Believe me, she was far angrier with me than she was with you; she looked at me like I was a dog that had just crapped on her best carpet. I guess the split-up was a little fresher in her memory.'

'But why does she even keep him on the database?' Teddy asked incredulously.

'I don't really know. I guess it's professional etiquette. He's a big name in the City – if he wasn't on the database it would look odd, I suppose, if clients asked about him, so she leaves him on, but just draws the line at his being considered for any job. If clients ever ask about him, she just says that she knows him to be untrustworthy.'

'Did they divorce recently?'

'No, years ago. Before Candida even started the business. When I put my foot in it, David Aston-Stewart took me out for a drink to tell me why Candida had gone off her rocker. Consider it a rite of passage in working for ARC. Every sucker has to mention Jack

Delavigne at some point, and you just did it sooner than most.'

'But why does she hate him so much?'

'I'm not sure. David said it was something to do with the death of their son – they had a baby who died, or something. I've never dared ask Candida.'

'God, how awful! You don't mean he killed their son?'

'You're getting carried away, my dear Theodora. He isn't in prison, he's just got a life sentence at Hayes Goldsmith. I don't know the story, I just know that the baby died, and that they split up, and that Candida goes as white as chalk if she ever hears his name mentioned. David said it was something to do with the little boy drowning whilst Jack was looking after him. Apparently, Jack just went back to work after the funeral as if nothing had happened.'

'Oh God. Poor Candida. No wonder she hates him so much. Has she never remarried?'

'Candida?' Jamie looked amused. 'Teddy, you may have learnt the business of headhunting very quickly, in fact, you've taken to it like a duck to Peking – but you have an awful lot to learn about Candida Redmayne. Candida marry? She doesn't marry men – ' he leant forward, his hands forming claws and his teeth bared ' – she eats them alive!' He took another large swallow of wine. 'For breakfast.'

Teddy was intrigued. Her opinion of Candida rose. To have lost a baby, and gone through a divorce from the man who was responsible, and to have then managed to pull yourself together and build a business! What a woman! It made her own little problems with Mike look ridiculous. At the same time, she wondered what sort of a monster Jack Delavigne was, to have let his son die, and then abandoned his grieving wife. She would certainly take him off the shortlist for FRG Barnekov, but she was determined to do a little bit more research into this awful man. Candida was right; he really didn't deserve to have a job at all.

JANUARY 14TH, 1984

It was a bitterly cold day. The doctor – if he could be called a doctor – practised in one of the large, anonymous houses that lined Harley Street.

A young, attractive woman paced restlessly around the large table that dominated the middle of the waiting room, taking in the other occupants: an old man, leaning heavily on a cane, a heavily pregnant woman, a family of two small girls and their clearly fraught mother. To stop herself staring, and wondering what had brought the other people here, she started to flip through one of the magazines that lay scattered on the mahogany table. Endless photographs of remote Scottish shooting estates, pictures of dogs and horses, portraits of young society women with frozen smiles, cunningly posed in three quarter profiles, so that their normally plain faces were granted some temporary distinction by the camera. Lost in contemplation of what seemed to be such trouble-free lives, the young woman jumped when the receptionist said from the doorway, 'Miss Redmayne? Mr Ballantyne will see you now.'

The room she was shown to was more welcoming than the waiting room had been, largely owing to the open fire that burned brightly in one corner. Candida contemplated the two large armchairs, but was unwilling to sit down until the doctor arrived; perhaps he'd sit behind the desk, or want to sit next to her on the small two-seater sofa in front of the fire. At least there wasn't a couch. She pretended to study the books that lined the walls of the consulting room, but was disconcerted to find that her vision was so *blurred by tears that she couldn't read the titles. Hearing a quiet cough behind her, she turned to see a tall, slim man with a slight stoop and greying hair. It was hard to pinpoint his age, but she guessed he was somewhere in his fifties. He motioned her to one of the armchairs without speaking or shaking her hand, and sitting down opposite her, began to polish his gold-rimmed spectacles with the corner of a white handkerchief. As Candida waited for him to speak, she felt the knots in her stomach tighten with apprehension. She spoke hurriedly, feeling that if she were silent any longer, her voice would crack, and that she would erupt into racking sobs.*

'I used to come to Harley Street all the time . . . to number ninety-six. To my obstetrician. Mr Rees-Williams. Do you know him?' *she spoke brightly, as if meeting someone at a cocktail party, and trying to find common ground.*

'I don't believe so, no.' *Mr Ballantyne's voice had a slight Scottish lilt, and Candida immediately pictured him with a labrador at his heels and a Purdey cocked over his shoulder on one of the Highland hunting estates featured in those glossy magazines downstairs.*

He continued, 'It's surprising how little the inhabitants of Harley Street do meet, actually. We run into each other constantly, of course, and I would probably recognise his face, but we really have very little to do with each other.'

'I suppose it's a very different field,' *Candida mumbled.*

'Oh, they're all related, actually. Any work that involves talking to individuals at length tends to share a lot of common points.'

He continued to polish his glasses, but looked up at her, and smiled. Candida was struck by the deep colour of his eyes, a blue that normally faded to grey in middle age. They sat in silence.

'*Don't you want to ask me why I'm here?*' she blurted out, almost uncontrollably.

'*I thought perhaps you'd tell me, but I'll ask if you like. Why are you here, Miss Redmayne?*'

'*I don't know. I mean, I know that my GP thought I should come, and he recommended you, and my husband thought I should come, and I suppose it can't do any harm, but I don't want to be here — I mean, it's not that I positively* don't *want to be here, it's just that I don't want to be here, if you see what I mean. I don't think I need help, exactly, I just need some time to be by myself. I need some time to think about everything . . .*' She paused, feeling the tightening around her throat, the constriction as tears threatened to spill over and take control of her once again.

'*I see. Would you like to postpone this meeting until you have had a chance to think things through?*'

'*No!*' Candida's voice rose. '*It's taken me three weeks to summon up the courage to come here — I won't ever come back if I leave now!*'

Mr Ballantyne didn't seem at all perturbed by her threat. Replacing his glasses, he picked up a notepad, and said, '*Would you mind if I made a few preliminary notes? Asked some background details?*'

She shook her head, mutely.

'*Is Redmayne your married name, or your maiden name?*'

'*Maiden.*'

'*And your christian name is Candida, is that correct?*' She nodded.

'*What is your married name?*'

'*Delavigne,*' Candida whispered the word.

'*How old are you?*'

'*Twenty-eight.*'

'*Do you work?*'

'No – well I used to. Not any more. I used to be a broker in the City.'

'Do you have any family?'

There was a long pause. Candida stared at one of her rings, twisting it round and round her finger as she struggled to control her voice. She swallowed hard, and replied without looking up, 'Yes. My mother is still alive. My father died when I was fifteen. My sister lives here in London, and I have a brother in Paris. My husband; I suppose he counts as family . . .'

'Tell me a little about your family. Are you the eldest?'

'No; my brother Philip is the eldest. He's two years older than me. He's married – happily, I'd say – and lives in Paris. He works for a French stockbroker,' she explained. 'My little sister Jessica is twenty-four. I've no idea what she's going to do; she doesn't seem to do much except go to parties.'

'Are you close to your brother and sister?'

'I'm very close to Philip – I miss him a lot now he's in Paris; it's not far away, of course, and we see each other often, but it's not the same.'

'And Jessica?'

'Oh,' she said with a sigh, 'of course I love Jess – everybody does – but she's just a baby. We don't have very much in common, really. She's very sweet, but it annoys me that she can't seem to get her act together. I've told her a thousand times that she has to grow up and make some plans for the future, but she just carries on partying. She seems to measure her whole life in terms of bottles of Bolly; that's Jess.' She shrugged her shoulders. 'But don't think I don't love her; I do. We're a very close family.'

'And your parents?'

'Well, they were both wonderful people, and good parents, but they didn't have a lot of time. They're both *quite career minded. At least Daddy was, and Mummy threw herself into a career after he died. He worked in the City – overworked in the City I should say. He had a heart attack when he was only forty-five. Mummy was only forty. I don't think she could face a life that had nothing in it but children – and we were all growing up anyway – so she started training to be a lawyer. She's done really well, given how late she started.'*

'Do you like her?'

'Of course I do! She's my mother! Look, I think you're barking up the wrong tree, if you don't mind my saying. You seem to think that the reason I'm here is that I have some miserable childhood history, that I hate my parents, or that my father abused me. Honestly, if you're looking for some sort of weird, Freudian hang-ups from my childhood you're going to be disappointed. It just wasn't like that. I had a very happy, secure childhood. We're a very happy, close family. It's a shame my father died, but he did, and we coped afterwards. There aren't any skeletons in the cupboard.'

'That's fine; now tell me about your own family.'

'I have.'

'No, I mean you and your husband. Do you have any children?'

'No.' She swallowed hard again.

'I'm sorry; I thought you said that you used to come here to visit your obstetrician?'

'Did I? If so, I meant gynaecologist.' Candida shifted in the chair, drawing her knees up and pulling them towards her. Mr Ballantyne continued to write.

'How long have you been married?'

'Five years. We married in '79.'

'Thank you. I think that's enough background for now.' Mr Ballantyne put the notebook aside. 'How would you describe yourself, Candida? May I call you Candida?'

'Of course. Describe myself?' She spoke slowly. 'Well, I've never really had to do that . . .'

'Do you consider yourself to be happy?'

'Happy? Moderately, I suppose. I've had an easy life, no real problems, I mean I'm not someone who's always bursting with joie de vivre, *you understand, but I think I would say, yes, I'm happy. It all depends on what you mean by happiness. I'm content.'*

'No specific complaints? No dissatisfactions?'

'Well, we all have those. . .I'd like to work again. I stopped a couple of years ago, and perhaps I shouldn't have. I'd like to be richer, but we're not badly off. I don't really feel that I have any goals at the moment – perhaps that's the problem. I normally have something to strive for – I need to have something to strive for – but I don't know what I want right now.'

'You said that you had had to steel yourself to come to see me today. Why did you find the prospect frightening?'

Candida laughed. 'Aren't all your patients frightened? It's not a particularly pleasant idea, going to see a shrink. And besides, I don't like talking about myself – I don't like being asked questions, it makes me feel rather nervous, rather embarrassed; well, out of control, I suppose.'

The more she talked, the more uncomfortable Candida became. She knew very well why she was here, why she had finally brought herself to see a psychotherapist, and now that she was in the room alone with him, she knew that the last thing she wanted to do was to tell him what had happened. She racked her brain to think of a plausible reason for her visit, and leapt on the first thing that presented itself.

'I shouldn't really have come to see you at all,' she continued with a bright smile. 'I think I really needed a different kind of counsellor – a careers counsellor, or a headhunter. My only real problem is that I shouldn't have

stopped work when I did, and now I have to decide whether to go back to my old job, or try to do something else . . .' As soon as the words died on her lips, she realised her mistake, and Mr Ballantyne was quick to pounce on it.

'Why did you stop work two years ago?' he asked blandly.

Candida looked at her hands, and began a makeshift manicure, pushing back the cuticles of each nail, buying time to answer. God, why had she come here? She ran her tongue around her teeth and licked her lips nervously. Her mouth felt bone dry.

'I don't know. Burn-out. I just felt like it. People get fed up in the City.'

'People get fed up everywhere, in my experience. Did you find your job particularly stressful?'

'No, I loved it.' Damn! She'd done it again! Opened the door a chink that was wide enough for him to slip through. She continued hurriedly, not wanting her inquisitor to proceed with his line of attack. 'I mean, when I say I loved it, that at times I loved it, but yes, it was stressful. Very stressful. Long hours, hard work, a lot of pressure to perform. A lot of stress. It's a very intense job. Brokers always have to strive towards something: a new client, a new commission target, a bigger bonus . . .'

'That's interesting. It sounds an ideal job for someone who acknowledges herself to be as goal-driven as you are.'

This time there was a long silence, and as Candida stared at Mr Ballantyne, she felt an uneasy sensation creep over her – the feeling that he already knew why she was really here, knew what had happened to her, and was deliberately tying her up into knots to squeeze it out of her. She had talked herself into seeing a therapist because she felt that Jack might be right, for once. It might be comforting to talk to some gentle old man, to do all her crying on the shoulder of a benevolent stranger. But this man wasn't comforting, and he wasn't benevolent. She felt frightened of him, felt that he was dangerous, particularly dangerous to her. She wanted him to like her, but she didn't want him to know her – not till she was ready, at least. She certainly couldn't tell him the truth, and he had an uncanny way of picking up the irrationalities in her lies. She stood up briskly and walked over to the bookcase.

'I liked the job when I was younger. I'm honest enough to say that I was very good at it, and I chose to leave it at the right time. Maybe it's the sort of job one just outgrows.'

Mr Ballantyne's eyebrows rose, almost imperceptibly, but enough for Candida to know that her story didn't wash at all.

'Twenty-six is a very young age to feel you're too old for something.'

'You're right. I think that's where I made my mistake. I thought I was too old for my job, and in point of fact I was too young for it! Too young to know better.' She continued her perusal of the bookshelves, unwilling to meet his eyes, and his soft voice resumed behind her.

'Careers are a very difficult choice for everyone. One never quite knows if one's doing the right thing.' Mr Ballantyne put down his pen and notebook, and walked over to sit behind his desk. 'Candida, I think I should tell you a little bit about how I work, and how I think we should proceed, and see if you agree with that?' He raised his eyebrows and looked questioningly at her over the rim of his glasses. She nodded, mutely.

'I think that we should meet once a week. I view the first four to six sessions as purely introductory; after that time, I hope that we will have covered some ground, and that I will be in a position to assess how you can best be treated, and how long such treatment might take. The issues troubling you may well be to do with your career choices, or they

*may not. I don't have any rules about what we should talk
about, that's entirely in your hands. The only rule that I do
have is that if you decide to stop coming to see me, you will
come for one final session to review the work we have done
together, and close off the treatment. Do you think you can
make that commitment?'*

*'Well, I don't know. . .I can't believe that this is all going
to take so long. I mean, I feel much better about things
already.' Candida's back went ram-rod straight suddenly,
as she felt a trickle of ice-cold water run between her
shoulder blades. She wheeled round to face him. 'You're
very good at your job. I already feel a lot better. I'm sure
you're right. I know it, in fact; you've just helped me to
realise it. I should go back to broking. I'm cut out for it,
and I've just been missing it.' She held out her hand.*

*'Thank you so much, Mr Ballantyne. You've been a great
help, and I hope I haven't wasted too much of your time. I
fear it was a rather silly little problem, after all.'*

*Mr Ballantyne had risen and taken her hand, but didn't
seem to be at all keen to release it. Candida struggled
against the urge to tug it away from him; the tightness
of his grip, and the calm gaze of his penetrating blue eyes
in their deep sockets caused a surge of panic.*

*'Candida, I feel that you are very hurt about something.
You shouldn't carry such a heavy burden with you. I want
you to agree to come back to see me next week, and I want
your earnest commitment that you will continue to come
to see me until we have formally closed our sessions. Do
you agree?'*

*'All right,' she gasped, and pulling her hand free, bolted
for the door.*

CHAPTER THREE

The weeks following Mike's return from Tokyo flew past. Mike was working extremely hard, and had many late nights at the office. He explained long-sufferingly to Teddy that he was being considered for partnership, and needed to put in a lot of long hours before the election in October. Teddy felt as if she were on automatic pilot. She rose with Mike, they had breakfast on the run, she worked, she went home, she waited for Mike, they slept. They did make love, but sporadically. Teddy had the impression that Mike was only doing it to please her, and that she was only doing it to please him. It wasn't exactly artificial, but it was somehow half-hearted. They did, however, set a date for the wedding. Mike wanted to marry the following January.

'Let's get the partnership election, and your first search, and Christmas behind us, and then 1993 will be for you and me.' She was immensely relieved. Ever since the Tokyo trip a small thought that Mike no longer loved her had been like a bruise on her mind that she couldn't avoid pressing. Once the date for the wedding had been fixed, her doubts vanished. After all, this was what real life was all about – juggling relationships and careers – and if she was going to 'have it all' she would have to put up with 'all of it' not being perfect all the time. Mike had also brought her a present from Tokyo; a pair of extraordinary square-cut emerald earrings to match her engagement ring. Teddy squashed the thought that Glory might have helped to choose them. Mike was right; they were both too busy to start planning a wedding, and 1993 was really only just around the corner.

Candida had been relieved, too; ARC was inundated with searches, and all five consultants were overstretched. At least Teddy wouldn't be going off on honeymoon immediately. She had even dropped her defences enough to allow Teddy a little glimpse into her past. 'Don't be in too much of a hurry to marry, Teddy,' she had drawled, 'I was once, and no good came of it. Women like you and me don't need to marry. I don't imply that we don't need *men*; we just don't need to marry them.'

It was now April. One morning, Teddy and Mike drove in to work together at the ungodly hour of a quarter to seven. 'I'll be at the office late tonight, Mike. I have to make a whole string of calls to the States, and I can't start them till I've finished the European ones.' There was no reply. 'Mike?'

'Huh? Sorry. I was miles away. That's fine. I'll be late myself. I'm seeing Fitz at seven.'

'Alex Fitzgerald? Why?'

'Oh, he wants to talk through a rearrangement of the department, nothing serious.'

'I always thought he was an absolute bastard when I met him.'

'He is; that's why he's so damn good at the job. I've got a lot of time for him. Anyway, I want him to support my election to partnership, so it helps to keep on his good side.'

Teddy shivered. She had come across Alex Fitzgerald only rarely when she had worked at Steinberg's but every time they met, she had felt as if she were standing in front of him wearing only her knickers. All the female staff of Steinberg hated him. After he'd looked a woman up and down, the only way of feeling clean again was a scrub with a brillo pad. She'd never forgotten the Steinberg joke that Fitz was at best one of the undead, and at worst, a not very distant relative of the devil.

'Well, I hope you've remembered your string of garlic and your crucifix . . . Shall I lend you mine?' she joked, pretending to remove the cross from around her neck. 'I'll see you back in Kensington, okay?'

'Sure, but stay at your place if you like; I'll be really late, and I know you've been longing to get back there.'

'Yes; I probably should. You haven't forgotten I'm off to Frankfurt tomorrow? I'm starting my interviews. I'll be gone till Friday.' Mike was clearly deaf to the note of wistfulness in her voice.

'Well, have an early night, and take care of yourself. And be a good girl, darling.'

He set her down at Finsbury Square, and drove on to Steinberg's.

Teddy popped her head into Candida's office, and was surprised to see her engrossed in a phone call. Candida must sleep in the office, Teddy thought. Unless she was on a trip, she was the first in and the last to leave, and always looked as fresh as a daisy. This morning was no exception. Candida looked positively elated, her normally pale cheeks suffused with colour, her blue eyes clear and bright. She was wearing an extraordinary outfit: a long, pencil-thin cream skirt that reached almost to her ankles, which still satisfied Candida's rule of displaying her best features by being slashed up the side nearly to the top of her thigh. An ice-blue silk shirt and tightly cinched broad belt completed the picture. Candida seemed to get bolder and bolder every day, and yet managed to look nothing less than elegant. Teddy was beckoned in to sit on the sofa whilst Candida finished her call. When Candida put down the phone, she shook back her mane of hair and stretched, like a large, languorous leopard. Her eyes sparkled.

'Teddy, we're on a roll. That was Alex Fitzgerald.'

'How uncanny! Mike and I were just talking about him five minutes ago. What does he want?'

'Oh, he wants us to do a rather special job for him. A bit of upgrading.'

'You mean someone's getting promoted? Is it Mike?'

Candida roared with laughter. 'I thought you'd know Steinberg's euphemisms. "Upgrading" means career re-aligning.' Teddy looked blank. 'Or career alternative enhancement; resource reallocation; career-change opportunity; decruiting; outplacement.' Teddy still looked confused. 'Sacking; laying off; giving someone the boot; the big heave-ho; passing the pink slip.'

Teddy was appalled. 'Why on earth do they call it upgrading, for God's sake? Can't you imagine the poor guy going in and being told he's being upgraded, and getting really excited?'

'Well, in this case, it's not a guy. It's a girl. Fitz likes her, but says she's not quite up to the job, so he wants to treat her gently, and has asked us to find her an offer she can't refuse. That way, she'll be able to feel she's leapt, rather than been pushed.' Candida looked down at her notes. 'She's a trader called Glory McWhirter.'

'*Glory*?' This was clearly going to be a day of surprises. 'I don't believe it! She's one of their best traders – works with Mike – she was only transferred from New York eight months ago!'

'Well, it looks like she's about to be transferred from London,' Candida spoke briskly. 'Anyway, don't worry about Glory. We'll find her a good home. In fact, I might just be able to kill two birds with one stone . . . do my old friend Malcolm Fairchild at Hayes Goldsmith a favour. He's lost so many people to Steinberg's, he should be delighted to get one back. God, I love this business, don't you?' Candida seemed lit from within.

Teddy nodded a little uncertainly.

'What do you think? Should you interview Glory, or should I?'

'You do it. I simply couldn't – I know her too well, and it would be embarrassing.'

'Right. I'll set it up. Now, you're off to Frankfurt and Paris, right? I can't wait to hear how they go. Just remember that the French are always arrogant, and talk their own book up, and the Germans always talk it down.' Candida was already back on the phone.

'Candida, it's seven-thirty in the morning! Who on earth are you calling?'

'Glory McWhirter. If she's as good as you say she is, she ought to be in by now, right?' Candida winked.

The next day, Teddy checked into the Frankfurter Hof Hotel. The lobby was bustling with business men and Japanese tourists, though why on earth any tourist should choose to come to Frankfurt was beyond Teddy's comprehension. Conscious that her list of German candidates would be uncomfortable meeting in such a public place – Teddy was ever mindful of Candida's analogy of the headhunter and the VD specialist – and aware that the Germans were even more neurotic than most about apparent disloyalty, she booked a small, private meeting room to ensure confidentiality, and prevent her guests' embarrassment.

Dieter Schleeman was her first appointment. He had agreed to meet Teddy in the bar of The Frankfurter Hof, and arrived exactly on time. He bent formally over her hand, and snapped his heels together. Teddy smiled to herself as she led him to the conference room; it was uncanny how frequently national stereotypes appeared to be true. After an hour's meeting, Teddy had not only satisfied herself that Dieter was a suitable candidate for the position at FRG Barnekov, but had managed to tempt him sufficiently to agree to meet her client without disclosing the actual name of the firm. What a stroke of luck that her very first interview should have progressed so smoothly, and had such a happy conclusion. Dieter had even admitted that prior to her introductory call, he had been thinking of making a career move, and her contact had strengthened his resolution. Teddy felt her confidence surge. She had been nervous about this trip. It was her first trial at flying solo, with neither Candida nor Jamie there to guide the interview or confirm her judgement, and she felt that so far she had passed with flying colours. She was, after all, only twenty-eight, and most of the candidates she had arranged to see were significantly older and more experienced than she was. At the beginning of each interview she felt a rush of adrenalin, and she used it to her advantage. Whenever she felt insecure, whenever she felt that she didn't really have a right to grill these strangers about their abilities and experience, she reminded herself that she was in the position of power. They had agreed to meet her because she had something to offer, and it was up to them to impress her. She was a natural at the job because she was a good listener, and she was a good listener because she was genuinely interested in people. Teddy's only problem as a headhunter was that she was inclined to set her expectations too high; she expected to be impressed by everyone she interviewed, and her day in Frankfurt proved to be something of an eye-opener. Teddy looked forward to her next meetings with keen anticipation; if they all went so well, she would be able to give FRG Barnekov a record-breaking shortlist of maybe fifteen names. They'd be spoilt for choice.

Fortunately for the directors of Barnekov, Teddy had been more than a little too optimistic. The remaining candidates that day were dismal beyond belief, and it had been a battle to conceal her disappointment and boredom from them. Candidates who had seemed interesting, even impressive, on the screen, had turned out to be the sort of men who made sheep look dynamic. It took her about ten minutes to decide if the candidate was a no hoper; after that, she focused her efforts on getting as much information about their colleagues as she could, without the candidate cottoning on to the fact that he was simply being pumped. This was how ARC's database had really been built up, and the method required an extraordinary degree of subtlety and artfulness on the part of the headhunter. If the interviewee smelt a rat, his mouth was likely to close tighter than a Scotsman's wallet. Candida had taught Teddy well, and by the end of the day, Teddy had amassed thirty new names to feed into the database. Thank God for Dieter, otherwise the day would have been a write-off as far as the search itself was concerned. By the time she had grabbed a sandwich and crawled into bed – removing the two chocolates that had been left on the carefully plumped pillows – she was too exhausted even to phone home and say good-night to Mike. She prayed fervently that the next day would produce some better interviews. Candida had warned her to be on her toes for Konrad von Budingen, whom she was due to meet for a seven-thirty breakfast.

Alex Fitzgerald had thought long and hard about his meeting with Mike Miccinelli. He wanted to sound out Mike without telling him too much, and he wanted to sow the seeds of doubt in his mind without driving the rather volatile trader into open rebellion against Steinberg Roth. It was a conversation that would demand all Fitz's powers of manipulation and tact; skills that he had developed in his eight years as a senior executive at Steinberg. He decided to play the role of Mike's buddy – his mentor – and appeal to the innate self-centredness that he had long ago recognised in the younger man.

They met in the small West End club that Fitz used for his most discreet appointments, and ordered drinks.

'Good of you to come, Mike. I've got a couple of problems that I want to get your input on, but before we talk about the department I would like to hear how things are going for you. How's the delightful Theodora?' Fitz had done his homework.

'She's fine, Fitz, just fine. She joined Candida Redmayne at ARC, you know, so if things ever turn sour at Steinberg I expect to be in the best place to get a lot of offers.' Mike laughed uneasily. He had told Teddy that he respected Fitz – which he did – but he was keeping up his guard until he knew exactly why he had been summoned for a personal chat. Strategy decisions were normally made by Mike and his direct boss, Norman Bell, and it was rare for Alex to talk to a trader without Norman being there. The two men circled round each other warily for a while, neither wanting to be the first to commit themselves.

'Mike, let me come right out with it,' Alex said finally. 'I have a bit of a problem with Glory McWhirter.'

Mike swirled the ice around in his glass, but made no reply.

'I think we ought to let her go.'

'She's a good trader, Fitz. She's better than a lot of people on the desk.'

'Sure, she's a good trader. She's a good trader because you trained her. You're a good boss – the best. But she's also expensive. She negotiated a high package to transfer from the States. On top of that, she puts people's backs up. You know how the London boys don't like interlopers from New York, and you must admit that Glory doesn't exactly make an effort to adapt.'

'Not many traders do.' Mike hadn't yet heard enough to know whether he should back his colleague or his boss. If Fitz was in the process of trying to run down the proprietary trading desk then Mike would fight him all the way; if, on the other hand, there was something in it for Mike, then he was prepared to listen to reason . . .

'I realise that. Don't get me wrong, Mike, I'm not going to make any decisions unless I have your total agreement. You run the desk after all, and you know who is really responsible for the profits you've been generating. I always assumed that ninety per cent of the desk's profits were coming from you personally, but if you feel that you couldn't keep up your performance without Glory, then it's a different ball game, and you need only say the word.'

Alex smiled to himself as he watched Mike swallow the bait.

'Now hang on a minute, Fitz. I said she was a good trader, but I'm certainly not dependent on her! She's learning fast, she does what she's told, but I still have to correct her judgement all the time. Maybe in another few years she would be able to make a real contribution to the desk, but at the moment, well, she's just learning.'

'That's what I thought. So if we let her go – to a good place of course, we could help her out with that – then you could keep an eye on her and when she was ripe, you could bring her back. But in the meantime, we can keep our overheads down and not worry Norm – '

'Norman? What's he got to do with it?'

Alex lowered his voice. 'Look, Mike. This is confidential, just between you and me. I promised Norman faithfully I wouldn't tell you about this. Norman's under a lot of pressure from the managing partners – we all are. This isn't going to be a good year for Steinberg's; problems on the investment banking side, losses coming from the equity desk. We've all been told to watch costs. To be absolutely frank, I don't think the future looks that bright for us for the next few years. It's no longer the old glory days of the eighties, when all you had to do to make a buck was to put on a smart suit and hand out your card. The only way to die rich these days is to shoot yourself before you go broke. We're all going to have to tighten our belts, I'm afraid.' He didn't look afraid at all. 'I think there are going to be a lot of surprises at the partnership election, and some people who may have been expecting election are going to be disappointed.'

'Are you talking about me, Fitz?'

Alex spread his hands wide. 'I don't know, Mike. If I did, believe me I'd tell you. Certain people just don't think Norman's doing that good a job. If it looks like he's prepared to make some cut-backs, and take tough decisions, it might just make him look better, and if he looks better, then the whole department will, you see? The election isn't for another six months after all, and anything can happen in six months.'

Mike sat silently, thinking through what Fitzgerald had said. Alex sighed; the time had come to play his cards *very* carefully.

'You know, Mike, off the record, if I were a younger man, I'd play my career differently. It's too late for me now, I am a partner, and I'm stuck with it. But in this sort of a market, and the way things are going at Steinberg's, if I was a young trader I'd look out for Number One. My objective would be to make as much money as I could in the short term and then set up independently. I shouldn't be saying this to you, of course. The last thing I could want is to have our best and most profitable trader leave, and anyway, there's every chance that you *will* be elected to partner this time round. I guess you should wait and see what happens. Anyway, we can talk about that another time. You know I'd always give you my best advice, don't you, Mike?'

Mike nodded, and Alex slapped him on the back.

'I've always kept my eye on you, Mike, you're going to go a long way. A real long way. It would gratify me just to know that I'd helped you along the right path.'

'Thanks, Fitz. I appreciate that.'

'And you agree about Glory? It's for all our sakes, hers too, in the long run.'

Mike nodded again.

'Terrific. Well, don't you worry about it any longer. I'll talk to Norman and Glory, and get things moving. You've got far better ways of spending your time. And don't worry about partnership, you've certainly got my vote, and without wishing to brag, that ought to count for quite a bit. If the others don't have the brains to know which side their bread is buttered, and elect you, then they're not worth working for, right? You look after that pretty fiancée of yours, okay? There's nothing so important as a good wife, hey? Give her a kiss from me, and make sure I get an invitation to the wedding, right? Right!'

As Mike stood at the door, about to leave the formal, oak-panelled sitting room, Fitz shouted, 'Buddy?'

Mike turned back, to see Fitz standing up, his chin pulled tight into his chest, his eyes meeting Mike's in a level and earnest stare. One arm was raised, the stubby index finger pointing directly at Mike.

'Buddy; you know I'd die on the cross for you; I mean it.'

Mike nodded.

As Mike walked down Pall Mall he felt angry with Norman Bell. Norman should have confided in him about what was going on at Board level; after all, it affected Mike's future as well as Norman's. He wasn't worried about Glory. She was as tough as old boots, and had an uncanny instinct for landing on her feet. Anyway, Fitz had given his word that he'd help her find a new position. It might even be the best thing for him to have Glory out of the office; she was getting a little too blatant, and a little too demanding. She turned him on, all right, but he would feel a lot happier if he could keep her a little bit more on the side. Most of all, it had been good of Fitz to confirm his support for Mike's election to partner. If Fitz voted for him, nobody else would dare to blackball it. It was as good as in the bag.

When Alex was left alone, he withdrew a filed report from the calfskin briefcase at his feet. It was a list of all those employees who had been recommended for partnership. Fitz turned to Norman Bell's list of candidates, and drew a thick black line through Mike Miccinelli's name. Five minutes later, Candida Redmayne sailed into the room, dressed to kill.

JANUARY 21ST, 1984

'How are you, Candida? Have you had a good week?'

Robert Ballantyne noted her red-rimmed eyes and wan face. She looked like a waxen image of a beautiful woman, the sockets of her eyes emphasised by soft purplish shadows, her cheeks hollow, her mouth turned down at the corners. She seemed deflated. She had shaken his hand limply, and seemed to have lost the hard, sinewy tension that had been so apparent at their last meeting.

'Oh, I'm all right. A little tired, that's all. I don't like January. It's an awful month.'

'Are you sleeping all right?'

'No; well, I don't know. I've never been a big sleeper — only about six hours a night. But recently it's been worse. I wake up five or six times during the night.'

'When did you start sleeping badly?'

She drew her hand over her face, massaging her eyes and temples.

'I don't know, really. A few weeks ago? I'm probably just getting flu. It's not important, anyway.'

'Candida, I'd like to hear a little bit of background about your husband. You mentioned last week that you had been married for five years.'

'That's right. My husband is called Jack Delavigne. He's a senior broker at Hayes Goldsmith. It's a merchant bank.'

'How did you meet?'

She smiled wanly. 'It was quite funny, actually. I was still a trainee broker at Drexel Burnham; I'd only been there for six months. I was sent to a presentation by a Swedish company. None of the analysts were able to go, and my boss told me to go and just take notes. I was absolutely terrified. The company was Astra — one of the biggest stocks in the Swedish market. I read all the research reports I could find, so that I wouldn't look like a complete idiot if I had to say anything, and then I sat down at the back of the room and tried to lose myself in the crowd. There must have been over a hundred analysts and salesmen there.' Candida's smile broadened, and a faint sparkle lit up her aquamarine eyes. 'I still feel sick with embarrassment whenever I think about it. The chairman opened the presentation, and then the finance director. I kept my mouth shut, though all the other brokers were being very aggressive — really giving them a hard time. Then the research boffins stood up to talk about their new drug licences and applications. I think I just got carried away by it all. I leapt to my feet, and they interrupted the presentation to answer my question. I made a total idiot of myself and asked them when they were going to get approval for Ventolin, which wasn't their drug at all. It was the rival drug launched by their biggest competitor.'

She laughed, and looked at Robert Ballantyne apologetically.

'*I'm sorry, it isn't very funny, is it? It's just one of those classic broker jokes. It seems so long ago and so unimportant now, but at the time it was truly terrible. The room erupted in laughter. I very nearly died of shame. Just as I was on the point of dashing out of the room, a man stood up in the row in front of me, and said, "What my colleague meant, is that surely the licensing of Ventolin recently secured by Glaxo will dramatically impact Astra's own launch of Bricanyl?" He wasn't my colleague, of course. I'd never seen him before in my life. I could have leant forward and kissed him if I hadn't been so mortified . . . That was Jack.*'

'*What a gentleman,*' *Ballantyne murmured.*

'*Oh yes; a gentleman, a dashing knight on a white charger, a fairy tale hero rescuing the damsel in distress from the dragon of the stockbroking community. Anyway, that was how we met. We married exactly a year later.*'

'*Did you want to get married?*'

'*Of course I did, or I wouldn't have done it. I wasn't under any pressure, if that's what you mean.*' *Candida had lost all traces of humour, and spoke in a clipped tone. 'Do you think I'm an idiot? Just because I made a mistake about pharmaceutical stocks doesn't mean that I didn't know where babies came from, or that I didn't know what to do about it. I suppose you think of me as some poor, little innocent virgin forced into a shotgun wedding?*'

'*Did you love Jack when you married him?*' *Robert Ballantyne remained, as always, unperturbed by her sarcasm.*

'*Yes. I worshipped him.*'

'*Do you love him now?*'

'*Yes.*'

Candida found the room stifling. Whether it was the heat from the fire, or the uncomfortable silence that followed her last assertion, or whether she was in fact coming down with flu, she felt faint, and longed to get out into the open air. She took a sip of water and lit a cigarette.

'Why do you think you love him?'

The therapist's question hung in the air with the wreath of smoke she had just exhaled.

'I don't really think that reasons for loving someone stand up to analysis.' Candida replied coldly, still feeling angry with him. 'I can tell you about him, what he's like, but I can't tell you why I love him. Could you tell me why you love your wife?'

'Yes, I believe that I could, but it wouldn't be relevant to our conversation. Tell me what Jack is like.'

'He's single-minded. He's devoted to his work, and very good at it. He sets very high standards. He's protective, responsible . . .' She paused, considering, 'perhaps a little distant. He doesn't get involved with many people. He's very English.'

'Is that a good thing, or a bad thing?'

'Neither. It's just a description, it's not a qualitative judgement. Anyway, he's been a good husband, all in all, and that's what concerns me.'

'You mentioned that he wanted you to see a psycho-therapist. Why was that?'

'We haven't been getting on very well recently. As I told you, I'm bored, and I want to go back to work. I'm clearly irritating Jack. He doesn't have time to deal with me, so I suppose he wants somebody else to handle it.'

'I see. Did he take an interest in your career after you married – before you stopped work?'

She shrugged. 'In his own way. We worked for rival firms, so it was rather difficult to talk to each other about what was going on in the office. You know, confidentiality rules and Chinese walls and everything. I suppose he was interested, yes, but neither of us had much time to sit around talking about the meaning of life.'

'*And now you do, and he doesn't?*'

'*It's not that simple. He doesn't want to talk about the same things I want to talk about.*'

'*What does he want to talk about?*'

Candida shifted uncomfortably in her chair, clearly displeased at the path the conversation was taking.

'*I don't know – you should ask him! I thought we were meant to be talking about what I wanted to discuss. If you want to hear Jack's sob story you can talk to him, and leave me out of it!*' *Candida snapped angrily. She sighed again, and looked at him wearily.* '*Look, I'm sorry. I really don't feel very well today. I must be getting something. Can we call it a day? I'll be all right next week.*'

When Candida left Harley Street she wandered aimlessly up towards Marylebone Road, and found herself entering Regent's Park. It had begun to rain, and the light snow had long turned to slush on the well-trodden paths. Candida gazed at a young mother sitting on a bench, chattering happily to an infant in a pram. It was only four p.m., but the lights in the park had already been turned on, their orange hue tinting the darkening sky. Candida wished the pubs were open. She had never gone into a pub alone in her life, but she longed for a large Scotch. On impulse, she hailed a taxi and directed it to her flat in Primrose Hill. By six p.m., Candida had fallen asleep on the sofa and the bottle of Glenfiddich was nearly half empty; some might have said half full, but to Candida's weary eyes, it was indisputably half empty.

Candida cancelled her appointment with Robert Ballantyne the following week, pleading a debilitating attack of flu, rather than a debilitating and recurrent hangover.

Whilst Teddy lay in one of the sumptuous bedrooms of the Frankfurter Hof Hotel, and whilst Mike, alone, celebrated his forthcoming election as a partner of Steinberg Roth

with a six-pack of Newcastle Brown, Candida Redmayne
and Alex Fitzgerald dined on oysters at Bill Bentley's, and
then retired to Candida's house for a nightcap. It was five
years since Candida had moved out of her original flat and
bought a large Georgian house in Primrose Hill. Without
speaking a word to Alex, she walked into the drawing
room and collected a bottle of champagne and two cut
crystal flutes, and then led Alex upstairs to her bedroom
which occupied the entire first floor of the house. Alex
sat down in one of the armchairs and watched Candida,
reluctant to break the silence that created an electric tension
between them.

Candida seemed to be in a trance. She undressed slowly,
leaving her clothes lying scattered on the floor where she
dropped them. First a chiffon scarf, in the softest shades of
pinks and greens, floated to the floor. Then she released the
tie of her wrap-around Norma Kamali dress, and draped
it over the back of the *chaise-longue*. Alex watched her
move about the room, wearing only a flesh-coloured silk
camisole, hardly daring to breathe lest he disturb her. He
felt supremely in charge, satisfied that this mysterious and
leonine woman was performing a show for his eyes alone.
He slouched in the chair, his eyes hooded. He was wrong.
Candida was no more aware of him at that moment than
she was aware of the rainfall level in the Netherlands. She
stood at the window and let the spaghetti straps of her
camisole slide off her marble shoulders, and then sat,
naked and unselfconscious, at the dressing table whilst
she brushed out her auburn hair. Alex started to count,
but gave up after thirty strokes. Candida rose and stood
before him, the bottle in her hand, a small, sweet smile on
her lips that belied the flame flickering dangerously in her
eyes. The pop of the champagne cork exploded in the room,
and they both laughed.

'So, Alex. All our little birds are coming home to roost.

It's taken eight years to get here. A long time to gather a little information. What is it they say in the City? Information is power.'

'No, Candida. Allow me to correct you. Information isn't power. Power is power.' Alex's voice was husky.

Candida handed him a glass of champagne, and straddled his lap. Alex pulled her towards him, the silken skin of her inner thighs rubbing roughly against the worsted of his suit.

'I'd like to propose a toast. To power. And to Jack Delavigne.'

The crystal glasses clinked, and they drank deeply.

JANUARY 21ST, 1984

'How's Candida?'

Jack played with his pen, sliding the top on and off rhythmically.

'She's bad, Dick. Awful. She insisted on moving out of the house. I told her I'd move out, if it would make her happier, but she said she hated it. I think that's pretty mild compared to how she feels about me. I simply don't think I can help her any more. God knows who can. She can barely speak to me on the phone. It isn't about Tommy any longer, it's about us — or about me, at least.'

Jack sat slumped at the table in one of the small dining rooms on the top floor of the Hayes Goldsmith building in Cannon Street. Richard Belton-Smith stood behind him, and patted him on the back. He was not usually a very demonstrative man, and had found it hard to express his sympathy to Jack over the past few months. The last thing that Jack needed, after losing his son, was to worry about his wife's mental health. Why the hell couldn't she pull herself together and get on with life? They were both young, there would be other children . . .

'I told her we could start another baby,' Jack continued, as if reading his boss's mind, 'and she nearly killed me. Went berserk. Grabbed a knife. I think she honestly wanted to kill me. Not her fault, of course; it's been such a strain on her.' He felt the gentle pressure of Dick's hand on his shoulder.

'Jack, there's no need for you to be here this morning. Why don't you go home? Take the day off, take Candida out somewhere. I'll deal with Fitzgerald.'

'No, she won't even speak to me on the telephone, let alone see me. I called her last night to see if we could meet. She called me a fucking assassin. I'd rather be here, thanks. What I would like to do is leave early today; I want to go over to Paris and see Candida's brother. Maybe he can help us through this, or at least help Candida.' He sighed heavily. 'Christ, it never rains but it pours. I've lost my son, I've probably lost my wife, and what do I have to do with my time? Sack a guy I really respect. You know, Dick, the worst thing about axeing Fitzgerald is that I like the man. He's refreshing to have around, and he's exceptionally bright, really creative. I'm sure he has a great future ahead of him. If only he could stop himself from pawing every woman in the office and calling our best clients "fucking cunts", I'd love to keep him . . .'

There was a tap at the door, and Jack visibly pulled himself together before opening it. Alex Fitzgerald stood uncomfortably on the other side, one hand shoved deep into his trouser pocket, the other hooking his jacket over his shoulder. Fitzgerald was renowned for being able to make a Savile Row suit look like something off the peg at Burton. Prejudiced people put it down to his being American, but it probably had more to do with having a fullback's physique. He flashed a smile, and sauntered across the room with his customary swagger.

'Hi, guys; what's for breakfast?'

Neither of the two men returned his smile, nor replied to his question. Jack pushed the coffee pot towards him, and looked at him gravely.

'Alex, I asked Richard to join us this morning because I felt you deserved to hear his opinions as well as my own. I have to admit that he and I have reached the same conclusions. You will remember that at your last review, we raised some doubts, not as to your professional ability, but concerning your personal conduct. I'm sorry to say that these doubts have resurfaced, and I have reached the unhappy conclusion that your personal style is probably not in sympathy with the image we try to project at Hayes Goldsmith.'

Fitzgerald leant back in his chair, and slowly unwrapped a pack of Marlboro cigarettes. The cellophane crackled noisily in the silence that met Jack's opening comment. After taking a deep drag on the cigarette, Alex met the eyes of the two impeccably dressed Englishmen opposite him. He misread their expressions, not for the first time, and probably not for the last, and decided to play the scene with bravado.

'Okay, guys. It's a fair cop. I've tried, really tried, to become a Brit over the past few months, but I can't do it all at once. I just can't shake the accent. Jeez, Jack, you've spent enough time on the other side of the pond, you know what hicks we all are – at least I'm going to the right tailor now!' *He laughed, but nobody joined in.* 'Whaddya want me to do next, start going to the opera? Playing cricket? Join Whites? Go to a voice coach? Level with me, guys!'

'It isn't that simple, Alex.' *Jack, sighing, pulled a grey folder towards him.* 'We have received various complaints, some from members of our staff, some from clients, about *your, ah, interpersonal relationships. Far be it from me to suggest that you should change. We simply feel that your technique might be better suited to a different sort of firm than Hayes Goldsmith. Perhaps you would be more comfortable in an American house?'*

Fitzgerald's eyes narrowed as he leant across the table, his dark, saturnine face became sullen. Jack continued.

'Clearly certain people respond very well to your motivational style, but too many of our own people find you difficult to handle, to say the least. It may, of course, be simply a question of culture, but I can't help feeling, for your own sake – '

'You asshole. You fucking, condescending, arrogant, patronising, English fucking prick!'

Dick winced as Fitzgerald spat out each word, as if the American were jabbing him in the stomach with each obscenity. Jack sat calmly. He had expected Fitzgerald to react badly; he wasn't a man who took criticism well, and in many ways Jack found this response easier to handle than if his criticism had been met by pleas for a second chance.

'You are quite right to be angry, Alex. In many ways, I should bear the responsibility for this. It was, after all, I who hired you. That's why we would like to offer you as much time and assistance as you require in finding a more appropriate post. We would like to help – '

'Fuck you!' Alex snarled. 'As we say back home, I wouldn't piss on you if you were on fire. Don't try to do me any favours, buddy. You think I need your help to get a job? There are ten firms out there begging me to join them.'

'I'm sure that's true. You have many talents, Alex, many, and we will be the poorer for losing you. I would also like to assure you that there is no question of our not paying you the bonus that you so richly deserve; we would like to make it an ex gratia payment – ' Jack's soothing tone *seemed to inflame Fitzgerald, who turned crimson with anger and leapt to his feet. Richard Belton-Smith also rose, ready to throw his towering frame between the two men if necessary. His authoritative presence seemed to dwarf the explosive American.*

'*Darn right, you're going to be a whole lot poorer. This business isn't finished. You wait and see.*' *Having made his threat, Alex Fitzgerald grabbed his jacket, picked up his cigarettes, and strode to the door. On the point of leaving, he swung back to face the man who had humiliated him.*

'*Hey, Delavigne. I've been meaning to mention. Didn't I hear your kid had snuffed it?*' *Jack didn't raise his head, but Belton-Smith laid a hand protectively on his shoulder.*

'*Lucky kid. What a break.*'

The door slammed shut behind him.

CHAPTER FOUR

There were about twenty people in the dining room of the Frankfurter Hof when Teddy came down at seven a.m. It was a large room, with one side dedicated to a spectacular buffet of breakfast foods: six varieties of eggs, smoked Westphalian hams, sliced cheese, pancakes, muesli, compotes of fruit . . . Teddy helped herself to an orange juice, and ordered a large pot of coffee. She didn't want to be caught eating when Konrad von Budingen arrived. She turned the pages of the *International Herald Tribune* nervously, watching the door.

After a few minutes, a man appeared in the doorway and surveyed the room. He was tall and broadly built, conservatively dressed in a dark grey suit and sombre tie. His fair hair was brushed high off his forehead. The waiters scurried around, as if his very arrival had triggered their frenzied activity. Teddy returned to her paper; this wasn't her guy. German bankers, in her limited experience, didn't have that sort of presence.

'Mrs Winnington?' She looked up. It *was* him!

He clicked his heels together and bowed over her hand as she rose to meet him. Teddy suppressed a smile; Candida was right about the heel-clicking.

'I am Konrad von Budingen. I hope I haven't kept you waiting?'

'No, you are exactly on time. Can I offer you some breakfast . . . coffee . . . tea?' He smiled at her, his grey eyes softening a little.

'No thank you; I am normally at my desk at this hour. I breakfast with my family at six a.m.'

He took a seat, and waited for Teddy to open the interview. She looked at him, and gave in to temptation.

'Konrad, tell me one thing; when you came in, you came immediately to my table. How on earth did you know what I looked like?'

'I didn't, but I am paid to make rational guesses. I expected to see a headhunter, English, and female. That narrowed my selection down to three. I remembered your voice on the phone, and judged you to be in your twenties, or early thirties; that narrowed my choice to two. I chose the more attractive.'

He spoke matter-of-factly, without any apparent attempt at flattery or suggestion. Teddy smiled. 'So you were lucky.'

'I am normally very lucky,' Konrad replied earnestly.

As the interview progressed, Teddy realised that she might have been wrong about Dieter Schleeman. Dieter was good, perhaps he was very good, but if so, Konrad was great. He spoke easily about his past, his education, his family background, his work at Delius-Zech. His confidence was natural and relaxed; few men she had met could talk so openly about their successes without either arrogance or insecurity sneaking through. His career was unsullied; one triumph after another, a client list that Goldman Sachs would die for, and yet he remained unaffected. He was the corporate financier *par excellence*; a man of strength, yet a man of discretion; at home with hard facts and figures, yet sensitive to business psychology.

'Konrad, tell me a little bit more about yourself. What do you regard as your greatest weakness?'

'My lack of real faith in God; that is certainly my greatest weakness.'

Teddy was silenced. She had expected the normal run of

semi self-congratulating faults – the standard list of inability to take no for an answer, intolerance of mediocrity (an old favourite), excessive drive and determination, spending too little time at home because they were too committed to the office. Headhunters were frequently presented with a list of faults that, with a flick of the wrist, could be turned into qualities. Konrad von Budingen wasn't playing silly games. He spoke earnestly, from the heart, and without forethought as to how Teddy would evaluate his response.

'Does religion mean a great deal to you?'

'Yes, I believe so; certainly the fact that my faith falters means a great deal to me.'

Teddy didn't want to pursue this subject. She was glad that Konrad had been so honest, but his revelation rather embarrassed her; it was almost more personal than if he had told her that he had a problem with premature ejaculation.

'Is there anything else? Are there any professional failings that you recognise, or that your peers or superiors might recognise?'

Konrad thought for a while without replying. 'Yes, there is something else. I believe that I lack "charm"; I believe that in these times, a good banker requires more than mastery of the financial instruments, more than a strong mathematical mind, and more than distribution, or "placing power" as our American friends call it. I believe a real banker needs *charm* . . . I doubt whether I possess it.'

Teddy felt as if she were falling in love, and reminded herself sharply that she was engaged to be married. She smiled warmly at him. 'I'm not worried about that. Trust me, I think you have more than enough charm.'

She proceeded to tell him about the position at FRG Barnekov, detailing the advantages of working for a truly global firm rather than one that was domestically focused,

such as Delius-Zech. Konrad listened carefully, asked
sensible questions, and agreed to meet her client. Having
written down the details of his CV, Teddy shook him by the
hand and said goodbye. She had a plane to catch, to Paris.

Charles de Gaulle airport pulsed with life; the concourse
was chaotic, teeming with would-be immigrants, tourists
and the ever-present mobile army of businessmen in their
dark suits. Whereas Frankfurt ran like clockwork, a model
of German efficiency, the administration at Charles de
Gaulle seemed to take pleasure in adding to the disarray,
changing landing gates at the last moment, closing passport
control and moving hundreds of delayed and grumpy
arrivals half way round the airport for no apparent reason.
Teddy was spitting with anger by the time she cleared
customs. It was already noon; her first appointment was
for twelve thirty, according to her schedule, and God only
knew how long it would take her to get into the city
centre. Elbowing her way rudely to the front of the taxi
queue, she slammed her bag into the back seat, handed
the driver an incentive of one hundred francs, and spat
out her destination. As they pulled off, Teddy heard an
Englishwoman in the queue say in a glass-shatteringly clear
voice, 'My God, the French are unspeakably rude!' That at
least brought a smile to Teddy's lips.

 When she arrived at the Hotel Georges V, she rushed to
the front desk and gave her name. The receptionist looked
slowly through his messages. 'Meese Winnington . . . yes.
There is a gentleman waiting for you in ze zentral 'all.'
He leant over the desk and pointed. 'Monsieur le Baron
de Clement-Grandcourt.'

 Christian de Clement-Grandcourt sat in one of the
brocade chairs that lined the central lobby of the hotel.
He was immaculately dressed, one leg crossed elegantly
over the other. He looked as if he owned the hotel. For

all Teddy knew, he did. He rose and smiled as Teddy came
to meet him.

'Christian? I am so very sorry to have kept you waiting.'

'It is I who should apologise on behalf of my countrymen.
Doubtless you have been a victim of our abominable
Parisian traffic.' His English was flawless, but he spoke with
the lilting French accent that Teddy found so gloriously
seductive.

'Perhaps we could move to somewhere more private? I
have reserved a sitting room.'

When Teddy and Christian had settled themselves in the
little salon provided by the hotel, been brought coffee and
chatted about whether the traffic was worse in London or
Paris, Teddy took out her notebook and pen and jotted
down a few apt phrases to describe the Frenchman.

'Sophisticated, smooth Euro-yuppy style. Blue-black,
straight hair. Piercing blue eyes – wonderful crow's feet.
Bedable. Tall. All the quintessentially French habits; white
socks, two-tone shoes, monogrammed shirt.' That was
enough of a sketch to allow her to remember his looks
when she got back to the office. She didn't think she'd
forget them in a hurry.

'So, Christian, where shall we start? Perhaps you could
give me a brief résumé of your career, starting with your
education.'

He shrugged. 'Of course; I'm afraid it's all rather pre-
dictable and boring.' He proceeded to outline a classic,
blue-chip French pedigree; the Lycée Louis le Grand,
then Assas, followed by Sciences Po, one of the *Grandes
Ecoles* of Paris, a year at INSEAD, and a stint with the
IMF before leaving to enter investment banking with
Chavaudret-Desforges, one of the few French banks that
could compete globally with the Anglo-American players.
His career path had been smooth and unusually fast, yet

he attributed this to being in the right place at the right time rather than to any particular talent of his own.

'So, you are . . . forty-three?' Teddy calculated.

'Yes; do you think I look it?'

Teddy looked at him carefully and answered seriously, 'No, I should say not.' She made a few more notes. 'Are you married?'

'Do I look married?' Again she studied his face, his smiling eyes accentuating the crow's feet, his thin upper lip and fuller lower lip parting to display a row of even white teeth.

'No; on reflection, I should say not.'

He laughed, and poured himself another cup of coffee. 'And I should say that you are a remarkably perceptive young woman.'

'So tell me, Christian; how do you see your career going on from here?'

'Clearly it is time for me to move on from Chavaudret, if I am to move at all. I have reached – how do you say it? – a critical point. I expect that I shall be promoted to the Board within the next year or two, and it is not *comme il faut*, in France, to move after that point. So, I have my nose to the ground, sniffing out opportunities.'

Teddy couldn't help chuckling at the bloodhound image this conjured up; she found it hard to imagine Christian's long, aristocratic nose sniffing anything so sordid as the ground.

'Let me tell you about the position I am trying to fill. Our client is one of the leading specialist merger advisors. I am afraid I cannot disclose the name at this stage in our discussions, but I can assure you that it's a very blue-chip use. What we're looking for is a partner to head up their forts in continental Europe; they have a partner for the US, for the UK, and for the Far East, and a specialist for Eastern Europe, so they now realise that the Continent must be their top priority. They have a truly impressive track record – as we get further along I will be able to show you a deal list. I really believe you should consider this very carefully; from what you've told me about your own view of the market, I think you have a lot in common with my client. Their commitment is unquestioned, and with the capital backing they have, the opportunities are genuinely limitless . . .' Her voice trailed off. Whilst making her pitch for FRG Barnekov, Teddy had not been unaware that although Christian maintained an attentive stance, most of his attention had been focused on her legs. She reprimanded him with a hard stare but Christian was far too smooth to appear embarrassed, and met her gaze steadily.

'It certainly sounds as if I should think about it. Now may I take the liberty of asking a few questions myself?'

'Of course; fire away. I will be as open as I can, but I cannot, you understand, give you any specific details about my client until I have drawn up a short list.'

'Why did your parents name you Teddy? I am of course familiar with Teddy Roosevelt, Teddy Kennedy, Teddy bears, even . . .' he drawled, 'but I have never before met a real woman called "Teddy".'

She laughed, disarmed by the question.

'Teddy is a nickname. My real name is Theodora. I doubt you've met any women called *that*, either.'

'Théodora. A beautiful name, and very fitting. I shall call you Théodora, in future, if I may be so bold.' Teddy inclined her head.

'And now for my next question. Have you made any arrangements for dinner tonight? I know a small place, not far from the hotel, that has a chef of genius. Allow me to invite you to taste the true flavours of France, and we can talk further about these opportunities.'

Teddy smiled. 'How kind of you. That sounds delightful,

but I am afraid that this is a whistle-stop tour. I have five other appointments today, and then fly overnight to New York, so with regret, I shall have to decline.'

'But you will return to Paris?' Christian asked with concern.

'Oh yes; provided, that is, that either you, or another of the candidates I am meeting today, decides to pursue talks with my client. Then I shall be back.'

'In that case, I have made up my mind. Most assuredly I would like to pursue talks with your client, and with you. So shall we, how shall I say it, make a date?'

Once again, Teddy laughed. This was certainly a candidate that should be kept at arm's length – and even that might not be far enough for safety.

'Let's leave it like this; when I return from New York, I will draw up my shortlist, in which I would certainly like to include your name. Then I will call you to arrange a second interview, and give you a little more information – '

'– and allow me to invite you to dinner.' Christian finished the sentence for her.

'Until then, I can only say it has been a great pleasure to meet you,' Teddy replied.

'The pleasure has been entirely mine.' Christian bowed over her hand, touched it briefly to his lips and left the room.

The Frogs and the Krauts; the hand-kissers and the heel-clickers.

'Candida, I have Glory McWhirter in reception for you.' ARC's receptionist buzzed through the intercom to Candida's office.

'Can you tell Jamie to join me, and then show her through, Julie.'

Candida liked to have Jamie sit in on interviews with female candidates; it was always useful to have a man's perception, even if Jamie wasn't always exactly discriminating when it came to the fairer members of the fairer sex.

The interview got off to a bad start. Glory breezed into the office, pushing past Julie, and opened with, 'Hey, I was expecting Teddy to be here!'

'She's travelling this week, Glory. I'm Candida Redmayne.'

'Good to meet you, Candy.' Glory flung herself into the armchair, leaving Jamie to assume the interviewee's place on the sofa, and ignored Candida's outstretched hand. Candida's face hardened slightly.

'Glory, may we start by your running through your career to date, and then we can outline some of the opportunities that we think might interest you.'

'Hell, no. I don't have the time, Candy, to sit around doing this. You know all that matters about me. I'm a proprietary trader at Steinberg's. You called me in, so put your cards on the table and tell me what you've got to offer.'

Jamie examined the pattern of the sofa fabric as if he were committing it to memory. There was a long pause. Glory took out a pack of cigarettes and lit up, then winked at Jamie and said, 'Could you get me an ashtray, hun?' He hurried out of the room.

'Glory, I realise that you have an *extremely* busy schedule,' Candida's well-modulated tones dripped with acid. 'We all do. Ten years' experience has taught me that the most efficient way of conducting interviews is to allow the candidate to speak first. In that way, we don't waste your time by suggesting positions that would not be of interest to you, or for which you might not be suitable. I would be immensely grateful if you would agree to do things my way.'

Glory shrugged. 'Okay, hun, but let's make it snappy. I've got places to go, people to see, money to make. I'm nearly twenty-seven, I come from the land of the free and the home of the brave.' Candida winced visibly, but Glory carried on unperturbed, 'I started with Steinberg in New York after college. I started as a broker, but it didn't take me long to realise that was a load of shit, so I nestled up to Miccinelli when he arrived in the Big Apple and managed to get transferred to the trading desk. Mike and I both realised that the heart of the foreign exchange markets had to be in London, so he came back a couple of years ago, and then begged me to come over and help him out. It was a hard call, believe me, leaving New York, but . . . when duty calls, Glory McWhirter answers! You know what I mean, Candy; we girls can't let the side down, can we?' She ground her cigarette out, and lit another one immediately.

'Explain why you didn't want to be a broker.'

'Hell, brokers are just glorified door-to-door salesmen, aren't they? Have you ever met a broker that didn't make you want to wring his neck?'

Jamie was on tenterhooks. Would Candida tell her that she herself had been a broker before setting up ARC? Probably not; Candida tended to make sure that she had the upper hand before she applied pressure. Anyway, he doubted that Glory could be made to suffer embarrassment.

'How would you distinguish the roles of a broker and a trader?'

'Easy. When a broker calls a client, he tells him what he's got, and then sells him what the client wants. When a trader calls, he asks him what he wants and then sells him what he's got. Mike taught me that.' She finished smugly.

'But you are now on the proprietary side, Glory; so you don't really have clients at all.'

'And thank the good Lord for that! They're all stupid as shit. No, the way we work is to invest our own money for our own profit; why should we help out the suckers with our ideas?'

'Why indeed? Now tell me about Mike Miccinelli. You and he work as a close team?'

'You couldn't get closer than me and Mike. We're like *this*.' Glory wrapped two of her scarlet-tipped fingers round each other.

'Is he a good manager? Do you like working under him?'

'I like working under him, over him, round him, side-by-side, back-to-back . . . we're *real* close, know what I mean, Candy? Mike and I have known each other – *intimately* – since we met in Sin City.'

'I think I do know what you mean, yes. That's very interesting. Do you think you have any weaknesses as a trader, Glory?'

Glory looked blank. Self-analysis was a new ball game to her.

Jamie stepped in. 'I think what, ah, *Candy* means is, is there any part of your professional life that you would like to improve?'

'Yeah, there are two things I'd like to improve. My salary and my bonus.'

Candida and Jamie's eyes met, Jamie's very amused, Candida's steely.

'Well, perhaps we should talk now about how you might be able to do that. Are you happy to stay in London for the next few years?'

'Happy? It makes me want to slit my wrists. Let's be frank, here, Candy; England sucks donkey dick. So do English men, present company excepted – ' another large wink at Jamie '– but the market's here, and a girl's gotta move with the market. So I'll stay, for a while.'

'We have been approached by a top class house to find a senior proprietary trader. It would mean a significant promotion for you, and a commensurate salary package.'

'Commen — what?'

'A bigger salary package.' Candida spoke as if she were explaining things to an irritating and under-developed five-year-old.

'How much bigger?'

'That depends, but I think we should be talking in the range of three hundred thousand plus, and an unlimited performance-related bonus; it's open to negotiation.'

'And we're talking sterling, right?'

'Absolutely.'

'Not bad. Who's the house?'

'Hayes Goldsmith.'

Jamie nearly choked on his coffee, and turned it into a cough. Never in all his time at ARC had he heard Candida try to recruit anybody for Hayes Goldsmith.

'I don't know. Aren't they an English merchant bank? I get the impression they are full of those huntin', shootin' fishin' wankers.'

'And that's exactly why they want somebody like you. They need a breath of fresh air — someone who can come in and shake them about a bit, sweep all the cobwebs away. I think you are just the woman to do it.'

Glory didn't look very convinced, so Candida continued.

'They've got good people, Glory. The department director, Malcolm Fairchild, is first class. He personally came to see me to explain their new strategy. It's dynamic, and they've got the capital to put it into action. What they haven't got is a star to run the desk.'

Jamie sat back, enjoying the spectacle of Candida — or Candy, as he would now think of her — in action. It was like watching a great actress wooing an audience, judging her timing and phrasing carefully.

'Finding a star, that's their only problem. There aren't may of them around — maybe two to three people in London of the right calibre . . .'

Glory was leaning forward in her chair, nodding her head in agreement, her cigarette forgotten.

Candida sighed. 'I know how excited they would be if I could put forward your name; Malcolm already mentioned you, but I warned him it would be tough to get you out of Steinberg's. He authorised me to say that he would pay whatever it took.'

'He did, huh? Sounds like a guy who knows how to treat his traders.'

'Oh yes; for you — I mean for the right person — he talked about an open salary, a guaranteed bonus, car of your choice, accommodation at Hayes' cost, full expense and health package, the works . . .'

'Sounds like I should meet him.'

'I think so, I really do,' Candida nodded earnestly. 'Jamie?'

'Oh yes. I think so too, Candy. I really do.' He joined in the nodding, the three of them looking like furry dogs on the rear shelf of a car.

'So that's agreed? I can give Malcolm the good news?'

'Yeah. Make his day. Tell him I'll talk. Let's suck it and see, hey, Candy?'

Candida smiled sweetly. 'Yes, Glory. You suck it and see. I'll be behind you all the way.'

The two women shook hands warmly, and Glory left the office, her hips swinging invitingly, throwing Jamie one last, suggestive wink. The door closed behind her.

'Is Malcolm Fairchild really desperate to get Glory?' Jamie asked his boss.

Candida snapped her file shut. 'He's never even heard of her. Yet.'

Jamie was troubled by Glory's none too discreet references to Mike. He didn't share Candida's automatic loathing for the American woman, instead finding her rather appealing and somehow vulnerable for all her

bravado. Her very brazenness left her exposed and unde-
fended in a way he found strangely touching, but right
now he was more concerned about Teddy's vulnerability
than Glory's. He couldn't believe that Mike was really so
stupid as to conduct an affair under Teddy's nose, but on
the other hand, what motive could Glory possibly have for
insinuating a relationship that didn't exist?

'Candida,' now that Glory had gone he didn't think he
could get away with Candy, 'what do you think we should
do about Teddy?'

'Hmm? What do you mean, "do about Teddy"? We
shouldn't *do* anything about Teddy.'

'Well, you know, what Glory was saying about Mike . . .
I think Teddy should know.'

'Know what? Know that her beloved fiancé is knocking
off the office bimbo in the run-up to his wedding? Know
that he's a jerk?'

'Yes; I think we should tell her.'

'Grow up, Jamie. Either Teddy does know, or she doesn't
want to know. What difference does it make anyway? Teddy
is going to have much bigger problems with Mike than a spot
of infidelity. Why should it matter who he's screwing?'

'So you do think it's true?'

'Oh yes, I'm sure it's true. Glory doesn't have the brain to
manipulate a situation. She just thought we'd be impressed.
And Miccinelli is not the kind of guy to turn down the
sort of offer Glory makes. Would you?' She looked at him
sharply, and Jamie blushed.

'I'm not engaged to be married.'

'No, well, wait till you are, and then you can start
pontificating about fidelity. You can do what you like,
tell Teddy if you want, but my advice is to leave well
alone and butt out.'

Jamie butted out of her office.

* * *

As Teddy was leaving the Georges V, she received a message to call Tom Pitt-Rivers, her erstwhile boss at Steinberg's, urgently. She called him from the airport.

'Tom? It's Teddy Winnington.'

'Teddy! How's my favourite girl?' His voice boomed out over the phone; half of Paris could have heard him.

'I'm fine, Tom, just fine, but I'm at Charles de Gaulle and just about to catch a plane to New York, so I wondered how I could help . . .'

His voice dropped to a whisper. 'Teddy, you realise that I'm at the office,' – conventional shorthand for 'I can't talk' – 'but I happened to hear about the, ah, *project* you are working on at the moment, and I wanted to let you know that I might be interested if you hadn't found anybody more appropriate.'

'Tom! I can't believe it! *You*, leave Steinberg Roth? It's unthinkable! Why on earth? Has something happened? I thought you were in your element – I would never have dreamt of approaching you!'

'Well, things change . . . circumstances beyond my control . . . other factors . . . things I can explain . . . a possible change of scene might be for the best . . .' He was whispering hurriedly.

'Listen, Tom, we can't possibly discuss it now. Of course you should be a candidate. Look, I've still got your home number – can I call you tomorrow night?'

'Bless you, Teddy. That's all I wanted to hear. Have a good flight.'

The phone clicked, and Teddy was left wondering what on earth was going on at Steinberg Roth. It had to be something dramatic to make a man like Tom leave – or consider leaving – but then Steinberg's loss could be her gain. She now had three leading candidates for the position at FRG Barnekov, plus a couple of back-ups. So far, luck had been on her side, but she wasn't too modest to give herself some of the credit. So, on to New York, and the end of the first stage of the search. Teddy felt relaxed. Even if none of the Americans were contenders, things were looking good, and she knew that FRG would be happy. She hoped that Candida would be happy. And most of all, she hoped that Mike would be happy; and proud.

The selection of American candidates had been more difficult than the Europeans. For one thing, not many Americans had sufficient experience of European markets to enable them to do the job; for another, not many Americans wanted, or were able, to move to London for an indefinite assignment. But Teddy had managed to find five people who were highly regarded, had at least the minimum requirements for the job, and, most important of all, were prepared to meet her. The first person she saw in New York was Stretch Logan. It took precisely fifteen minutes over a cup of coffee at the Carlyle for them both to realise that the meeting was a waste of their time. Stretch – he was well over six feet tall – was polite, matter-of-fact, and business-like. He expressed some interest, with the reservation that he would talk further so long as Teddy's client wasn't FRG Barnekov. Teddy's face fell, and he shrugged.

'To be frank with you, Teddy, if I'd realised your client *was* FRG Barnekov, I wouldn't have wasted your time. I've known Paul Driver for a long time, and there's no chemistry between us. He wouldn't want to work with me any more than I would want to work with him.'

He had the courtesy to suggest a few other names that he thought might be suitable, and to wish her a successful conclusion to her search before leaving for his second 'power breakfast' of the day. Her second appointment was with Bob Brauchman, a banker from the Mid West. He was keen, but Teddy ruled him out.

He was simply too old for the position, a nice, paternal man with twenty-five years' experience in banking who had long lost his passion for the job, if he'd ever had it. Teddy lunched on a pastrami sandwich with the third candidate, Jim O'Brien. He was impressive — well advanced on the fast track and determined to win — but he believed his power base lay in the States for the time being, and although he agreed, somewhat reluctantly, to consider a move to England, Teddy knew instinctively that his considered answer would be no. As he was leaving, he said abruptly, 'If I were you, I'd talk to Esther Levenson at Solly's.'

'That's interesting — why?'

He shrugged. 'She's very good, that's all. I know her pretty well. I like her, and I rate her. I get the impression she might not mind leaving New York. It's worth a shot.'

They shook hands briskly, and he was gone.

Esther Levenson was already scheduled as Teddy's next appointment. When Teddy had arranged the meeting, Esther had insisted that Teddy come to her office at Salomon's, rather than meeting in a hotel. This had surprised Teddy. Few people wanted to have a headhunter come to their office, and she had suggested to Esther that it might be more discreet to meet elsewhere.

'Discreet? Who needs discretion? It's not illegal to see a headhunter — hell, I'm showing more loyalty by staying at my desk than by sneaking off for some hole-in-the-corner meeting!'

So Teddy, now suffering from jet lag after so many flights and so many cups of coffee, duly turned up at Salomon Brothers and asked for Esther Levenson.

She was shown into a large, open office, dominated by a huge desk, behind which sat a small, dark-haired woman shouting into a telephone.

'For Christ's sake, Bill, I asked for this weeks ago! How

long does it take you schmucks to come up with a couple of charts? It's not like I'm asking for the earth, for God's sake. I'm simply asking the in-house research department to come up with a little in-house research!' She waved Teddy to a seat opposite her desk. 'Okay. Not four o'clock. Three o'clock.' There was a pause. 'Three fifteen. That's my final offer.' Another pause, and she started smiling. 'And I love you too, Bill. Three fifteen. *Hasta la vista.*' She hung up, pushed her large, horn-rimmed glasses on top of her head, and beamed at Teddy.

'Thanks for coming to see me here. I'm up to my neck trying to get a client presentation finished, and the bozos in the research department aren't exactly pulling their fingers out. When did you fly in? Good trip? Want a coffee?'

She spoke faster than Teddy had ever heard anybody speak, and seemed to be doing ten things at once, checking the Reuters screen, glancing at her diary, shuffling papers on the desk, yet she didn't make Teddy feel that she wasn't paying attention. She found what she was looking for – a small box of slim cigarillos – and offered one to Teddy. 'Smoke?'

'No thanks.'

Teddy watched while Esther Levenson lit a cigar, inhaled deeply and pushed her chair back. 'That's better. I gave up cigarettes two years ago and a friend of mine suggested switching to cigars to kick the habit. Now I smoke twenty of them a day. I've given up all my other vices – I don't drink, I work out, I maintain a low fat, low cholesterol diet, I recycle my garbage, I go to therapy, I've even done EST, though I drew the line at primal screaming, but the no smoking thing just never really appealed to me. So, let's get down to business.'

It took Teddy a while to get herself in gear to interview Esther. She'd never met a cigar-smoking female banker before, and was already enjoying the vision of how Paul

Driver would react to her. She made her standard opening speech.

'Esther, as I mentioned on the phone we have been retained to find a senior partner for our client to run a blue-chip operation in Europe. Several people suggested that I speak to you – we've heard some very good things about you – '

Esther's face cracked into a broad grin. '– and some very bad ones, I'll bet!' she finished for Teddy.

'No, not at all. But I have to admit that I don't know an awful lot about you, and I would be grateful if you could fill me in on the details.' She had her notepad and pen poised. Esther wasted no time asking for more details about Teddy's client; she started again, at machine-gun pace, barely drawing breath.

'Sure. I'm thirty-nine. I grew up in New York, on the Lower East Side, if that means anything to you. My dad was a baker – best bagels south of Gramercy Park; my mom died when I was ten years old, so I spent a lot of time looking after my kid brother and sister, and helping Dad out. I did get a scholarship to Columbia, and I went back to night school and did my MBA, but I didn't have a lot of time to study, you understand me? Anyway, I worked my proverbial butt off – sadly, not my real one – ' she slapped her somewhat generous backside '– and for my pains, I ended up three years ago in charge of this circus. I've got a team of six people – good people – and we try our damnedest to cover everything that moves in Europe. It's been uphill work; you know Solly's aren't known for mergers specialisation, but I think we're getting there, and we're doing our best. When I joined the department, clients used to laugh when I went to see them. All I ever heard was, "We work exclusively with Goldman Sachs." "We work exclusively with Steinberg Roth." "We work exclusively with Bergdorff Weintraub." Turkeys. Well, we didn't work exclusively with *anyone* – no one should – but now we're up there.' She finished simply and succinctly. 'People don't laugh anymore when I call them.'

Teddy could see very clearly why not.

'And the future, Esther? How do you see your career developing?'

'Well, that's where I hope you come in, Teddy. I've got certain reasons, personal reasons, for wanting out of New York. I've set my heart on Europe, it's high time I soaked up a bit of culture, you know what I mean? I can't go anywhere else with Solly's – they are pulling people out of London, and can't justify sending me over. I've made my position clear to them, there are no bad feelings on either side. Maybe there isn't anything else available that would make sense, but I'm hoping you might be able to suggest something.'

'I think I can. Could you tell me first why you want to leave New York?'

'Sure. It wouldn't exactly be fair on you if you didn't have the whole story. Look. I've spent eighteen years of my adult life in this hell hole, sweating away to try and make a decent living. So long as you call a decent living a professional career and money in the bank, then I've been successful. To succeed in this business, in this city, you have to play the game; you have to sit up and beg; you have to roll over and play dead; you have to be in the right spot at the right time; above all, *you have to play the game by their rules*, particularly if you're a woman. You have to have the right attitude – or, even better, no attitude at all. But over the past couple of years I decided that that wasn't a decent living – it wasn't enough. I'm thirty-nine, Teddy; no spring chicken. In my twenties, I didn't have time to do any dating; the past few years I've done my fair share, but let me tell you, it's harder to find a good single man in New York than it is to sell sand to a Nomad. Six months ago I decided that when I hit fifty it wasn't going to be enough to have twenty merger mandates to show for my life's work.' She jerked her thumb towards the the stack of deal tombstones that lined the shelf behind her desk. 'I want to have a baby – or maybe more than one. I want to stay in touch with my feelings – or rather get in touch with them; there's got to be some good reason for being female, for Christ's sake! It's not easy to do that in New York; hell, it's not easy to do it anywhere. When we get to the bottom line, I haven't found a man in New York who's a good enough dinner companion, let alone a good enough husband or father. If I haven't found *one* in thirty-nine years, I'm not likely to find one in the next few years, am I? Don't get the wrong idea, Teddy, I'm not a quitter, I'm a fighter; but I'm smart enough to know when I'm really beat.'

Teddy had listened carefully to Esther; she was deeply impressed by the older woman's openness and honesty, but hoped that Esther Levenson wasn't being too optimistic about her romantic prospects in London.

'Esther, why do you think it would be easier to find a good man in England?'

Esther laughed out loud. 'I don't. I just told you, I've given up on finding a good man.'

'But having a baby – when do you think you will start a family?'

Esther glanced at her desk diary.

'I've pencilled in December twenty-four. If my obstetrician isn't a complete jackass, it should be Christmas week, whatever.'

Teddy looked at her blankly.

'I'm four months pregnant. I told you, Teddy, I'm not a quitter.'

Teddy had no doubt that Esther was up to the job at FRG Barnekov; it was a question of whether FRG were up to hiring her. She had stayed with Esther for well over an hour, and had been sorry to leave, enjoying the woman's company. Esther was lion-hearted. She had calculated exactly the obstacles she would have to overcome, and had evaluated all the risks in her plan before she made her decision. It was not that Salomon's wanted her to leave now that she had embarked on motherhood; they were more than happy to give her maternity leave, and keep her position open. It was nothing to do with the father; he wasn't even aware he was going to *be* a father. Esther simply felt that she had chosen a new course, and wanted to mark the change radically. Her commitment to working was unchanged; if anything, she now had even more of a reason to strive for success, in that she would soon have someone to be successful for. Esther had been a dutiful daughter and sister; she had enabled her father to retire early and move out to the warm sunshine of Florida; she had put her brother and sister through college, and seen them launch independent careers. She had been a dutiful employee, regularly working sixteen-hour days. She wasn't proposing to slack off now.

'The way I see it, Teddy,' she had said, 'if they will let me start in say, September, October, I could put in a couple of months learning the ropes and finding my feet before taking a month off to have the baby.'

'How do you know you'll want to go back to work after the baby?'

'Because I won't have any choice. Maybe there's a choice if there are two of you bringing up a kid, but if I make the decision to have a baby alone, then I take on the responsibility of caring for it all the way. I wouldn't let FRG down, because I'm never going to let my baby down.'

'I'm sure FRG will realise that.'

Teddy had sounded reassuring, but she suspected she would have a tough time convincing Paul Driver that she wasn't completely off her head. It was going to be a risk to Teddy's credibility simply to put Esther forward. Female, American, unmarried and pregnant – it wasn't *exactly* the criteria that FRG had given her.

It was fortunate for Teddy that Candida had not accompanied her on the trip to New York. Candida would have been less sympathetic to Esther Levenson's situation, although Teddy knew that her boss would have appreciated Esther's guts and strength of character. But Candida was preoccupied with placing her own candidate. She had arranged to meet Malcolm Fairchild for a drink at Langan's. As she predicted, he leapt at the chance. Malcolm was wrapped around her little finger, a position he had assumed more than twelve months previously, and one he showed no sign of wishing to leave. Candida treated him as one might treat a trainee gun dog; she was sparing with her praise, and quick to reprimand, and yet his devotion was constant. After all, he was occasionally allowed to sleep on his mistress's bed.

That evening, Candida was in a tolerant mood. She kissed Malcolm warmly, and even allowed him to hold her hand as they sat in a little alcove at the back of the bar.

'Candida, darling, I haven't seen you for three weeks . . .'

'Two weeks, Malcolm. We went to Covent Garden two weeks ago.'

'Well, it feels like longer. It feels like for ever. Anyway, watching bloody *Turandot* doesn't count as seeing you. When are you going to let me take you away for a weekend?'

'It's just too frantic at the moment; I've got Teddy in America, Jamie in Paris and Louise and Philip God knows where. I even dragged David away from his books and made him come back and help me with a search. I spend most nights and every weekend on the phone. Once the summer arrives we'll be able to get away, I promise. Anyway, we're together tonight, and that's what counts. Let's enjoy it. As it happens, I've got some rather good news for you.'

Malcolm nearly panted with anticipation.

'Let's get some champagne, and then I'll tell you all about it . . . it's a little idea I had, a bit of a brainwave if I say so myself . . .'

The champagne arrived; was poured; was drunk. Malcolm lapped up every word that fell from Candida's lips. She told him about Glory McWhirter, told him that this staggeringly successful trader had walked through her door, and asked Candida to find her another job. She was fed up with Steinberg's, she didn't want her CV punted around, she simply wanted Candida to approach a few key names and inquire about terms.

'You know how rare it is to get a good walk-in, Malcolm? Nobody's moving these days. Glory just decided she'd had enough; there's a senior trader at Steinberg's she doesn't like, and she thinks the organisation's going downhill. I remembered what you said last October when you were so cross with me about moving Bill Burrage and the others, and I thought, here's my chance to make amends; I'll offer Glory to Malcolm. So here she is, on a plate. Probably London's best trader. With my compliments.'

She signalled to the waiter to bring another bottle of champagne. It didn't take Candida long to convince Malcolm that Glory *was* the best trader in London. Within an hour, he had not only thought out the provisional terms of the contract, but also convinced himself that the whole thing had been his own idea. They drank to his genius, and Candida modestly accepted his thanks for her part in the coup.

'So, Malcolm. I'll arrange for Glory to come and see you this week, and we should be able to speed through a decision. Now tell me what else has been going on at Hayes Goldsmith . . . what's the gossip?'

A couple of hours in Candida's company, and well into his second bottle of champagne, Malcolm felt nurtured and trusting.

'It's tough, Candida. Sales and trading profits are well down on last year – Jack's being a total shit about it – but I guess that won't come as a surprise to you. He's pretty much in charge of the firm now. Belton-Smith is in semi-retirement, still there as a figurehead, but he leaves all the decisions up to Jack. I've got to admit, Jack's not doing too bad a job on the corporate finance side; he's managed to drag in a few new clients – good ones – '

'Who?' Candida asked quickly.

'He's got into Bouygues – managed to persuade them we should lead their Stock Exchange listing. Stole it from under Steinberg's nose, in fact. He's working on some very hush-hush merger deal for a UK client – the counterparty is Italian, but he barely tells me a thing about it. He's such an arrogant arsehole; he treats me like I'm a child, sometimes. I'm damn well going to prove to him that I can run my own team!' His ginger eyebrows bristled with irritation.

'I'm sure Glory will help you do that. Even Jack will have to admit that snatching Glory is quite a coup. Who is his UK client . . . on the Italian deal?'

'Come on, darling, let's not waste our precious evening talking shop, and let's not talk about Delavigne. It's going to put me off my dinner.' He picked up the menu and began to study it.

Candida complied, and glanced at the menu, but her thoughts remained on Hayes Goldsmith. She wanted to know everything that happened there, every deal Jack won, every move he made. But there was no point pushing Malcolm beyond his capabilities. He was pretty well trained, but it looked like it was time for a reward rather than a new lesson. She considered whether she should sleep with him tonight. Malcolm wasn't exactly *bad* in bed, but he wasn't exactly good, either. He tried hard to please, and had paid enormous attention to learning what turned Candida on. The problem was that nothing turned Candida on so much as talking about Jack Delavigne, and for some reason Malcolm had an aversion to discussing Jack in bed.

Suppressing a sigh, she turned to Malcolm with sparkling eyes. 'What did you say, Malcolm darling? I was a million miles away.'

CHAPTER FIVE

Teddy had been bitterly disappointed not to have more time in London, but Candida had insisted that she return to Paris almost the day she landed back from New York. FRG were in a real hurry to sign up the candidate, and Candida's experience had taught her that when a client was hot to sign a contract, they would hire a baboon if you put one in front of them. Anyway, other than spending some time with Mike, Teddy had no excuse for delaying the search. She and Mike spent one night together before she was back on a plane to Charles de Gaulle.

Mike had been disappointed too, but had managed to cheer himself up by taking a quick and dirty eight million pound profit on the French franc. Glory had insisted on going out to celebrate, and was coming round to Mike's Kensington flat to pick him up for dinner. Knowing Glory as he did, Mike knew what to expect, and awaited her in jeans and a twill shirt.

Glory arrived in the skimpy red sequined dress that she had worn to Mike and Teddy's Mexican party, her dead straight blonde hair flowing down her back, her arms weighed down by two enormous carrier bags. She dumped them on the kitchen table, and unpacked a bottle of iced Stolichnaya pepper vodka, which she shoved into the freezer, two bottles of champagne, a kilo tin of Beluga caviar, blinis, an onion and two lemons. Mike leant against the kitchen doorway.

'I guess we're not going out to celebrate?'

'I thought it would be a drag . . . why swap an empty

flat for a crowded restaurant? I called up that Kaviar Kaspia place you told me about, and the schmucks wouldn't deliver, so I just brought it with me!'

'Are you expecting friends?' Mike eyed the enormous tin of caviar.

'No, it's all for you and me, hun.'

'A kilo of Beluga . . .'

'Yeah; I like round numbers. I put it on my Steinberg gold Amex card.'

'Sounds like you need a Kryptonite card, Glory; you're going way beyond the platinum credit limit.'

'Well, you're worth it . . . and you sign off on my expenses, don't you, darlin'?'

Glory was at home in Mike's flat. She knew exactly where to find the lead crystal shot glasses, helped herself to an ashtray, and stalked into the drawing room. When Mike joined her the glasses were full of vodka, Bruce Springsteen belted out through the discreet speakers, and Glory had made herself comfortable on the white damask sofa, leafing through one of Teddy's magazines.

Mike watched her, admiring the contrast that her red dress and blonde hair made in the pure whiteness of the room. When Teddy relaxed, she lay curled up like a kitten, her head frequently nestled against his shoulder, her feet tucked under her. Glory lay stretched out prone, the short dress barely covering her backside, one leg thrown up along the back of the sofa, one slim, tanned arm dangling a cigarette, her hair spilling luxuriously over the edge.

'Come on, Miccinelli, take a pew and let's party.' Glory spoke huskily, raising her glass in a toast, and patting the space beside her on the sofa. Mike felt his apprehension slip away as the burning vodka slid down his throat. He didn't like the way Glory took control of scenes, he didn't like the way she made decisions without consulting him, and he didn't like the way she took his willingness for granted. But he loved to look at her. He loved the way her cat-like, sherry-coloured eyes, so different from Teddy's, went narrow and hooded, the flecks of yellow making them tigerish. He loved to fill his hands with her tumbling blonde hair, loved the way he could feel her inner muscles tighten when he stroked her. He loved the rasp of her voice, the soft growl of her accent. She was large, and powerful, and dangerous. Being with her, hearing her say 'Miccinelli' in that raspy voice made him feel large, and powerful, and dangerous, and it felt good. They had fallen into a pattern, when they were alone together. Glory let him know when she was ready, and Mike took his time to come to her. She was just clever enough to let him make the final decision.

Tonight, Mike sat opposite her, resisting the invitation to join her on the sofa. This was not reluctance on his part – he wanted her hunger to develop an edge, wanted to see Glory's eyes darken with desire. For a moment he thought of Teddy, her wide-eyed trust and sweetness, but he dismissed the image from his mind. Teddy was in Paris, or Frankfurt, or some other Godforsaken continental dump, he couldn't remember which, and was doubtless far too busy to be thinking of her.

'So tell me about this amazing job offer.'

'I'm not one to blow my own trumpet, Miccinelli, but they want me *bad*. I went to see Malcolm Fairchild, and he was just about on his knees begging me to go. We're talking serious money. I'd be pretty much my own boss. D'you think I should take it?'

Mike shrugged. 'It's up to you. Sounds like a decent offer. Hayes Goldsmith doesn't have the clout that Steinberg's have, but you'd be a big fish there, and I guess you'd do pretty well.' He replenished their glasses. 'Don't know how you'd cope without me to hold your hand and keep you on your toes, but you're a big girl now, and I'd be just on the other end of the phone.'

Glory bristled, as he had hoped she would. 'Can it, Miccinelli. The real question is how *you* would cope without *me*.'

'Hell, Glory; I've never depended on anybody in my life. To tell the truth, I've been getting a bit tired of having a trainee around,' he could see her lip curl, and could almost hear her snarling, 'but I would miss you. A bit.' He grinned at her.

'So d'you think the market's big enough for the two of us?'

'We're just going to have to try it and see. I just didn't want my little girl to be scared, that's all.'

'When did you last see me scared? I haven't been scared since my mom took me to the dentist when I was six years old.'

'What happened then?'

'I just about bit his hand off. I wasn't scared after that. But you can bet your sweet ass he was.'

She laughed, a rich, self-satisfied laugh that made Mike's blood tingle.

'Why don't you come over here and show me what you did to him?' It was now Glory's turn to feign reluctance.

'But what about dinner, Miccinelli? It'll get cold.'

'It's caviar, baby; it's meant to get cold. And if you don't get your ass over here, I'm the one who's going to get cold.' He spoke slowly, his tone menacing.

Glory took her time, rising slowly from the sofa, flinging her hair back, and never taking her eyes off him. She paced silently across the room towards him, swinging her hips and unzipping her dress as she walked, so that it fell to her feet when she stopped in front of him. She wore a pair of lacy white briefs, a suspender belt and stockings, and high-heeled red shoes; otherwise she was naked. Her large breasts were tanned, with no trace of a bikini line, the nipples puckered and raised. Mike didn't touch her.

He looked at her silently for a moment, gazing at her full bosom, flat stomach and gently curving hips.

'The curtains are open, Glory. Do you want the whole world to see?'

'Why not? Why not let them share in your good fortune, Miccinelli?'

He didn't really give a fuck about the neighbours. Not moving from his chair, he ran his hand over Glory's golden, taut stomach, and checked between her legs. Her pants were warm and damp. Her skin glistened with tiny beads of perspiration.

'Take off your shoes,' Mike ordered.

Glory bent over before him, her breasts falling into his hands. Mike traced the curve of them with cold fingers, and heard Glory's intake of breath. He unfastened the four little lace clips that held up her stockings, his hands lingering over the swell of her buttocks, and she rolled her stockings down slowly. Bending over him, she removed his tie, and unbuttoned his shirt, trailing long fire-engine red fingernails through the dark hairs on his chest down to his abdomen. Her hands rubbed clumsily against his erection as she tried to undo the belt of his jeans. Mike let her struggle for a while, enjoying the way her teeth chewed at her lower lip in frustration, before pushing her away and rising to stand up and strip off. They were well matched, physically, her golden head only an inch or two below his own dark one, both long-legged, muscular; two lean, long bodies pressed together, separated only by the white slip of Glory's briefs. In a moment she had removed them.

Glory's hand immediately encircled his hard cock, moving slowly and expertly, her head bent as her tongue caressed his chest, licking and biting gently at the jut of his collar bone, his strong neck, moving down to tease his nipples. She sank to her knees, taking his penis into her soft mouth, working like a professional, not hurried, not hesitant, but steady and determined, intent on her work, her large mouth full of him.

Mike groaned with pleasure, directing Glory's head, massaging her scalp, his hands tugging at her tumbling hair. He suddenly pushed her roughly away from him on to the floor, and lay over her, ramming his knee into her crotch, pressing against the pubic bone. His mouth explored the swells and hollows of her body, its muscular tension, savouring the slightly sour, salty taste of her skin. Every inch of her body responded to his touch, her hips arching to rub hungrily against his own, her head turning from side to side on the pillow made by her hair. His fingers slipped into her easily, warm and wet, as her breathing quickened and became shallow. He stopped, supporting his body athletically on the palm of one hand, and raising his head to look at her met her narrow cat's eyes, golden and desperate. He entered her then, driving into her with the sudden force he knew she needed, seeing her eyes blinking quickly, as if surprised, feeling the instant inner tremble as he possessed her. Mike was in control, his mouth set in a thin, hard line, concentrating on Glory's face, on her wild eyes, on her rasping breath.

He began to speak, quickly, in a rough, angry voice. 'So you don't need me any longer, huh, baby? So you've learnt enough?'

'No Miccinelli, you bastard, I do need you,' Glory whispered.

'I can't hear you, baby; say it again.'

'I need you, Miccinelli; I need you I need you I need you . . .' She was whimpering, repeating her need like a mantra, her eyes shut tight, her teeth biting into her lower lip, her delicious breasts heaving, her legs wrapped tight around his waist.

Mike nearly withdrew, teasing her, and thrust deeply into her again, seeing her eyes open wide in shock, her hands flying to his back, pulling him closer and deeper into her, frightened that he would leave her empty.

'Remember, Glory . . .'

'I know. No marks.' In the midst of her passion, she raised her arms, laying them back over her head, in a position of complete subjugation and surrender. It was his favourite moment. She moaned and shuddered, still whispering as she came, 'You bastard Miccinelli, you bastard, you bastard, you bastard . . .'

'That's right, baby, I *am* a bastard and now it's my turn. Turn over.'

It had taken all Teddy's determination to refuse dinner with Christian de Clement-Grandcourt. She had lunched with him on her return to Paris, and had steadfastly refused to respond to his flirtation. When he asked what time he should collect her for dinner, she told him again that she had a prior engagement. It was true; Charlie was on business in Paris, and they had agreed to dine together. Christian looked heartbroken; secretly he was delighted. He loved all women; the ones who fell into his lap like over-ripe plums at the first shake of a tree; the ones who fought him off like wildcats; the ones who remained aloof and *noli-me-tangere*; they were all worth the chase, and sometimes the longer the chase, the more thrilling his ultimate victory. After all, he knew he would get them — all of them, every type. In the end.

Teddy had finally agreed to meet Christian later for a purely social drink, and had promised not to mention the name of FRG Barnekov. She was meeting Charles at the Closerie de Lilas on Boulevard Montparnasse at eight o'clock that evening, and agreed to see Christian at seven. She dressed carefully, telling herself that it wasn't for Christian's sake; she simply wanted to enjoy a night out in Paris with her oldest and dearest friend. She chose a floating printed silk skirt that had cost her an arm and a leg in the Nicole Farhi sale, with a matching bustier and jacket, and folded her hair into a loose chignon, leaving tendrils stroking the nape of her neck. Charles probably wouldn't even notice her efforts, but Christian certainly would. Feeling guilty at the very thought, Teddy called home to speak to Mike, but was forced to leave a disappointed message on the machine.

The Closerie was teeming with the fashionable young – and not so young – things of Paris. Teddy saw Christian guarding a table in one of the corners of the crowded bar, and squeezed her way through to him. He kissed her hand.

'You have taken my breath away. Such a vision of beauty, such elegance. How can I face the knowledge that you are not to spend the evening with me? I will have to consider abducting you, stealing you away from this Mr Bartholomew of yours.'

It was hard not to enjoy Christian's charm. Over the past few months Teddy had been starved of male attention and flattery, and she blossomed like a rosebud under Christian's experienced hands. He had a knack of taking control, and yet leaving her with the sensation that he was simply responding to her every whim. His eyes never left her face, unlike Mike, whom she sometimes had to shake to make him listen to her. His attentiveness was perhaps the core of his appeal. Christian was on his best behaviour; courteous, witty and suave. He wanted to know every detail about her, and was visibly crestfallen when she told him she was engaged to be married.

'Oh, you are beautiful, Théodora, but you are too cruel! How could you let me see you so lovely, and then tell me that you are to be married to another man! Is there no end to these men? Mr Bartholomew, and now the awful English fiancé ... Didn't one of your English poets say that women should only be as beautiful as they are kind?'

'I've never heard that, but I *have* heard that it is better to be beautiful than to be good ... or so Oscar Wilde thought.'

'Perhaps he was right. But in your case, I know you are beautiful *and* good.' He took her hand and held it between his own, leaning closer to her.

'Hey, Christian, you old frog! What are you doing here?'

A large, and obviously English, man in a pin-striped suit and red braces slapped Christian heartily on the back. Without turning round, Christian raised his eyes to heaven, and said, 'Théodora, I would like you – or rather, I would *not* like you – to meet my old friend Philip Redmayne, one of the greatest *rosbifs* in Paris.'

Philip pulled up a chair and squeezed his large bulk into the tiny gap next to Teddy.

'And who's our lovely friend?' he asked, his eyes on her alone.

'Her name is Théodora Winnington. And she is *my* lovely friend, not yours, and we were in the middle of a very private *business* meeting before we were very rudely interrupted by a fat Englishman.' Christian's tone was slightly acidic, but basically good-humoured. The two men were clearly old friends, and fell into a natural banter that seemed to consist largely of attacks against their respective nationalities.

'You don't want to spend your time with this filthy old frog, Théodora. Remember Nelson? It is the duty of every Englishman – and woman – to hate a Frenchman as he hates the very devil. How on earth did the old bugger manage to get a girl like you to talk to him?'

'We really *were* having a business discussion. I'm a headhunter.'

'Is that so?' Philip helped himself to Christian's glass. 'My little sister's a headhunter.'

Teddy leant forward.

'Didn't you say your name was Redmayne?'

'That's right; but call me Philip.'

'Well, Philip, your little sister happens to be my boss.'

'You don't say! What a coincidence! Well, I say, this calls for a celebration! Be a good chappy, Grandcourt, and get us a bottle of fizz!'

Within moments, Philip Redmayne had insisted that Teddy join him and his wife for dinner that night.

'Any friend of Grandcourt's is a friend of mine, and any colleague of Candida's is a friend of mine, and any friend of mine is a friend of my wife's, so you simply have to come.'

'I'm sorry, I'd love to, but I am expecting someone to join me for dinner at any moment – '

'So bring him – or her – too! I won't take no for an answer. You can even bring Grandcourt, if you absolutely insist. What do you say, old chap?'

Christian declined. 'No, Philippe; you have already destroyed my *tête-à-tête*; I draw the line at you destroying my entire evening by monopolising Théodora.'

Teddy also tried to escape Philip's invitation, but when Charles Bartholomew entered the bar, Philip befriended him so warmly, and was so persuasive, that Teddy and Charles agreed to accompany him home. They all made their farewells to Christian, Philip giving him another comradely slap on the back, Charles giving the stranger a rather curt nod, and Teddy offering him her warmest smile and her outstretched hand.

Christian drew her towards him, and bestowed a kiss on each cheek. 'We will meet again, Théodora. We have many things to discuss. In private.'

By the time that Philip, Teddy and Charles arrived at

Philip's flat, it was nearly nine o'clock. As they walked in the door, a fragile, dark-haired woman with flashing black eyes flung herself into Philip's arms.

'Pip, my darling, we had decided that you had abandoned us! Come, you must be a host and greet our guests . . .'

She looked brightly at Charles and Teddy, and continued, 'Have you come to dinner? How lovely! I am Bertine, Philip's wife. Let me take your things, how lovely of you to come, I am so very happy to meet you.' She embraced both of them as if they were old friends, rather than complete strangers who had arrived uninvited to her dinner party. Teddy began to make apologies, but was rapidly silenced by Bertine.

'No, my dear, you must not be sorry; Pip does this as a great treat for me – he knows I love to meet new people.' She clasped Teddy's hands in her own. 'You are most welcome to our house. Now come – Philip will get some drinks for you – come and meet our other friends.'

She drew Teddy into an elegant and intimate drawing room, draped with rich antique brocades, where a small group of people were talking. She turned first to a chic blonde, 'Delphine, this is our friend Teddy – Philippe was lucky enough to persuade her to join us tonight.' Next stop, a small, dapper Frenchman with a tiny beard, 'Teddy, this is Hervé Bilancourt, Delphine's husband, and a colleague of Philip's.' Next, a rather gaunt Englishman, 'Teddy, this is our dear brother-in-law, Jack Delavigne. Jack, may I introduce you to Teddy Winnington?'

Teddy shook hands, as she was expected to. She felt rather flustered, and looked over her shoulder for Charles' support, but he was already deep in conversation with Delphine Bilancourt. Philip and Hervé appeared to be arguing, so she was left with Philip's bird-like wife and Jack Delavigne. Bertine almost immediately excused herself to check the progress of dinner with her cook, and Teddy was left with Candida's former husband.

'Are you in Paris for business, or pleasure?' Jack asked politely, leaning down from his great height to talk to her.

'Business I suppose. Look, I'm a little embarrassed to meet you – actually, I work at ARC. With Candida. Your ex-wife.' Teddy spoke bluntly. She didn't like the man, and could see no reason for pussy-footing. 'I only met Philip an hour ago. It's quite accidental that I'm here at all.' She was being uncharacteristically rude. If Jack Delavigne was aware of it, he certainly didn't show any discomfort.

'I hope you weren't interviewing Philip; I should imagine he makes a most difficult subject.'

'No, I wasn't. I met him quite accidentally,' Teddy repeated, her chin jutting out belligerently as she spoke to Jack. She found his very courtesy and composure distasteful; he could at least have the grace to look chastened when she mentioned poor Candida's name.

At the first opportunity, when Bertine fluttered back to them, Teddy moved away to join Philip and Hervé in a heated debate about the Maastricht Treaty. It wasn't exactly riveting, but she was not prepared to enter into pleasant chit-chat with Jack Delavigne.

The dinner was excellent, largely thanks to Bertine's skills as a hostess. The Hungarian porcelain was heaped ever higher with tempting morsels, Philip kept the crystal glasses brimming with a selection of fine wines – all Australian, as he told Hervé smugly – and conversation flowed in a mixture of French and English. Charles and Philip were natural allies in a tongue-in-cheek assault on the inadequacies of the French, tossing out the bait that Hervé snapped at like a greedy fish. Philip leapt on every topic – even the traffic – finding an excuse for an unflattering comparison between the British and the French. Hervé talked to Teddy about his last trip to London.

'I lurve London very much, but ze traffic is *exécrable*. What do you call it – your M25 . . .'

'No one going to the right places would ever use the M25,' Charles interjected in mock horror. 'The only places one needs to go to are the City, West London, Heathrow and the Cotswolds. No need to go on the M25 at all.'

'Absolutely right. Anyway, it's a bit rich to talk about the M25 when all you frogs have to offer is the *périphérique*.. more bloody *pathétique*, I'd call it!' Philip Redmayne roared with laughter at his own joke as Hervé groaned.

Conversation ranged from Mrs Thatcher's much lamented fall from grace to Christian Lacroix's latest collection, until the persistent wailing of a small child in some back room of the apartment broke the babble of voices.

Philip raised his eyes to heaven. 'My God, it's a tie-straightening experience having a toddler around! I'd rather take on the stock market any day!' They all laughed indulgently, but as Bertine made as if to excuse herself, Jack Delavigne rose to his feet, saying, 'May I, Bertine?' He left the dining room, and shortly after, the high pitched weeping subsided and was replaced with happy chortling.

The conversation resumed. When Jack returned to his place at Bertine's right hand, she squeezed his fingers, and said, 'Bless you, Jack. Marie-Claire was so upset that she wouldn't see you tonight; I knew she would find some way of enticing you into her room.'

'I would have been equally upset not to see her. She's growing up so fast – she's really a little girl now.'

Teddy spoke crisply from across the table, making no attempt to muffle the edge in her voice, 'I take it you are fond of children, then?' The question was uncharacteristically hostile.

Jack looked at her curiously, his grey eyes reprimanding

in their gravity, making Teddy feel uncomfortable; but he replied gently and seriously.

'Yes, I am fond of children, but I am particularly fond of babies. Babies are very, very nice. Much nicer than we all are.'

Teddy looked away, embarrassed by his sincere response to her barbed question, but she caught the glowing approval in Bertine's smile. Clearly Bertine would warm to any ogre who showed an interest in her children, Teddy concluded, and hardened her heart towards Jack.

Having arrived so late, Teddy and Charles were careful not to overstay their welcome, and withdrew to the Deux Magots for a nightcap. Even at that late hour, the bar was full of people, and they had to fight for a table. The encounter with Jack Delavigne had not improved Teddy's mood. Her natural inclination was to label people – good, bad, indifferent – and she was struggling hard to pin Jack down like a butterfly specimen into her 'bad' box; the effort made her irritable. Teddy didn't like enigmas; she felt that her loyalty was to Candida. Candida had clearly been badly treated by this man, and instead of softening her opinion of him, the encounter had made her unsettled and angry. Bad people ought to be visibly bad; she didn't like it when they appeared to be nice, and she didn't like the fact that Charles had been so easily impressed by him. That was the problem with Charles; he always took things at face value. She considered it an irritating form of naïveté.

'You were bloody rude to him, Ted. That business about being fond of children. Have you got some sort of axe to grind?'

'No. I mean, I don't personally, but Candida does, and I see no reason why he should present himself as such a wonderful father figure after what he's done. It's a question of principle. Anyway, I don't want to talk about him anymore.' Dismissing Jack Delavigne from her mind, she turned the subject to Glory.

'Come on, Charles, you promised you'd tell me about your date with Glory.'

Charles signalled for two more Calvados, clearly needing extra fortification. 'It was an, ah . . . interesting experience,' he began noncommittally, 'a very interesting experience.' Teddy waited patiently, accustomed to the way Charles liked to develop a story. 'I just don't think she's my type, that's all.'

'What, too much hard work? Come on, tell me what happened! Spill the beans! You didn't manage to get her in the sack, is that it?' Teddy prodded him in the ribs, and he looked at her crossly.

'That is an extremely offensive accusation, young lady, and a rather unladylike one, I might add. As a matter of fact, you're wrong. I *did* get her in the sack, and no, it wasn't hard work, either. It was extremely easy; I didn't even have to buy her dinner. She suggested we stayed in.'

'So?' Teddy was on tenterhooks. 'What happened? You didn't fancy her? You couldn't get it up, when push came to shove?' She was laughing now, and Charlie pretended to be offended and superior.

'You are becoming increasingly vulgar with age, Theodora. God only knows what your sainted grandmother would say. I can see, however, that I will have to lower myself to your level. No; you're wrong on both counts. I would say that young Glory rates rather high on the fuckability scale, as we chaps like to call it, and I had no problem performing. None whatsoever.' He sounded, and looked, extremely pompous.

'So what's wrong with her?' Teddy persisted. 'She sounds like your dream come true.. attractive, easy to pull, cheap . . . I've got it! It's her mouth! She didn't let you get a word in edgewise!'

Charlie leant across the table conspiratorially.

'To tell you the truth, Ted, if there's one thing that I wouldn't complain about with Glory, it's her mouth — and I'm not talking about what comes *out* of it. That woman has got a mouth that could suck a golfball through a hosepipe . . .'

'You are *disgusting*, Charles!' Teddy was laughing, and Charles, warming to his task, continued.

'No, the real problem is that for the first time in my life, I thought she was just too keen. She couldn't keep her hands off me. It made me feel — I don't know — it made me feel like a *woman*.' Charlie's face looked such a picture of injured pride that the bar rang with Teddy's throaty laugh.

'That is the most ridiculous thing I've ever heard!'

'And there's something else about her, Ted. I got the impression that she's not too discriminating about who she sleeps with.'

'Evidently not, if she slept with you!' Teddy guffawed, and heads turned to look at them curiously.

'Shut up, I don't mean that, I mean I think she sleeps with women . . .'

'And you'd call that undiscriminating? That's a bit rich! Did she tell you that she was bisexual?'

'Not exactly, she just talked a lot about other women . . . in fact, she talked a lot about Mike. But even more about you.'

'So big deal, so she has a healthy fantasy life. Honestly, Charles, you get straighter and straighter and more and more pompous every day! I don't believe a word of it, anyway. You're the one with the fantasies . . .'

Charlie looked serious, now, all jesting set aside. 'I admit it, Teddy. I *do* fantasise about you when I'm with other women — at least some other women. I always have, and maybe I always will. But mark my words, there's something funny about Glory McWhirter. She's funny about you. I shouldn't make a great buddy out of her.'

Teddy looked down at her glass as she swirled the Calvados.

'Mike thinks a lot of her. He sees a lot of her. Much more than he sees of me. She thinks I'm holding him back, restricting his career.' Her voice was small and suddenly melancholy, and when she looked up at him, her eyes were dewy with tears. Charlie felt a stab of irritation. Why the hell was Teddy's heart wrung by a man like Miccinelli? Who the hell was he to wring anybody's heart? The last thing he wanted to talk about was Michael Miccinelli.

He replied dismissively. 'That's rubbish, Teddy, and if you had an ounce of sense you'd know it was. You bring more to Mike than he could have dreamt of.'

'I don't know, Charles. I've got the feeling recently that he doesn't really love me any more. He seems so – detached. And this search doesn't help – we've hardly seen each other for weeks, he doesn't talk to me about his work any more . . .'

'Listen, Ted, if you are going to marry the man, you're going to have to deal with this sort of thing for a long time to come. Don't worry about it. I'm sure he loves you.'

Teddy's eyes shone wistfully through the tears. 'Are you? Are you really sure?'

Charles had long avoided discussing Mike with Teddy, fearful that any attack on Mike would simply result in the end of their long friendship, but Philip Redmayne's fine claret, and the Calvados, had put fire in his belly and added fuel to his sense of injustice, and he threw caution to the winds.

'Well, if you put it like that, no, I'm not sure. If you *really* want to know what I think, I think he probably doesn't love you. I think he only loves himself. I think he's a shit, and a jerk, and quite probably a bastard, and I think you are a fool to talk about marrying him. There! That's what I think!'

Teddy had pushed her chair back, and the tears now flowed freely down her pale face. 'I'm leaving. I'm going back to my hotel,' she gasped.

Charles ran after her, and caught the door of her taxi as she was about to close it.

'Teddy, I'm sorry. I shouldn't have said that. I don't know what the hell Mike thinks of you – I'm sure he does love you – I'm sorry. I'm just jealous, that's all. I love you too, sweetheart. I can't help myself. You're my best friend and I only want what's best for you . . .'

Teddy jerked the door out of his hand, nearly breaking his wrist in the process, and slammed it.

Charles cursed himself. His first instincts had been right. He should never have told Teddy what he really thought.

FEBRUARY 4TH, 1984

Candida didn't even remove her coat. She sat down, huddling in the chair next to the fire, and stared into the flickering flames.

'My baby died.' Her voice broke, but Robert Ballantyne didn't leap to his feet, or offer her his handkerchief, as she had envisaged. He continued to write, continued to keep his eyes on the paper in front of him.

'When?'

'Three, four months ago. Last October. He died when we were on holiday.'

'How old was he?'

'Nearly two.'

'He died whilst you were away on holiday?'

'No. He was with us. We were all on holiday. He drowned. In the hotel. In the pool.'

'*I'm so very sorry.*'

She could feel his eyes on her face, could actually feel them penetrating her, could feel the warmth of his sympathy wrapping around her like the warmest of blankets, but she couldn't bring herself to look at him. The tears poured silently and unchecked down her cheeks.

'*I'm sorry. You'd think I would have stopped crying by now. It's been so long . . .*'

'*Not long at all. I quite see why you are crying. Do you want to tell me what happened?*' *His gentle voice seemed to be coming from a great distance.*

Candida leant back in the chair, her eyes closed, the tears streaming . . .

'*I'm insisted that we went on holiday. It was really all my fault in that sense. If I hadn't forced it, Tommy would be alive now. My husband had been working so hard, you see, he rarely spent any time with Tommy, and I thought we all needed a break. Jack was exhausted – so was I – and Tommy so needed to spend time with us together. Jack said he didn't think he could get away, but I insisted. I said I'd arrange everything – even call Dick, his boss – and force him to let him go. He wouldn't let me. He did, finally, persuade them to let him go. He hadn't taken any real holiday since our honeymoon, only a few days here and there. Dick's not a bad guy, he just depends on Jack so much. Everyone depends on Jack.*' *A sliver of bitterness crept into her voice.* '*Anyway, I booked two weeks at a hotel in Mexico, where we spent our honeymoon. It seemed right to take Tommy to the Presidente – we'd been so happy there. The first week was wonderful – the weather was perfect, and Tommy was loving it; he loved his father so. One day, we had a long lunch. I'd been up most of the night with Tommy – he didn't sleep well, you know – and I was so tired. Jack told me to go back to bed. He said he'd go swimming with Tommy. Tommy laughed and laughed.*

"Good-night, Mummy, time for bed," he said. "Daddy go swimming with Tommy." We all laughed.'

Candida opened her eyes and stared up at the ceiling. A small patch of damp in one corner caught her attention, and she focused on it. She felt as if she were in a different place, as if she were a stranger describing a scene in a film. She continued to speak in a flat, wooden voice.

'Up in our room, I stood on the balcony and waved to them. The room overlooked the pool. It was such a bright day, so blue . . . I always think of that bright clear blue as a Mexican blue, not a Mediterranean blue. I bought a rug that shade of blue, actually. It's in the spare room. The Med's so green . . . I waved to Tommy in the pool. He loved the water. Jack was holding him and I shouted out, to tell him to put his arm bands on. He heard me. I know he did — he nodded and smiled. I went to sleep. I don't know how long I slept. When I woke up, I drew the curtains of the window and went out on to the balcony again. I saw Jack first. He was lying on the lounger. Face down. He was asleep. Then I saw Tommy . . . He was floating in the pool. Face down. I think I screamed then. I nearly jumped off the balcony. Jack went in. It was too late. He was dead. People always say that drowned bodies are bloated and blue, but Tommy wasn't. He was very white, and there was a green tinge around his mouth. Not blue at all.'

The room was so silent that Candida could hear the clock ticking on the mantelpiece, and could hear Mr Ballantyne's even breath. She couldn't hear her own, and for a moment it occurred to her that she had stopped breathing.

'How do you feel?'

'How do I feel?' she repeated numbly, leaning forward to face the therapist for the first time in their conversation, and gripping the arms of the chair, white-knuckled.

'How do I feel? I want to kill him!'

'Who?'

The word sank in the silence of the room, and Candida collapsed back in the chair. 'Jack. I want to kill Jack. He killed my son.'

CHAPTER SIX

After landing at Heathrow airport, Teddy went through passport control in a daze and waited for her bag at the carousel. She felt utterly deflated; tired, confused and quite alone. The impersonal atmosphere of the airport made her isolation all the more intense. There was no one to turn to. Charles had betrayed her, attacking her on the one front where she felt most vulnerable. She didn't believe what he had said about Mike – she couldn't believe it. Surely Mike loved her; they had been together for two years now, and had had many good times; all right, maybe he was a little obsessed by his work – but wasn't she? The more people she interviewed, the more certain she felt that professional success required a touch of obsession. She thought about the candidates she had shortlisted for FRG Barnekov: Esther Levenson, Konrad von Budingen, Christian de Clement-Grandcourt; they were all attractive characters, and yet they had made sacrifices in their personal lives, dedicating their time single-mindedly to the pursuit of professional excellence. So it was natural that Mike should do the same, and natural that she should follow suit. But why did she feel so damn miserable? Maybe it was just jet-lag; maybe it was just that she had developed an aversion to international airports, she thought as she heaved her bag off the carousel. She passed through customs and walked into the arrivals hall, a small dispirited figure carrying the weight of the world on her shoulders, oblivious to her surroundings.

It seemed as if somebody was calling her name from a

long way away. And there he was. So handsome, so vibrant, so much her own dear Mike.

'Teddy!' His face lit up with a huge lopsided grin. Shoving back the forelock of black hair that fell over his brow, he flung his arms open wide, letting armfuls of flowers fall to the ground at his feet, and swept her in to the air as she ran into his welcoming embrace.

'God I've missed you, sweetheart.' She was crushed in a huge bear hug before he set her down on her feet. 'Let me look at you. You look absolutely terrible. What's wrong? What's happened?' His eyes were full of tender concern, his arm braced around her supportingly, as he studied her face.

'Nothing's wrong, Mike, I'm fine now I'm home, and you're here. I'm just a little tired, that's all.' Despite her brave words, the tears that she had stifled ever since her conversation with Charles were starting again.

'Teddy, Teddy darling; hush now, don't cry. It's all right, sweetheart. We're going home. I'm going to take you home now.'

'I've got to go into the office,' Teddy sniffed uncertainly.

'Out of the question. We're going home. I've taken the day off work, and I called ARC and told Julie I'd be picking you up. I'm going to pop you into a hot bath, then feed you a warm meal – you look like a ghost – and then I'm going to tuck you up in bed and you're going to have a long sleep. That's an order.'

She closed her eyes and gratefully allowed him to take control.

'Now give me your bag, Teddy, and you can pick up your flowers. I didn't bring them all the way out here for you to trample on them.' Flowers were scattered on the floor at their feet, small white roses, gracious lilies, ivy wrapped tightly around their stems, fragile pale blue delphiniums lay neglected on the dirty linoleum of Terminal Two.

'Oh, Mike! They're so beautiful!' Teddy bent down to sweep up the delicate blossoms.

'So are you, Teddy. So are you.'

Teddy leant back, eyes closed, in the soft leather seats of the Ferrari as Mike steered it cunningly through the London traffic. Her fears and doubts ebbed out of her slowly as she remembered again and again the image of Mike standing tall and straight, arms overflowing with flowers, eyes searching for her face in the crowd. Thank God she was home at last ... She was oblivious to the Talking Heads music thumping away on the car stereo.

Mike was as good as his word. When they arrived at his flat, his first move was to call Julie at ARC and tell her that Teddy was laid low with flu and wouldn't be in to work that day – and possibly not the next. Then he switched the phone over to the answering machine, and ran Teddy's bath, helping her to undress, washing her back, and drying her as one might dry an infant. He dedicated the entire day to her, ministering to her needs with kindness and consideration. When Teddy awoke refreshed from a deep sleep, he took her shopping, insisting that she needed cheering up, and that he wanted to buy her something glamorous. The shop assistants at Harvey Nichols were thrown into confusion by Mike. Every time Teddy tried on an outfit, and paraded for Mike's approval, he would close his eyes and shake his head. 'No; it doesn't do you justice.' 'No, it's too old for you.' 'Nope, too business-like.' 'No, you're too pretty for that.' Finally, they settled on a pale chamois wrap-around skirt in a suede so soft that it clung like silk, a bisque silk body by Donna Karan, and a long, close-fitting tabard waistcoat in hand-stitched matching suede. The soft honey colours of the outfit brought out the lights in Teddy's ash-blonde hair, and reflected the warm glow of her complexion. She felt pampered, and spoiled, and cherished, and secure for the first time in several months.

'Now; I'd say it's time for a glass or two of fizz, and then dinner. Where do you want to go, darling? The Gavroche? Tante Claire? Bibendum?'

Teddy nestled into his shoulder as they walked arm in arm down Sloane Street.

'I think I'd like an Indian take-away. Chicken Jalfrezi. Lamb Karahi. Muttar Paneer. Prawn Puree. A bottle of Brouilly. And I'd like it in bed. If that's okay with you?' She looked up at him shyly.

'Your wish is my command.'

That night, Mike made love to Teddy as if it were the first time, or perhaps as if it were the last time. He was exquisitely tender, and seemed to revel in every part of her, paying attention to her small, elegantly turned ankles, the arch of her foot, caressing the nape of her neck, stroking the tendons of her forearm. He knew from experience that such thoroughness paid high dividends.

Later, Teddy lay curled in the comfort of Mike's arm, her eyes closed, her breathing light and steady.

'Ted? Are you awake?' Mike whispered.

'Um-hmm . . .' she murmured contentedly.

'Ted, will you marry me?'

She opened one eye. 'Hey, buster; it's me, your fiancée. I *am* marrying you.'

'I know. I mean will you marry me now?'

Teddy propped herself up on an elbow to see Mike's face better in the gloom of the bedroom. The street-light reflected on his face, and his expression was uncharacteristically wistful.

'Now? You mean tonight?' Her tone was joking, but her eyes looked serious.

'Not tonight; you haven't got your wedding dress yet. But let's move the date forward, okay? I don't want to wait much longer to call you my wife.'

Teddy leant over him, kissing the corners of his mouth

with light, butterfly kisses. 'As soon as you like, Mike. I can't wait much longer to *be* your wife.'

As the increasing darkness took hold of Mike's large, airy bedroom, Teddy began again to make love to him.

When Teddy walked into Candida's office the next morning, Candida flung her arms wide and embraced her. 'Welcome home, stranger! How'd it go?'

'I think I've got a great list – von Budingen, Clement-Grandcourt, Levenson, Tom Pitt-Rivers – ' Candida's eyebrows rose '– and some good back-ups if they fall through. Tell you what, I'll write them up on the computer and then bring them in so you can have a look. I'd like your opinion about who to push hardest with FRG.'

Teddy started updating her candidate files, putting in a brief summary description for each candidate so that she wouldn't forget them when talking to her client. She turned her mind first to Konrad von Budingen. She deleted the last screen comments, and tapped in:

'A real mover and shaker. Serious and determined, part of the inner circle in Frankfurt. Highly Teutonic. Dedicated corporate man, loyal but rational; great integrity. The jewel in Delius-Zech's crown – calls all the shots there. They just don't come much better than this. Probably mobile – shortlist for FRG Barnekov.'

She turned next to Christian:

'Smooth, sophisticated, jet-set. Naughty but nice. Makes and has lots of money. Has the gift of the gab, but not all talk – intellectually rock-solid. Superb client man – made to market, born to broke. Don't be misled by this book's glitzy cover – the guy's a real heavyweight. Only question is, would his style function in the UK as well as it does in France? Shortlist for FRG.'

Now for Esther:

'Small and explosive – a dynamo of a woman. Bags of potential in the right house. Very bright and packs a punch. 100% energy in motion – should be called 'Hurricane Esther' – won't take no for an answer, and never, *ever*, says die. A street-fighter in the investment banking world. Wiz with balance sheets, works 24 hours a day.'

Teddy paused, chewing her bottom lip. How should she end the description? Chain-smokes cigars and is four months pregnant? She decided against it, and typed rapidly,

'Not much experience of European markets, but takes to challenge like the proverbial duck to water, and should be given a chance. Shortlist for FRG.'

And now dear old Tom:

'Eton drawl and slouch, but the very best of the old school. Also known as Shit-Rivers – a misnomer, as he's one of the world's great gentlemen. Natural team leader – a true mentor, versus a tormentor. Long term Steinberg's star (now in a hurry to move . . . begs the question why?) they call him a licence to print money. Right image for FRG Barnekov; shortlist.'

For the sake of the other ARC consultants, and the

sake of future searches, Teddy was now obliged to put in her comments on the less appealing candidates she had interviewed. She flipped through her notebook.

Lawrence Able: 'Totally underwhelming. The original invisible man.'

Philippe Armand-Delille: 'Stocky and cocky – will never leave Paribas.'

Brad Mischkin: 'Fat and tired, and thinks he's better than he is . . . he's lost his bite; well past his sell-by date.'

Stretch Logan: '100% Wall St. Likes the limelight. Tons of talent. Personality clash with Paul Driver.'

Gordon Gould: 'Greasy, spotty Northerner – no charisma, a cup of cold sick.'

Bob Brauchman: 'A thoroughbred, but put out to pasture. At least he's a has-been, and not a never-was.'

When she had completed all the other entries, she shuffled the print-outs into order and went into Candida's office. Candida was very approving of her work.

'They all look good, Teddy. My instincts tell me that FRG will go for Konrad; he's probably got the most high profile reputation of the four, and somehow the Brits tend to work better with the Germans than the French. I guess Tom Pitt-Rivers is a serious contender, but why is he itching to leave Steinberg's?'

'Beats me; we're due to have lunch tomorrow, so I'll try to find out what's going on. To be honest, I think they're all good, but I kind of favour Esther, myself.'

'Really? It seems to me that you have some sort of reservations . . . saying she ought to be given a chance. It sounds like there's some reason why she *won't* be given one.'

'Wee-ll,' Teddy sighed, 'I *do* have reservations. She's pregnant, Candida. And unmarried.'

'Then you should cross her off. This is no time for caring about sisterhood, Teddy; it's a professional decision, and if she chooses to have a baby, knowing it's going to undermine her career, then she's going to have to pay a price for it.'

'Come on, Candida. You of all people know how hard it is to get on for a woman. If *we* don't have faith in her, who else is going to? If a man was starting a family, it wouldn't affect his chances for the job, would it?'

'Don't be so naïve, Teddy. The man wouldn't be suffering from morning sickness, either. Don't misunderstand me; I'm not saying women shouldn't have men's jobs. But you've got to remember, that for now, at least, they are still *men's jobs*. If a woman wants one, then she ought to be prepared to do whatever a man does – she ought to start peeing standing up, if that's what it takes.'

'I don't agree. If people like you and me keep saying that, then you just prolong the *status quo*. Honestly, Candida, you know as well as I do that men have helped each other up the ladder for centuries. They constantly advance someone they went to school with, or play cricket with or whatever. It's just not fair!' Teddy sighed. 'Look, I know I'm sounding naïve and childish. I don't really *mean* it's not fair. I just think we should be doing more to promote women.'

'Listen to me carefully, Teddy. If this were a theoretical argument, then this is my view: men do promote men, but they promote them for a reason. Whether it's the old school tie, or Freemasons, or because they support the same football team, it doesn't matter; what matters is that there is a reason for the alliance. What you are talking about is positive discrimination purely because Esther is a woman. That's not good enough. If you came in and told me that she was your second cousin, or you played hockey together, or you went to the same hairdresser, I might be more sympathetic. But you cannot recommend people purely because of their sex. I've been around a lot longer than you have, Teddy, and if I've learnt one thing that I can pass on to you, it's that excellence brings its own rewards. Mediocre men don't succeed, and nor should mediocre women. The only difference for men and women in the City is that women should be advised to forget about being women, forget about discrimination, sexism, chauvinism, and just get on with doing the job as well as they can. Sex doesn't matter. It is irrelevant.'

'But it's not irrelevant to the clients! They constantly reject candidates because they are female!'

'Are you absolutely sure of that? Can you cite examples?' Candida asked sharply.

'No, but you know it's true. It's up to us to show people that times are changing.' Teddy's chin was raised belligerently.

'And when they've changed, I'll change too. For the moment, this is purely theoretical, and I'm not interested in theory. I am interested in doing a job as well as it can be done. FRG hired ARC because we're good headhunters, not because I'm a woman, and I hired you because I believed you would be a good headhunter, not because you are a woman. We have been hired to find the best candidate for our client. Do your job, Teddy, and leave your feelings out of it. I'll be very surprised if FRG think that the best candidate is a forty-year-old unmarried mother.'

'Thirty-nine,' Teddy corrected.

'Okay, thirty-nine. Let me ask you one question, Teddy, and think carefully about it before you answer. If Esther Levenson was a man – or if the three other candidates were all women, who would you say is the best candidate?'

Teddy thought for a moment and then sighed. 'I just don't know. I can't think of Esther not being a woman, because a lot of the assets she brings to the table are *because* she's a woman, and because she's had to fight against prejudice. It's just that she's really good; she's thought through how she'd handle being pregnant, and I trust her. I'm not saying we should conceal it from FRG – hell, she's not going to be *able* to conceal it much longer – I just think they should meet her first before we tell them. Then if they reject her straight off, we don't have to say anything, and if they love her, we'll tell them, and maybe they'll accept it. That's not exactly dishonest, is it?'

'I don't give a damn about dishonesty, I just don't want to blow the deal.' Candida looked at Teddy over the rim of the large tortoiseshell glasses which she wore for reading. 'Okay. It's your call; you can decide how to handle it. But I'm warning you, Teddy, don't try to play God. And don't waste your time and your talents being some sort of latter day suffragette. It doesn't pay the rent, do you understand me? Talk it through with Jamie; his instincts are pretty good. Just remember, at some point you're going to have to tell Paul Driver he's potentially hiring two, not one.' Candida turned back to her papers. 'Oh, by the way – as you are so concerned about women's rights, you'll be interested to know that we saw your friend Glory while you were out of town. Ghastly woman. But Hayes are going to take her.'

Teddy stuck her head into Jamie's office on her way past.

'Jamie, can you spare me half an hour to go through the FRG candidates?'

'Sure thing, oh gorgeous one. From what I've heard, they sound like the perfect cast for a joke, you know, "Heard the one about the Englishman, the Frenchman and the German . . .?"'

'You're forgetting the American. Give me ten ticks and I'll be with you.'

Teddy couldn't resist the temptation to have a look at Glory's screen and see what Jamie and Candida had made of her. She detected Jamie's hand in the assessment:

Name:	McWhirter, Glory
DOB:	14/4/61
Sex:	F
Nationality:	American
Languages:	Eng. (barely recognisable as such)
Current Employer:	Steinberg Roth, London
Previous Employer:	Steinberg Roth, New York
Prof Status:	Asst. Vice President
LOB:	Proprietary Trading
Product:	Foreign Exchange
Mobility:	Definite, for money
Last salary:	£200k +bonus
Last Interview:	2nd May, 1992 (see records)
Rating:	B++ (JF/CR)
Relationship:	F:M Miccinelli
Comments:	Looks like an aerobics instructor. Pneumatic. Mega-yank. Feisty. Brazen. Unsophisticated – closest she's come to culture is the yoghurt in the fridge. Arrogant but appealing. Natural trader.

Teddy smiled. Jamie had clearly fancied the pants off her. The relationship cell referred to Mike, presumably as it was their friendship that had introduced Glory to ARC. She was guiltily relieved it didn't say, 'Friend: T Winnington'; after all, one wasn't forced to embrace *all* one's husband's friends, and she had the feeling that she and Glory weren't destined to be bosom pals.

Jamie was extremely helpful on the candidate write-ups. He agreed with Teddy about Esther Levenson, and started to rough out the detailed analysis that would accompany each candidate on their interviews with FRG Barnekov. Teddy left it in his reliable hands while she concentrated on drawing up their CVs. At the door of Jamie's office, she paused.

'Hey, Jamie; remind me what F stands for in the relationship code – I haven't filled them in yet for these new guys . . .'

'Teddy, you have a brain like a sieve.' Jamie said long-sufferingly, not looking up from his computer console. 'For the last time, M is for Married, E is for Engaged, B is for Brother, S, amazingly enough, is for Sister, C is for Chum, and F is for Fucks. Got it?'

Teddy closed the door of his office, and made it as far as the corridor outside. She leant against the wall. She felt physically ill. Her legs were jelly-like, trembling, and threatening not to support her. Cramps seized her stomach so that she almost gasped with pain as she struggled to the bathroom. Thank God it was deserted. She retched into the bowl of the loo as wave after wave of nausea hit her. After it had passed, she sat on the floor of the cubicle, her forehead resting against the cool porcelain, for what seemed like hours. She couldn't cry; she couldn't think. All that went through her mind was that she felt so sick that she might be dying. Her mouth was filled with the sour, acrid taste of bile. She dragged herself up off the floor and stared into the mirror. She looked exactly the same; a touch paler, perhaps, her eyes slightly reddened, but she looked exactly the same as she had looked yesterday in the mirrors of Harvey Nichols. She picked up her bag and briefcase and walked slowly back to Candida's office.

'Do you mind if I take the rest of the day off? I feel rather sick, suddenly.'

'You certainly don't look too hot. Go on, go home, and

don't come in tomorrow if you don't feel up to it. Is Mike around to take care of you?'

'Oh yes; he's bound to be. I'll be fine.'

Teddy went straight to the car park. Her stomach was still in knots, but her head had cleared. Feeling numbed, she pulled Mike's red Ferrari out through the exit, and drove down London Wall, following the traffic to Steinberg's glass and steel offices near St Paul's. Above the three, large revolving doors, silver letters announced 'Steinberg Roth International Ltd' under the world-famous logo of the solitary silver star. She pulled the car straight up on to the pavement outside the entrance, so that the front wheels came to rest on the fourth step leading up to the impressive foyer. Leaning forward to reach the hidden controls by her feet, she switched on the car alarm and stepped out of the car as the alarm started screeching. Five or six people had gathered, watching her in amazement. She flicked the button on the car keys – Mike had automatic central locking, *of course* – looked around her, and dropped the keys into the nearest grate. The awful noise of the alarm had attracted people into the hall of Steinberg Roth, and she saw others gathered at the windows that faced the street. She hoped they recognised Mike's car. Teddy coolly stepped into a taxi, and gave the driver the address of Mike's flat.

'Spot of trouble with your car, ducks?' he said as they pulled away from the growing crowd.

'No; I was just returning it to a friend.'

When she arrived in Kensington, the phone was ringing. She let the answering machine pick it up, as she proceeded to throw her few belongings into yesterday's Harvey Nichols bag. She left the suede skirt and jacket, but on impulse took the silk body. Glory's tits were too big to fit into it. She heard Mike's voice on the machine speaking into a void.

'Teddy? Teddy pick up the phone if you're there, for

Christ's sake . . . Teddy?' The machine clicked. His voice sounded strange – irritated and clipped – but nervous. He clearly felt he couldn't shout at her in front of his colleagues, Teddy thought bitterly. She looked around the flat. There was really very little she was entitled to take. She helped herself to a bottle of champagne from the fridge, and took the precaution of removing Mike's spare set of car keys from his desk drawer – thank God he was so organised – slipping them into her pocket. Another short taxi ride and she was home.

Her own answering machine blinked furiously at her . . . four – no five – calls recorded. She ignored it. It was a lovely, early summer's afternoon. The light poured through the window of Teddy's little kitchen. She was bathed in the warming sunshine as she leant her hip against the counter, pulling the champagne cork. Taking one solitary crystal flute, and the chilled bottle, she made her way out into the private gardens. Teddy wanted to get drunk. It wasn't a question of drowning her sorrows – she knew perfectly well that they weren't going to stay drowned, but would keep bobbing up to the surface – but for an hour she didn't want to think. She didn't want to think about the future; didn't want to think about her family's reaction to her broken engagement; didn't want to think about what Charlie had said just two days ago in Paris; didn't want to think about Mike . . .

But of course it *was* Mike that she thought about. It hadn't for a moment occurred to her to doubt what Jamie had said, because somewhere in her heart she had known that Mike was cheating on her for a long time. Far from thinking of him as a bastard, as an ogre, she thought of the man she had loved, and still did love. She was prepared to admit some responsibility for his affair. Her mother Laura had always told her that it was a woman's duty to dedicate herself to her man, to devote her time and her energies to his satisfaction, and to keep up her appearance for his sake. Laura wasn't advocating a doctrine of female inferiority; her theory was entirely founded on self-interest. Laura couldn't believe that any real woman wanted to work, and certainly that no real woman wanted to sleep alone, and the easiest method of avoiding such an unspeakably awful fate was to ensure the willing enslavement of a suitable supporter. But here Teddy was pulled up short. Even by Laura's rules of play, Teddy hadn't jettisoned the game. It wasn't the fact that Teddy was working that had forced Mike into Glory's ever ready arms, and it wasn't as if she had let her looks slip. Teddy stared at the simple fact; Mike had slept with Glory because he *could* sleep with Glory. There wasn't anything that Teddy could have done about herself or their relationship that would have made him unable to sleep with Glory. It was just in the nature of things. By her fifth glass of champagne Teddy wasn't sure whether she even cared about Glory. She was beginning to feel intensely embarrassed about how Mike had publicly humiliated her. If Jamie, and therefore Candida, knew about Mike and Glory, who else had Glory told? The whole of Steinberg Roth, thought Teddy, her stomach beginning to churn again. She went inside and switched on the answering machine.

'Teddy? Where the fuck are you? I don't know what the hell has gotten into you, but I haven't got the spare car keys and I can't switch off the fucking alarm – it's driving everyone mad. Ring me.'

Click.

'Teddy, it's Mike. Look, I don't know what the hell I'm supposed to have done, but whatever it is, I'm sorry. Really, truly sorry. Please call me, darling; I'm sure there's been a misunderstanding.'

Click.

'Théodora, this is Christian de Clement-Grandcourt. I

have taken the liberty of calling you at home as your colleague gave me your number and thought you wouldn't mind. I will be coming to London next week and hope that you might be able to arrange an interview with your client. Perhaps that would give you enough grounds to accept my invitation to dinner to discuss interviewing strategy? Please call me at the Paris office.'

Click.

'Teddy. It's me again. Where are you? I'm leaving the office and going back to Kensington. I'm worried about you. Has something happened to your gran – to Matilda?'

Click.

'Teddy, it's Jamie. Look, I realise what happened about Glory's records. I feel like a total shit. Please let me try to explain.'

Click. The tape whirred as it rewound automatically.

As Teddy sat by the telephone, motionless, it rang again, making her jump.

She didn't touch it, simply listened to Mike's voice: 'Teddy? For Christ's sake, what's going on? I've just come home to get the spare Ferrari keys and they're gone. If this is all some sort of a game, it's not a very amusing one . . . Teddy? I'm coming round right now to your place to sort this out.'

Teddy doubled over on the sofa, her arms clutched around her waist, succumbing again to nausea. She knew she should see Mike and hear him out, but she didn't want to look at his face and hear his explanations now. She wanted to hear the facts. She scratched a note explaining that she had gone out, shoved the spare car keys into it, and stuck it on the front door. She then retreated to the sanctuary of her bedroom and dialled the number of ARC's office.

'Teddy, how are you feeling, you poor lovey? My Bill has

come down with the same thing, weak as a kitten, he can barely get out of bed,' Julie's sympathetic voice rattled in Teddy's ear.

'I'm all right Julie, really. Can you put me through to Jamie?'

Teddy waited until she heard Jamie's soft Scottish accent. 'Teddy, hang on a minute, I just want to shut my office door.'

'Why bother? This whole subject seems to be a matter of public discussion for everyone except me.' Teddy's tone was clipped and cold. Jamie sighed audibly.

'God, I am so sorry Teddy. I've been a complete idiot. I wanted to talk to you first about Glory privately, and I just didn't think that you were going to look at her screen. I realised what had happened the second Candida said you'd gone home, and I went into your office. I'm so sorry; it's all my fault. I could shoot myself.'

'It's not your fault at all. It's Mike's fault. You were simply the bearer of bad tidings.'

There was an uncomfortable pause before Teddy continued. 'So. What did Glory say, exactly?'

'She didn't *exactly* say anything. She just made it perfectly clear to us that she and Mike had a special relationship, and that it was far from platonic. I got the impression it's been going on since Mike was in the States.'

'What did Candida say?'

'She said she was sure that you knew, in your heart of hearts, and that if you didn't, it wasn't up to us to tell you.'

Teddy's mouth twisted as she listened to him. 'Well, for once Candida gave me more credit than I deserved. I didn't know — at least I think I didn't know. And I'm glad you told me. It makes everything much simpler, in a way. God bless the integrity of the candidate computer records, eh, Jamie?' Jamie had never heard Teddy speak so bitterly, and his heart sank.

'Teddy, I don't think you should jump to any conclusions . . . give yourself some time, let things calm down a bit, get some perspective . . .'

'Oh, that all sounds *frightfully* mature! The only problem is, Jamie, that I don't want to be mature. I'm fed up with being calm, and having perspective, and giving people the benefit of the doubt, and behaving nicely. I'm fed up with being dignified. If there are conclusions to make, and there are, then why the fuck not jump to them?'

Concentrating on her conversation with Jamie, Teddy was oblivious to the sound of her front door opening and closing. It wasn't until her bedroom door opened that she realised that Mike was in the house. She'd given him her door keys months ago.

As she sat on the edge of the bed, the phone pressing hard against her jawbone, she looked at Mike, his large, handsome frame filling the doorway, his face wearing the crooked, diffident smile that she had fallen in love with.

'Jamie, I've got to go. There's something I've forgotten to do. I have to put the rubbish out. I'll talk to you later.' She hung up.

Mike came towards her, his arms outstretched in the same welcoming gesture that he had used so recently at Heathrow airport. Teddy tensed involuntarily as he sat down beside her and took her hand in his.

'Darling, what's the matter? What's upset my little girl?'

'I'm not a child, Mike. Don't use that tone of voice to me.'

'What's this all about?'

'It's simply about your affair with Glory. That's it. Nothing complicated. Yesterday I didn't know about it; today I do.'

Mike laughed and stood up, turning his back on her for a moment. 'Affair with *Glory*? God, for a moment I thought it was something really serious.' He put his hands on his hips, assuming a comical expression, and said humorously, 'And what has given you the idea that I'm having an affair with Glory?'

Teddy closed her eyes.

'Stop it, Mike. Stop it right now. I've told you I know. It doesn't matter how – that's not the issue. All that matters is that I don't want to be with you right now, and I don't think I'll want to be with you in the future.' She felt Mike trying to take her hand and jerked it away, letting it lie limply in her lap. She heard him draw in his breath over his teeth.

'All right, I'm sorry. I had one stupid and terrible one-night stand with Glory. I made a mistake, and I regret it. I didn't want to sleep with her. I just – '

Teddy opened her eyes wide in feigned amazement. 'You didn't *want* to? What happened? Did she rape you in the office?'

'No, I don't mean that. I just mean that she made it very difficult for me. I didn't think anything of it, you were away – '

'Oh, I *see*. Well, that's an entirely different story, then. You mean I wasn't sitting in the next door room while you laid her? Thanks. That makes me feel a whole lot better. Thanks very much.'

'Teddy, listen to me! There was a leaving drinks for one of the traders on the desk . . . I was pretty trashed, I admit it. Glory said she'd drive me home, we had a few more drinks, one thing led to another. It was really because I missed you so much, I just needed – '

'Oh, for God's sake Mike, don't make me sick on top of everything else! How many bloody traders have left Steinberg's in the past two months? Ten? Twenty? Don't lie to me any more! You taught me an important lesson once, remember?' Teddy's voice rose uncontrollably as she spoke. 'Miccinelli's Law of Holes: when you're in one: stop digging. Well you're in one up to your neck. I'd be grateful if you could handle this with a little bit of dignity. For once in your life. I'm trying to preserve mine.'

Mike swiftly changed his tactics. He had arrived at Teddy's not knowing what was up, but suspecting that somehow she had found out about Glory. He had decided to deny everything, unless her evidence was watertight, in which case he would be suitably contrite and beg her understanding and forgiveness. But he wasn't prepared to be patronised under any circumstances. In a situation like this, attack was definitely the safest form of defence. He turned nasty.

'Oh *excuse me*! I forgot I was talking to the Virgin bloody Mary! The problem with you, Teddy, is that you're so fucking holier than thou – I don't suppose you've ever made a mistake in your life, right!' He began to storm down the stairs, and Teddy followed him, now shouting.

'Oh yes, I've made a few mistakes all right! It was a fucking big mistake to think I could trust you! It was another fucking big mistake to get engaged – that was *my* big mistake!' It sounded stupid, and cheap, and childish, even to Teddy's ears, but she couldn't stop the words pouring out of her mouth. All her tension and pain knit into a ball in her chest and exploded in rage.

'How long have you been fucking her, Mike? Just tell me that, and then you can fuck off. Just tell me how long! Ever since you left New York?'

'I was fucking her, as you put it, long before I left New York! At least Glory knows how to treat a man – at least she's not bloody Julie Andrews!' They were standing in the hall.

'Don't you dare walk out of here, Miccinelli. You don't even have the guts to listen to what I'm saying!'

'You were the one who didn't even want to let me in!

Now you're telling me I can't fucking leave? That's really dignified, Teddy. I'm impressed.'

'D'you want to know what really upsets me, Mike? The fact that it was Glory. If you had to screw anyone, you could have chosen somebody with some style, but no, you end up with some stupid tramp from the gutter. I guess she makes you feel right at home, is that it? Common enough for you, right?'

Mike froze, and turned to face her, his face white, black eyes blazing. 'You arrogant little bitch. You've never forgotten that I come from the wrong side of the street, have you Teddy?'

They were at the front door. They stood inches apart, both breathing heavily. Teddy regretted what she had said, and felt her anger evaporate into a thin mist of misery.

'I'm sorry, Mike. I didn't mean that. I'm just so hurt . . .' The tears began to pour down her drawn face. Mike put out a hand, hesitantly, but she shrank away, shaking her head silently, and looking at the floor.

'I know, I know,' Mike said quietly. 'You bruise too easily.'

'No. You hit too hard.'

She heard the front door close with a soft click, and was alone.

CHAPTER SEVEN

Although Teddy couldn't stop thinking about Mike, fortunately she had far too many other engagements to allow her life to grind to a halt over the breaking of one. She had scheduled lunch with Tom Pitt-Rivers, had an appointment to see FRG Barnekov with Candida, and had to make a decision about how to handle Christian de Clement-Grandcourt. She had invited Charlie to dinner to try and rebuild some bridges – although she hadn't let on how right he had been about Mike – and she had invited her grandmother to stay for the weekend. On top of everything else, she had been asked by New College, her Alma Mater, to make a presentation to the current undergraduates on career opportunities in the City. The Master of the college had contacted her, having heard that she had become a headhunter, and was extremely keen that Teddy should dispel any lingering notion that the City discriminated against women. She was not at all sure that this was a notion that deserved to be dispelled, but she had agreed to do her best. Teddy was glad that her diary was so full; the last thing she wanted was to be sitting in front of the television alone every night.

Paul Driver was an ideal client as far as ARC were concerned. Although somewhat lacking in charisma, he was extremely efficient, respected the service his headhunters provided, and knew exactly what he wanted them to achieve. Whereas some clients changed the brief of the search every week, Paul had thought everything through before he retained ARC, and never wavered from his original goal. When Teddy and Candida met him in one of FRG's conference rooms he listened carefully as Teddy talked through the candidates that ARC had interviewed, and explained how they had arrived at the current shortlist.

'The candidates that you should see first, Paul, are Konrad von Budingen and Christian de Clement-Grandcourt. As I know Tom Pitt-Rivers personally, we haven't as yet interviewed him formally; I'd like to find out exactly why he's thinking about leaving Steinberg's before suggesting he meet you, and I will be having lunch with him later today to find out what the story is there.' Teddy looked down at her notes. 'There's one other candidate I consider top class: an American woman, Esther Levenson of Salomon's. We'd like to bring her over to London to see you.'

Paul jotted down the four names. 'Tom Pitt-Rivers I know, and would love to bring him on board, but you're right, Teddy. Let's find out what's going on first. Konrad von Budingen and Clement-Grandcourt I know only by repute, and I'm delighted that they're interested. Well done, ladies.'

Teddy and Candida exchanged a brief glance. There was always something slightly patronising about being called 'ladies' in that tone, but it was a hell of a lot better than if he had said, 'Well done, girls.' You had to be grateful for small mercies. 'Go ahead and schedule a round of interviews through my secretary. I want each of them to meet me, and the other three division heads, so you're going to have trouble finding us all in the same country at the same time. Now, Esther Levenson; can't say the name rings a bell. Why are you so keen on her?'

'She's excellent, Paul. Very committed, a lot of experience, and she's done wonders for Solly's name in Europe. It's not easy building a client list in Europe from a New York base, particularly when Solly's don't exactly have a broad range of equity products, and she's done it. I think she's a miracle worker and, equally important, I really like her.'

'What do you think, Candida?'

'Well, Paul, I haven't met her, as Teddy did the New York interviews alone. My first reaction would be that a European would tend to have more clout in continental markets than an American, and much as it goes against the grain to admit it, I think that certain corporate CEO's still have trouble taking a woman seriously.' Paul nodded in agreement. Candida glanced over at Teddy, and then continued smoothly, 'On the other hand, I think it would be an advantage for FRG to have a senior woman executive on the board, and I trust Teddy's judgement. If Teddy says she's exceptional, then I'm sure she is, and that it would be worth your meeting her. You know it's one of our key principles at ARC that we never waste a client's time.'

Paul nodded again slowly, and continued to look through the list of candidates that ARC had ruled out. 'Okay, let's start with Budingen, Clement-Grandcourt, Pitt-Rivers and Levenson . . . I just want to be sure we aren't leaving anybody off that stacks up to the other four. What about Jack Delavigne, Teddy? I don't see his name here.'

Candida stepped into the breach. 'I advised Teddy to cross him off without an interview, Paul. I don't think he'd fit into your culture here at FRG.'

Paul Driver's thoroughness, the very characteristic that made him such a desirable client, occasionally resulted in his being a difficult one. He rarely accepted things at face value.

'Why not, Candida?' he asked directly. 'I've met him, not at length, but at various receptions and conferences, and thought he came across very well. His reputation is first class, and his clients seem loyal to him personally, despite the trouble Hayes are having at the moment.

Those seem to me to be good enough reasons to approach him.'

The two women were silent.

'Unless, of course, you have a specific reason for excluding him that you haven't mentioned . . . other than a feeling that he might not fit in?'

'I can't give you any hard facts, Paul. It's more a question of instinct. I simply don't consider him to be reliable. I think in the past you have been quite satisfied with my judgement of people,' Candida replied haughtily.

'Absolutely; but in the past you've given me chapter and verse to justify your conclusion. If you can't do that for Delavigne, then I think we should give him the benefit of the doubt and see him, don't you?'

Candida was tight-lipped, and Teddy came loyally to her rescue. 'Paul, I think it's highly unlikely that Jack Delavigne would consider a move. He's spent his entire career at Hayes Goldsmith, and appears to be very loyal to his team there . . .'

'Perhaps you're right, Teddy, but you're not going to know that unless you ask him, are you? Anyway, it's precisely his loyalty and leadership that appeal to me.' He looked at them for a moment, and then said briskly, 'So, ladies, we're agreed. I will tell my secretary to give you priority in my diary, and one of you will contact Delavigne first thing. Good. Thank you for your time, and what looks like a job well done.'

As they travelled back to the office Candida was silent, clearly preoccupied by the prospect of having to interview Jack. Teddy tentatively suggested that she would contact him, if Candida preferred.

'Yes; I would prefer it, thank you. There's something you should know, Teddy, before you speak to Jack. I don't know if Jamie mentioned this to you, but I used to be married to Jack, a long time ago.' She stared out of the taxi window. For a moment, Teddy thought that that was all she was going to say, and didn't want to pry. She was quite surprised when Candida continued.

'If you are going to interview him, you should probably know a little bit about what happened. Our marriage failed when my son died. It was an accident; he drowned when we were on holiday in Mexico. I haven't talked about it for a very long time.' She covered her eyes with one hand. 'Jack was meant to be looking after him, and Tommy drowned.' Teddy put her hand on Candida's arm in a gesture of sympathy. Candida's skin was icy to the touch. 'It's all right, Teddy; it was all over a very long time ago. I have never felt able to see him since then, and I just don't think I can talk to him now.'

'Of course you can't! It must have been terrible for you!'

'It was terrible. It was also my fault. I should never have trusted Jack, and I knew that long before the accident. So, quite simply, it *was* my fault. And I paid everything I had for that mistake.'

'And Jack?'

'Jack paid nothing. Men never do. Jack just decided to throw himself into his work and couldn't understand why I didn't want to be with him any longer. I think he was afraid that Tommy's death and our divorce might somehow jeopardise his perfect career record. Anyway, he was wrong about that. It's women's careers which get ruined by children and marriage – even if the children die and the marriage breaks up. Even if the children don't die and the marriage stays together. Men just go from strength to strength. I think Jack actually benefited from it all; Dick Belton-Smith was so bloody sympathetic he couldn't wait to promote him.'

Teddy squeezed Candida's arm gently. 'I know how you feel.'

Candida looked at her strangely. 'You do?'

'Yes. I've just broken off my engagement with Mike. He was having an affair with Glory McWhirter.'

'Oh, *that*,' Candida spoke dismissively. 'You shouldn't worry about that, Teddy. It's not important. I always knew you couldn't trust men on the little things, but it's the big ones you should worry about. What they do with their pricks is neither here nor there.'

Teddy felt rebuffed by Candida's lack of sympathy; she would have welcomed a return squeeze, some gesture of solidarity, but Candida didn't speak again, and Teddy gazed out of her own window, both women distracted by memories.

JANUARY 19TH, 1981

Mystry Cottage was a small, pink thatched cottage not far from the Suffolk coast. Candida and Jack had arrived there that morning to spend the weekend with Jack's friends, Mary and Stephen Mallinson. Jack and Stephen had been at New College together, and Jack had been best man at Stephen and Mary's wedding. Stephen had not been able to return the favour when Jack and Candida married, as Mary was expecting their fourth child at the same time and had actually gone into labour on the morning of the wedding day. Candida had been relieved that the Mallinsons couldn't attend; she really didn't want three toddlers disrupting the solemnity of the occasion, but knew that she couldn't refuse to invite them. It would have hurt Jack too much not to have one of his best friends there, and Mary was certainly the type to turn down any invitation that didn't extend to her entire family. But God had been kind to Candida by taking

*the decision out of her hands through the vehicle of
Mary's fecundity and – how could one put it politely?
– Catholicism.*

Dinner that night was a chaotic affair. They had spent
the early evening in the large family kitchen, trying to help
Mary and Stephen feed their five children, which mainly
involved dodging chunks of bread hurled by Lucy, now
a year old, and trying to persuade the older children that
setting fire to the dog's tail was not the ideal pursuit for a
Saturday evening. It was nearly nine by the time Mary had
the children in bed and started to cook their own dinner.
Jack and Stephen sat in the cosy sitting room in front of
the fire, drinking Tesco's own label whisky and discussing
the proposed reforms in trade union law. Stephen was a
barrister, and disagreed with the government's case that
the reforms would be enforceable. Bored, Candida took
her glass of wine into the kitchen on the pretext of seeing
if Mary needed any help.

Candida sat at the farmhouse table, her legs elegantly
crossed, swinging one sleek leather boot as she watched
Mary at the Aga. Her hostess was wearing a pair of old
jeans, summer sandals with argyll socks and what seemed
to be one of Stephen's sweaters, patched at the elbows
and staggeringly moth-eaten. Her long brown hair was
pulled back with a pink velvet ribbon that clashed horribly
with the sweater. She had refused Candida's half-hearted
offer of help, saying brightly that she was absolutely fine,
although the smell of burning was unmistakable. Candida
didn't repeat her offer, but refilled her wine glass and lit a
cigarette.

'How on earth do you cope without a nanny, Mary?'

'Oh, you know, we have some help in London during the
week, but it's so much fun to come down here at weekends
and just be family, you know?' Mary stared unconvinced
into the smoking saucepan and tipped in the contents of

her wine glass and what looked like half a pound of flour. The pan sizzled ominously.

'But five children under the age of eight! I don't know how you cope!'

'Oh, you'll see for yourself soon enough; they're tremendous fun, really. Patter of tiny feet and all that. Peter Rabbit. Jemima Puddleduck. Bubblebath. Trips to the zoo. Crescendo. Mother and toddler groups.' *Mary was now in a fully-fledged babble.* 'And if we had a full-time nanny, I'd never spend any time with them. I think it's so important that the parents are involved at this stage, don't you? And I'd simply hate to miss out on all the high jinks.'

'I suppose so,' *Candida agreed doubtfully. She looked at Mary's ragged clothes and straggling hair, at the debris of plastic building bricks and bits of lego which covered the kitchen floor, and the hunks of sweaty cheese, well past their prime, that Mary had already dumped on the kitchen table. Candida picked a few dog hairs off her otherwise spotless cashmere sweater.*

'The key thing is just to relax and enjoy everything.' *Mary pushed the hair out of her eyes with one hand, stirring furiously with the other.* 'You couldn't just fill my glass up could you, Candida? Thanks.' *Her face was flushed from the steam.*

'Well, I must say I admire you. It seems like an enormous amount of work to me.'

'But so much fun!' *Mary repeated.* 'I would simply hate to go back to proper work now.'

'What did you do before the children?'

'Oh, this and that. I worked as a paralegal in Stephen's chambers for a while, and I worked at the Oxfam shop two afternoons a week — nothing high-powered, like you. Oxfam was fun because the people were all so decent and I got first crack at all the clothes that came in.'

*Candida resisted the temptation to say that that was
quite obvious; Mary was still wearing them.*

*'But then when Charlie was born I just couldn't face the
idea of going back to work, and Stephen was so sweet and
understanding about it, he said I simply had to stay with
the baby. I mean you can't do two things well, can you?
So we decided that he would work, and I would raise the
children.'*

'And you've never regretted that?'

*'Not for a moment.' Mary placed a large casserole full of
brown lumps and strange floating black bits on the table.*

*'Well, I do admire you,' Candida said again. 'I don't
know – the idea of all those years being pregnant, and the
pain, and the breast-feeding – I'd be so worried about my
figure . . .'*

*Both women's eyes fell immediately to the other's waist-
line, Mary's tummy bulging slightly under the enormous
sweater, Candida's flat as a board, encased in leather
trousers that fitted like a glove.*

*'Yes. Well. There are other compensations,' Mary said
briskly. 'Shall we call the men? You don't mind eating in
the kitchen, do you? It's so much cosier . . . Dinner is
served!' she trilled brightly down the little corridor.*

*Dinner was served, but barely touched, by Candida at
least. The stew managed to taste floury and burnt at
the same time; the little black bits that Candida had
eyed so suspiciously were charred mushrooms. The pota-
toes were underdone, and the cauliflower leaked greenish
water on to their plates. 'Ah, Boeuf Bourgignonne! Mary's
Boeuf Bourgignonne is legendary!' Jack said cryptically to
Candida, with a wink. Mary blushed, well pleased, but
apologised profusely and frequently for everything until
they had all assured her that it was absolutely delicious.
Jack and Philip left spotlessly clean plates. For dessert,
Mary offered the children's left-over raspberry jelly which*

she had tried to dress up by beating in whipped cream and sticking in a few sprigs of mint. It looked like it had been vomited by one of the children earlier. Candida, smoking to kill her hunger pangs, watched in amazement as her husband ate it with gusto, washed down with a 72 Sauternes that he had brought as a gift.

After a cup of disgusting coffee that left a dark sludge in the bottom of their cups, Mary and Stephen retired to bed. 'The children are up at six, I'm afraid, even on a Sunday . . .' Stephen said apologetically. 'You two lie in as long as you like.'

With various strange admonishments regarding tiptoeing up the stairs, and shutting doors extra quietly, and refraining from flushing the loo, so as not to wake the baby, their hosts left Candida and Jack to finish the Sauternes in front of the fire.

Candida waited until she heard the floorboards creaking in the room above them and then rolled her eyes and banged her head against the wall. Jack laughed until they both shushed each other simultaneously, collapsing in giggles on the sofa.

'Never again!' Candida gasped. 'We can never come here again. I'd starve, for one thing . . .'

'I've got some chocolate in the car, if you want it . . .'

'No, I'll stick to the booze. It's the only thing that hasn't got doghairs or baby sick on it in the whole house.'

Jack pulled her towards him, and they sat gazing into the fire. 'Do you really think they're so awful?' he asked, whispering.

'No – at least he's not. He's quite sweet. But Mary! What a drudge!'

'Now, now. She's really a splendid woman, and lots of fun; it's just hard work entertaining and looking after so many children. And besides, I think she's rather beautiful.'

'You do, huh? Well, you only say that because she

reminds you of your mother . . . God, she certainly looks like mine. She obviously hasn't washed her hair in a week, and hasn't had it cut in a year. She's completely exhausted, and she tears around like she runs on batteries . . . I kept wanting to pull the plug out!'

'Bitch,' whispered Jack lovingly. 'Seriously, Candida, I do rather envy them. There is something awfully appealing about family life, don't you agree?'

Candida pursed her lips. 'There's family life and family life, Jack. I mean, if they had one kid, they'd still have a family, but they'd also have some life left. There's got to be another way of doing it, surely. Like birth control, for instance.'

They went to bed, wincing at every creaky floorboard, and freezing like statues outside the baby's room as they heard a snuffle. Their bedroom, under the eaves of the house, was ice cold. Candida sat up in bed, the blankets pulled around her, and dug Jack in the ribs to show him how her breath condensed. 'The least they could do is provide bloody hot water bottles,' she muttered through clenched teeth.

Jack began to rub her warm as she shivered against him. Her small breasts were icy, the nipples hard, as she clutched the covers up around her ears, pulling them greedily off her husband. He nuzzled her neck, his breath soft and warm against her ear.

'I'm afraid there's only one way of getting really warm, darling . . .'

'Do it, quickly, for God's sake. I'm going to die of cold and if you don't hurry up I'm going to put on all your clothes and my tracksuit, which I don't think you'll find very attractive . . .'

'Forget about very attractive, I won't be able to get inside it,' Jack mumbled into her left breast.

'I'm sure you'd find a way.'

'Where there's a will . . .' Jack rolled on top of her, and Candida mimed a scream.

'Get off!' she hissed. 'You feel like a block of ice! I'd even prefer to have that disgusting dog on top of me!'

'Sometimes I wonder how perverted you are, my darling wife . . .' Jack had remained firmly planted on top of her, and had her shoulders pinned down to the lumpy mattress.

'If I have dirty thoughts about the dog it's only because he's got more body hair than you have, and because your bloody friends keep their house like a fridge . . . Misery Cottage, what a bloody appropriate name – awful food, god-awful bed, and as cold as the fucking North Pole . . .'

'Mystry Cottage, darling, as in mystery, secret, unknown –'

'Well, it's a bloody mystery to me why we're here, and I wish it had stayed bloody unknown as well as far as I'm concerned.'

'If you don't shut up, I'm going to give you one –'

'Promises, promises . . .' Candida teased, but parted her knees accommodatingly. Jack was as good as his word and proceeded to make love to his wife without exposing any part of his or her bare flesh to the chill. When they were both ready, and he was about to enter her, Candida laid a finger against his lips. 'Now remember, whatever you do – DON'T WAKE THE BABY!' As soon as the words were out of her mouth, she shoved Jack off her and sat up. 'Jack! I forgot my diaphragm!' she hissed.

'Well go put it in, for Christ's sake!'

'I can't; I left it in the car. It's in the glove compartment.'

'What the fuck is it doing in the glove compartment?'

'Oh, I just shoved it in there when we left London – I thought I might need it.'

'In the car? God, you were hopeful! Well, go get it.'

'*I can't. I can't get out of bed. It's too cold.*'

'*So I have to get it, right?*'

Jack leapt out of bed, stubbing his toe in the dark and hopping silently up and down, his face contorted with pain. Grabbing Candida's dressing-gown – he hadn't bothered to bring his own, and needed some protection from the night air – he bent down over his wife's huddled form to whisper in her ear.

'*Let it never be said that I wouldn't go to any length to make love to you, Candida,*' he growled.

Candida heard him inching stealthily down the corridor and giggled; it gave a rather new interpretation to the concept of corridor creeping when you were already married, she thought. When Jack reached the top of the stairs, a floorboard crunched suddenly, and the foul dog set up a furious barking.

'*Shut up! Shut up, damn you!*' She could hear Jack's furious whisper, and so could everyone else.

Mary appeared from her bedroom, her hair tousled, wrapped in an old towelling robe that had clearly been washed with several pairs of black wool tights.

'*Jack? What is it? Are you all right?*'

Jack clapped his hands over his still firm erection.

'*All right? Yes, absolutely. First rate. Couldn't be better. I was just going . . . to get a glass of water.*' He finished lamely.

Mary rubbed her eyes, and took in the vision of Jack in a satin and lace shell-pink dressing-gown.

'*The bathroom's over there. There's water in it,*' she said, half asleep.

'*Ah yes! Of course! Splendid!*' Jack turned on his heel and padded back towards the bathroom, but it was too late. A noise like an air-raid warning came from Lucy's room. Mary looked daggers at him.

'*Sorry . . . so sorry,*' he hissed, and slipped back into the *guest bedroom. The mound of blankets on the bed was heaving with Candida's laughter.*

'That was your fault entirely. I'm glad it afforded you so much amusement.'

'Oh Jack! You have no idea how funny you look! You've got a stiffy sticking out like a flagpole! And in my dressing gown!' She was nearly hysterical with laughter. Jack resumed his position on top of her.

'I am not, positively not attempting to go downstairs again, is that clear? We will just have to make do without the diaphragm.'

'Jack, I do not, positively not, want to get pregnant. Can't you hold back, or improvise, or something?'

'Improvise?' Jack roared, and then dropped his voice to an outraged whisper. 'What do you want me to improvise? A screw? A condom? Are you thinking about using your bath cap, or what? Is that in the car, too? Listen, I'll do my best, okay? I don't see why it would be such a problem if you did get pregnant, but I promise I will do my best. Satisfied?'

And Jack had done his best, considering the circumstances.

It was that weekend at Mystry Cottage that preyed on Candida's mind as she and Teddy rode back to Bishopsgate.

Before Tom Pitt-Rivers met Teddy for lunch, he had to make his regular call to Steinberg's New York office to brief the salesmen on what was going down in Europe.

'Good morning, my lovelies!' he bellowed down the squawk box with his customary greeting, and was answered by a series of unintelligible grunts from the assembled American salesmen. 'It's a bright and sunny day in London town, and we're looking at doing a hell of a lot of business today, so let me run you through the new issues we've got piping hot and ready to be gobbled up by those ever hungry punters. Starting off with a tricky one, we've got to place forty mill of SKF – that's Swedish for ball bearings for all you happy campers who aren't quite awake. Due to the fact that the Turnips are in a spot of financial crisis, it's not going to be that easy a deal . . . Any salesman who moves this heap of junk gets the yellow jersey for the week, and earns the undying gratitude of yours truly . . .'

In some ways, Tom Pitt-Rivers wouldn't compromise. He didn't bother to explain to the Americans, who probably didn't know that a swede was a root vegetable, that Turnip was a nickname for a Swede . . . He didn't bother to explain that the yellow jersey was something to do with the Tour de France. He just sold his story, and expected them to understand, and by and large, because they knew him, and because they loved him, and because he was one of the finest salesmen in the world, they did. In other areas, Tom Pitt-Rivers did compromise. He had suggested meeting Teddy for lunch at a small Italian restaurant in Islington, somewhat off the beaten track and therefore likely to afford a little more privacy than most of the standard City haunts. Tom greeted Teddy very warmly. He had been fond of her, although she was right to think that he had reservations about women's commitment to work. He was ready to make exceptions in Teddy's case, however, and clearly wanted her professional advice.

'The fact is, Teddy, that I'm really perfectly happy at Steinberg Roth; I like the job, I've invested a lot of time in it, and it isn't easy for me to face throwing it away and starting over again. But there are circumstances that force me to consider it, and when I heard on the grapevine that you were recruiting for FRG Barnekov,' he raised his eyebrows, waiting for Teddy's nod of confirmation, 'I just felt I had to put my cards on the table and talk to you about it.' He drained his glass of Perrier and cleared his throat nervously. 'This isn't easy for me to talk about; it's a rather personal matter.'

'Tom, you know you don't have to tell me anything you don't want to, if it's private. All I need is one good reason why you should leave Steinberg's; you could say it's to do with company policy, or new business prospects or anything you like.' Teddy was trying to ease his obvious embarrassment.

'But it isn't anything to do with Steinberg's, *per se*, Teddy. It's to do with Alex Fitzgerald. Do you remember him?'

'Beelzebub? How could I forget him?' Teddy shuddered.

'D'you remember Annie?'

'Your wife? Of course I do! How is she?'

'She's fine, just fine. At least she is now. The thing is, Teddy, she and Fitz had an affair.'

Teddy looked aghast. She couldn't imagine any reason that any woman would want to have an affair with Fitz, let alone Tom's pretty and charming wife. 'Tom, that's awful . . . I don't know what to say.'

'The affair didn't matter; it was very brief, and finished over a couple of years ago. Annie told me all about it. I don't hold it against her at all. I think it was the old seven year itch . . . it's just a shame that she chose Fitz, that's all. To be honest, I don't think she chose Fitz at all; I think he chose her. But it's water under the bridge. Annie and I understand each other; we have much too much to throw it all away over something like an affair. In some ways it's even been good for us. I love her very much, you see, and I don't think she understood that at the time.'

'It makes me feel sick, Tom. Why Fitz?'

'He's not unattractive, Teddy. He's very clever, much cleverer than I realised. He knows how to make women feel safe, which is something I clearly failed to do. He can be very charming. I agree that when Annie first told me, I couldn't understand the appeal at all, but when I thought about it and tried to look at him objectively, I began to see

what had happened. You've got to admit he's good-looking
– or so women tell me – and he's American to boot, which
can be appealing, and he talks straight. I think he seemed
exciting after seven years with me.' He looked so sad that
Teddy felt her heart twist. 'Anyway,' Tom sat up straight
and spoke decisively, 'it's all in the past and my present
concern is the future. Fitz isn't prepared to let sleeping
dogs lie. I don't know if he ever really cared about Annie.
Maybe he did, and that's why he bears so much resentment
towards me now. I don't know; he's married himself, and
I can't believe he would have left Nancy – he could never
have given up her trust fund for a start – not for Annie,
anyway. But ever since he's tried to block me at every
step. I'm one of the newest partners at Steinberg's. I've
got a very hard slog ahead trying to prove myself and earn
my points over the next couple of years before partnership
really begins to pay off. Fitz is doing everything he can to
undermine me, whether from malice or because he truly
doesn't think I come up to scratch is irrelevant. He's a
couple of years ahead of me, he's going from strength to
strength, really expanding his power base, and I just don't
know if I can take him on in hand-to-hand combat. He's
a powerful adversary.'

'I know that. What did the corporate finance desk call
him? They had some funny nickname . . .'

'The Terminator. Two days after he made partner, he
sacked thirty per cent of his department without batting
an eyelid. He's built up quite a reputation for doing that
– other partners call him in to consult on dismissals.' Tom
managed a smile. 'So you see my predicament, Teddy? If I
hang in there, and lose, I'll have nothing in three years. So
unless I'm sure I can beat him at his own game, it's looking
as if I should make a break now. And I don't think I can
play Alex's game, let alone beat him at it. I never learnt
the rules.'

Teddy patted his hand maternally. 'There's no reason why you should. FRG will be delighted to see you, and there's no reason for you to tell them any of this. I'll make something up.'

When Teddy left Tom, she didn't immediately return to the office. Instead, she walked to Highbury Fields, a dull and rather ugly park to the north of Islington. She felt extremely angry, but in an absolutely miserable way. What was wrong with men like Alex and Mike? Why did they need to have 'illicit' sex to make them feel better? She questioned her own reactions to Mike's infidelity; had she just been horribly naïve, and was she even now repeating her initial mistake? The affair itself hadn't seemed to bother Tom unduly; she thought about what Tom had said: *Annie and I understand each other; we have much too much to throw it all away over something like an affair*. She didn't understand how he could say that. Clearly, whatever he had thought he had with Annie had been a mistake, and Annie had shown him how wrong he was, just as Mike had shown her. Try as she might, Teddy could see no excuse for Annie; if she loved Tom, then she had been stupid to the point where it became immoral, and if she didn't love Tom, then it was he who was being stupid. Pacing around the park did nothing to alleviate Teddy's growing frustration. It seemed as if everything that she had taken for granted, friendship, marriage, trust, were being held up and exposed as nothing but a sham. Look at poor Candida, and what she had suffered; then Mike, who had betrayed everything Teddy had committed to his care; and now Tom and Annie Pitt-Rivers! She kept telling herself that it was none of her business how Tom and Annie had managed to patch up their relationship, it didn't reflect on her own relationship with Mike. But it did. Didn't Tom's magnanimity make her own censoriousness look narrow-minded and misguided? *We have much too much to throw it all away over something like an affair.* Perhaps Tom was right; but what had she and Mike ever really *had*?

She felt utterly confused. One part of her said that Tom was indeed right, when it came to his own marriage, but in her case, she and Mike had never reached a point of sharing where there could be such understanding. Could she forgive him for abusing her trust before he had even earned it? Another of Tom's phrases haunted her: *I love her very much, you see, and I don't think she understood that at the time.* Was it her fault rather than Mike's? Had Mike doubted, in some way, that she really loved him, and if so, wasn't she simply proving by her rejection that his fears had been well-founded? Teddy felt that there were so many questions that she needed answered in black and white, and yet nobody could really answer them; she certainly couldn't. Whatever she decided was going to be a leap in the dark. It would take an act of faith to take Mike back, and she didn't know where she would find the strength to do it. But if she didn't . . . was it a cowardly act of self-protection? Somebody had to have the answers. Teddy had an awful feeling that she was going to have to come up with them herself.

Late that afternoon, Teddy caught the train from Paddington to Oxford. Walking up George Street and down The Broad towards her old college, she felt strangely at peace, as if the past seven years had slipped quietly away and she was back in the happy sanctuary of university life, when her greatest problem had been finding a new excuse for why she hadn't completed her essay by the tutorial deadline, and her greatest stress had been directing a production of *Love's Labours Lost*. Oxford never seemed to change, except that the students tearing past on bicycles looked ever younger, and the façade of Blackwell's looked ever older. The porter at the lodge of New College was the same old John, and when she leant through the little hatch to get her room key, he simply said, 'Evening, Miss Winnington. Staircase Five,' as if she had just popped out that morning rather than seven years before. The alumni guests were to assemble for drinks with the Master, proceed to the high table for dinner, and then meet the third year undergraduates for an informal question and answer session in the junior common room.

Teddy couldn't help but laugh when her old tutor handed her a glass of sherry. Without any preamble, or any comment on her career since leaving Oxford, he embarked on a lengthy discussion about the relative merits of F Scott Fitzgerald versus Hemingway, the subject of her special paper at finals. He portrayed the very image of an ivory-tower academic, dishevelled hair, an ill-fitting and worn suit, nicotine-stained fingers, and a strange, fluting voice.

'I myself have always agreed with Henry James that American novelists suffer from the lack of a subtly articulated society with a historical tradition out of which to write. But of course, Theodora, if I remember correctly, you were always an admirer of the nostalgic quality in *Gatsby*; I myself preferred the more muscular strength of Hemingway.' He tapped out his pipe against a table leg, the ashes falling on to the carpet. 'I find Fitzgerald's obsession with the unending quest of the romantic dream somewhat tiresome. At best, an overly sentimental portrayal of the search for self-orientation . . . "Gatsby believed in the green light, the orgastic future that year by year recedes before us . . ." I myself have *never* believed in the green light. Do you still see its glimmer, Theodora?' His eyes twinkled mischievously behind his thick-lensed glasses. Teddy was about to launch a spirited defence of her erstwhile literary hero when she saw Jack Delavigne walking towards them across the room. Damn! She had known from the brief

CV on file at ARC that Jack had gone to New College, but it simply hadn't occurred to her that he would be here tonight, and she hadn't bothered to ask the Master which alumni would be attending.

'Ah, Jack, old chap!' Professor Miller greeted him warmly. 'Have you met Theodora Winnington, another of my former undergraduates, but after your time with us?'

Jack inclined his head. 'We have met, but I hadn't realised that Theodora had also suffered under your tyranny, Douglas. It's good to see you again.'

Teddy smiled politely as she shook his hand.

'Now Jack, if I remember correctly, was always a Hemingway man.'

'That doesn't surprise me one bit,' Teddy said impulsively, provoking a raised bushy eyebrow from her old tutor.

'Not really a Hemingway man, Douglas, although I preferred him to the other Americans . . . the Metaphysicals were really more my cup of tea . . .' They continued to talk about the English syllabus until they were interrupted by the Master of New College, who wanted Jack's opinion on a new scheme he was launching to boost the college's endowments. Teddy didn't have a chance to speak to Jack again until after dinner, when they assembled in the junior common room for the question and answer session. There were about forty undergraduates gathered in the large room, and they divided roughly into two camps. In the front rows were a selection of soberly suited young men and women, who clearly viewed the meeting as an opportunity to accelerate the interview procedure; one particularly earnest looking young man even clutched a copy of the *Financial Times* under his arm. At the back were a handful of obvious dissidents – lounging on the sofas, smoking and preparing for battle. In the middle sat a nervous gaggle of students who couldn't decide which was more important, the esteem of the back row brigade or the chance of an early job offer.

Jack naturally assumed control of the session. He introduced the other alumni briefly, and gave a short presentation on the structure of the City, and how the banks had evolved through the 1980s, before soliciting questions. A forest of hands rose from the front rows.

'Are my career opportunities likely to be greater with a merchant bank or an international investment bank?'

'How would you value a background of accountancy qualifications against legal training?'

'I want to go into mergers and acquisitions; where should I start?'

'What is the starting salary at Hayes Goldsmith?'

Jack answered all the questions succinctly, turning to his colleagues on the panel for their comments.

'What do you look for in a CV?'

'I think Theodora has the best qualifications to answer that,' said Jack, passing Teddy the baton.

'Well, at the undergraduate level, the first thing we would look for would be indications of excellence . . . they might be academic, or sporting, or social. Anything that sets your CV apart from the crowd. Then we would look for signs of leadership: a willingness to be in a position of authority, such as election to the JCR committee, student union politics, the debating society, head boy at school, et cetera. Finally, any indications of originality: interesting hobbies, a lot of travel, some sort of hint towards your professional motivation.' Teddy paused. 'What you have to realise when you write a CV is that it's a selling document; what you *don't* say is just as important as what you *do* say.'

'What you are telling us is that, if I want to get a job in the City – though why any thinking person should want to is another question – I *shouldn't* say that my dad's doin' life in Brixton, that I went to the local comp, and that I don't have a fucking blue in rugger? Is that about right?' The voice belonged to an aggressive young man at the back of the room, sporting a black leather jacket and a belligerently spiked haircut, whose consciously coarsened accent betrayed his Etonian roots.

'No, that's not what I'm telling you. I'm telling you to stand out from the crowd in any way that you are comfortable to do so. If most of the applicants to a City firm came from the local comp, and didn't have a fucking blue in rugger, then your CV might not arouse much curiosity, so you would need to stress your father's, ah, experience, to differentiate yourself. Does that make it any clearer?'

Jack smiled at Teddy approvingly.

By half past ten, the session was drawing to a close, and seemed to have been a success. Some of the undergraduates lingered to ask for more specific advice, two of them (including the be-denimed Etonian) thrust their CVs into Teddy's hand, but most drifted off to the undergraduate cellar bar. Teddy decided to approach Jack about interviewing for FRG Barnekov. Much to her surprise, given her rudeness to him in Paris, he agreed to an interview, and suggested that they retire to his rooms for a drink and conduct the interview then and there.

Jack had been allocated a set of rooms in the oldest quad of New College. After removing his tie he poured Teddy a whisky from a bottle that his now ancient scout had thoughtfully placed in the sitting room, and then strolled into the little bedroom to change into jeans and a sweater. He left the door open, and Teddy couldn't help admiring his broad back as he peeled off his jacket and shirt; she then looked away discreetly. He came back into the room, now wearing jeans and smoothing his tousled fair hair.

'Theodora, would you excuse me for just a moment

whilst I have a word with John the porter? I need to order a car for tomorrow.'

After he had left the room, Teddy prowled around, but Jack had obviously brought very little with him for an overnight stay. His discarded clothes were tossed in a heap on the floor, a compact leather bag lay open on the bed, and a small photograph of a little boy had been propped up on the bedside table. Teddy realised at once that it was a snapshot of Candida and Jack's son. A pair of trusting eyes, so like Candida's, stared out at her from under a broad, smooth forehead that he had clearly inherited from his father. As Teddy heard Jack's steps on the stairs, she hurried back to the sitting room, and started turning the pages of a college magazine idly.

'Sorry to keep you. John hasn't lost his taste for a gossip.' He refreshed her glass, and poured himself a large shot of whisky. 'I must say, it's a relief to get away from the office for a bit.' He sighed. 'Now what do you need to know, Theodora? Shall I run through what I've done to date?'

Despite the fact that it was late, that they were sitting drinking Scotch out of cafeteria tumblers in a room that had barely changed since the fifteenth century, and despite the fact that Jack for one was clearly on the point of exhaustion, he answered Teddy's questions as professionally as he might have done had they been sitting in her office with a cup of coffee. He was unequivocal about his commitment to his work, but had no illusions as to the problems Hayes Goldsmith faced.

'This is an extremely difficult time for the bank; we have to make some definite strategic decisions about how we are going to compete in the nineties. To date, Hayes has tried to offer the full range of products and services that Goldman Sachs or Steinberg Roth offer. We're certainly inferior to both of them on the trading side, but on the corporate finance side we compare pretty well. It's my belief that we need to specialise further, cut out – or at least cut down – most of the market making, and concentrate on where our skills are strongest. Some of my colleagues on the board disagree, as they feel that the bank's survival depends on being multi-product. I'm not convinced; we're in the middle of discussions at the moment. That's probably why it's such a relief to come here and get away from all the argument.'

'Why don't you just leave? Your reputation is very good – you could move pretty much anywhere . . .'

'Don't tempt me! I've thought about it, of course, everyone does. I suppose nothing especially attractive has ever come up when I'm in the mood to jump ship.'

'Well, maybe now's the right time. We're looking for someone to take over a corporate finance function for a specialist firm; they've gone down the road of offering highly specialised advisory services, much as you were suggesting Hayes should do, and the strategy seems to be working.'

'FRG Barnekov, right?' Jack guessed, and Teddy nodded reluctantly. As soon as she began to describe the job, most people in the business had guessed which firm she was recruiting for. 'Yes, they are very much an example of what I had in mind for Hayes. They have good people there; Paul Driver knows what he's doing.'

'He says the same about you. He suggested that we approach you.'

'It wasn't Candida's idea?' Jack looked up hopefully.

Teddy shifted uncomfortably in her chair. 'No; Candida didn't think you'd be interested. Paul felt we should ask you directly.'

Jack made no response, and Teddy felt obliged to fill in the silence in the room. 'Of course, we all felt that your qualifications were appropriate, Candida too, she simply felt that you might be too committed to Hayes Goldsmith.'

Jack laughed hollowly. 'Candida *always* felt I was too committed to Hayes Goldsmith.'

'Yes, well. The point is,' she paused, struggling to continue, 'the point *is* – '

'It's all right, Theodora, I think I know the score – probably even better than you do. The point is that Candida didn't want to consider me for the job, because she doesn't want to do anything that might be considered as beneficial to me, and Paul Driver insisted that you ask me. It's all right, really. I do understand. I'm sorry that you should be embarrassed like this.'

Jack was standing by the stone window, looking out at the pitch black sky. Some students ran across the quad, and their high-spirited laughter floated up into the room. Jack turned to face her, and Teddy noticed how pale and drawn he was, two frown lines deeply etched into his forehead. Jack crossed the room to replenish her glass, but she shook her head, leaving him to refill his own. He sat down opposite her, and leant forward, so that his face was only a foot from her own.

'Has Candida told you what happened? Why we divorced?'

'Yes. Well, no. Not exactly.' Teddy felt intensely uncomfortable. She unconsciously sat right back in her seat to put a little more distance between herself and Jack. The atmosphere between them was strange, tense and yet very intimate. She wanted to hear what Jack had to say, and yet she didn't want to hear it. She didn't want to hear him say that he was responsible for his son's death. Teddy didn't like even thinking about something so horrible, and the more she had talked to him tonight, the more she wanted to like him. He intrigued her. But she couldn't like him if he talked about his son.

'Did she tell you about Tommy?' Jack was still leaning forward, looking at her intently.

'Not really.' Teddy stood up restlessly, and moved across the room to the fireplace. She felt very cold, although it was now midsummer, and wished that the scout had laid a fire in the grate. 'She told me that your son had died in an accident. I'm sorry. It must have been awful for you both.' She avoided looking at him.

'I'd like to tell you about it, if I may.'

Her heart sank at his words, and she tried to stop him. 'Please don't feel that you have to – it's none of my business. It's certainly not relevant to FRG Barnekov.'

'I think it *is* relevant.' Jack ran his hands through his fair hair. 'When Candida and I were married, we never talked about whether or not we wanted to have children. I mean we never talked about it specifically. I think we both assumed that we would have children eventually, when the time was right. It seemed the "normal" thing to do, and we were both very "normal". Then, when Tommy was born, I realised – in some way – what an extraordinary liability it is to have a child. It was a very frightening realisation.'

Teddy shivered. This was it; he was going to tell her that he had realised that he hadn't wanted to have children in the first place. Christ. Poor, poor Candida.

'Very frightening,' Jack repeated, in a strange, flat voice. 'Candida seemed to adapt to it all naturally. For me, it was much more difficult; Tommy changed our lives so radically, you see. And then, when he died, I couldn't change things back. I thought I could make everything just as it was before we had a baby, when it was just the two of us, but I couldn't. We had changed; Tommy had changed us. And even when he wasn't there any more, when everything should have been back to "normal", everything was different. I'm not really explaining this very well, am I?'

Teddy shook her head mutely. She didn't trust herself to speak.

'I'm sorry. This isn't at all fair on you. You see, once Tommy was gone, I tried to make things normal with Candida. I failed. So the only *normal* thing I had left, the only thing that had always been there, that Tommy hadn't changed, was my work. I threw myself into the job. Maybe it was the wrong thing to do. At the time, I didn't feel that I had any choice. It was the only way I could cope. So Candida left; I agreed to the divorce. It was the least I could do for her to make up for everything. I lived and breathed Hayes Goldsmith. They stood by me, you see; nothing else did. That's why I feel I can't let them down now. That's why I can't honestly consider moving to FRG Barnekov or anywhere else. I'm responsible for what happened, you see.'

Teddy still refused to look at him.

'Responsible for what?' she asked, in a small voice. Perhaps if he didn't hear her, he wouldn't attempt to answer the question that she had to ask.

'Responsible for everything. I can't ever forgive myself.'

'But forgive yourself for what? For the fact that Tommy died?'

'For the fact that he died. For the fact that he was born. For what it all did to Candida. I *was* responsible.'

Teddy turned round, and walked unsteadily back to the armchair to pick up her handbag. 'I'm sorry, Jack, I really have to leave now.' Jack rose to accompany her. She tried to brush him away. 'No, no; it's all right. I quite understand. I'll explain to Paul that it's not the right time for you to move. That's fine. We'll be in touch. I'm sure something else will come up to suit you. Thank you for your time. Thank you for being so honest.'

She was backing away from him towards the door, but Jack insisted on accompanying her to her own staircase.

They walked across the dark quad in silence. At the foot of her staircase, Jack took her arm above the elbow, holding it gently but firmly enough to turn her towards him. Teddy felt an involuntary shiver run down her spine, leaving her skin tingling. She was shocked to recognise a feeling of arousal, and confused to see a responding flicker in his own troubled grey eyes. She felt desperate to get away from him.

'Theodora; I doubt very much we will meet again, but I would like to thank you for listening to me. I had no right to unburden myself, and no excuse. I'm grateful for your kindness.'

'Not at all.' Teddy pulled her arm out of his grasp and ran up the stairs two at a time. She felt twenty years old again.

After she had undressed, she went to the window to draw back the curtains, and saw Jack Delavigne, walking purposelessly round the silent quad, his head bowed. She was trembling. Jack had told her that he had never wanted his son; he had told her that he was responsible for his son's death; he had as good as told her that he wanted Tommy to die; he had told her that all he wanted was to resume his life without his son. She felt sickened that anybody could feel so callously, and be able to admit it to a stranger. Most of all, she felt sickened that having heard it, she herself could feel attracted to the man. She didn't love him; it wasn't as if she even liked him. But when he had touched her arm, the pit of her stomach had burned with that strange, hungry ache of desire. Some treacherous chemical reaction had occurred to render her overwhelmed by the urge to feel his skin against her own. After watching his solitary pacing for a few moments, she turned away from the window, leaving the curtains drawn.

She didn't like him *at all*. She didn't respect him. She wasn't attracted to him. She hated him. She longed to be in bed with him. Such is the way the body plays games with the mind and the heart.

CHAPTER EIGHT

The following day, Teddy told Candida that she had accidentally bumped into Jack, and had interviewed him for the position at FRG Barnekov.

'I suppose he leapt at it. He always lands on his bloody feet,' Candida snapped bitterly.

'No. He actually said that he couldn't consider a move at the moment; loyalty to Hayes Goldsmith, I suppose.'

'Did he talk about anything else?' Candida's clear blue eyes glinted dangerously.

'No, it was all very brief. He implied that he was in the middle of trying to turn Hayes around, and that he couldn't leave now. That's all he said.'

Teddy left the office; she wasn't sure why she had lied; it certainly wasn't out of respect for Jack, but something stopped her from describing his admission of responsibility. She knew what it was, too. It was guilt. She felt that she had been disloyal to Candida simply by listening to Jack's story, and that she had been virtually treacherous in warming to him. She hadn't seen Jack again before she left Oxford. She had deliberately left for the station early that morning, and had avoided going into breakfast in case she might bump into him. She didn't know that he had passed through the lodge gates only moments before her for precisely the same reason. Teddy didn't expect ever to see him again, and the thought filled her with a strange relief. She put a call though to Paul Driver to confirm that she had seen Delavigne, and that the answer was no. So that was that; the shortlist was final.

Teddy was meeting Christian for dinner tonight to brief him on his interviews the following day; Tom Pitt-Rivers and Konrad were scheduled for the next week, and then Esther was due to arrive in London for a whirlwind round of introductions to the FRG team. One of them was sure to go through. Teddy couldn't decide who she hoped it would be; her instincts told her that Konrad would be the safest choice, but she wanted to help get Tom out of what was clearly a dead-end for him. If Esther were chosen, it would represent some sort of justice, some sort of minor triumph for women, and Teddy liked the idea of having a friend like Esther around town. Still, she couldn't deny that her personal preference would be for Christian. She felt so utterly lonely since breaking up with Mike. She felt like being courted. She felt she deserved a fling. It was an awful thing to admit, but if a by-product of this search was going to be either helping an old friend out, or having a new female friend in town, or having a new potential lover, she would go for the lover. She was that lonely. It would surprise many of her friends and suitors to know that she was lonely, but it was true. And it was the dangerous, frightening loneliness that often follows the end of a long-term relationship.

Christian had arranged to meet Teddy at Leith's on Kensington Park Road. Teddy had been delighted by his choice; the restaurant was two minutes' walk from her home, which would give her enough time to rush home and change before meeting him. Life at ARC was so hectic at the moment that she rarely had a chance to change out of her suit before going out in the evening. It was hard to know what to wear; the dinner was not exactly social, and yet not strictly professional. She wanted Christian to continue his flirtation, and yet didn't want him to know that she wanted him to continue it. By the time she left her house, there were fifteen different outfits strewn across the bed; she had opted for a stark linen dress that fitted her like a glove and left her arms bare. It was the conventional little black dress, and yet it didn't make Teddy look at all conventional.

Christian was waiting for her in the bar off the main restaurant, talking to the *sommelier*. Teddy caught her breath as she saw him. He was so utterly polished, from his gleaming black hair to his shining black shoes. He rose to meet her, and kissed her on one cheek, letting his lips linger for a fraction of a second where her jaw bone met her ear. He slipped an arm around her small waist and led her to a quiet table at the back of the restaurant.

'I hope I haven't taken you out of your way, Théodora. This is one of the few restaurants in London that I believe compares — at least adequately — with Michel Rostang or Jacques Cagna, but I hope it wasn't too far for you to come?'

'Quite the opposite, I live just around the corner . . .' Teddy looked at him boldly. A waiter brought a bottle of champagne to the table, and melted away discreetly.

'Would you allow me to order for you?'

'I'd be delighted.'

'Good; are you hungry?'

'I'm starving! I always am.'

Christian smiled, his white teeth flashing. 'Even better; I like to watch beautiful women eat. A lovely woman and beautiful food is one of the sublime marriages, I have always thought.'

Teddy began to tell him about Paul Driver and Martin Beckwith. She spoke animatedly, willing him to share her enthusiasm for the job, and Christian complied, his head bent attentively towards her, making sure that her glass was regularly replenished.

'Paul is a good man, but very straight; you won't find him a barrel of laughs, but I'm sure you'll get on very well.

He's the ultimate safe pair of hands. Martin is far more initially appealing – he's larger than life, looks a bit like Philip Redmayne, in fact: extremely jolly, very English, but only in a good sense. The two of them make a good team, they complement each other. Jan Strakowski is the partner in charge of Eastern Europe; I've only met him once, but I was very impressed. The same goes for Hector Fuller, who runs their Far East business.'

'I'm sure I will be impressed; I believe you and I share the same taste in many things. Tell me, Théodora, what have you told them about me?'

She answered him seriously. 'Well, I told them your track record, I passed on your deal list, which of course they will handle confidentially. I told them that you were head and shoulders above the rest of the French candidates, but that I thought it would be a hard sell to get you to leave Chavaudret-Desforges.'

'And how did you describe me personally? I assume that you gave them a "flavour" of me, in the same way that you are giving me a flavour of them.'

'Yes, of course. Well,' Teddy drew in her breath, and took another sip of champagne. 'I told them that you are very charming, very sophisticated, very polished. That you are an excellent marketer, and that you are good with clients . . .'

'But not a safe pair of hands?'

'I didn't use exactly that expression, no,' Teddy said with a smile. 'I said you were very professional.'

Christian looked crestfallen. 'You make me sound like a boring businessman.'

Teddy laughed in response. 'You *are* a businessman! A banker, at least. That's why they are seeing you, don't forget. That's what you're meant to be, and what they want to hear!'

'But it's not what I want to hear, not from *you* at least.

Is that how you see me, Théodora, as just another banker in your portfolio of international bankers? Is there no way that I can stand out from the crowd?'

'Of course you stand out from the crowd, or I wouldn't have recommended you!' Teddy felt slightly embarrassed and ill at ease. She was attracted to Christian, and she was considering the idea of some sort of relationship – something light and amusing to restore her confidence – but this was going a little too fast. She was acutely aware of Christian's fingers, which were holding her wrist lightly. She unconsciously tried to pull her hand away, and only realised she had done so when his grip tightened. She met his eyes. He had a mesmerising stare. After a few seconds, which seemed like an eternity to Teddy, he released her hand with a casual shrug.

'I see I was wrong. I had hoped there was some special spark between us. I was sure I felt something when we last met in Paris, but I was wrong, and that makes me sad. Clearly no man stands out from the crowd for you other than your fiancé. What a rare and wonderful man he must be. And what a very fortunate one.' His eyes hadn't left her face, and Teddy felt the warmth rise into her cheeks.

'Yes, well, perhaps. I don't really know. Anyway, Christian, tell me more about you. Do you like London? Would you be happy living here?' She spoke brightly, praying that he would accept her attempt to change the subject. He did, but only partially, and Teddy began to realise how persistent he could be.

'Yes, I do like London, but I am a Frenchman, and I have never before seriously considered leaving Paris. Until now. As I told you, Théodora, I am enamoured of two things, beautiful women and good food, and these are not things that are easy to find in London. And sometimes, even if you are lucky enough to find them, you have to wait a long time to get them.' He snapped his fingers at the waiter, who had still not brought their first course. 'For beautiful women, I can be patient. If I have to be. For food, less so.' He spoke tersely to the waiter in French, and the poor man, after a frenzied bobbing and bowing, scurried away.

Teddy knew that she should leave the subject of beauty and women well alone, for her own comfort's sake, but couldn't resist a small gibe at Christian. 'I wouldn't have expected you to be guilty of such a clichéd bit of stereotyping, Christian. Surely there are as many beautiful women in London as there are in Paris?'

'I genuinely think not. In my experience, which is far from limited, most of the beautiful women in London are not actually English. I'm not saying that English women are not beautiful, but they do not dedicate their time to their appearance the way that so many French women do. They do not appear to understand that the art of attraction is a skill, and one that takes hard work and much practice to perfect. When an English woman is truly beautiful, it is, how should I say, almost an accident.'

'Well, that's certainly put me in my place! Are you always so blunt, Christian? It never occurred to me, the last few times we've met, that you could be insulting.'

'Insulting? Excuse me, Théodora. It was not my intention to be rude. I simply state the truth. When I see a woman as lovely as you, I say that your beauty is accidental because it is unconscious. It is not laboured, it is as natural and accidental as the Grand Canyon or Niagara Falls. It is a work of nature, of God, if you like. Deliberate, conscious beauty is also very appealing, but beauty like yours is infinitely less common. It lies in the heart, and I must confess it frightens me a little. That is why I say your fiancé must be very rare . . . and very fortunate. To be able to hold *such* beauty . . .' He sighed. 'That is good fortune indeed.'

Stung by Christian's reprimand, the waiters served them

with punctilious efficiency, and Teddy was enjoying the meal. Her only problem was that she didn't know how to react to Christian. Whenever she teased, he disconcerted her by his sincerity; when she tried to be serious, he was suave and urbane. Teddy knew she wasn't that beautiful; she knew she was attractive, pretty, and could look lovely when she made an effort, but she wasn't prone to self-flattery, and generally disliked men laying it on thick. But Christian was different from the others. She didn't go so far as to believe that she was truly an outstanding beauty, but she believed that she was in Christian's eyes. And after all, she told herself, that was what counted. Mike had never once told her directly that he thought she was beautiful. If she were to consider an affair with anyone, then she'd like him to be as different from Mike as was humanly possible. However much she told herself that it didn't really amount to a hill of beans if a woman were beautiful or not, Christian's words gave her confidence, and her confidence made her glow. She cleared her throat, and spoke with calm assurance.

'Christian, just to set the record straight, I should tell you that I'm no longer engaged. Mike and I broke it off a little while ago.'

Christian stared at her in disbelief.

'It was for the best. There were all sorts of things wrong with our relationship, and I'm much happier now being free and footloose.' She smiled at him, feeling a little brazen, but what the hell? She was in control of the situation for once.

'What can I say? I am astounded. And delighted. I said that he was rare and fortunate, but I can only think now that he was a rare fool, and that perhaps fortune will smile at me.' Christian took her hand again, and raised it to his lips. 'My poor Théodora; has it been very hard for you?'

Teddy couldn't speak for a moment. She swallowed the lump in her throat, and pressed her fingers against her temples. She damn well wasn't going to cry over Mike again, but she couldn't really carry off an act of being bright and breezy. 'Yes, it has been hard, but it's over now, and I don't regret it. It was my choice. Have you ever been involved, I mean in a long relationship, Christian?'

'Yes, just once.' Christian looked away across the restaurant, clearly thinking of a lost love. 'Just once,' he repeated, and Teddy left it there. They had both been hurt – probably everybody had, and everyone recovered from it.

'Now Théodora,' Christian turned back to her, flashing his brilliant smile, 'I want to see you happy and laughing again. The night is young, and you make me feel young as well. Where may I take you now? Shall we go to dance? At a club, perhaps, or would you like to dance in the park? I, at least, have something to celebrate.' His eyes were laughing, his expression was boyish, full of energy and enthusiasm, and Teddy was grateful to him for so artfully changing the mood.

'Christian, I simply can't! I'm really too tired, and anyway, you have to be on your best form tomorrow for your interviews. It would be irresponsible of me to keep you up tonight.'

'It would be irresponsible of you to send me back to my hotel when I am only just getting to know you. I would be forced to sit in the bar all night drowning my sorrows and trying to find someone to keep me company.'

Teddy giggled. 'I don't imagine you'd have much trouble doing *that* . . . but no, dancing is out of the question. When you sign a contract with FRG, then we'll go out dancing. But not tonight. It's been a lovely dinner; I enjoyed it very much.'

'Then don't let it end now! You must play by the rules, dear Théodora. We met in Paris, and you abandoned me for your English friend. You promised me that if I interviewed with FRG you would let me take you out, and now you say that only if I sign a contract with FRG will you really let me take you out.' He shook his head, feigning bewilderment. 'Perhaps my English isn't good enough. Perhaps I misunderstood. You should be kinder to foreigners. You will have to speak very slowly and clearly. Will you let me take you dancing?'

Teddy smiled at him. 'No. N. O. NO. *Non*, if you prefer. *C'est pas possible. Absolument non*; *c'est hors de question*. Do you understand now?' Her words refused him, but her eyes were sparkling with encouragement.

'Oh, Théodora! Now you have made it worse than ever! How can I leave a beautiful woman who speaks French to me in such a way? Never! You will never be free of me now!'

'All right, all right! You win; but we're not going dancing, okay? Just a drink, one nightcap. Come back to my place; it's only a minute's walk away.'

Christian's eyes held a look of deep satisfaction as he summoned the waiter for the bill.

Teddy was surprised when Christian said he would prefer a malt whisky to an armagnac or calvados; she had expected him to be resolutely Gallic, and was slightly disappointed that he had acquired certain British tastes. He admired her grandmother's collection of Meissen figurines, particularly delighted by a depiction of Andromache weeping over the ashes of Hector. He prowled around the room, picking up and examining one piece after another, studying the rather eclectic collection of books on the shelves, and flipping through her CDs.

'Would you like me to put some music on?'

'Yes; I see you have a recording of Georges Moustaki. I am a great fan. May we hear it?'

'Certainly; I don't know him, I can't think where that disc came from – it certainly isn't one of Mike's. I don't think he'd hold with French crooners.'

'Then he is a Philistine as well as a fool. But I am not surprised that you don't know Moustaki, Théodora. You must have been in nursery school when this was recorded.'

'Well then, you can't have been very old yourself!'

'Oh yes, I was; I was already trying to seduce pretty young girls when I first heard this. It added to my success in no small measure, I believe.'

He smiled at her as the soft, soulful tones of the French singer filled the room. Christian leant against the wall, his glass held loosely in both hands, his blue-black hair slicked back over a high forehead. He raised his glass to her in a toast: 'To you, Théodora. To your beauty, and happiness, and fulfilment.' His eyes never left her face, his stare was expressionless, the thin smile on his lips impossible to read. Teddy smiled back at him in acknowledgement, her hair slipping out of the loose chignon to fall across one side of her face. Christian crossed the room, quickly and silently, and removed the combs from her hair, letting his fingers rest for a moment in its softness. He removed her glass from her hand, and pulled her to her feet.

'Dance with me?' he whispered softly against her hair.

They began to dance, moving gently in time with the music. Teddy's eyes were closed, her cheek lying against the the cool, crisp cotton of Christian's shirt.

> *'Tu portes ma chemise*
> *et je mets tes colliers*
> *je fume tes Gitanes*
> *tu bois mon café noir . . .*
>
> *Je ne sais pas où tu commences*
> *tu ne sais pas où je finis . . .'*

Teddy felt weak; if Christian's arms were not wrapped

around her, she would slump to the floor, unable to support herself. The lighting was soft, the music seductive and her head was spinning. It wasn't the wine . . .

'Do you understand what he is singing, Théodora?'

'Most of it . . . I think.'

Christian began to sing, or rather to speak the words in a rough, throaty voice, his breath warm against the hollow of her cheek,

> *'Tu as des cicatrices*
> *là où je suis blessé*
> *tu te perds dans ma barbe*
> *j'ai tes poignets d'enfant*
> *tu viens boire à ma bouche*
> *et je mange à ta faim*
> *tu as mes inquiétudes*
> *et j'ai tes reveries*
>
> *Je ne sais pas où tu commences*
> *Tu ne sais pas où je finis.'*

His lips pressed against her cheek, and then lightly on her throat. Not daring to open her eyes and spoil the dream, Teddy raised her face, longing to feel his lips on her own. She was trembling, whether in anticipation, or fear, she was beyond knowing. Christian strengthened his clasp around her waist, and caressed the back of her neck with his other hand, rubbing away the tension, his lean thigh pressed against her hip, their bodies swaying together. He didn't kiss her mouth.

> *'Tes jambes m'enprisonnent*
> *mon ventre te retient*
> *J'ai ta poitrine ronde*
> *tu as mes yeux cernés . . .'*

They continued to dance dreamily, so that Teddy was only partly aware of his hands caressing her back, her shoulders, her face. Teddy felt as if she were on the edge of a precipice, aware of the danger, and yet longing to throw herself over the edge and float gently downwards. She felt frightened, but it was a delicious fear.

As the music finished, Christian picked Teddy up in his arms, without a word, and walked up the stairs as if he had been in her house a hundred times. He pushed open a door into the guest bedroom first, and then moved down the corridor to Teddy's own room. Teddy opened her eyes for a moment, dragged back to reality as she remembered that she had left piles of discarded clothes scattered all over the room. Too bad. At least it didn't look as if she had *planned* to bring him home, as if she had *planned* to be so easily seduced . . .

Christian put her gently on her feet.

'Christian, I think we ought to talk,' she said dutifully. The last thing she wanted to do was *talk*. 'I don't want to do anything that would jeopardise our relationship – personal or professional – ' She knew she should be having second thoughts, but she didn't really have any thoughts at all.

Christian silenced her with a finger across her lips.

'Stop talking, Théodora. Stop thinking. This is not a time for talking.' His hands were warm on her bare arms.

'I don't want you to think that I'm just on the rebound from Mike – ' his lips brushed hers lightly, silencing her.

'Théodora, listen to me. When you look at me, are you thinking about Mike?'

'No.' Teddy answered, almost truthfully. The whole truth was that it *did* make her think about Mike; it made her feel a whole hell of a lot better about Mike.

'Good. Then you are not on the rebound. Not that I would care if you were. Now, as far as our professional relationship is concerned, it is nearly at an end, is it not? As of tomorrow, I will handle it directly with FRG Barnekov.'

'That's true, I suppose.' She admitted it a little reluctantly.

'So all that could concern you is our personal relationship. Can you think of a better way to get to know me than by making love to me, or at least allowing me to make love to you?'

Teddy shivered involuntarily. 'No, I can't.'

'Good. Neither can I. So we have resolved your questions, no? Now. Let me tell you something about me. Let me tell you what *I* know. I know that I want you more than I have ever wanted any other woman. I know that I want to see you smile, and laugh. I know that I can make you happy. Right now, tonight, and here in this room, that is all I want to do, and all I want to think about. If I make you unhappy, if you are unwilling, I will leave you now, and you can decide if you would like to see me again. It is your choice, Théodora.' His eyes had darkened with desire. She looked into them and felt mesmerised.

'I just feel a little nervous, Christian . . .' She closed her eyes, resting against him, as his hands moved to the zip of her dress. 'I don't feel very in control . . .' Her voice was faint and breathless.

'You *are* in control, Théodora. You are in control of yourself, and in control of me.'

For the first time, he bent his mouth to hers, his cold lips pressing firmly against her own before her mouth opened to allow him to kiss her deeply. He unzipped her dress, pushing it off her shoulders, and traced the line of her collar bone with light, feathery kisses, whispering words she didn't understand, but loved to hear. When Teddy was naked she moved to the bed, whilst Christian stood up and undressed quickly. Teddy watched him from under her lashes. She wasn't exactly nervous, but it was a long time since she had been in bed with anyone other than Mike, more than two years, and she still felt too shy to look at him boldly. He was tall, and more heavily built than she had expected. He folded his clothes methodically and placed them on the armchair next to her bed, unsnapped the watch from his wrist and put it on top of the pile of his clothes. He seemed perfectly at ease, perfectly comfortable to be standing naked in the middle of her room. His very confidence made Teddy feel wickedly, deliciously brazen, and yet . . . She reached up self-consciously to switch off the light. His hand covered hers on the switch, stopping her.

'Please, Christian . . . turn the light off,' she whispered.

'No, my darling; then how would I be able to see you? Trust me, Theodora. Let me show you how I will love you.' He bent forward over her and unscrewed the cabochon emerald earrings that Mike had given her on his return from Tokyo, and placed them next to his watch. He sat on the bed beside her, and examined her body, his hands following the line from the arch of her foot to her hip bone, and over the gentle curve of her buttocks.

My bottom's too big, Teddy thought instinctively, her head turned into the pillow, and then she heard him say, 'You are perfect. Perfect. All I have ever dreamt of. Look at me, Teddy. Look at yourself. See how beautiful you are.'

Teddy did look, and saw how white she was against his own golden skin, and saw how their bodies complemented each other. She felt how gently Christian touched her, the infinite care he took in each caress, and slowly, her shyness melted away, as she rose to meet him.

Christian was for a moment taken aback by Teddy's passion. He had expected, and planned, this seduction as that of the experienced older man with a sensual but inexperienced young girl, and had played his part to the letter. He had nearly called a halt to it when she had told him that she had broken off her engagement; he really preferred his women to be attached, and the knowledge of her imminent wedding had somewhat fuelled his ardour. But his curiosity was too strong to pull out at that point. He had a vision of what Teddy would be like in bed, how fragile, how submissive, how girlish. She had surprised him by her willing acceptance of the seduction, had moved him by her open admission of desire. And now, she moved him again, by the force of her abandoned hunger. He had watched her face change from the pretty, winsome look she had worn in the restaurant, to the steady gaze she had worn as she allowed him to undress her, to the wild-eyed voluptuous siren that now straddled him. And Christian, for all his world-weary, jaded cynicism, was overwhelmed by a different sensation of release, one that he had not felt for a very long time.

Jack was having a bloody awful day, and it didn't look like it was heading for improvement. Another of his team, one of the junior associates, thank God, had handed in his resignation that afternoon. Jack had done his best to persuade him to stay, but when it came to the crunch, he believed that the young man was probably better off at Merrill Lynch anyway. God, five years ago he would have roared with laughter if anybody had said Merrill Lynch was a better house to be with than Hayes Goldsmith. Well, every dog has his day. To add insult to injury, the associate had implied that Merrill were eager to talk to Jack himself about a move. So he had potential job offers coming out of his ears, and there was just no way he could jump ship. There was more at stake here than one merchant bank against another, more at stake than a pay cheque. For starters, there was his friendship with Dick Belton-Smith. Dick had stood by him when he needed support, and Hayes Goldsmith was Dick's life. Second, there were the people that Jack had brought into the bank who had stayed with him, and who continued to prove their loyalty daily, despite the fact that headhunters now popped into Hayes as if it were their local grocery shop. Above all, it was a question of his integrity. It wasn't so much that his friends and colleagues wouldn't be able to get other, and possibly better, jobs; it wasn't as if clients of the bank were going to lose out; it was simply that Jack had taken over the helm of Hayes Goldsmith, and people trusted the bank because they trusted him. As far as he was concerned, even if he did get a good position at FRG Barnekov or Merrill Lynch, it would be at the price of his integrity.

On days like this, it didn't seem such a big price to pay. Jack had spent much of the morning talking to the finance director of Bouygues, who was getting cold feet about the timing of their London listing. He had lunched with an Italian executive of one of Hayes' clients, who was beginning to question Hayes' capital muscle, and had then done an interview with a journalist from the *Financial Times* who was writing a profile on Hayes. Jack hoped to God he had managed to convince the man that morale was improving. He had just sat down to look at the week's trading accounts when the young associate had come in, sheepishly carrying his letter of resignation. Jack had spent an hour with him, mainly spent trying to ease the boy's conscience rather than persuade him to stay, and had then turned his attention to the bank's proprietary trading report. When he saw the positions, and the size of them, his heart sank. He decided to try to catch Malcolm Fairchild in his office, although the fool would almost certainly have gone home by now. Malcolm was one of Dick Belton-Smith's only mistakes. Dick had hired him years ago, largely because Malcolm had been at school with him and was some sort of first or second cousin, and he had never had the heart to fire him. Jack was sorely tempted to do so. Malcolm had been a mediocre trader, and that made him a disastrous head of trading, and the fact that it was common knowledge that he was conducting an affair with Candida didn't endear him to Jack's heart. But at this stage, the last publicity Hayes needed was the sacking of one of its most senior directors. Jack picked up the computer print-out and took the lift down to the trading floor.

Malcolm hadn't left; he was sitting on the desk, one foot resting nonchalantly on the arm of Glory McWhirter's chair. Jack recognised the pose from years of watching Malcolm Fairchild at work. Malcolm regularly sat on the desk so that he wouldn't look short, and so as to have a better vantage point to look down the shirts of his female traders. He simply didn't hire women who wore polo necks. Jack walked up behind them, but Malcolm was so engrossed in his conversation that he didn't see his approach.

'Well, I'm really glad you're settling in so well, Glory. I must say, it was a lucky day for us when you decided to join us here.'

'Well, boss, like I told you, I like working for a man who knows what he's doing . . . I never felt that about Norman Bell — he ain't exactly Stormin' Norman, know what I mean?'

Jack watched Malcolm puff up with pride like a bullfrog before interrupting the *tête-à-tête*.

'Malcolm, could I see you for a moment? We need to go through some of these positions you're running.'

'Sure, Jack. Glory and I were just running through a few positions ourselves.' He leered at Glory. 'Come and take a pew.'

'Malcolm, perhaps we should discuss this in private?'

'You know me, Jack, I never hide anything from my right-hand men, or women . . . and Glory probably knows more of the details than I do.'

'I can believe that,' Jack said drily, and sat down in the chair next to Glory's. 'Right. I'm no trader, but it seems to me that you've got a very large position long the weaker ERM currencies, particularly sterling,and short the D-mark, at the moment, and I'd like to hear the case for being so bullish on the pound.'

'Hell, Jack baby, it's in the blood; either you're a trader or you're not. You've got to take a punt sometimes, and my instincts tell me the pound's gonna swing dramatically. That's what it's all about, you know? Following gut feeling.'

'No, I don't know. Could you explain your reasoning to me, Glory?'

'Volatility. That's the name of the game, and that's what makes some guys make out like bandits, and some guys make out like turkeys at Thanksgiving.'

'I understand what volatility is, Glory. I just don't understand why you've put over two hundred million pounds of the firm's capital at risk on this position, and I'd like a rational answer. Why do you think sterling's going to strengthen against the mark?'

'Instinct. I've listened to what Norman Lamont and the other guys have got to say, and I think when everyone stops busting their asses about Maastricht, they'll all realise that sterling's in for the long haul and stop the speculation. That rational enough for you, Jack, hun?' She exhaled a thin stream of smoke into Jack's face. He stood up.

'Malcolm, could you come with me a minute?'

They walked to the lifts together. Once they were in the privacy of the hall, Jack turned to Malcolm and said coldly, 'Listen to me. We've got enough problems here not to be running dangerous risks with the trading book. We cannot afford to take a big loss on currencies, do you understand me, Malcolm?'

'God, Jack! You've got to take a chance in this business! How are you going to make money if you don't take a chance?'

'Yes, well it seems to me that we've got two chances of making money on this one, Malcolm: slim and nil.'

'What are you saying exactly? Are you telling me to tell Glory to close the position down? Do you realise how that's going to make me look? She's just joined, for Christ's sake. I guaranteed her she'd have a lot of capital to play with.'

'*Play with*?' Jack's voice rose in anger. 'Play with? What the hell do you think we're doing here, Malcolm? Do you think this is some kind of new edition of Monopoly? Lose two hundred million, and collect three hundred million when you pass go?' He controlled his voice with difficulty. 'Listen Malcolm. I'm not trying to overrule you, and I don't want to undermine you in front of your team. I just want you to exercise some caution, that's all. If you want to run with the position, so be it; I'll accept your decision. But I want you to be completely aware of what you are risking.' Jack stepped into the lift.

'Who the hell is running this department? You or me?' Malcolm was red in the face, and breathing heavily.

'You are. For the time being.'

The doors closed.

Teddy awoke to find herself alone in bed. She stretched luxuriantly, smelling the sharp, citrus scent of Christian on the sheets where he had slept. Before she stepped into the shower, she looked at herself in the full length mirror, running her hands over her stomach and over her breasts, and shaking out her tousled hair. She liked what she saw, and on impulse, leant forward and kissed her own reflection. She switched on the radio to listen to Brian Redhead, and then stepped under the steaming water, humming to herself. When she emerged from the bathroom, Christian was sitting on her bed, fully dressed, looking as bright and shining as he had the first time she saw him.

'I thought you'd gone,' Teddy said, slightly shy. 'It's nice that you haven't.'

'Didn't you see my watch? I left it, so you would realise I'd be back. I never leave without my watch.' He snapped it back on to his wrist. 'I went to make you some coffee.'

He held out his hands to her for inspection.

'What do you think of them now, Théodora? Would you call them a safe pair of hands?'

'I'd call them a *very* dangerous pair, Christian.'

Teddy turned one of his wrists in her hand so that she could see the face of the watch.

'My God, Christian, you've got to go! Your interview's in half an hour!'

'I know. I have a taxi waiting outside. I simply wanted to wish you good morning.'

He kissed her, a long and thorough kiss, not the quick peck on the cheek that Mike used to deliver. 'May I see you tonight?'

'Well, I suppose we really *ought* to have a debriefing session; it's the very least I could do. Aren't you going back to Paris?'

'Not if I can see you. I will have to go back on Friday – I told the office I would be in by tomorrow lunchtime.'

'So tonight is our last night together? Then I'd love to see you. Yes please.'

'So once wasn't enough? You have not tired of me?'

She shook her head slowly.

'Excellent. What time should I report for duty?'

'Why not come and have dinner here, say at around eight o'clock? I could cook for you.'

Christian laughed. 'I will come at eight. But you won't cook for me. I told you last night, my darling, I love beautiful women and good food, but I have *never* found them combined in one package. I don't want to – how do you say it? – push my luck. You may provide the beauty, but *I* shall provide the food. Rather, I shall allow you to choose the restaurant.' He touched her hair fleetingly, and left.

Candida was not amused by Teddy coming into work at half past nine in the morning, and was even less amused by the fact that Teddy proffered no explanation.

'This is the crucial time in a search, Teddy. I thought you'd learnt enough by now to know that. You should be doing everything in your power to keep the candidates on their toes, Clement-Grandcourt, at least.'

'I *am* keeping him on his toes, believe me, but I don't see how I can possibly do it for all of them . . . certainly not Esther Levenson . . .' Teddy replied cryptically.

'I have no idea what you are talking about, and I don't want to, either. Just don't drop the ball, Teddy. Just don't drop the ball . . .'

'Oh, I wouldn't do *that*, I assure you!' said Teddy with a laugh, and virtually skipped down the corridor to her office.

She had barely settled herself when Julie put through a call: 'Teddy, it's your friend Charles Bartholomew on the line. He's *so* charming. Will you introduce him to me?'

'Absolutely not, Julie. He's a dangerous old lech. Put him through and I'll have words with him.' There was a click on the line, and then she heard Charles' familiar voice.

'Charles, haven't you got anything better to do than flirt with my receptionist?'

'Frankly, no I haven't. You are clearly avoiding me, for starters. You leave a message on my machine saying we have to have dinner, and that you need to talk to me, and sound desperately sad, so I bust a gut calling you every day for a week, and you don't bother to return my calls! What the hell's going on, Ted?'

'Nothing. Everything,' she giggled. 'I do want to see you

though. I've got something to tell you. Mike and I have broken up.'

There was a long pause on the other end of the line.

'You sound mighty chipper about it.'

'Well, *you* don't! I thought you'd be delighted, I thought it was what you wanted me to do . . .'

'I did. I do. But it seems a little bit strange to me that when *I* suggested it, you nearly scratched my eyes out, and just about broke my arm in the door of the taxi, and now you are sounding like the cat that got the cream.'

Another pause.

'Ted? There's someone else, isn't there? That's it. Oh my God. I don't believe it. You've dumped him for someone else, and I'm not going to get a look-in. Great. That's just dandy.'

'Oh, Charlie, don't be such a spoilsport! Be happy for me, for once, would you?'

'Be happy for you?' he said incredulously. 'How can I be happy for you, Ted? Even setting my own feelings aside, even if I act wholly altruistically, how can I be happy for you? You just go on and on repeating the same mistakes . . . this time I haven't even had a chance to pick up the pieces before you go hurling yourself over the edge again! No, I don't even want to discuss it with you. Case closed. You're a cow, that's all. A stupid old cow, and I hate you. But I need a favour.'

Teddy's high spirits were irrepressible. 'Ask away, my darling. Ask and you shall receive.'

'I have to go to a dinner. Tomorrow night. Steinberg Roth are hosting a shindig for some organisation or other – the Association of International Bond Trading Arseholes, or something – and I have to take a guest. As most of my girlfriends are either under the age of consent, or couldn't identify a long bond if it bit them in the ankle, I thought I'd take you. Not that I want to spend any time in your company, you understand. But at least you won't disgrace me. Or there's a decent chance you won't. So how about it, dogbreath?'

'I have never received such a charming invitation, Bartholomew. Thank you; I'd be delighted to accept.'

'Fine. I'll pick you up at seven sharp. Black tie . . . that applies to me. You should wear a dress.' He hung up.

Down the corridor, Candida was talking to Malcolm Fairchild. 'No, Malcolm, I can't come with you.' 'I can't come with you because I'm already going myself.' 'No, I don't know who you should take!' 'No, I don't really care who you take.' 'Malcolm, you are beginning to *really* annoy me.' 'What does it matter who I'm going with?' 'It's a previous engagement, that's all.' 'No, I can't get out of it.' 'No, you're right, I don't want to get out of it.' 'Fine. I'll probably see you there, then.' 'Malcolm, I am absolutely sure I'm not going to change my mind.' 'Malcolm, either we change the subject, or I'm going to hang up right now. How's Glory getting on?' 'Good; glad to hear it.' 'Yes, I think she *is* quite a risk-taker.' 'Sterling? Yes, I'll keep my fingers crossed.' 'Bye. See you Friday.'

Candida cradled the phone in the crook of her neck as she tapped out another number.

'Alex Fitzgerald's office?' A clipped, English voice answered.

'Louise? It's Candida Redmayne here.'

'Oh, Miss Redmayne, I'm afraid that Mr Fitzgerald is out of the office today. Do you need to reach him urgently?'

'No, I wanted to speak to you, actually. Do you have the guest list for Friday's reception in front of you?'

'I do indeed.'

'Can you tell me if Jack Delavigne was invited?'

'Let me check. I'm almost certain he was . . . yes. Here it is. Jack Delavigne, Hayes Goldsmith and Partners.'

'And did he accept?'

'Oh yes. There's one tick, so that means he'll be coming alone.'

'Fine. Thank you very much, Louise.'

Candida stared into space. So she *would* be seeing Jack again, after all.

FEBRUARY 11TH, 1984

'*Of course I don't want to actually kill him, and I know he didn't exactly kill Tommy. It wasn't as if he took a knife out and plunged it into his heart. But he let him die, and it's the same thing, isn't it? Isn't gross negligence the same as murder? It should be.*'

Candida took her cigarettes out of her bag, and lit one slowly. She no longer needed any prompting from Robert Ballantyne. '*I can't understand why those bastards who kill people through drunk driving aren't put away for life. It is murder, isn't it? It's just the same – it causes the same pain, the same death, the same destruction . . .*'

'Was Jack drunk when Tommy drowned?'

'*No, I don't think so. I don't know. It doesn't matter any longer. Tommy's dead, there's nothing I can do to reverse it.*' Candida took a deep drag on her cigarette. '*For weeks, no, months, all I could think about was that it hadn't really happened. I used to lie in bed and screw up my eyes and think that if I could concentrate hard enough, or pray hard enough, or just do something hard enough, I'd wake up and find him next to me. I used to dream about him all the time; it was such agony waking up. Even awake, I could hear his voice in the house, hear him laughing. It was intolerable. There were so many photos of him. Every day I seemed to find some little reminder; a sock, a scribble, the wheel off one of his toys. The house was full of him. I*'

*put everything I could find into his room. Oh, don't bother
to tell me how bad it is to make shrines. I know all about
that. Everyone told me. One day Jack and Jess — my sister —
cleared everything out. They just piled it all into boxes and
sealed it up. Like a coffin. I went mad, ripped them all open
with a knife. Whilst I was ripping them open, that bastard
actually suggested that we should have another baby. Just
like that. 'Let's have another baby, darling,' he said. Like,
'Let's have another cup of coffee.' He didn't really love
Tommy — not the way I did. He considered him a nice
thing to have around — an amusing plaything, just so long
as it didn't interfere with his work. Jack has never really
cared about anything except his work. Do you know, I
actually used to worry that he'd have a stroke? Like Daddy
did.' She looked at Robert accusingly. 'Now I long for it.
But he won't. He's as tough as old boots, if you'll forgive
the cliché. He's a workhorse. He'll go on and on, plodding
away, doing one bloody deal after another.'*

'How are you coping with him day to day?'

Candida's bright, glittering eyes widened in horror.

'My God, you don't think I actually live with the man,
do you? I moved out of that damned house as soon as
I could. He stayed there, of course.' Her bitterness was
rasping. 'He stayed there as if nothing had happened. I
haven't set foot in the place for three months. He phones,
of course. "How are you, darling? Please let me come and
see you, darling,"' she mimicked a concerned tone of voice,
biting with sarcasm.

Robert Ballantyne leant forward in his chair, and,
unusually, took one of her hands in both of his. He
very rarely touched her, preferring to keep a professional
distance.

'Candida, I believe it might help you to come to terms
with your bereavement if you and Jack came to see me
together; it might help if the three of us — '

'No!' she shouted, leaping to her feet in horror. 'No! Never! I never want to see him again! I never want to set eyes on him, I never want to hear him, I don't even want to hear his name spoken! I only want to hear about him if he's dead.' She resumed her customary pacing up and down the small space, furious, and wild, and trapped. 'Don't you see, that's the only way I can get over this. If I see him, I'll remember Tommy. I don't want to remember Tommy any more. It hurts too much.' She turned, back against the wall, and lashed out at him illogically, 'Do you think I can ever forget him? Do you really believe I can forget my own baby? I gave birth to him, for Christ's sake! That's more than Jack ever did! I gave him life, and Jack just took it away. I'll never forget seeing him lying in that pool – I'll never get that out of my mind, d'you hear! Isn't it enough that I have to live with the image of my baby lying face down in a swimming pool? Why do you want me to see the bastard who killed my baby and ruined my life?'

She was panting with effort. The fury that had seized her had passed, and left her spent. She collapsed, exhausted, into the chair and sat hunched over, shielding her eyes with one hand and shaking her head slowly backwards and forwards.

'I'm sorry, sorry, sorry. I'm sorry I lost my temper. I never used to do that. Do you know, I've changed so much? Well, of course you don't. I'm being stupid again. You didn't know me before this happened. I feel like I'm drying up, slowly, day by day. I hardly even cry anymore. Sometimes I want to howl at the moon like some sort of wild thing, but I don't cry. That's one blessing, isn't it? I wish, I wish . . .' her voice trailed off, and she took her hand away, looking straight at the therapist, her pretty face hollowed by grief, bright, feverish roses burning in her cheeks, and her eyes haunted.

'I just wish I'd never married him,' she finished simply.

'Then you would never have had Tommy, never have known him, however briefly.'

'I know; I wish I hadn't, that's all.' She lit another cigarette. 'Robert, I don't want to talk about Tommy any more. You said that I hadn't come to terms with my bereavement, but you're wrong, I have come to terms with it. That doesn't mean that I don't still wish it hadn't happened – I wish none of it had ever happened – but it's over, finished. I accept that. What I have to do is build a new life. I want a life that has nothing to do with Tommy, or Jack.' She flicked her ash into the ashtray, using a long wine-red thumb nail in a technique that Robert Ballantyne had always found madly sophisticated and alluring. After undergoing years of psychotherapy himself, in order to qualify, Robert Ballantyne now understood why he was attracted to deadly women, but it had done nothing to quell the attraction itself. Candida spoke calmly, fully in control, in a confident, measured voice quite unlike her recent outburst. 'You said that part of our agreement was that I could decide what we talked about?'

'In a sense, yes.'

'Well, I've reached a decision about what to do with my future. I'm going to start my own company in headhunting. I think I'm going to be very good at it.'

'I hardly even know what it means, Candida. I assume you're not going to head off to darkest Africa and stick a bone through your nose?' He was rewarded by a laugh.

'No; I'm going to identify the bright sparks in the City and place them in lucrative new positions, whilst taking a hearty slice of their ludicrously high packages myself. I'm rather a good listener, you see, although it's ironic that I should be telling you that when you must see me as a ranting neurotic fruitcake; but I assure you I am good with people, I'm a good judge of character, a good deal-maker, and I have a lot of contacts in the City.

I understand the business; it's just broking again, with a different product range.'

'I'm sure you would be very successful at anything you decided to commit yourself to; but the City? Will that not bring you into rather close contact with your husband?' the therapist probed cautiously.

Candida ground her cigarette out efficiently. 'No. The City is a big place, big enough for us to avoid each other indefinitely. Anyway, he's not my husband any longer. Or he won't be in six weeks' time. Didn't I tell you? I've divorced him. The decree nisi came through a few days ago. It's just a formality now.'

'What grounds did you cite for the divorce?'

Candida tucked her cigarettes neatly into her handbag, and closed the clasp with a sharp click. 'Mental cruelty,' she replied briskly.

Teddy's second evening with Christian was in some ways even more delightful than the first. At ease with each other, after only one night, they no longer needed the discreet privacy of Leith's to feel alone. They dined at Kensington Place, not wanting to stray far from home, and despite the crowds and noise, they both felt as if they were perfectly alone. Such sudden intimacy was a rare and delicious treat for Teddy; there were few people that she felt so completely relaxed with, and normally those were members of her family, or old friends that she had known for years, but she felt that she could say anything to Christian, and that he would understand. He seemed so much older than Mike, so much more sophisticated, so much more exciting. He seemed dangerous, and Teddy felt like flirting with danger. Christian too was relaxed, and if the fine polish of his manner occasionally seemed a little tarnished, he also allowed his guard to drop — a little. Having fallen for Alain Delon, Teddy now discovered a real man, with warmth, and humour, and a temper, underneath the playboy good looks.

They were celebrating Christian's first round of interviews. Christian cautiously said that he felt they had been satisfactory; Paul Driver had enthused loud and long on the telephone to Teddy.

'It's in the bag, Christian. Trust me. They'll make you an offer, you just wait and see.'

'We'll see. They said they had three other people to see before they could make any decisions.'

'I know that! It's my shortlist! But they'll pick you. I'm sure of it. Who wouldn't?'

'Théodora, my darling, you are very sweetly confident. But next time you put your lover up for a job, you had better make sure that the rest of the shortlist compares unfavourably,' he growled at her.

'You weren't my lover then,' she reminded him.

'You can hardly accuse me of not trying . . .'

'Anyway, there won't be a next time I put my lover up for a job. You'll join FRG, and we'll live happily ever after. Then, if you get tired of them in say four or five years, we'll think where you'd like to go next, and I'll arrange it. Easy.' She spoke flippantly.

Christian didn't reply.

'You know, I thought of something else,' Teddy chattered on. 'Whilst we're waiting for FRG to make the offer, you'll save a fortune in hotel bills for Chavaudret-Desforges, so they'll benefit too.'

'What do you mean?'

'Well, you can stay with me, of course!' She looked at him, worried for a moment, and then relieved by his broad smile.

'Of course I'll stay with you, but I think I'd better keep a room at the Meridien. We don't want to arouse suspicion, after all. I don't think Chavaudret would be thrilled to find that I was sleeping with a headhunter during business trips to London.'

'Okay. So, you're going home tomorrow, and then when are you back? Next week?'

'I'm not sure. I will have to check my calendar, and see what commitments I have in Paris. FRG said they needed to see me again in a fortnight's time.'

'Oh well, if you can't come over next week, I'll just have to come to Paris. I'm sure I can find someone who urgently needs to be interviewed!' She looked up at him, and saw that he had stopped eating and had pushed his plate away. 'You're not eating? Is there something wrong with it?' She sounded concerned, as if the failure of a restaurant represented the failure of London, and therefore her own failure, to please him.

'It's fine, but I've lost my appetite. Looking at you makes me lose my appetite for food, Théodora. I've thought about you all day – all through my interviews. Now I want to be with you. I want to feel you, and know everything about you.'

'I thought you found out everything about me last night.'

'No. Last night was simply the very beginning of the journey; we have a long way to travel yet.'

His thigh pressed against hers under the table.

'I think I must be falling in love with you, *chérie*. I want you, Théo. I want you all the time.'

'And I suppose what Christian de Clement-Grandcourt wants, he gets?'

'You, young lady, are very astute.'

Teddy hated to see Christian go, even though they had agreed that they would meet again, somewhere, within the next week. When she woke up with him on Friday morning, she envisaged a courtship of walking beside the Seine in the moonlight, of small restaurants with red-checked tablecloths, of bottles of champagne in bed, of *café au lait* and croissants in bed, of *saucisson sec* and *baguettes* in bed. Christian had been amused when she painted this picture for him, and had teased her that her fantasies of romance in Paris seemed so centred on food . . . and bed; no mention of the Louvre, or the Musée Picasso. She had blushed furiously until he had hugged her and told her how flattered, how proud, how honoured he was to play such a role in her fantasies. Teddy had confessed that never before had sex meant so much to her, never before had she felt so free.

'And it will continue to get better, my darling girl. The miraculous thing about making love is that it always does get better, so long as it starts off right. The tragedy is that you haven't experienced it before. You must never, never again sleep with a *rosbif*. Promise?'

She had promised him, laughingly, and handed over his watch. Teddy cautioned herself severely not to take things with Christian too seriously. She had embarked on the affair because he was attractive, and charmed her; because he was seductive, and she was in the mood to be seduced; because she wanted to prove that she didn't need Mike, and didn't care about his betrayal. The last thing she wanted to do now was to fall in love with Christian.

Charlie arrived on Friday evening, late, looking uncharacteristically elegant in black tie. Teddy, still in a bathrobe, ushered him in and grimaced. 'It's going to be another one of those ghastly English occasions where all the men look fantastically debonair, and all the women look like frumps dressed up in their grandmother's curtains . . . you know, like you see at every English wedding you've ever been to.'

'I don't know, but you're going to go in that bathrobe if you don't get a move on.'

Teddy was back downstairs in a flash, and pirouetted for him.

'I have always admired your grandmother's taste, Ted, but more so tonight than ever.'

Teddy wore a skin tight, ivory-coloured dress that clung to her hips and then plummeted into heavy folds of ivory satin, glinting with flecks of gold. She was ebullient, nearly dancing down the steps of the house to Charles' waiting car.

'I don't know what's happened to you, Ted. You seem different. You look different. Have you lost a few pounds? Had your hair done? Been in for colonic irrigation?'

'Oh shut up, Charles! You're disgusting. I told you. I've met this man – '

'You didn't tell me, I guessed. And I don't want to hear another word about the bastard. All right?'

Teddy nodded obediently.

'And you can take that smug smirk off your lips too,' Charles snapped. He looked hard at her, sighed in resignation, and leant over to snap on her seatbelt, taking the opportunity to deposit a quick kiss on her cheek. 'You look gorgeous, darling. Absolutely, simply, radiantly, divinely and infuriatingly gorgeous.'

To the extent that City parties ever get into full swing, the AIBTA, as Charlie insisted on calling it, was approaching it when they arrived at the Grosvenor. Charles and Teddy did a circuit of the room, nodding and smiling in well-established royal family fashion, Charles greeting colleagues and rivals as if they were all long lost friends. As they turned away, Charles would whisper, 'He's an arsehole; he's a trainee arsehole; he's a would-be arsehole, but he hasn't made it yet; *he's* not even an arsehole, he's just a prick.' As they completed the circuit, Charles pointed at the entrance to the ballroom. 'And here come's the man who epitomises the very essence of the word, the Great King Arsehole himself.' Teddy turned, following Charles' finger, to see Alex Fitzgerald coming down the stairs with Candida on his arm. 'And I think we both know his lovely consort,' Charles muttered. 'Come on, Ted, let's get in line to pay homage to the King and Queen.'

Candida did not justify Teddy's prediction about English women at black tie functions. She was wearing a straight, ice-blue dress, covered with thirties-style beading, that fell in a column to her feet. Her alabaster neck rose swan-like, her chin tilted up as she scanned the room for familiar faces. She smiled when she saw Teddy coming towards her, and kissed her on the cheek, every inch a Grecian heroine. 'I thought you might be here, Teddy; I meant to ask. Charles.' She inclined her head graciously.

Charles and Alex were busy slapping each other on the back, and congratulating each other on their most recently publicised deals. Alex kissed Teddy on the mouth. 'Teddy Winnington! My, my, don't you look edible!' Teddy tried not to flinch away. 'And how's Mike? Keeping an eye on you, is he? He can't be far away . . .'

'Mike Miccinelli? You probably have a better idea than I do, Fitz. I haven't seen him for a while.'

'What's this? Something upsetting love's young dream? Must be pre-wedding jitters. Now I want you to be gentle with him, Teddy; I can't have Mike getting upset. It might mess up his trading performance, and we can't allow *that*, can we now? You come and tell your old Uncle Alex all about it . . .' He drew her away much against her will, and Charles and Candida were left together.

'So, Candida. How's tricks? Business good?'

'We're doing pretty well, Charles. Teddy's doing well, about to close a deal, and I have a few things up my sleeve as well. We're taking on a new consultant, a man from County NatWest. I'm hoping he's going to open some doors into the trading side of the business. That's why I'm here, tonight, really. Just doing a bit of homework.'

Charles looked at her strangely. 'You never stop, do you, Candida? You never stop thinking about the business. Don't you ever, just once, want to run screaming from the room, and tell them what arseholes they all are?'

'No, Charles, I'll leave that sort of behaviour to you. But before you do it, you should go and rescue Teddy. Somehow, I don't know why, I get the feeling that she doesn't really like Alex Fitzgerald all that much.'

Charles looked across the room to see Teddy peeping round Alex's back and making gagging signs. 'I see what you mean. Catch you later.'

'That man makes my flesh creep,' Teddy said with passion. 'I mean, *really* creep. What the hell makes him so bloody successful?'

'I told you. He's the biggest arsehole of them all, and until a bigger one comes along, he's on top of the heap. There's another of your old friends over there.' He nudged her in the direction of Mike, who stood alone, ill at ease in black tie, glowering at everyone who approached. 'Want to go and say hello, just for old times' sake?' Charles goaded her.

Teddy turned her back, but was too late. Mike had seen her, and for a moment his face lit up before becoming sullen again as he recognised Charles.

'Hello, old man!' Charles shouted heartily. 'Not a bad beano, eh?'

'Would you mind if I spoke to Teddy alone, Charles?'

'Not a bit, not a bit . . . I'm getting quite accustomed to being sent off. I'll just stand in that corner over there, shall I? If you need me, Ted, you know the signal, don't you?' He mimed the gagging action, bringing a smile to

Teddy's lips and a scowl to Mike's. 'Toodle-pip, chaps.' Charles shimmied away.

'How are you, Mike?'

'I'm fucking awful, Teddy.'

'I know you're fucking awful, Mike. I didn't ask you *what* you were, I asked you how you were.' She smiled her customary sweet smile.

'Teddy, please. Can't we get out of here and talk? I *have* to talk to you. It's only fair.'

'Don't talk to me about fairness, Mike. You can talk to me all you like, but don't you dare mention the word fairness.'

'I'm sorry,' he mumbled. 'I just want to tell you how sorry I am. God, these past few weeks have been a nightmare. I've been miserable without you. I'm really sorry. Sorry about Glory, sorry about how I treated you.'

Teddy looked at him closely. 'Do you know, Mike, I really do believe you for once. I really do believe that this time you're sorry. But it's that old, old story, isn't it? You're not sorry for what you did, you're just damn sorry that you were caught. Well, you see, I'm not sorry. In fact, I'm positively delighted. I haven't been so happy since the day I met you. And now, if you'll excuse me, Charlie's making signs.'

Mike swung round angrily to see Charles innocently whistling in the air, twiddling his thumbs. He walked away, his shoulders slumped.

'Poor chap,' Charles murmured, watching his departing back. 'So, farewell, Mike Miccinelli. I always rather liked him, you know Ted.'

'If we weren't in company, I'd smack you for that comment, Bartholomew.'

'If we weren't in company, I wouldn't have dared to say it, Winnington.'

By dinner, the evening had degenerated into a bunfight

of three hundred men and a handful of female traders swapping stories about mighty trades and shitty clients. Teddy and Charles couldn't help but notice Malcolm Fairchild, accompanied by Glory, strutting around the room, although it must be said that it wasn't Malcolm that caught their eye. Glory was once again wearing the fire-engine red, skimpy little dress that she had worn when Teddy had first met her.

'For God's sake, doesn't she have anything else in her wardrobe?' Teddy hissed.

'Now, now, claws away, Teddy. Though I must admit, when she and I had our little, ah, *encounter*, she was sporting the same frock. I found it rather appealing, I must admit.' He contemplated Glory until Teddy dug her elbow into his ribs.

'We're being called into dinner, Charles. Move your butt, and stop dribbling.'

As Teddy was about to take her allocated place at one of the tables for eight, Candida appeared at her side. She looked deathly white, and seemed to be trembling. 'Teddy, could you do me an immense favour?'

'Of course, what is it?'

'Could you and Charles swap places with us? I'm afraid there's been a bit of a mistake. Alex needs to sit at this table. Something to do with some client. Could you, please?'

Teddy was surprised by the note of desperation in Candida's voice.

'Of course,' she assured her. 'Nothing could be easier.' She hauled Charles out of his chair, and followed Candida's directions to table twelve. There were only two men sitting at it, one on each side of the table. One was Mike, and the other was Jack Delavigne.

'Oh my God!' said Teddy, under her breath.

'Michael! Oh joy! Now we'll have a chance for a proper

heart-to-heart,' said Charles, unable to resist goading him. They were quickly joined by four other people: a bond salesman whom Teddy had interviewed three weeks previously, who pretended they had never met, and sat as far away from her as possible; his girlfriend, a pretty blonde whose face was a mask of studied boredom; a Japanese banker who distributed seven cards and seven bows before he even sat down, and finally a grey-haired, grey-eyed and grey-faced representative from the Bank of England.

Charles rubbed his hands together in anticipation. 'So; our little band is assembled; I can see we're going to have quite a jolly little party at table twelve!'

Teddy delivered a sharp kick under the table but Charles had already turned his attention to the expressionless blonde who sat between him and Mike.

'What do you do? Let me guess; convertible bond origination? No? Hmm; French equity warrant sales? No? Mortgage-backed securities? No? Let me see; perhaps something more esoteric. I've got it! Zero-coupon bonds – a deep discount woman, am I right?'

She looked at him blankly. 'I'm a model,' she said, in a voice as flat as a pancake.

'A *model*! That must be tremendously challenging work! A model! Well, aren't we honoured! Lucky old table twelve!' Charles had developed a knack of taking sarcasm to such an extreme point that his listeners tended to take him at his word; no one, other than Teddy, could believe that he would be intentionally so rude to a complete stranger. The model began to preen a little, and the ghost of a smile flitted across her empty face.

'It's good to see you again, Teddy,' Jack said quietly. 'I believe I owe you an apology for what happened in Oxford.'

'Not at all; you clearly wanted to talk, and I'm paid to listen. That's my job.'

'None the less, I'm sorry that I involved you in my problems. I took a liberty.'

'Think nothing of it. How are things going at Hayes Goldsmith?'

Jack sighed. 'As well as can be expected. How are things going at ARC? How are you getting on with your search?'

Teddy could feel the bond salesman across the table flinching as he heard the name of her firm. He was clearly listening intently to Teddy and Jack's conversation whilst pretending to discuss the future of the Nikkei with the Japanese banker. Teddy decided that he deserved to squirm a little more.

'Not bad, not bad at all. As you can imagine, Jack, every search involves interviewing a handful of no-hopers. I saw a man a few weeks ago who simply *defined* the word mediocrity . . . I can't for the life of me remember his name. He's probably here tonight.' She pretended to gaze around the room, letting her eyes sweep slowly over the man across the table. She paused. 'No, I can't seem to see him. What a relief! But we all have our own trials and tribulations, don't we?'

She turned back to Jack. Charles and the model were chattering like old friends, the Japanese banker was making polite enquiries about bank regulation of the central banker, and Mike and the broker stared morosely at their plates of *sole véronique*. Teddy could see Candida, a few tables away, watching them. Jack followed her gaze, but as soon as his eyes met Candida's, she looked away. Teddy caught the expression of misery in Jack's grey eyes, and the realisation hit her that he was still in love with his ex-wife. Her heart, instantly sympathetic to those suffering from unrequited love, went out to him, and she instinctively covered his hand with her own. As she did, she missed the flash of anger pass over Mike's face, and missed him throw his linen napkin down and leave the table without a word to anyone. You can't watch all the people all of the time.

'Jack, you mustn't dwell on the past. It doesn't help, believe me.' His hand trembled momentarily under her own, and she gave it a squeeze of support, not really understanding why. Jack Delavigne was not a man who ordinarily inspired sympathy, after all. He was a successful banker, at the peak of his career, whatever his temporary problems at Hayes, and on top of that, he was handsome, doubtless wealthy, and well-respected in his own field. He had it all; he had it made. There were thousands of people who would kill to be in his position. And yet, and yet . . . there was something in his shadowed eyes, something that haunted him that Teddy found painful to watch. The knowledge, which he himself had given her, that he was responsible for his own ghosts, that any scars he bore were self-inflicted, didn't make it any the easier to witness his pain. And so Teddy, unable to harden her heart against him, unable to forget how the skin on the back of her neck had tingled when he had held her arm in the New College quad, unable to bear the sight of his longing for Candida, turned away.

'Ted, you will never guess – *never* – what Jaine – that's J-A-I-N-E, with an i you understand – is going to be when she stops modelling. She's going to be – a fashion photographer!' Charles' eyes sparkled mischievously. 'I am simply overwhelmed with admiration. Aren't you, Ted?'

'Down, Fido, down,' Teddy said quietly.

'Ted, did I tell you the great joke I heard last night?' Charles waited until he had the attention of the entire table. 'It's a cracker.' Everyone looked at him, half smiling in anticipation. 'What's your definition of the ideal woman?'

He paused, enjoying being centre stage. 'A woman who fucks until three a.m., and then turns into a pizza!'

And that just about summed up the rest of the evening.

CHAPTER NINE

Teddy began work on a new search, looking for a head of global strategy research for Morgan Stanley. She was still preoccupied with the outcome of her work for FRG Barnekov, but everything had ground to something of a standstill. Both Christian and Tom Pitt-Rivers had received very positive feedback from the partners of FRG, but Paul Driver did not want to proceed to the second interview stage until he had seen Konrad von Budingen and Esther Levenson. Konrad had had to postpone his interview for another week due to commitments in Frankfurt, and Esther was due to arrive in London in ten days' time, so there was little Teddy could do except twiddle her thumbs and kick her heels. And go to Paris to see Christian, with the excuse of doing some first round interviewing for Morgan Stanley.

Paris, and more importantly, Christian, lived up to Teddy's expectations. The only thing to blot her happiness was that Christian refused to allow her to see his apartment. He explained that it was being refurbished, and told her that she would have to wait until the work had been completed before passing judgement. Teddy was disappointed, having been curious to see how Christian lived when alone. He was insistent, and she was amused that he was so nervous of her opinion. Christian himself had moved out of the flat when she arrived in Paris, and had taken up residence in a hotel on the Left Bank, the Saint Simon. He had booked Teddy a room next to his own for the sake of propriety. The charm of the romantic little hotel went a long way towards dissipating Teddy's frustration at not seeing Christian's flat, and the intrigue of their affair added spice to the romance. Each evening, as they returned from dinner, they would bid each other a formal good-night in front of the receptionist, before making their way separately to their rooms. Moments later, they would be in each others' arms, and stay there until morning, when they would arrive separately on the little terrace where breakfast was served. Christian, the perfect model of etiquette, would wish her a good morning, inquire as to how she had slept, and ask her if she would care to join him at his table. Teddy would initially decline, and then give way under a little gentle pressure. She realised that all the hotel staff must have known, from the second morning at least, that their relationship was far from formal.

Teddy knew in her heart of hearts that they were not conducting a 'normal' relationship. 'Normal' relationships were based on who would pick up the dry-cleaning, who was going to sack the cleaning-lady, who was going to do the washing-up, and who had forgotten to buy fresh milk. A romance conducted against the backdrop of hotels, restaurants and Paris by moonlight was not a trial run for learning to live together. But they would have plenty of time for the mundaneness of all that later, when Christian moved to London. Occasionally, she reminded herself that this was a fling – a very pleasant and powerful one, but a fling none the less – but the reminders were becoming less and less frequent. For the time being, Teddy wallowed in everything being special, and in feeling so special, so prized, herself.

Teddy could have flown back to London on her own wings. She wished she had been able to stay on for the weekend in Paris, but this was the weekend that Matty was due to visit, and nobody, not even Christian, could persuade her to cancel her grandmother. Christian had in fact been very understanding about it, almost relaxed. Teddy went straight from Heathrow to the office, although at four p.m. on a Friday, she really would have been entitled to call it a day and head for home. However, she didn't want Candida to feel that she wasn't pulling her weight, and she also wanted to talk to Jamie; she had barely exchanged a word with him for weeks, since they were both flitting around the globe. When she arrived at ARC, she found a pile of messages on her desk, and leafed through them before starting to catch up on her paper work. She needed to update the files with some salary data. There were three messages from Esther Levenson — Teddy prayed she wasn't going to back out of the interviews — and curiously, two messages from Jack Delavigne. Teddy chose to call Esther back first.

'Esther Levenson's line?'

'Hello, is Esther there, please?'

'Sure she's here, she's speaking to you.'

'Esther! It's Teddy Winnington. I thought I'd got through to your secretary . . .'

'Hell, no; we're not such fat cats that we pay people to sit around picking up the telephone . . . I just pretend I've got a secretary to look important. How you doing, Teddy?'

'I'm fine; more to the point, how are *you*?'

'Fatter. Happier. Excited about coming to London.'

'Great. I was worried you were going to say you couldn't make it.'

'Wild horses wouldn't keep me away. No, I was just calling 'cos I didn't know if you'd told the boys at FRG about my waistline or not.'

'Actually, no, I haven't. Do you want me to?'

'You're the headhunter. I'll trust your judgement.'

'Then I'd say no. Wear a girdle. We'll tell them later. Maybe at the christening.'

'You're a woman after my own heart. I can still get my

skirts on, so long as I leave the zip undone and wear a longer length jacket. Take care, Teddy. Gotta dash – I can't seem to stop peeing. Think that FRG will be suspicious if I keep rushing to the john?'

'No. They're men, after all. It would take a woman to put two and two together and come up with four. FRG will come up with three, and assume you're a sweet, nervous little thing.'

Teddy heard a gale of laughter before the phone clicked.

She didn't feel like talking to Jack, and decided to put it off till Monday. She guessed he was calling to say he'd changed his mind and wanted to talk to FRG after all. She hoped not; first of all, she didn't want Christian's chances diminished, not now, when things were going so smoothly between them. Second, she would feel somehow let down if all his talk about duty and loyalty didn't amount to a hill of beans, if Jack sold out like all the others, though she had no good reason for expecting him to be any different than all the rest of them. No good reason, just a hunch . . .

Teddy tapped the salary information into the computer, and keyed in the confidential code that would stop anybody else looking at it. She wandered down the empty, silent hall to the computer room where the shredder was kept. All the ARC consultants were diligent about destroying any hard copy evidence of confidential reports. Whilst waiting for the shredder to warm up, Teddy gave in to the temptation to glance through the piles of paper that lay waiting for Julie to shred on Monday. On top of the pile was a photocopy of a Steinberg Roth internal memo; Teddy recognised the silver star logo at the top of the page, and picked it up. What the hell was it doing at ARC? Teddy skimmed the memo. It was directed confidentially to the partners of Steinberg Roth, and contained a list of members of staff who were being considered for election to partnership. Michael Miccinelli's name was fourth on the list. There was a thick black ring around it, and an arrow leading to a handwritten message which said: 'Watch this space, Candida. You and I have other plans for this guy; let's make him really hungry, right? And when he's foaming at the mouth, we'll let him loose on JO.'

Teddy read the memo again. It didn't make any sense. It was clearly sent to Candida, but why? Somebody at Steinberg might have thought Candida would be interested in who was up for partnership, but why single out Mike like that? It couldn't be Fitz; Mike had told Teddy that Fitz was supporting him at the election. And what was JO? Teddy couldn't remember the term being used at Steinberg's. Well, what did it matter; Teddy didn't give a shit about Mike's future anyway. She was about to feed the paper into the shredder when she changed her mind, folded it, and slipped it into her pocket. Teddy wasn't given to acts of vengeance, but she wouldn't mind having a little bit of ammunition against Mike if she ever needed it. Before she left, she fed the rest of the pile of papers into the shredder, watching it regurgitate illegible little scraps. Candida would have killed Julie if she'd discovered that the receptionist had left the shredder tray full over a weekend.

As she was about to leave the office, she saw the phone blinking, and picked it up. 'Aston-Redmayne Company; may I help you?'

'Teddy – it is Teddy, isn't it? It's Jack Delavigne.'

'Oh, Jack.' Teddy didn't know what to say, and wished she'd left the office a few minutes earlier. 'I've only just come in from Paris.'

'So you didn't get my messages?'

'Messages? No.' Teddy hoped she didn't sound too artificial.

'Listen, I really need to talk to you, but I can't talk here. Would it be okay if I called you at home?'

Teddy's shoulders slumped despondently. Thank God

no one had introduced video phones yet. It was obvious that Jack had changed his mind and wanted to see FRG. Bugger it. 'I suppose so.' She couldn't exactly refuse, could she? 'My number's 727 – ' she *could* always, accidentally, give him the wrong number. No, she couldn't. She sighed long-sufferingly, '727–6643.'

'Thanks. May I call you tonight?'

'Yes, all right. I'll be home in about half an hour, and in all evening.'

'Talk to you later.'

Sod's law, thought Teddy resignedly as she drove home. Just when everything was working out so well, Jack Delavigne had to put his bloody great foot in it. She thought about how she could describe him in such a way that, without exactly lying, might make Paul Driver less enthusiastic to hire him. She couldn't say he was incompetent; she couldn't say he was unreliable; she could, perhaps, say he was a shit, but how would she prove it without disclosing the whole of Candida's story? Jack didn't come across like a shit. It made Teddy increasingly uncomfortable just thinking about it. Well, she didn't have to think about it until he called, and with any luck, his phone might be out of order. Indefinitely.

As soon as she got home, Teddy called the Saint Simon to speak to Christian, to be told that he had checked out of the hotel. Teddy's French wasn't good enough to brave asking where he had gone; she assumed he had either moved into the flat, or was away for the weekend, in which case he'd be back at the hotel on Monday. The receptionist seemed to think not, but Teddy put that down to misunderstanding. Maybe he would call her. She felt like having a long talk with him, but there was nothing she could do except prepare for Matty's visit. She had planned a rather hectic itinerary: lunch on Saturday at the Belvedere, a trip to the new wing of the National Gallery, which Matty was keen to see, dinner with Charles at Le Suquet. On Sunday, Matty wanted to go to matins at St Paul's, and had to catch a train back to Salisbury at four-thirty; they would just have time for a quiet, private lunch together. Teddy put fresh flowers in her spare bedroom, and carefully laid out towels, new soap, a carafe and water glass. Chores done, she wandered aimlessly around the house, waiting for Christian to call. At ten o'clock she poured herself a drink, and put on the Georges Moustaki CD. When it got round to 'their' song, the phone rang. Teddy picked it up excitedly. 'Christian?'

'No; it's Jack. Jack Delavigne.'

'Oh, Jack.' Teddy couldn't conceal her disappointment.

'I'm sorry, Teddy. Were you expecting another call?'

'Not exactly expecting, no. Just hoping. What can I do for you Jack?'

'Well, I don't really know how to put this. I just wanted to talk to you. I know I don't have any right . . . I've been thinking about you, and I thought we might be able to get together, for dinner or something.' He spoke hesitantly; Teddy couldn't really believe that this was the confident, controlled man of the world she had met at the Grosvenor last week. Jack continued. 'Is there any chance of getting together over the weekend, or are you tied up?'

'I'm afraid I am. My grandmother's staying, and we've arranged a lot of things . . . I'm sorry.'

'I see. That's quite all right, I understand. Another time, perhaps.' His voice was dejected.

There was a silence on the line.

'Jack? It's not that I don't want to see you – don't misunderstand me. Is there any way I can help? Do you want to see FRG after all? Just say the word.'

'No. It's not that – I haven't changed my mind about that.' Teddy nearly sighed out loud with relief. 'But I just feel that maybe talking to you would help. I'm sorry, Teddy. It was a silly idea. I shouldn't have called.

I always seem to be apologising for something whenever I talk to you.'

'You don't owe me any apologies. If there's anyone you should apologise to ...' She didn't feel that she could say it.

'Yes? If there's anyone I should apologise to it's Candida? Is that what you were going to say, Teddy?'

'Yes, I *was*. But it's none of my business. I don't have any right ...'

'Let's not talk about rights, Teddy. You have every right. I involved you after all. I have *tried* to talk to Candida, you realise.'

'And she won't talk to you?'

'Not a word. Not a word in eight years.'

'Jack, I do feel sorry for you, but I can't say I blame her. She's still very upset, you know. She might never get over it. I think it's even harder for a woman to lose her child than for a man.'

'Is it, Teddy?' His voice was low and quiet, the emotion controlled.

'So they say. Perhaps the kindest thing you could do is to leave her alone. If you want to be kind.'

'I know. I've tried. Sometimes I get the feeling that she won't leave me alone, though. Whatever we do, this isn't going to go away, it will always be with us. Oh, Teddy. I wish ...' He seemed incapable of finishing the sentence. 'Look, I'd better go,' he said briskly, 'and let you take your other call.'

'Don't worry about that, Jack.' For some reason, Teddy didn't want him to hang up, not just yet. In a strange way, she felt that she had known Jack all her life. She really knew nothing about him, other than the tragedy of Tommy's death, and yet it seemed perfectly natural to be talking like this, late on a Friday night. 'He probably won't call anyway.'

'I'm sure he will, Teddy. I'm sure he will. Take care of yourself.' He was about to hang up.

'Jack? Call me next week — about dinner, I mean. You know you can always call me if you want to, okay?' Why on earth had she said that? She didn't mean it.

'Thank you. Maybe I will.'

Teddy stayed up until well past midnight waiting for Christian to call. After the sixth listening, Georges Moustaki didn't sound quite as convincing as he had the first few times. It wasn't really the sort of music you could listen to alone.

Teddy had a very good weekend with her grandmother, as she always did. After lunch on Sunday, they had a chance to talk before Matty had to leave to catch her train. Teddy told her grandmother everything that had happened with Mike, and Matty had listened quietly, apparently intent on her embroidery, although Teddy knew she was listening to every word, and was simply reserving her comments until Teddy had finished the story. Teddy described their final row, and bravely told her grandmother what she had said about Glory being more of Mike's class. The old lady didn't look up; she rethreaded her needle with a different skein of silk.

'I shouldn't have said that, should I, Matty?'

'No, I don't suppose you should have.'

'I always remember you saying that one should never say anything unless it is kind, unless it is true, and unless it is necessary.'

'And was it?' Matty asked mildly.

'Well, at the time I thought it was true, but I knew it wasn't kind or necessary. And now, I don't even think it was true. So I suppose I shouldn't have said it, should I?'

'You know the answer to that, Theodora. But remember that you are not an angel; you're a young woman, and you experience anger as much as we all do. Don't try to be a paragon of virtue all the time; it's not a very attractive characteristic.'

'So what do you think about my breaking off the engagement?'

'I don't really know until I've heard the end of the story.'

'But you have! I've told you everything that happened!'

'Have you, Teddy?' Matilda Winnington-Smythe looked at her granddaughter with the piercing green eyes that were so like Teddy's own. She continued to stitch, working on the delicate petals of a peony. 'If that was the end of the story, I would expect you to be more upset, and to be more concerned with your decision. But you don't seem to be; you seem to be surprisingly unaffected, happy, even.'

And so Teddy confided in Matty, and told her about her sudden and thrilling affair with Christian, and how Christian had more than filled the gap in her life that Michael had left.

Again, Matilda took her time to reply. 'It seems to me that it was the right decision to break off your relationship with Michael, if you have found it so easy to replace him in your affections.'

'That's what I think, too. And what do you think about Christian?'

'I can't possibly make any judgement of that. Time will tell, I'm sure.'

There were many things Matilda might have said to Teddy about her new passion, but if they were true, if they were necessary, even, they probably weren't very kind, and Matilda had more experience than her granddaughter in controlling her reactions.

The next few weeks flew past. Teddy tried to keep herself busy with the Morgan Stanley search, and enjoyed Christian's constant admonishing that she was not to jump into bed with any of her new candidates. He threatened to accompany her on her interviews, so as to protect her from the merest hint of flirtation. When Teddy assured him that his own interview had been the exception rather than the rule, and that even the most daring candidates confined themselves to an approving look at her legs, he feigned outrage.

'How dare they look at your legs, Théodora? Does the very fact that they are being interviewed by a woman entitle them to examine you like a piece of meat? Do you look at *their* legs, I wonder?'

'Of course not! I hardly look at them at all . . . unless they are terribly attractive,' Teddy teased him.

'Seriously, my darling, doesn't it offend you?'

Teddy blushed a little. 'I suppose it's wrong of me, Christian, and not very liberated, but I have to admit privately that I find it a little flattering. I know it's wrong, but I can't help liking people liking me. Candida doesn't. She despises them all.'

'Then I wish I were in love with Candida, and not with you,' Christian growled, pulling her into his arms.

'Oh no you don't!' Teddy laughed. 'She'd eat you up for breakfast. Or so Jamie says. I don't think men understand Candida, really. I think she's desperately attractive, but most of them seem to find her rather frightening. God knows why.'

Christian had met Candida, albeit briefly, when he had stopped at ARC's offices to pick up Teddy for lunch. Teddy had seen them measuring each other up, and was curious as to Christian's reaction to her boss. He had been noncommittal, admitting her good looks, but saying that he wasn't personally drawn to her. When Teddy had pushed him to explain, he had simply said that he could only be attracted to one woman at a time, and he didn't expect to have any availability for some time to come.

Christian had come over to London for his second
round of interviews. Paul Driver was torn between the
four candidates. As Teddy had expected, he had been very
impressed by Konrad von Budingen, but had found him a
little severe. Tom Pitt-Rivers had gone through on the nod
with all the FRG partners – he had been at Harrow with
one of them, was a member of Whites with another, and
he and Paul both hunted with the Heythrop. Paul's only
reservation was that it might strengthen FRG's marketing
effort to have an oily continental, as he put it, rather than
an upstanding Brit. Esther Levenson's interviews had been
the most contentious; Martin Beckwith and Jan Strakowski
had both loved her, but Paul and Hector found the idea
of a female partner a trifle unsettling, particularly one as
forthright as Esther. 'I'm not sure about her, Teddy; you
were right in saying that she's very impressive. She is. She's
tackled a hell of a lot of obstacles to get where she is. I'm
just not sure that she has the right *style* for FRG.'

'Why not, Paul?'

'Well, she is American, after all . . .'

'That doesn't seem to have caused any problems with
her current client list.'

'True, but we tend to handle a rather more conservative,
more traditional client list than Solly's.'

'And you don't think they would respond to an American?'

'It's not that exactly, Teddy, that I'm frightened of . . .'

Teddy knew what it was, exactly, that Paul feared. It
wasn't that Esther was American. It was that she was
female. And that she was Jewish. She wasn't going to
make it easy for Paul to reject her, though.

'I'll tell you what, Paul. I've done a bit of checking on
Esther, spoken to some of her European clients about her
work – just to get some professional references. Of course,
I didn't tell them she was interviewing with you, I just said

we were curious about her reputation. They have all – every one – given her glowing reports. Let me fax them through to you, okay?'

Let him wriggle out of that one, she thought with satisfaction.

Whilst Teddy busied herself with research analysts, and keeping her FRG candidates – particularly Christian, who had had to return to Paris almost immediately – informed about the progress of her interviews, she considered the idea of having dinner with Jack Delavigne. She thought she saw a way of helping him, and helping Candida at the same time. What a coup that would be, if she could bring them back together! It would put her into the *Guinness Book of Records* as fairy godmother *par excellence*. She decided that she would accept Jack's invitation to dinner, when he called. The only problem was, he didn't.

Jack hadn't forgotten his conversation with Teddy. Several times a day, he picked up the telephone to call her, and then put it down again. One problem was that he didn't know exactly what it was he wanted to tell her, and the other was that he didn't know exactly why he wanted to tell her anything at all. Another slight hitch was that he was working eighteen hours a day and barely had the energy to drag himself home to bed at night. He didn't feel that he would be a very lively dinner companion. His concerns over Hayes' trading account were growing. Malcolm, or rather Glory McWhirter, had decided to keep their account long on sterling, despite growing pressure on the ERM from market speculators. Jack faced a dilemma. If he forced Malcolm to close the position, they would register a small loss, but Hayes could survive that. What the bank might not survive would be the resignation of the director in charge of trading, and the almost certain resignation of Glory, Hayes' new star, whose recruitment had been publicised with such a fanfare. There would be no way he could hire decent replacements quickly; working for Hayes Goldsmith was increasingly regarded as being as promising an option as planting roses in the desert. On the other hand, if they let the position run, Hayes faced losing their shirts – all for the sake of Glory and Malcolm's egos. Jack sat with his head in his hands. It was a tails I win, heads you lose situation, and he had the sickening feeling that he himself had tossed the coin. Jack couldn't even discuss it with Dick Belton-Smith. Dick had taken a three month sabbatical, leaving the bank in Jack's safe hands. Only now, Jack felt like a wicket-keeper with both hands tied behind his back. It wasn't the time to get involved with Teddy – even if she'd let him, which he doubted very much. Fingers still on the telephone, he sighed, and dialled the number of Gordon Allinson, a member of the Hayes Goldsmith board and one of the bank's largest private shareholders, other than Dick and Jack himself. It was time to sound out support.

Alex Fitzgerald was also drumming up support. He took Mike Miccinelli out to lunch, on the pretext of having heard about his bust-up with Teddy. The two men sat in Corney and Barrow on Moorgate, toying with their *saltimbocca alla romagna*. Mike was a little suspicious of Fitz's paternalistic concern; Fitz wasn't known for involving himself in his staff's private lives, but he did seem genuinely more interested in Mike than in any of the other traders, and Mike was feeling sufficiently full of self-pity to welcome any condolences.

'Let me give you a bit of advice, buddy. I've had a lot of experience with the fairer sex,' Fitz winked slyly, 'and there's one rule that must never be broken. It doesn't matter what you do, what you think, or what you say, so long as you always let them feel that they are the most important thing in the world. That's all that matters to women. You gotta make them feel good, even if you feel like shit. That's what they call being a gentleman, and believe me, if you do it, it works a treat every time.'

'Yeah, I believe you Fitz. The problem is, Teddy found out about something . . .'

'Let me guess. Another woman, right? Glory, right?' He refilled Mike's wine glass, and Mike reached out for it automatically. 'Can't say I blame you, Mike. I wouldn't mind a piece of that action myself, know what I mean? Anyway, the point is, you screwed up twice. First of all, you let Teddy find out, and second, I bet you didn't explain it in the right way.'

'I told her I was sorry,' Mike muttered grumpily.

'Exactly. Wrong explanation. What you should have said is that you didn't feel *worthy* of Teddy; that you felt under such a helluva strain, because every time you looked at her, you just couldn't work out what the hell she saw in you. You should have told her that you only felt good enough for Glory, that Teddy was just too precious, and that after it had happened, you realised you couldn't face life without her. That'll do it, every time. You call her up, and tell her that. First, she'll get all self-righteous, and then she'll start feeling guilty about making you so insecure, and then she'll feel great because you adore her. Even better, write her a letter. All women like getting letters. Here – have another glass of wine, not bad stuff, is it?'

At nearly forty-five pounds a bottle, it should have been pretty good stuff.

The two men talked like old comrades-in-arms, swapping battle stories. Fitz even told Mike about Annie Pitt-Rivers; the story amused Mike, despite the callous way Fitz talked about Tom and Annie. Fitz had seduced Annie during a managers' weekend at Chewton Glen. Tom had been kept late at a meeting on, ironically, selling skills, and Fitz had found Annie drumming her heels in frustration in the hotel bar. 'It didn't take me long to locate the source of *her* itch, if you get my meaning, Mike . . . in fact, it took me less than half an hour!' Both men guffawed with laughter. 'We had a pretty good time, until the silly bitch decided to tell her fool of a husband.'

The conversation turned to Steinberg Roth. Alex pressed Mike on his view of the markets, and Mike admitted that for once in his career, he was nervous.

'I just feel like there's going to be a real catastrophe . . . there are so many guys out there jabbering for blood, and the stakes are getting bigger and bigger. I don't give a shit about the little guys – they're going to lose whatever happens – but I've heard rumours about some of the big boys, Soros, Tiger, Jones, that type, and it's making me pretty uncomfortable. I've got a pretty flat book, and I think it's going to stay that way.' He gulped at his glass of wine. 'Norman's edgy; doesn't want us to take any risks, doesn't like the look of the market, or rather the feel of it.'

'Oh, I don't think you should pay much attention to Norman Bell, Michael. You trust your own instincts, I'll stick with you. Don't forget, we've gotta do something to make the department look good, and it's up to you and me – Norman's not going to pull his finger out, is he? Talking of the markets, Mike, how's Glory getting on at Hayes Goldsmith?'

'She's crazy. She hasn't really got anyone holding in her reins, and she's got her neck way out. She called me today to try and convince me why sterling is such a good buy. Fucking headcase. In a few weeks' time, the only people supporting sterling are going to be the Bank of England and Glory McWhirter, courtesy of Hayes Goldsmith. She must have a few hundred pounds riding on it already, and she's putting in more.'

'That means a few hundred million, right? Trading desk talk.' Mike nodded.

Fitz rubbed his hands together. 'She's a big girl, Mike. Big in lots of ways, am I right, or am I right?' He held his hands out, as if he were comparing the weight of two watermelons.

Mike colluded in the joke. 'Even bigger than that, Fitz, believe me. And pretty big in other areas, too.' Abruptly, his face became serious. 'I wanted to ask you something else. How do you think my chances are looking for partnership, Fitz? Tell me the truth.'

'The truth?' Mike nodded, his mouth set in a thin line. 'Not good, buddy. I told you I'd do everything I could, and I am, and I'll keep on doing it, but I get the feeling that the trading desk just aren't flavour of the month.'

'Not fucking flavour of the month! I've made millions for those arseholes, Fitz, fucking millions, and you're saying I'm not flavour of the month?'

'Cool down, Mike. I know what you've contributed, and I'm gonna make damn sure you're rewarded for it one way or another. Give me a bit more time. I'll promise you one thing straight up. I'm not going to let you go up for that election like a dumb sucker. If you're not gonna get it, I'll let you know beforehand, and I'll let you know why. Then you can make your own choices. Make *informed* choices, okay?' He patted Mike on the back. 'You worry about the currency crisis, and you worry about Teddy; let me worry about you, okay? Is it a deal?' He held out his hand across the table. 'Shake on it, Miccinelli.'

Mike slowly shook his hand. It wasn't all bad. At least he had Fitz fighting his corner.

Teddy, Candida and Jamie were discussing their schedules, seeing who had the most time to take on yet another new search that Morgan Stanley had assigned ARC.

'I just wish Adrian was up and running and ready to head a search,' Candida said, 'but he's not, and Louise and Philip are still bogged down in Spain, so one of us has got to take it. Teddy, how are you getting on with the strategy head?'

'Frankly, Candida, I'm up to my neck. Besides, I think it would be a mistake for me to take on two different searches for Morgan Stanley – I'll end up torn between two departments, and they'll both think I'm giving priority to the other . . .'

'True. So it's you or me, Jamie – '

The intercom buzzed.

'Yes, Julie?' Candida picked up the phone. 'Put him through.' She signalled at Jamie and Teddy to stay. 'Fitz, good to hear you. Yes, I enjoyed last week very much, too. We must get together again sometime soon.'

Teddy shuffled through some papers and pretended not to be listening, but she was always surprised by how warmly Candida talked to Alex Fitzgerald. It was true he was a client, but Candida treated most of her clients coolly, and Teddy couldn't work out why Fitz of all people merited the deluxe service. It seemed as if every time she came into Candida's office recently, her boss was taking to Fitzgerald.

'No, I hadn't heard that. How very interesting.' Candida started making notes on her pad. 'I'll check with Malcolm about it. I'm sure he'll tell me. Have you talked to Mike yet?'

Teddy looked up; there were a hundred Mikes at Steinberg's; they weren't necessarily talking about *her* Mike. She unconsciously fingered the sheet of paper she had rescued from the shredder, which was still in her jacket pocket. Why should she care, anyway?

Candida laughed suddenly, a long, spontaneous laugh. 'Yes, Fitz, I'll keep my fingers crossed. It's a bit of a one way bet, though, isn't it?' 'Well, I'd put money on Glory to screw up any day.' Candida seemed oblivious to Teddy's presence. 'I'm quite happy to leave it in your hands. You just say the word when you want me to do anything.' 'Yes, I could be free tomorrow. Late, though. I have an eight o'clock meeting.' 'Okay, see you there. Keep it up, Fitz.' She laughed again, a soft, suggestive ripple of laughter that seemed totally out of character, and put down the phone.

Teddy was no longer making any pretence that she wasn't listening to Candida's conversation. Both she and Jamie stared at Candida, who met their astonishment with a satisfied smile. 'What's the matter with you two? You both look like you've seen a ghost.'

'Candida, do you really like that man?'

'Like him? Why do you ask that?'

'Well, I'm sorry, but I couldn't help listening, and you just sound so friendly with him, and I don't see how you can possibly like him. He's totally immoral, and corrupt, and evil. Whenever I've talked to him, I thought he sounded like Dracula, or one of the undead . . .'

'And you're beginning to sound like Julie Andrews. Don't judge things you don't know anything about, Teddy.' Candida spoke crisply, her good humour evaporating, and the accusation stung; it was, after all, almost a direct echo of Mike's. 'Now where were we? I remember; we'd just decided that Jamie was going to handle the new Morgan Stanley search.'

Teddy and Jamie looked at each other blankly, before Jamie said, 'I think we were just starting to talk about whether it should be me – '

'Good; that's settled then.'

Teddy left the office with her tail between her legs, Jamie with his shoulders slumped in resignation.

Left alone, Candida shut her office door, and stretched out on the 'interviewing' sofa. She crossed her feet at the heels, resting them on the arm of the sofa, and lit a cigarette. She felt like sending Julie out for a bottle of champagne. It was all going to work out all right; she just knew it. Fitz was eating out of her hand, and Mike was eating out of Fitz's, and Glory would eat out of Mike's. It was neat, it was clean, and above all, it was just. She blew the smoke out in a cloud above her head, and as it cleared, she felt she could see the future for the first time in many years. It amused her that here she was, stretched out on a couch, just like people did in the movies when they went to see a shrink. But her shrink hadn't solved any of her problems; she had solved them herself. It had taken her a long time to track down the ghost of her past, but here he was at last, and she was going to bury him once and for all. All those years of work and worry had been worth it. All those tears. All that sobbing. Alex was a good partner; she didn't fool herself into thinking that he was a good man – let Teddy worry about that – all that mattered to Candida was that he did what he had said he would do. She didn't give a damn about his motives, didn't care what he thought or felt. They had formed an alliance, each for their own purpose. If Alex wanted to fuck her a couple of times, that was fine by her. She could even, in her own way, enjoy it. It brought her closer and closer to her goals. And if there was one thing undeniable about Candida, it was that she was goal-driven. And her goal was so astoundingly simple: an eye for an eye, a tooth for a tooth. That was what her father had always said. It hadn't got him very far, but things were going to be different for her. She was in the home stretch, she'd been given her head, and no one was going to stop her now.

Alone in her office, happily alone, Candida closed her eyes and drifted into sleep, a sweet, heavy, dreamless sleep.

FEBRUARY 18TH, 1984

Candida looked like a different woman when she arrived,

late, at Robert Ballantyne's office that Thursday afternoon. The worn jeans had been replaced by a short tartan skirt and blazing red hunting jacket. She wore her auburn hair up, accentuating the fineness of her cheek bones and strong jaw line, and emphasising the length of her slender neck. Nothing, however, could alter the weariness in her eyes, or hide their blue hollows.

'What do you think?' She pirouetted for him. 'I'm pulling myself together at last, hmm?'

'You look very nice, Candida. Are you sleeping any better?'

'Yes. My GP gave me some pills. They help a lot . . . except for the dreams.'

'Tell me about your dreams.'

'There are several that recur – not exactly the same way – but they are identifiable as the same dream. Basically, I dream that I'm on a staircase, or in a lift – there's always some sort of vertical aspect to it. There's somewhere I'm going. I don't know where, because I never get there. Whilst I'm trying to get there, a figure appears on the stairs. It's not anybody I know – certainly not Jack, so don't get excited, Robert – it's definitely a man, older, well dressed . . . it might even be you! I'd never thought about that before!' Candida laughed, a natural, clear, flirtatious laugh. 'Anyway, I rush down the stairs – or up the stairs, it varies – and I feel that I'm looking for something I've lost – but it isn't Tommy – I don't dream about Tommy any more. It's more mundane than that, something like a handbag, or a set of car keys or something. I know where it is, through a door at the top of the stairs, which goes into an entirely different place. I know that this man is going to stop me getting there. I know that he wants to hurt me. I turn on the stairs, and take out a knife, and stab him again and again. There isn't any blood. I just know he's dead. Then I wake up. That's it.'

'What do you think these dreams are about?'

'Oh, Christ, Robert, I don't know. I'm not really sure that I care. I think they are probably just to do with having a lot of stress about setting up this new business. The man on the stairs is probably my lawyer, for God's sake!' She laughed, but Robert looked grave.

'Look, I'm doing my best to focus my thoughts on my company. I'm trying to decide what to call it. "Redmayne & Associates" seems a little dull — I don't want to sound like a law firm — and "The Search Partnership" sounds a little pretentious. What do you think would be a good name?'

'I'm not sure . . . Candida, I was very moved when you told me about Tommy's death. I would like to talk about that day again, and explore your immediate feelings a little further . . .'

Candida didn't reply, but her lips tightened perceptibly.

'When you first looked out of the window, and saw that Tommy wasn't wearing his arm bands, did you feel any sense of fear?'

'No; why should I? I told Jack to put them on; I thought I could trust him.'

'And when you saw that Tommy had drowned?'

'I didn't think about Jack then, not for a while at least. I couldn't think about anything except that somehow it couldn't be true. I just kept saying to myself, it's not true . . . it can't be true, God wouldn't let this happen. It just didn't seem real. Nothing about it seemed real. We were far from home, in an other-worldly sort of place . . . I just didn't believe it. For a moment, there was nobody there except the three of us. Then suddenly, the place was full of people, all the hotel staff, a doctor, police, I think. Jack and the doctor were kneeling over Tommy, I suppose they were trying to revive him. Later, I don't know when, the doctor gave me an injection. I think it must have been a sedative. I slept, I suppose.'

'How did you react to the shock? Were you hysterical, or silent?'

'I just don't remember. I suppose I was hysterical, and that's why the doctor sedated me. I do remember Jack telling someone to help me – but I just can't remember much else until the next day.'

'And the next day? How did you feel then?'

'Guilty.'

'Why?'

'Because if I had stayed with Tommy, it wouldn't have happened. If I'd just trusted my instincts and gone back down to the pool when I first looked out, and saw that Tommy didn't have his arm bands on, Tommy would be here now.'

'Did you instinctively feel, then, that Tommy was in danger?'

'No. I told you; I trusted Jack. That was my big mistake. That's why I felt so guilty.'

'Had Jack ever let you down before?'

'What do you mean?'

'Did you have any reason not to trust him before Tommy's death?'

'How can you ever tell that you shouldn't trust somebody until they let you down? No, of course I trusted him until then. I told you, Jack is a responsible man, he'd always been very reliable.'

'I see. Now the day after Tommy's death, what happened exactly?'

'I can't remember. Jack went to the hospital, I think. I couldn't go. He made all the "arrangements". It was very complicated. We wanted to bring Tommy home.'

'How did you feel towards Jack?'

'I began to hate him. The more I thought about it, and the more I realised that Tommy wasn't going to come back, the more I hated him. It was so selfish, you see.

If he had just stayed awake, if he had just cared enough about Tommy to stay awake for a few minutes ... The coroner said that Tommy had drowned moments before I shouted. What's a few minutes' sleep compared to the life of your only son?'

Candida twisted a handkerchief in her hands, but she wasn't crying.

'How did Jack react?'

'Oh, he was very calm, very much in control,' Candida said sarcastically. 'He was doing his white knight bit again. I don't really think he reacted at all. He went back to work the week after we returned, right after the funeral.'

'How did you feel at Tommy's funeral?'

'How do you think I felt?' she said angrily. 'I felt I was dead. I just felt dead. I suppose I wanted to be dead. It seemed that everything was over. Everything is over.' She repeated the phrase in a dull, flat voice.

'Candida, I think we should leave it there for today. I'd very much like to continue talking about this next week.'

CHAPTER TEN

When Teddy took Paul Driver's call the next morning, and heard his decision, she was perfectly composed, the model of a professional headhunter.

'I see, Paul. Yes, I think your reasoning is absolutely correct. I quite take your point about Konrad. After all, what matters most is that you're happy with the choice. You're the one who's going to have to live with it.'

'Well, don't say anything to the other candidates just yet. I want to get a contract signed before we reject the rest of them. Things can always go wrong at the last minute, Teddy. You know that better than anyone.'

'I couldn't agree more. No, I'll present the offer, and let's take it from there. So let me just make sure I've got the terms straight: we're saying a base salary of two hundred thousand sterling, right?'

'Yes; I'd even go for it in the dollar equivalent if there are any concerns about exchange rates, but I'd rather keep it in sterling. I'm also able to pay half of it offshore, so there's an added tax benefit. And if it comes to the crunch, I guess I'd up the offer, if the signing depended on it.'

'Right. Understood. We'll start negotiating at the two hundred level. And bonus?'

'I'll guarantee a minimum take home for the first year, as it's bound to take a while to establish a new client list. After that, it'll be performance related. He's going to have to clock up partnership points, but he'll be looking at take home of around a million sterling. The key point to make is that none of us take much more than that out of the firm, because of the partnership interest. Our normal cash draw is probably around two hundred per cent of salary, plus the profit share, plus stock, and stock options which can be converted at any point within the next three years. I'll talk it all through with him.'

'Sounds good.'

'What are our chances, Teddy? Will he sign?'

'We'll have to wait and see, Paul. You know nothing's ever a sure thing, but it's a good offer. Let me try, and I'll get back to you tonight or tomorrow.'

Teddy put down the phone, her hand shaking. Moments later, Jamie heard a whoop of delight, followed by Teddy bursting into his office.

'They picked him! FRG have just made me an offer for Christian Clement-Grandcourt!' Her eyes were shining, her cheeks flushed with excitement. Jamie was genuinely pleased for her.

'That's fantastic news, Teddy. Well done! So what's the fee on that?' He pulled over his calculator and tapped figures in rapidly. 'Let me see . . . base of two hundred k, plus fifty per cent minimum – '

'No, we agreed to do it on the average, which is going to be seventy-five per cent – '

Jamie whistled. 'Okay, now we're talking. Two hundred plus seventy-five per cent is three hundred and fifty thousand, times thirty-three per cent, that's one hundred and fifteen thousand, five hundred pounds, less the retainer – which was?'

'Thirty thou.'

'So our net is a grand eighty-five thousand, five hundred pounds . . . not bad, Teddy, not bad at all.'

'Oh, it's much better than that, Jamie. You've forgotten the equity kicker; Monsieur le Baron de Clement-Grandcourt is going to be taking home just about a million pounds at the end of his first year . . .'

Jamie closed his eyes. 'I can taste it, Teddy; I can taste it already.'

'What?'

'The celebratory dinner you are going to treat me to.'

'Okay, it's a date. When do you want to go, my little haggis?'

'What's wrong with tonight?'

Teddy blushed. 'Oh, Jamie, I can't tonight. I want to go to Paris – ' her cheeks reddened further ' – if Candida will let me, that is.'

'Aha! I thought you had another reason for being so happy other than the prospect of filthy lucre. So you and the Frenchman will be celebrating, will you? Tripping the light fantastic, hey? I do hope you haven't been guilty of any bias, here, Teddy; perhaps pushing one candidate a little harder than the others?'

'I swear not, cross my heart and hope to die, Jamie. It's just that Paul Driver and I seem to share certain tastes . . .'

'Hmm. Lucky old Clement-Grandcourt. Hope he deserves all this faith, Teddy, that's all I can say. Now. Let's see when we're going to have that dinner.' He flipped open his diary. 'I'm a busy man, you know, much in demand. Next week I could do . . . Monday? Or Tuesday?' he mused. 'As a matter of fact, I could do Wednesday . . . Thursday, and at a pinch, Friday.'

Teddy hugged him.

'You are precious, Jamie. I love you.'

'But not like you love Monsieur Grenouille, I fear.'

'Not quite. Let's make it Monday.'

Teddy didn't tell Christian why she was coming to Paris.

She simply told him that she had to be there, and was very keen to see him. Christian had been a little put out by the lack of notice, but had rather grudgingly agreed to cancel his other arrangements and meet her for dinner.

'Let's go somewhere really special, Christian. My treat, okay?'

'If you insist.'

'And can I see your apartment tonight?'

'No,' he stalled. 'That won't be possible. There has been some sort of problem with the, ah, *plomberie* – the floors are ruined. It's very inconvenient, is it not?'

'But I thought you were living there? The hotel said you'd checked out ages ago.'

'I have been staying with a friend. I couldn't afford to live in a hotel any longer. I will book two rooms there tonight, however. Meet me there at seven thirty, *ça marche*?'

'Book one room.'

'I will book two rooms, Théodora. I am concerned about safeguarding your reputation, even if you are not.'

Teddy heard the phone click, and hugged herself. Christian didn't even suspect what she was going to tell him.

Teddy left the office early and caught a taxi to Heathrow. She didn't even bother to stop home and pack a bag; she would be in Paris early enough to do a little shopping, and she had decided that the occasion justified a new outfit. As the taxi crawled through the streets of the City down to the Embankment, it passed the offices of Hayes Goldsmith. Teddy peered up at the windows, and realised that Jack had never called her back. For some reason, it dampened her spirits, so she pushed it to the back of her mind, and thought about where she would go shopping.

In the end, it took Teddy only ninety minutes and three stops to equip herself for her one-night stay in Paris. She went first to Azzedine Alaia, and bought a dress that was so sculpted, she felt as if she had been melted down in order to fit into it. She stopped at Maud Frizon for a pair of strappy shoes that cost nearly as much as the dress, and finally at Sabbia Rosa, her favourite shop in Paris, on Rue des Saints-Pères, just around the corner from the Hotel Saint Simon. The shop was a veritable temple of worship for lingerie lovers; unable to choose between a silk teddy in palest apricot, or a bra and pants in primrose silk, Teddy took them both, and threw in a white camisole and silk boxer shorts for good measure. She rushed to the hotel, and dressed with more than her normal care. She sat on the terrace overlooking the hotel garden, enjoying the early evening sunshine, and waited for Christian.

He was late. When he walked on to the terrace, lines of irritation were etched into his face, making his thin mouth look drawn. His eyes were hidden behind dark glasses. He kissed Teddy rather perfunctorily before removing his shades and sitting next to her.

'You look . . . different,' he spoke curtly. 'You look like a temptress. *Jusqu'au bout des ongles.*'

'Don't you like it?' Teddy was taken aback; she had expected Christian to love the sleek, sultry lines of the black dress. He was normally so appreciative of anything she wore.

'Yes, I do, I like it very much.' He rubbed his eyes. 'Forgive me, *chérie*; I am very tired. I have a lot of work on at the office, and I am a little, how do you say – *préoccupé.*'

'Well, relax! Have a drink, take your jacket off, and let's enjoy the evening.' Teddy smiled secretively, and kept her news to herself. She wanted to let Christian unwind a little from the rigours of the office before she told him about FRG's offer.

'You *do* look lovely. That is Alaia, no? *Très chic. Très seyant.*'

'Christian, you must be tired! What's happened to your English?'

'You must give me a moment to adjust.' He stroked the hair at the nape of her neck.

'All the moments you like, darling Christian. What would you like to drink? Champagne?'

He snapped his fingers at the hovering waiter.

'Whisky soda,' he ordered.

'How appropriate! Much more fitting than champagne, really, under the circumstances.' Teddy smiled at him; she couldn't contain her news much longer.

Christian raised an eyebrow quizzically. 'Appropriate? How is a whisky appropriate? And what are these circumstances?'

'Oh, never mind! I'll tell you later. Now tell me what you've been up to that's worn you out so much. I hope you haven't been having too many late nights?'

Christian struggled to revive his lover's role. 'How could I have had late nights whilst I have been so lonely in Paris, and you have been in London? The only thing that has kept me awake is my absence from you.'

Teddy leant against him, rubbing her cheek against his shoulder like a cat. 'Oh, Christian! I have missed you so much . . . I long for you to be in London, and then we can spend much more time together . . .'

She didn't feel Christian's muscles stiffen under the smooth linen of his suit jacket. She looked up at him through her long lashes, and spoke in a low murmur. 'Darling, how long do you think it would take you to leave Chavaudret? What's your notice period, I mean?'

'Ah, I don't know. I have never really looked into it.

Three months from resignation – possibly six. It depends. They could let me go earlier, but I believe the maximum legal notice period is six months.'

'But they wouldn't hold you to that, would they?' Teddy looked concerned.

'I think not. My uncle Henri is on the Board; they would not care to offend him. Neither would I.'

'Well, I think maybe it's time to start finding out exactly what your situation is . . .'

'Why? Your people at FRG still have to see the American lady, and the German . . .'

Teddy made no response. He put his hand under her chin and tilted her face up to look into her eyes. She was smiling. 'Théodora?'

'Oh, it might just be sooner than you think. We English make our minds up pretty damn quickly, you know. I certainly did, when it came to you.'

'*Chérie*, have you heard some news?' Teddy mistook Christian's tension for excitement, and shrugged, enjoying the momentary power she had over him.

'Well,' she drawled, 'you *could* say that. News, in a way, yes.' She dragged her fingernail across his shirt, drawing tiny, concentric circles.

'Théodora. You must tell me what you have heard.'

'Must I?' she teased.

'I order you to tell me.' He held both of her hands tightly in his own.

'Oh, I love it when you get dominant . . .' Teddy purred at him.

'Théodora!'

She gave in to the note of urgency in his voice. 'Okay, okay. Paul called me. This morning. They want you. You've got the job.' Her eyes were shining. Christian stared across the balustrade over the gardens, his eyes avoiding Teddy's.

'But they haven't yet made an official offer, am I right? They haven't yet talked about terms?'

'Oh yes they have! Two hundred thousand pounds basic, plus a guaranteed bonus, plus stock, plus equity options. You're going to be looking at a take home salary of around about a million pounds.'

It was Christian's turn to glow. His eyes narrowed, and a smile spread slowly across his face. '*Ça n'est pas mal . . . pas mal du tout . . .*'

'Not bad? It's bloody marvellous! It's more than thirty per cent up on your current package, and that's without even valuing the equity kicker. It's a triumph. And you have *me* to thank for it.'

Christian was still distracted, looking away from her. Teddy was bubbling over with excitement. 'So where shall we go to celebrate, my darling? It's my treat. Or rather, it's ARC's treat. I'm sure Candida wouldn't begrudge you a slap-up dinner on this occasion.'

Christian didn't reply, and Teddy assumed he was reluctant to allow her to foot the bill. 'We can even do a little business if that makes it easier for your inflated male ego to let me pay — we could discuss contract terms, whatever.'

'Hmm?'

'Where shall we go to eat, Christian? Or would you like some champagne now?'

'Yes. We shall order a bottle of champagne,' he said decisively. 'A Veuve Cliquot, I think. Suddenly, I do not feel very hungry.'

Teddy laughed delightedly. 'We could, of course, pass on dinner and drink in bed.' She spoke in a low, suggestive voice.

Christian kissed the inside of her wrist. 'That is an excellent idea. I should have thought of it myself.'

'And we can dine on the food of love . . .' Teddy coiled her arms around his neck, and kissed him deeply.

The two waiters loitering at the edge of the terrace looked at each other knowingly. They had wondered how long it would take for the Englishwoman to abandon her pretence that she was not sleeping with Monsieur le Baron.

Up in Teddy's room, Christian poured the champagne, and watched Teddy undress. She had completely lost any sense of shyness before him, and seemed to revel in every sensuous experience: the crispness of his cotton shirt as she slowly undid his buttons, the citrusy smell of his skin, the icy chill of the champagne glass as he trailed it lingeringly down her throat and over the swell of her breasts, the murmur of his voice in her ear, the taste of the sweat on his skin. Christian pushed her back on to the floor. Her nipples hardened under the soft primrose silk as she arched her back with pleasure, feeling the floorboards under her shoulder-blades. Christian's hand slipped inside the top of her stocking, and caressed her, his thumb rubbing against the lacy scrap of silk. As his fingers reached inside her, he jerked her head back roughly and kissed her throat, making Teddy moan with aching desire. He took her hand and pulled it down between her legs.

'Feel how lovely and warm and sweet you are, *chérie*, my lovely, my precious, my sweet little girl, my darling one . . .'

The rhythm of his endearments beat inside Teddy's head like a drum, matching the natural pace of their bodies. His touch was thrilling, her skin shivered under his artful fingers, her lips were bruised beneath his own. He rolled her over so that she was on top of him, her hair tumbling wildly over her face. He held her hips and guided her gently on to him, and Teddy became absorbed in her own pleasure, almost unconscious of Christian beneath her, feeling that she held him entirely in her body. She was not aware of Christian holding himself in check, watching her face intently for the moment of her orgasm. She was not aware of his hands continuing to guide her, urging her towards fulfilment. When she came, her body shuddered uncontrollably, and she fell forwards on to him, sobbing. Christian held her close, stroking her hair, stroking, stroking, his hands becoming more insistent, not allowing her to regain control over her body even for a moment. For the second time she was lost in the current, and Christian joined her, calling out something in French that she couldn't really hear, and yet understood perfectly.

Later, they lay together on the bed, their bodies entwined. Teddy's cheek rested on Christian's chest as it rose and fell, and the sound of his soft breathing lulled her to sleep. When he was sure she was sleeping quietly, Christian moved her gently off him, and dressed rapidly. It was midnight. He sat down at the escritoire to write a short note:

'My Théodora,
My mind is blank when I lie next to you. You fill my thoughts. I can think of nothing other than my hunger for your touch. I must take some time to think about this offer, quietly and alone. Go back to London, my darling. I will call you within twenty-four hours. Until we speak, hold me in your heart.
Yours ever,
Clement-Grandcourt.'

He strolled nonchalantly through the lobby, and walked briskly down the dark quiet street.

Teddy awoke in the middle of the night to find herself alone. She called Christian's name in the silence of the bedroom, and then found his note. She understood. He was taking an important step, and needed to come to terms with leaving Chavaudret and leaving Paris. She wanted him to make the decision without any pressure from her, and knew without a shadow of a doubt that he would accept. She stretched out across the width of the bed and smiled to herself. His formality of signing himself Clement-Grandcourt after hours of abandoned intimacy touched her to the heart.

Mike stared at the screens in front of him. Every bone in his body warned him to back off and clear out of the market. If ever there was a time to take a holiday, it was now. The market was going crazy. Traders all over the world were rolling up their shirt-sleeves and taking on the Swedish Central Bank. The Swedish currency was under severe pressure; statistics were forecasting lean years ahead, the economy was juddering to a virtual standstill, and government borrowing was set to go through the roof. The krone didn't even have the security net of the ERM. It was in freefall, and there were simply no grounds to do anything other than short the currency, and gain where Sweden lost. But he didn't like it. Mike was a big, bold player. He liked to place large bets, and the krona wasn't a big enough currency for him to play rough with. If he bought krone, he would simply be funding every other trader's bonus; if he sat on the fence, he would be accused of missing a trick that had been handed to him on a platter, courtesy of the Sverige Riksbank. It went against the grain to follow the market's lead; he wasn't called *Il Duce* for nothing. Mike knew that every trade, every profit he ever made, caused somebody else to take a commensurate loss. That's why he didn't like to follow a trend: you might just be on the losing end of the game. But you had to swallow your pride sometimes and jump on the bandwagon with everyone else, and this time the loser was almost certainly going to be the Riksbank. Almost certainly. He pushed the button which connected him automatically to the currency desk of Morgan Guaranty.

'JD? It's Miccinelli. Give me your price in four yards of krone against the mark.'

'Norwegian? Danish?'

'If I was looking for Danish I'd go to the bakery on the corner. No, budgie-brain, the Stocky.'

These currency traders were no fools; they knew the capital city of every European country.

'This will takes us a while to quote, Michael. That's no small order.'

'Fine.'

'And you realise that there's going to be a big spread for that size?'

'Yep.' Mike waited for a few minutes.

'Three seventy-four and a half to three seventy-five and a half.'

'Good.'

'Have I ever *not* been good in size for you, big boy?' JD Mitchell simpered affectedly.

'Done. Yours. At three seventy-four and a half I sell you four yards of Stocky against the mark.'

Mike booked the trade, time-stamping the dealing ticket, and marking the counter-party as Morgan Guaranty. He always felt better once he had taken a trading decision – particularly when it was going to make him a shit-load of money. He breathed in deep, filling his lungs with the stale air of the dealing room. It smelled sweet. Yet somewhere, somewhere, there was the distinct odour of rat wafting around.

Candida strolled across to the credenza in the corner of her office where the hard copy records of all candidates, and potential candidates, were stored. She extracted the CV's of four people: Jack Delavigne, Malcolm Fairchild, Glory McWhirter and Michael Miccinelli. She looked through them casually, amused by how much they had in common. For a start, they were all single, apparently focused on their careers. When Candida had set up her headhunting business, she had believed that 'Marital Status: Single' would be an advantageous phrase on anyone's résumé. It implied that you were not only single, but single-minded, someone who wouldn't have to be subject to the demands of a sick child, or a partner relocating to another country, or any of the practical inconveniences of family life. It was Alex Fitzgerald who had taught her otherwise. Fitz liked nothing better than to scan a résumé and see the golden words 'Marital Status: Married; four children'. If you hired someone like that, you knew you had got them cornered for life. You could work them to death, pay them badly, walk all over them, and they were never going to throw up their hands and tell you to get stuffed. You could keep them in the office until the small hours, make them work three weekends out of four, and it was okay; they weren't rushing off at dusk to seduce some hot little number. Oh no. They would crawl home, well after two a.m., to find that their dutiful wife had left a bit of charred chicken and some soggy broccoli in the oven, and gone to bed with the baby. They had already kissed goodbye to freedom and independence, and had been in slavery so long that they had forgotten what individual choice was all about. A married man was a sound investment. When it came to a choice between two male candidates, Fitz always, but always, opted for the married man. And it certainly wasn't because he upheld family values. Married – or marriageable – women faced a much tougher time getting into Steinberg Roth than their male counterparts; the scenario reversed.

Candida thought about this principle as she scanned the CVs on her desk. How easy would it be for these four to find new jobs? A lot depended on how Alex handled things. There was a good chance that Mike and Glory wouldn't be in the job market for at least a couple of years. They'd either be sunning themselves on a beach in Acapulco, or they'd be in some cosy minimum security prison. She didn't really care; they weren't relevant to her long term plans, so long as they did as they were told. As for Malcolm . . . well, Malcolm's future was likely to be in her hands. If she felt tolerant, she knew she could find him another job somewhere. Candida felt inclined to be tolerant. Malcolm had been more helpful to her than he would ever realise. The one whose CV she studied most carefully, the one who really concerned her, was Jack. If all went according to plan, he'd be out of Hayes Goldsmith within six months, if not before. The question was, what would he do next? His track record was just too damn good to rule out the possibility that somebody else would offer him a job, but Candida knew her ex-husband well enough to doubt that he would accept it. No; if Jack blew everything at Hayes, if he felt he'd let everyone down, his team, his shareholders, and himself, then she was confident that he'd bow out gracefully and call it a day. And that day would be hers . . . the day she had been waiting for. At last she would be in control, calling the shots. It wasn't that Candida had become a headhunter in order to destroy her husband. She had promised herself a long time ago that Jack would suffer, would lose something that really mattered to him, in the same way that she had lost Tommy. She had not foreseen that her career as a headhunter would help her ensure that this promise was kept, but if that was one of the perks of a job well done, then so be it. Candida prided herself on the fact that she always kept her promises, all except that silly little promise she had made about going back to see

Robert Ballantyne, and breaking that one certainly hadn't caused her any problems.

FEBRUARY 25TH, 1984

As soon as she had settled herself in her regular armchair, Candida looked at her watch and told Robert that she was pressed for time. She had a meeting with her lawyer in forty-five minutes.

'You simply wouldn't believe the paperwork that goes on before you can start doing business!' she explained apologetically.

'How's it all going?'

'Well, I've got the backing. It's mainly my own capital from the divorce settlement, but my family have rallied around marvellously — my mother says she's always wanted to invest in one of her children, and Philip, that's my brother, the one in Paris, has not only provided capital, but is also going to be my first head — I mean the first candidate I try to place! He's been working for a French broker for six years, Tuffier, and is massively underpaid and underchallenged. I'm already planning who to send him to, if I could just get all the legalities out of the way.'

'You certainly haven't lost any time.'

'There's no time to waste. I wish I'd done this years ago. I've done a lot of homework; there are plenty of headhunting companies that cover the financial sector as well as the corporate sector, but there are very few specialists. I'm going to build a really dedicated, professional firm; I'll only hire people who have worked in the City themselves, and even then, they must have been successful in it. So many headhunters are just no-hopers. I've been to see about twelve since I saw you last — pretending that I was going back into the City myself, you know, looking *for a job, and they were all God-awful. The market's wide open, you see? There just isn't any serious competition, so long as I stick to the straight and narrow.'*

Her enthusiasm was contagious, and Robert Ballantyne found himself caught up in it. 'It sounds tremendously exciting, Candida. I applaud you. Will you be working alone?'

'Oh, no; I've persuaded an old friend of mine, David Aston-Stewart, to come in as my partner. He has a lot of corporate finance experience, which I don't, and an excellent reputation. I thought I needed an old school tie sort of person – there are plenty of City types who wouldn't take kindly to being interviewed by a twenty-eight-year-old woman. They'll come round in the end, but I think the company will be easier to launch with David around, and we'll hire one or two consultants right away. You need to build a critical mass.'

'Well, it certainly sounds as if you've done your homework. But I would expect that of you; you're clearly someone who likes to plan ahead. Why do you think this business is so important to you?'

'There are three reasons. One, I need to make a living. Two, I want something that is just mine – that nobody can take away – something I am solely responsible for. And three, well, the third reason isn't really important.'

'What is it?'

'Nothing. There isn't a third reason. Look, Robert, I really have to be making a move. I'm sorry to be so rushed, but you know how it is . . .'

'All right, Candida. We won't really count this as a proper session. When we meet next week I think we should talk about the early years of your marriage to Jack, about your relationship before Tommy was born. I think that might help you to put things in perspective, and see what went wrong.'

'Nothing "went wrong"; he killed my baby, and that killed our relationship. It's that simple. There's no point in looking for complicated explanations. I told you, all of that is finished.' Candida looked stony. She had turned cold on him again.

'I understand; but I would like to explore the ground to see if there were signs of a problem that might have emerged regardless of Tommy; let's try next week, all right?'

'No! It's not all right! All you want to do is talk about Tommy, and talk about Jack! You're meant to be interested in me, godammit! I've been trying to tell you about something that really matters to me, and you just don't want to hear. I really don't think there is any point in my coming back here if you won't even have the decency to listen to what I am saying!'

'I am listening, Candida. But I've also listened to you talk about Tommy and about Jack, and I'm very interested in what you have to say about them. I think it would be valuable to discuss them more deeply before we proceed further.'

'Well I don't. I don't think it would be valuable to discuss anything,' she shouted, her eyes flashing, her chin raised, daring him to challenge her again.

'Candida, when we first met, you agreed that if at any point you decided that you did not want to continue therapy with me, we would have a final session to wrap things up. I am very sorry that at this preliminary stage, you feel reluctant to continue. I would ask you to think about it very carefully, as I am absolutely sure that you would benefit from further work. However, if you are determined not to proceed with therapy, then I must remind you of your commitment to have one final session. Do you agree to return next week, as you promised, and review the ground we have covered?'

'All right,' Candida agreed perfunctorily.

Robert Ballantyne heard her heels clicking hurriedly down the corridor, and heard the quiet clunk of the heavy black door shut behind her as Candida stepped out into the winter sunshine.

On the fourth of March, she did not turn up to her appointment. Robert Ballantyne phoned her several times during the ensuing weeks, and after he left five messages on her answering machine, she had her number changed. She never returned to Ninety-one, Harley Street.

Teddy could hardly sit still waiting for Christian to call her. Her restlessness got through to Jamie, who finally banned her from his office after she had destroyed his store of paperclips by nervously unbending and straightening each and every one. When Jack phoned, and tentatively suggested dinner that night, she leapt at it, knowing that she couldn't bear to sit at home next to the telephone. As soon as she had arranged where to meet, she panicked; what if Christian did call, and she wasn't in? She couldn't reach him – she didn't have his friend's number, and she had sworn not to call him at his office again as his secretary was getting so suspicious. She raced home, praying that he wouldn't call her whilst she was in the car, and could hear the phone ringing as she fought to get her key in the door. She snatched the phone off its cradle, breathless.

'Teddy, it's Charles.'

'Charles, you have got to get off the phone this instant! I'm expecting a terribly important call.'

'From yet another new lover, I suppose.'

'Wrong. It's a business call, if you must know.'

'Well, I've told you before, you ought to get call waiting; then you could chat away to me, and when your ghastly, spotty little candidate called up to cry on your shoulder, I'd hear a discreet little bleep, and you could go.'

'Charles! I've just had a brilliant idea! What are you doing tonight?'

'Well, now you mention it, I was calling to see if you fancied tying on the old nosebag with me.'

'No, I can't. I have to go out to dinner. For business, really. But you could do me an enormous favour . . .'

'Yee-eess?' He dragged out the word into two syllables, each one laden with suspicion.

'Could I borrow your mobile phone? Just for tonight? You see, I simply can't afford to miss this call, and I can't afford to miss the dinner, and so I'm in a bit of a quandary.'

'All right, of course you can. You can pick it up on the way to dinner.'

'Charles, darling,' Teddy wheedled, 'you couldn't be an absolute sweetheart and bring it round here, could you? I just dare not leave my phone until I've got the mobile, so I can leave that number on my machine . . .'

'God almighty, Theodora, is there no end to your bloody cheek? What'll you give me if I say yes?'

'What do you want?'

'A night of unadulterated, mad, and preferably deviant sexual passion.'

'Done. Provided you and the phone get here within fifteen minutes, you're on.'

'My God, Winnington, you must be desperate. If you'd do that for the loan of a mobile phone, what would you do if I gave you one of your very own?'

'That's for you to wonder about, Charles . . . but don't forget our deal depends on timing – you've only got fourteen minutes left, so you better get your arse over here.'

Charlie hung up without even saying goodbye.

Jack was waiting for her at the River Café when Teddy arrived half an hour later. She was breathless and her excitement showed in her flushed cheeks and sparkling eyes. Almost forgetting how little she really knew Jack, she impulsively kissed him on the cheek, and plumped herself down in the chair next to him. The restaurant was cool despite the humid August evening. A slight but welcome breeze drifted in off the Thames through the large open windows. Teddy fanned her face and unbuttoned the first two buttons of her linen shirt.

'You look like you need a long, cool drink. How about a Pimms? Or a gin fizz?'

'D'you know, Jack, what I would really kill for is a mint julep. Do you think they would make one for me?'

'Leave it to me.' He spoke quietly to the Italian waiter, and when met with a confused look, and a heavy shrug of the shoulders, gave him detailed instructions on how to make the cocktail. Now that she looked at him, Teddy realised how infinitely tired Jack looked. He was pale, and the lines were heavily etched around his eyes, with two deep creases of tension above the bridge of his nose.

'Jack, you look like you could really do with a holiday. Are you going away this month? Surely there can't be much going on in August?'

'Well, you know what they say, Theodora, no rest for the wicked. To be honest, I haven't made any plans for going away. Perhaps in September, when things cool down . . .'

Teddy didn't know if he was referring to the weather, or to the climate at Hayes Goldsmith. She was about to encourage him to book a break when the mobile phone buzzed loudly. As the heads of their fellow diners turned in some curiosity and some disapproval towards the noise, Teddy mouthed an apology to Jack, and flipped open the little wallet-sized contraption.

'Yes? Teddy Winnington?'

'Ted? Just checking up to to see if it's working.' Charles spoke jauntily.

'For God's sake, Charles, we're in the middle of dinner! It's working fine!'

'You can't blame me for checking up on my collateral,' Charles drawled. 'I didn't want you backing out of our deal because I had provided faulty equipment.'

Teddy snapped the phone shut.

'Sorry, Jack. I had to bring this awful thing because I'm expecting to hear back from a candidate about whether he's going to accept FRG's offer or not. I'm desperate to wrap it up.'

'But that wasn't him I take it?' Jack was smiling.

'No, that was a nuisance call. You remember Charles Bartholomew? Well, he's become a sort of dedicated heavy breather.'

Teddy drank her cocktail, which came in an ice-frosted glass in authentic Kentucky tradition, and began to relax. She had forgotten why Jack had even asked to meet her. They talked so easily and naturally, and discovered that they had many tastes in common: a genuine love of the country; a shared passion for English literature, despite their differences of opinion about F Scott Fitzgerald; a hatred of City social functions such as the dinner that Steinberg's had hosted at the Grosvenor House.

'You should have seen Candida's face when she realised that she and I had been put at the same table.'

'I did; she looked like she'd seen a ghost.'

'Not quite, Teddy. She would have looked a great deal happier if she thought I had been a ghost. Candida probably fantasises about my being six foot under.'

They laughed together, although Teddy knew that it was no laughing matter. Both Candida and Jack clearly suffered a great deal from the bitterness between them, particularly Jack, who clearly loved his ex-wife. She hoped that Jack wouldn't dwell on his relationship with Candida. It was bad enough that she was meeting Jack at all, going behind

Candida's back as it were, without their discussing the relationship. Teddy justified seeing Jack by telling herself that the more she knew about him, the more she might be able to help Candida and Jack resolve their differences, but it was an inadequate excuse and she was relieved that as dinner progressed Jack seemed to have no more interest in pursuing that particular topic than she did. As they talked, Teddy realised one thing with absolute certainty. Whatever had happened between Candida and Jack, and however their son had died, Jack Delavigne was not a bastard. This understanding didn't make Teddy's position any easier. She still felt sympathetic to Candida; she still felt that her boss had suffered a hideous experience, but that Jack could no longer be held strictly responsible. He was simply too decent a person. What she couldn't understand was why Candida, whom Teddy considered an excellent judge of character, was unable to recognise what was so obvious to Teddy. After a delicious meal of pan-fried monkfish with peppers, they waited before ordering dessert, savouring the end of a bottle of Brouilly. When the phone squealed again, Teddy jumped in surprise. She had forgotten all about it, had even forgotten all about Christian, but the sound of his voice was thrilling. She was conscious of being overheard, although Jack began to study the dessert menu with the utmost tact, so she spoke rather more formally than she would have liked to.

'Christian. It's very good of you to call me back. I'm on the mobile as I didn't want to miss your call.'

'You mean you are not alone?'

'That's right,' Teddy spoke carefully.

'Then I will be brief. I very much regret to say, my darling, that I am unable to accept the offer.'

Teddy's hand tightened on the phone.

'I'm sorry. It's rather a bad line. I couldn't quite hear you.'

'I cannot move to FRG, Théo. I hope that you will understand.'

Teddy swallowed hard, then cleared her throat nervously. She could feel heat rushing into her cheeks. 'No, I don't understand, Christian. Why not?'

He sighed. 'It is very hard for me to explain. Perhaps I should call you later.'

'If it's a question of remuneration, Christian, I should make it clear that I can go back to Paul Driver. As I explained, we have quite a lot more room to negotiate.'

'No, Théodora. There is no more negotiation. I am confident that this is the right decision.'

'How can you say that? We haven't even really discussed it together!' Teddy's voice rose, but she was oblivious to the attention she was attracting. '*Why* won't you accept it?'

'I think perhaps you have not understood me. I did not ever intend to leave Chavaudret. However, it would have been foolish not to see what, ah, *price* I could command.'

'I can't believe what you're saying, Christian,' Teddy shook her head, as if Christian could see her. Her free hand began to drum the table. 'You have made me look like a complete idiot. Do you realise how unprofessional it is to solicit an offer purely so as to go back to your current employer and negotiate a raise? I cannot believe this of you, Christian.'

'Théodora.' There was a note of warning in Christian's tone. 'Do not lecture me. You have done your job, and I have done mine. I do not consider this lecture appropriate.'

'Not *appropriate*? Who the hell do you think you are talking to?' Teddy shook off Jack's restraining hand. 'You owe it to me to tell me why you aren't coming to London. We had arranged everything so well, made plans – '

'No, Théodora. Perhaps you had made plans, but I had made none.' He spoke coldly.

'I made them for us. Please tell me why you've changed your mind.' Teddy was pleading, her ears straining to hear what Christian said. She could, perhaps, accept him turning down the job so long as she understood why, so long as it wasn't anything to do with her. If Christian loved Paris so much, if he couldn't face leaving, then she could understand that. In time, if all was going well between them, she could transfer to a French headhunter, or maybe Candida would consider opening a Paris office, she thought wildly, waiting for him to explain.

'I am unable to leave Paris. I would prefer not to say why. This is not a conversation we can have on the telephone.'

'Please, Christian. *Please*. I just don't understand.'

'There are many things you don't understand, my sweet Théo.'

'So explain them to me. Please.'

There was a very long silence. Teddy could feel tears pricking against the inside of her eyelids. 'Please,' she whispered.

'Théodora. I cannot move to London. My wife would not contemplate leaving Paris.'

Teddy closed her eyes. Her hand seemed frozen around the telephone. Everything else felt numb. Her mind felt numb, dulled and stupid with the shock. She made an enormous effort to speak, and heard her own words emerging slowly.

'I see, Christian. Thank you. I am sorry to have bothered you. I understand. That's fine. Good. We'll speak soon, perhaps.' Her hand, rigidly holding the phone against her cheek, dropped suddenly to the table. Jack leant forward, removed the phone from her now limp fingers, and closed it, cutting off Christian. Teddy opened her eyes – they felt sore, but remained dry – and stared at Jack. Her voice sounded odd to her.

'He doesn't want the job. Do forgive me, that was terribly rude. I hope I didn't embarrass you awfully.'

'Of course not.' He returned the phone to her.

'I am afraid that I have to leave now.'

'Of course. Did you bring a car?'

Teddy shook her head. She felt so limp, so flat, so miserable. She couldn't make the effort to speak.

'Then I shall take you home.'

Teddy waited silently while Jack paid the bill, and then led her to his car and helped her in. He started to drive, and only spoke to ask for her address. She was grateful for his silence, and also grateful that she was not alone. When they arrived in Stanley Gardens, he stepped round the car to open her door. Teddy stayed in the car. She felt utterly stupid, incapable of doing anything.

'Teddy, what would you like me to do? I don't want to intrude, but I don't want to leave you like this. Can I help you at all?'

'I honestly don't know Jack. I feel like my brain is numb. I just can't seem to think of anything at all. I'm sorry.'

'Give me your bag.'

He extracted her keys, opened her front door, and came back to help Teddy out of the car and into the house.

'What about coffee, Teddy? Should I make you some, and then leave? Get you a drink, perhaps?'

'No, Jack. I don't want anything, thank you.' Teddy sat motionless on the sofa.

Jack watched her for a moment. He had initially tried hard not to overhear her conversation in the restaurant, but the urgency in her voice had compelled him to listen. For a moment he had believed that she was simply a very dedicated headhunter, but after that moment, God knows what her relationship was with this man. She had seemed to be angry — rather too angry, from what he understood about headhunters — with him for turning down the offer, and Jack had concluded that he was her only candidate for the job. But when Teddy had said – what was it? – 'I made plans for *us*,' when Jack had heard that, and heard the pain and confusion in her voice, he had known that he was eavesdropping on something much more personal than a headhunter reprimanding a client for bad behaviour. As he watched her now, he felt a surge of pity. She looked so forlorn. Her eyes were downcast, and from where he stood, her eyelashes appeared to brush her cheekbones.

He sat down next to her, and took one of her hands in his own.

'Teddy, I don't know what happened back there, but you are clearly unhappy. If I can help you – I'll do anything I can. But if you would like me to leave, you have only to say the word.'

She looked at him, her large green eyes clear if dull, and her voice was controlled and calm when she spoke. 'That's very good of you Jack. I don't really think there is anything you can do. The problem is that I've been a silly little fool – not for the first time. I've been sillier than I'd care to admit. I'm just a little bit shocked by my own stupidity. I'll be okay. Nobody likes staring at themselves in an honest mirror, that's all.' A smile passed across her face, lifting her cheeks so that her face, for a moment, looked heart-shaped. 'I don't think I want you leave, though. Would you mind staying for a little? Perhaps we could have that drink, after all.' A spark flickered dangerously in her eyes. 'Perhaps we should have a lot of drinks.'

Jack rose, relieved by her regained composure, and strangely relieved at being allowed to stay. He went over to the table where he could see an assortment of bottles. 'What can I get you? A brandy? Whisky? Calvados, perhaps?'

Teddy shuddered, then spoke passionately. 'I think I've had a lifetime's supply of Calvados, thanks very much.

Champagne, please, Jack. I feel like celebrating! There's a case of something under the table.'

Teddy raised her glass high in the air, and proposed a toast: 'To Monsieur le Baron, Christian de Clement-Grandcourt. And to me. To my utter stupidity.'

'I don't want to drink to that,' Jack said, 'but I'll drink to you.'

They sat in companionable silence for a while, nursing their drinks. Jack sat in the armchair opposite the sofa, his long legs stretched out in front of him. Teddy had never met a man who was so easy to talk to, and so easy to be silent with. He gave the impression that he was waiting for her to speak, and yet didn't care if she chose not to.

'Do you believe in luck, Jack? Do you believe that some people are born lucky, and others aren't?'

He thought before replying. Jack always seemed to consider things carefully; he rarely spoke off the cuff, but gave his attention to every question, however banal, as if it were something he had never considered before. 'I don't think so, Teddy, no. To me, luck is restricted to betting on the horses. I think certain actions can be lucky, but I don't think people are. I think we make our own decisions, and then live with the outcome. People never consider themselves the beneficiaries of good luck, do they? We're all quite happy to take the credit for things working out well. No, it's only bad luck we're victim to. It may be comforting to blame it on bad luck, but it doesn't ring true to me.'

'I rather agree with you. That's why I feel so awful. It would be so nice to say this was all bad luck rather than bad judgement. But you see, I can't even be angry with Christian, because in a way it was all my own mistake. My own crass stupidity. I could kick myself.'

'That he didn't accept the job?'

Teddy laughed hollowly. 'No. It was my mistake that I didn't do my research more thoroughly. I spoke to so many people about him, checking up on his references, seeing what people in the market thought of him. You'd think one of them might have mentioned that he was married. I guess I just didn't ask the right questions. I said, "D'you think he'd make a good manager? D'you think he has the loyalty and respect of his clients? How do you rate him as a business manager?" With hindsight, I should have forgotten about FRG and asked if he'd make a reliable lover.' She assumed her interviewer's voice. 'How does he rate in the sack? Could you possibly tell me if he's married . . .?' Her voice faded away into silence and self-condemnation.

'Didn't he tell you himself?'

'I was just thinking about that as we drove back in the car. I asked him, of course, when we first met, and he asked me if he looked married. I said no, he said thank you, and that was that. He never lied, exactly, he just didn't quite tell me the whole truth. I jumped to conclusions because I wanted to jump to them, and because I wanted to fall in love, I suppose . . .' She didn't look him in the eye, and Jack realised that she was embarrassed to be admitting all this to him. He stared into his glass, swirling the golden liquid around, and allowed Teddy the time and space to continue. 'I just can't believe that I did what I did. Don't get me wrong, I never thought I was in love with Christian, I just thought that it was all very nice, and that I was in control of everything, and that it was a fun way to pass the time. I felt like I deserved some fun after Mike. Now I don't even know if I was ever in love with Mike. I seem to have done things without a thought – for myself, or anyone else. I feel like I was swept away in a current, and didn't even try to grab on to anything. And the worst thing of all is that I don't seem to have learnt from my mistakes. You'd think that having felt so betrayed so recently, I'd have the sense not to hurl myself at a complete stranger a couple of weeks later.'

Jack had no idea what she was talking about, but he

recognised her pain and her anger, and his heart went out to her in the desire to comfort.

'We all repeat the same mistakes, Teddy. Perhaps we're programmed to make the same mistakes over and over again. We don't have an in-built, self-correcting mechanism.'

'I can't believe *you* make mistakes, Jack! You're so controlled, so together – what mistakes have you ever made? You can't possibly think that Tommy's death was really your fault – surely you would put that sort of thing down to bad luck?'

'*Bad luck?*' Jack's grey eyes darkened in anger.

'Oh God – I didn't mean to sound so crass. I just meant it wasn't anybody's fault. It was a terrible accident, wasn't it?' The question was phrased rhetorically, and Teddy longed to hear Jack confirm it.

'It was terrible, all right. As to whether it was anyone's fault, I don't know any more. For a long time, I believed it was my fault. But that may be one of the mistakes that I recurrently make. I am programmed, perhaps, to accept responsibility for things.' He massaged the spot between his eyebrows with his fingertips.

'I'm sorry, Jack. You're so tired, and I'm keeping you up moaning on about my screwed-up love life. And I ruined our dinner! How selfish of me!'

'Teddy, I cannot tell you how good it feels to sit here and listen to you, and talk to you. It's no hardship, believe me. For the first time in months, it's taken my mind off my own problems. But I don't believe your love life is as screwed up as you say. I can't look at you and believe that. There must be hundreds of men dying of love for you!' He spoke reassuringly, and Teddy wished, for a moment, that he wasn't being quite so paternalistic.

'Yes, but it's the way I pick 'em!' Teddy said flippantly, and they both laughed.

'I'm not going to worry about you, Teddy, so long as you keep a sense of humour. You'll be fine.'

'And *I'm* not going to worry about *you*, Jack.'

They smiled at each other, a warm conspiratorial smile. They had made a pact. They were friends. She had nothing to hide from him. She hoped he felt the same. Jack finally gave in to exhaustion, and made moves to leave. Teddy walked him to the door. 'May I take you to dinner again, Teddy?'

'I'd like that. Very much. I enjoyed the evening, Jack. I'm sorry about all the interruptions.'

'Don't even think about it. We'll end up spending our lives apologising to each other, and that would be a terrible waste.'

'Yes, it would, wouldn't it?'

On the doorstep, Teddy had to stretch on tiptoe to kiss Jack's cheek. As he bent his head to kiss hers, they bumped awkwardly, aiming for the opposite cheeks so that their lips brushed. For an instant, Jack was motionless, his lips cold and still, but then he gathered her into his arms and kissed her hard and long. As Jack felt her lips open beneath his, he drew away, and held her at arm's length. Teddy could see a look of shock, almost of horror, in his eyes, and she said good-night hurriedly.

Safely inside her house, she leant heavily against the front door.

Okay, it had been an accident. A clumsy accident. But talk about making the same mistakes . . .

CHAPTER ELEVEN

Mike groaned when the phone went. It was the fifth time this week he had been woken up in the middle of the night. It was bound to be New York, freaking out over their positions and needing his advice. He half-crawled over Glory's dormant body to reach the phone.

'Uhh,' he grunted.

'Michael?' He couldn't place the voice immediately in his semi-conscious state.

'Yeah, this is Mike Miccinelli.' He rubbed his eyes. The fluorescent face of the alarm clock glowed in the dark at him. It was four thirty a.m.

'Michael, this is Sven.' Michael searched his memory in vain. 'Sven from Skandinaviska-Enskilda Bank. I am in Stockholm.'

'I don't give a flying fuck where you are. Christ Almighty, Sven, it's four o'clock in the bloody morning! What the hell do you want?'

'I want to do you a favour, my friend. Listen carefully. The Riksbank is going to raise the overnight interest rate on the krona to seventy-five per cent. Perhaps even higher.'

'Sven, if this is a windup, you're a dead man, understand?'

'It is not a windup, Michael. We have sources – unimpeachable sources, as they say. I tell you this because you are my friend, and you may be able to get out of your position in time. There will be an announcement before the market opens, but you can try to trade out through Tokyo, or Helsinki, perhaps. I doubt you will have much success, but I wish you luck. You *are* short the krona, no?'

'I'm short the krona, all right, about as short as a fucking midget. Sven, are you sure of this?'

'Does a bear shit in the woods?'

Mike groaned.

'Good-night, Michael, my friend. Sleep well.'

Mike pulled himself together and sat on the edge of the bed, his head in his hands. Sven wouldn't lie to him; he'd helped the Swedish trader out a couple of times, reversed a trade for him once even, and Sven clearly felt that he owed him a favour. Mike looked down at his cock hanging small and limp between his legs. He was going to need a fucking big swinging dick to get out of this one. He shoved Glory in the back, and she mumbled in her sleep. His irritation deepened as he looked at her.

He had tired of Glory the instant that Teddy had found out about his fooling around, but Glory didn't want to call it a day, and Mike hadn't bothered to make an issue of it. After all, it was easier to carry on, for the time being, than end it. Glory had an almost insatiable libido. The traders at Steinberg's openly referred to her as Ever-Ready, after the batteries. When Mike had told her about the nickname, she had been delighted. 'I bet they don't know I'm rechargeable, too,' she had drawled. He looked at the clock again. Four forty-three. He didn't have time to worry about Glory. She wasn't short the krona anyway; he knew that Glory had staked all her capital on a sterling rally. Let her sleep.

By five twenty, he had showered, dressed and driven to Steinberg's offices at St Paul's. The night-shift security guard was surprised to see anyone coming in so early, but waved him through when Mike flashed his security pass. Mike sat down at his desk and lit a cigarette. He had perhaps two hours – at the most – to cover a four billion krona short position. Before he touched the phones,

he began to calculate what his maximum loss was going
to be. He had sold four billion krona that he didn't own.
He had been expecting to buy the krona at a lower price
when the economic prospects for Sweden had sunk home,
and everyone else had sold krona. Everyone expected a
major devaluation. The difference between the two prices
could have made a him a substantial profit. It had been a
pretty safe bet. There was nothing the Swedes could do to
support their currency without shooting themselves in the
foot. But the Swedes had been brave; they had decided to
blow both their own legs off. By putting their rates up to
seventy-five per cent for overnight money, they would force
every trader in the world to buy the currency, and that was
going to push the exchange rate sky high – far higher than
where he had sold it. When it came down to the bottom
line, all that mattered was that he was going to lose a lot
of money. Mike looked at his valuation. He stood to lose
up to twenty million pounds if he did nothing. That would
really impress the partners. Twenty million pounds, unless
he could find some sucker before the markets opened and
unload the position. He lit another cigarette and tapped a
number on to the dialling pad.

When Teddy woke up, she was surprised how well she
felt. She had slept soundly, and had not woken up until
eight a.m. Putting on her dressing-gown, she took a cup of
coffee out to the garden, and sat for a moment in watery
sunshine. It looked like it was going to rain – yet again.
She wondered if Christian would call her again, or whether
she should call him. It didn't seem very important. She also
wondered if Jack would call. God knows what had come
over them on the doorstep last night; loneliness? Lust?
Mischief? She smiled to herself. Whatever had provoked it,
she was glad she had kissed Jack. She had been wondering
for a long time what it would feel like to kiss him, and it

had felt very good. At least until she had seen his horrified face. It had been a perfectly natural accident; they might have bumped noses and laughed it off, but instead he had kissed her, and she had, however fleetingly, kissed him back. It was no big deal. A kiss; no more, no less. Teddy would have to think about why he had looked so shocked – Jack certainly wasn't a prude. Maybe he thought she was a complete tart. And maybe he was right. For the time being, she enjoyed the memory and told herself sternly that it wouldn't happen again. She and Jack were well on the way to being good friends, and she wanted to preserve that at all costs. The smile left her lips as she thought about Candida. She had been – until the kiss – toying with the idea of talking to Candida about Jack, but that now seemed impossible. She might have been able to justify befriending Jack as a way of reconciling him and his ex-wife, but she didn't see how she could explain away snogging Jack on the doorstep. The story was more than a little lacking in credibility. No; it would be better to say nothing at all about Jack to Candida; and nothing at all about the kiss to Jack.

Teddy and Candida made short work of their first appointment that morning. Teddy had become a skilful interviewer, and she and Candida worked well together. Candida was trying to recruit a senior bond salesman for Steinberg Roth, and had recalled one candidate for a second interview because she was interested in getting Teddy's judgement of the man. Before he arrived, Candida briefed Teddy on the first interview. She was torn between whether the guy, Richard Barton, was a real talent with an unfortunate manner, or whether his brusque and arrogant style masked nothing at all. They decided to play a good cop, bad cop routine. Candida, as she had met him before, would be all sweetness and light, and Teddy would be tough.

When Richard arrived, Candida led him into her office, and explained that as Teddy had herself worked at Steinberg's for several years, she thought that it would be valuable for him to hear what Teddy had to say about the firm. This was the first deception. Barton would be lulled into thinking that ARC had already decided to put him up for the job, and were trying to sell it to him. If all went according to plan, he would drop any attempt to sell himself, and they would see him in his true colours. Barton fell for it, and he trotted to the slaughter with his little lamb's tail wagging.

Richard Barton was a heavy-set man with a face like a bullfrog. As Candida stroked and pampered his ego, Teddy sat quietly, taking a few notes and holding her fire.

'You see, Richard, when we come across a candidate such as yourself, whose credentials are so outstanding, all we really need to ascertain is whether you would be happy in the culture of Steinberg Roth. I'm rather hoping that Teddy here will be able to convince you of that.'

'I have very high standards, as you know, Candida. I hardly need to tell you how many times I've been headhunted – and most of the offers were a complete waste of my time.' Barton puffed up visibly.

'I can quite imagine . . .' Candida soothed him. In five minutes, Candida had him stripped and laid out on the slab, ready for Teddy to dissect him.

'Richard, could you begin by telling me your commission levels for the last three years?' Teddy deliberately kept her eyes on her notepad, asking the question casually.

'I see no reason whatsoever to disclose that.'

Teddy looked up to see Barton's jaw set hard. She smiled to herself, but outwardly feigned innocent surprise. 'Why?'

'My track record speaks for itself.'

'So why not let it speak for you? I'm only asking for three simple numbers . . .'

'I can't remember three years' worth of commissions – ' he began to bluster.

'No? How strange! We always ask salesmen what they have earned in commissions, and generally the big earners – people such as yourself – always remember what they earned to the last red cent.'

'Maybe equity salesmen tell you that, but in the bond market it's confidential.' Barton was now visibly sulking.

'How curious! Why do you think there is such a difference in the way that bond salesmen and stock salesmen behave?'

'Well, equity salesmen can't understand numbers, can they? I bet most of them can't even count up to ten. All they do is tell stories.'

'And I suppose bond salesmen can't follow a story line, is that it?'

Barton glowered.

'Now, Richard, let's get back to these commission levels, as you have such a good head for figures. We're quite able to assure you that it won't go beyond these four walls.'

'I can't give you exact figures . . . I was the top earner last year . . . probably the year before . . . my client list is the best in the business . . .'

'Well, could you give me approximate figures . . .' Teddy persisted, enjoying his discomfort.

'No, I've told you. I'm not some begging junior salesman who has to prove himself to a headhunter – '

'Well, I suppose I'll just have to assume a ballpark range. Shall we say 250 to 300 thousand?'

'It's far higher than that!'

'How much higher?' Teddy said sharply.

Candida timed her intervention perfectly, turning round to Teddy and saying in a calm and soothing voice, 'Teddy, I really don't think Richard deserves this sort of interrogation . . . I'm quite sure that we can be confident that his commission levels are satisfactory, don't you?' Teddy shrugged, and prepared to shut up for a while – long enough to allow Barton to recover his cool.

Candida turned back to the victim with a warm smile. 'Now, Richard, I think we've talked enough about business. Tell us about your other interests. I have a feeling that you are a multi-faceted young man . . .'

The word 'young' worked magically. After a bit of huffing and puffing, and a few dark looks directed towards Teddy's bent head, Barton, who was pushing forty-five and looked it, began to pontificate about his activities for the local Tory party. Teddy couldn't resist a smile as she heard Candida say, 'How absolutely riveting! I can see you standing for Parliament yourself in the not too distant future – I'm sure you'd be elected. However do you find the time to be so productive?'

Ten minutes later, Candida started wrapping up the interview. Barton, engrossed in himself, had made the fatal error of not asking a single question about the job, or about Steinberg Roth.

'Well, Richard, if you don't have any further questions . . . I think we can leave it there,' Candida said brightly, 'unless you have anything else, Teddy?'

'Just a couple of things. You mentioned your clients, Richard. Could you just give me a list of your top five firms, and the names of the individual fund managers that you speak to on a daily basis?'

The noises that came out of Richard Barton's mouth were hardly describable as words – more like the death throes of a stuck pig. Candida patted his arm, and showed him the door. When she came back into the office, she adopted the manner of a Eurovision song contest presenter: 'And now the marks from London. *Londres*?'

'*Ici Londres*,' said Teddy.

'*Les points pour la Norvege*?'

'*La Norvege . . . nil points.*'

'*Nil points*,' Candida confirmed with a smile. The two women burst out laughing.

Whilst Richard Barton returned smugly to his office, confident that he was on the point of receiving a major offer from Steinberg's, some of the staff of his prospective employers were in less happy mood. Seconds after the announcement of the dramatic hike in Swedish interest rates had flashed on Reuters screens around the world, Norman Bell was at Mike's desk, incomprehensible with terror.

Mike let him rant for a moment. He was absolutely exhausted, having survived the most nerve-shatteringly intense two hours of his trading career. He handed Norman a stack of dealing tickets. Each one detailed a purchase of Swedish krona, and the times of the trade, scribbled in Mike's almost illegible hand, ranged from five thirty-five a.m. to seven twenty a.m. London time.

'Shit, Mike! Did you sell off the whole exposure?' Norman collapsed with relief into the chair next to Mike's.

'Not all; we were still short five hundred mill when the markets opened. I just dumped it, and we'll take a bath on that.'

'We're down to five hundred mill? From four billion last night? How the hell did you do it, Mike? Did you know what was coming?'

Mike looked at him silently, and Norman read the message in his eyes. If Mike had traded out of a disastrous position on the back of inside information, it was nobody's business but his own.

'Don't answer that question. I don't want to know,' Norman said quickly. 'You are a fucking miracle, Miccinelli. A fucking miracle.' Mike and his boss sat in silence together, both numbed by the idea of how close they had been to the brink of disaster. The tragedy was, no one was going to thank them for losing three million pounds rather than thirty million. There was an unwritten rule in trading: you didn't get the credit for avoiding huge losses. You only got the credit for making huge profits.

'What are you going to do now, Mike?' Norman asked quietly.

'Do? The first thing I'm going to do is short sterling. Then I'm going to sit here until twelve o'clock and smoke my way through this packet of fags. Then I'm going to go to El Vino's and drink myself fucking unconscious. You got any problems with that?'

'Save me a seat, buddy. And a patch on the floor.'

Paul Driver was disappointed that Christian Clement-Grandcourt had declined his offer, but remained stoical.

'Well, you win some, you lose some, Teddy. It's not going to break my heart.' Well, if it's not going to break yours, Teddy thought to herself, it sure as hell isn't going to break mine. 'So I guess we've got to make our second choice, right? If Delavigne is out of the running, and Clement-Grandcourt, then we've got Herman the German, Pitt-Rivers, and the American girl, right?'

'I'd hardly call Esther Levenson a girl,' Teddy said drily.

'Okay, don't burn your bra on my account, Teddy. The American *woman*.'

'Thanks.'

'It's a tough choice. I like Tom, but something tells me that when push comes to shove, he's probably not going to leave Steinberg's. He joined them to take the safe option, and however good FRG's prospects are, we're new and untested, and we need someone who's a true risk taker. I just don't know if Tom's got the balls.'

Whilst she listened to Paul's pondering, Teddy was doodling on her pad, playing a game that she hadn't played since she had left school. She had written out her name, Theodora Winnington, and beneath it she had printed Jack Delavigne in capital letters. She crossed out all the matching letters in both names, and counted up those that were left: love, like, hate, adore. Love, like, hate, adore. Love, like, hate, adore. So she adored him. As Paul droned on, she totted up the letters left in Jack's name. Love, like, hate, adore. Love, like . . . hate. Fuck. She crumpled up the paper, and started again. 'So we've got Konrad, who I know could live with the risk, because he wants greater access to non-German markets, and we've got Tom, who might not.'

'And we've got Esther. She's the real risk taker – more than the other two, I'd say.' Teddy forced herself to concentrate on her client. He didn't reply. 'Paul? What have you got against Esther?'

'I haven't got anything against her . . . but she *is* American . . .'

'Yes. I don't deny that, but we agreed that could be an advantage. What else, Paul?'

'She's a bit feisty . . .'

'Beckwith and Strakowski loved that. They said you could do with a bit more spunk at FRG, if you'd pardon the expression.'

'Sure, Teddy, but don't you think it's a bit ironic that Esther should be the one to provide spunk?'

'No, I don't think it's ironic. I think it's pretty telling. I think that any woman who's got to the point she's got to without making very serious compromises probably has a great deal of spunk.' Teddy nearly spat on the last word. 'Listen, Paul. What's your real problem here? That she's female? Or that she's Jewish?'

'Calm down, Teddy! Don't rant at me. It's not that she's female *per se*, it's the *way* that she's female.' Paul couldn't see her, but Teddy rolled her eyes in exasperation. A woman couldn't win this game. If she was gentle, and submissive and conventionally feminine, then they said she didn't have the balls. If she was feisty and tough and a hard-hitter, then they said she was a ball-breaker.

'Listen, Paul,' Teddy said resignedly, 'if you ask my opinion, which I'm aware that you haven't, exactly, then I would pick Esther. But you are the client, and it's your choice.'

'I'd like you to make the same offer to Konrad von Budingen, Teddy.'

'Consider it done.'

Teddy put down the phone. Before she called Konrad, there was something she had to resolve. She drew a clean piece of paper towards her, and wrote down Teddy Winnington-Smythe, and Jack Delavigne. Love, like . . . Fuck! It was even worse! Now they hated each other. Perhaps she should count the hyphen as a spare letter, but then she'd be back to adoring him whilst he hated her. One more shot . . . Teddy Winnington, and Jack Delavigne. This really classified as cheating, if she remembered the rules of the game, but then, she was only doing it for fun, so what did that matter? It was an improvement. It meant she liked him, and he adored her. But it still wasn't the perfect result. She gave in to impulse and called him at Hayes Goldsmith.

'Jack? It's Teddy.'

'I was just about to call you. I wanted to thank you for last night.'

'I wanted to thank you. It was your treat, after all. I enjoyed it very much.'

'So did I.'

Neither of them made any reference to how the evening had ended.

'Jack, I needed to ask you a quick question. What's your full name?'

'Why on earth would you want to know that, Teddy?'

'Oh, I'm just writing up the final report for FRG and we have to use the full names of all the people we approached,' Teddy lied easily. She'd had a lot of practice.

'How very bizarre. Well, it's not a pretty one, so prepare yourself; my parents, for reasons known only to themselves, christened me John Arthur Mungo Delavigne.'

'Mungo?' Teddy roared with laughter.

'Yes. Mungo. And I'd be grateful if you would keep that to yourself, if at all possible.'

Teddy was still laughing.

'Teddy, can I call you tonight?'

'Of course you can, Mungo.'

'Shut up. Talk to you later.'

Teddy looked at her pad. John Arthur Mungo Delavigne. It gave her a whole new range of combinations to try. She'd save them till she got home.

Mike sold sterling short to Glory. He didn't like to take advantage of her – he felt sure she was going to lose out – but he didn't know anything she didn't know, and it was her own lookout. She was clearly building a big position in sterling, and was happy to do the trade. That done, he headed off to El Vino's, a popular watering-hole, with Norman Bell and a couple of other traders. None of them had anything to celebrate, exactly, other than not losing their shirts, but they worked their way through three bottles of champagne in half an hour. It seemed a shame not to, when Steinberg's were picking up the tab. Mike made a private toast to Sven Pedersen as he swallowed his first mouthful. He was still nervous; it would take a lot more than alcohol – or maybe just a lot *more* alcohol – to make him recover from the morning. He called into the office on his mobile phone to check that no one else had made any shock announcements.

'No, it's pretty quiet over here, *Duce*.' Spig Hall was

manning the desk. 'Fitzgerald has been trying to get hold of you, though.'

'Fitz? Did it sound urgent?'

'Hard to tell, he wouldn't say what it was about, but he's called a couple of times since you left.'

'Okay, Spig. I'll call him. You doing okay on your own, or d'you want one of us to come back?'

'It's as quiet as the grave, Mike. Too quiet, if you ask me. You guys drink one for me, though.'

'Any problems, Mike?' Norman asked before ordering another bottle.

'Nope. Fitz has been calling, though. Asking for me.'

'Why does Fitz want to talk to you, for Christ's sake?' Norman was instantly suspicious. Office politics were rampant at Steinberg's, and those who didn't watch their backs were frequently left with a gaping hole. Mike wondered how much he could confide in Norman. Probably as much as he could confide in anyone. In three words, not at all.

'He's been trying to get me to sign on to some charity scheme or other . . . the United Way, I think he said.'

'Are we talking about the same guy, Mike? Alex Fitzgerald? Involved in a charity? The only charity Fitz would give money to is the Society for the Elongation of Pricks.' They all laughed, and turned to other, more interesting topics, like the inverse yield curve of the Treasury bond. Mike slipped off to the men's room to call Fitz.

'Hey, buddy! Having a good day?'

'Shit, Fitz. You know what the bastard Swedes did. You know what my position in krona was. It's been a fucking awful day.'

'Yeah, but I also know you dumped most of the position early this morning. Way to go, Miccinelli.'

'Is there anything you don't know, Fitz?'

'I like to stay informed, Mike. And I like to keep my key people informed. That's why I thought you and I should

get together. I've heard something on the grapevine that I
think you ought to know about. Where are you now?'

'El Vino's. With Norman.'

'Yeah? Well, you better just stay put, and I'll join you
there for lunch.'

Mike didn't want to see Alex at the moment; he was
clearly going to blow him apart for the krona position.
Mike stalled. 'I'm not very hungry, to be honest, Fitz.'

'Did I say I'd make you eat, Mike?'

'Okay. I'll see you here.'

'Yeah, and Mike – don't mention this to Norman,
okay?'

Mike strolled back to the dark little bar, where his
colleagues sat telling jokes.

'Here's one for you, Miccinelli.' Fatty Fields, one of the
options traders, stood in the middle of a circle of men,
waving a bottle of Bollinger that he had gripped by the
neck. 'The devil visits a foreign exchange trader. He says,
"Have I ever got a deal for you! I'll make sure that every
trade you do for the next ten years is a winner – every single
trade, spreads, outrights, options, shorts. *Everything* will
make you a shit-load of money. However, after ten years,
your mother will die of cancer, your wife will be raped and
stabbed, and your kids will be kidnapped and slain." The
trader thinks it over really carefully, and then asks, "What's
the catch?"'

The room exploded in laughter. Most traders' jokes
played with the theme of corruption. The best humour is
often the closest to the bone. Whilst Norman and his boys
remembered other jokes, Mike's eyes watched the door of
the bar. When Fitzgerald appeared, and motioned him to
the back room, he went without disturbing the party.

The back room of El Vino's was dark, cramped and
oppressive, but full enough to afford a little privacy.

'You look like you could use a drink, buddy. What'll it

be? You going to stick to the champagne, or move on to something with a little more bite?'

'Whatever you're having will suit me, Fitz.'

'Bring us two vodka martinis – and you know what to do with the vermouth: just wave it over the glass, okay? And no fuckin' olives, cherries or twists of anything, you got it? And get rid of these menus; we don't know if we're gonna eat yet.'

Fitz waited until Mike had knocked back half his glass of virtually neat vodka and signalled for a second round before he began to talk. 'Okay, Mike. So you've had a bad day. But you saved it. We're doing all right. Steinberg's can live with a little hit. Don't worry about it. Put it out of your mind, okay? I give you ten out of ten for managing to get out of a hole.'

Thank God at least someone on the executive board gave credit where it was due.

'I've got other things to talk to you about. More important. More long term. I've made some progress on the next partnership elections.' Mike's eyes widened in surprise, and he sat forward, eager to hear how Fitz was fighting his corner at this of all times. 'Hey, sure you don't want to eat, buddy? I could eat a horse. That's probably all this shit-hole serves, anyway! You want a steak?' Mike shook his head, and Fitz placed his order. 'I'll take a steak. Rare. No fries, no rabbit food, no nothing. And bring us another round.' He looked at Mike expectantly. 'What were you saying, buddy?'

'Nothing, Fitz. You said you'd heard something – made some progress – '

'It's not what you'd call progress, Mike. Kinda more of a setback. I just meant I had some news. I'll give it to you straight. You're not going to make partner this year.'

Fitz let the words sink in. Looking at Mike's face, Fitz couldn't work out why this guy had such a great reputation.

You'd have thought traders had to be a bit more streetwise, a bit more cunning, a bit poker-faced, but here was this kid looking like he was on the verge of tears. What a jerk.

'To tell you the truth, Mike, I don't know if you're going to make partner any year.'

A flash of anger crossed Mike's face. 'What do they want, Fitz? I've performed better than any other trader on the desk. What do they fucking want? Do they think it's easy making money in markets like this? Even with the krona loss, I'm still well up this year. I'd like to know how many other traders in this fucking town can say that.'

'Calm down, Mike. Stay cool. This decision isn't anything to do with you. Norman Bell blackballed you – '

'Norman *what*?'

'– but it's across the board. Steinberg's are thinking of shutting down proprietary trading altogether – maybe just doing a bit from New York, but otherwise closing down.'

'That's crazy.' For a moment Mike forgot his own concerns. It seemed an act of strategic suicide to shut down proprietary trading. Trading was the only hope investment banks had of making serious money these days.

'Don't I know it, buddy. I've done everything I can to fight it, believe me. And it may not go through. But there are some jerks around who are trying to push it through the board; Freeman, Hirsch, and whilst that ball's still up in the air, they aren't going to elect any traders to partner. Period.'

Mike wondered if the day could get any worse. He'd had a bad night with Glory. She'd been all over him, wanting to do it in the bath, on the kitchen table, up against the wall. And Mike hadn't been able to do it at all. It was probably just overwork – he'd never had any problem getting it up with Teddy – but the fact that Glory had laughed like a fucking hyena hadn't helped. Then the call from Sven. Then the desperate unloading of his position, when his nerves had settled like a tangle of wires in his stomach. And now, just when he thought he was going to hear some good news, Fitz laid this on him.

'Fitz, if you don't mind, I'm going to call it a day and go home. I've got to think all this through.' The hubbub in the bar was beginning to make his head spin.

'That's just what I'm not going to let you do, Miccinelli. And I'll tell you why. I've already thought it all through. I want to talk to you for ten minutes, okay? For ten minutes, I want you to listen to me real carefully, and not interrupt. If you still want to go home after that, I'll let you, but you've got to hear me out.'

Mike nodded reluctantly. There wasn't anything Fitz could say that was going to make things better, but he might as well sit here and drink as sit at home and drink.

'So here it is. I know my reputation, Mike. I'm not known as a nice guy – no, don't interrupt, I know everyone thinks I'm a two-faced shit – and they're right. I'm out for myself, and so is anybody with any sense. So forget about your position for a minute, and take a look at mine. I've been a partner for four years. I'm doing okay. I'm responsible for sales and trading at Steinberg's, and for the proprietary book in London. I've got some money in the bank, but not enough, know what I mean? Hell, who's ever made enough?' He laughed. 'Seriously, Mike. It's not going to help me one bit if they shut down proprietary trading. It's not going to help me if they piss off my best traders so bad that they all quit. I need to come out of this looking good and smelling like a rose. That's why I put up such a fight for you. I reckoned you were the guy who would make me look best. And I haven't changed my mind about that. Besides, I like you. You remind me of myself. So what I'm telling you, Mike, is that I'm not doing anything here out of philanthropy – I've got a big personal incentive, you read me?' Mike nodded. At least Fitz was honest, which you couldn't say about some of the other bastards. Like Norman Bell. 'So last night, I was thinking. Thinking about the trading desk, about you, about how small my power base is going to be by the end of the year. And I thought, hell, Fitz, you're in too far with Steinberg's to get out, know what I mean? I'm too old to move – and partners don't move anyway. They either strike it rich, or they get carried out with the garbage. And I'm not prepared to climb into the trash compactor. Well. I've got something else up my sleeve. This is just between you and me, okay Mike, because it's really confidential. We've been looking at a little acquisition. More like taking a stake, really, in a British merchant bank. If we can get it real cheap, and very quietly, it'll strengthen our corporate finance department, and we could make a killing on the principal investment side. So I've been looking at ways to build that stake. And last night, I was thinking about it, thinking how am I going to pull this off – how am I going to save my traders – how am I going to buy that stake – the two thoughts just circled round and round in my head, you see what I'm saying? And suddenly I thought, bingo! Like that. Eureka! And I saw how I could do them both in one go.'

'I don't follow you, Fitz.' Mike was mesmerised, but he didn't see how this had anything to do with him, or why Fitz was telling him about it.

'That's why I'm going to spell it out for you, Mike. It's very simple.' He picked up the salt cellar. 'Let's call this the target, the merchant bank, okay?' He moved it into the centre of the table, and picked up the pepper grinder. 'And let's say this is Steinberg Roth, you got it? What happens to the stock price of this salt cellar if there are bad rumours about it? It goes down, right?'

'Of course. You don't need an MBA to see that.'

'Right. You don't need an MBA to wipe your ass. Now. What happens if a proprietary trader at Steinberg Roth,' he waved the pepper grinder, 'puts on an enormous trade with a trader at the target bank,' he waved the salt cellar, 'the kind of trade that might make the target bank lose one or two hundred million pounds?'

Mike was absorbed in the simulation. 'Well, it would depend on the size of the merchant bank – how much capital they could afford to lose. If it was say, Barclays, it would hurt, but it wouldn't be terminal.'

'It ain't Barclays. Say it was one of the old, smaller British banks.'

'One or two hundred mill loss could burn them up.'

'Exactly. So what would happen to the stock price?'

'It would collapse.'

'Good! You're right with me! So the pepper gets to buy a lot of salt, right?'

'Yeah, but there's a problem, Fitz. That trade you talked about. If the merchant bank was prepared to do that big a trade, then they had to have good reason for thinking it would move in their favour. How are you so sure that Steinberg's takes the profit?'

'Don't worry about that. Let's say that we knew, for certain, that the trade would work our way. For certain. What would happen then?'

'If we knew for *certain* it would work in our favour, then at least one, and probably both of the traders would be looking at doing five to ten years in prison. My calculations might be out, Fitz, it's a long time since I checked up the prison sentence for fraudulent trading, so that's just a guesstimate.'

Fitz laughed, and leant across the table to slap him on the shoulder. 'That's my boy! And that's precisely why my plan fell through. Then this morning, I came in to the office, those two ideas still pounding in my brain – remember? How am I gonna buy a stake in this target, how am I gonna keep my best boys happy. Then I saw the news about the Swedish central bank. Then I called Norman, and he told me that you'd managed to dump most of the position before seven-thirty. And then I saw how we could do it. Why should the trader here,' he again waved the pepper, 'and the trader here,' he flourished the salt, 'actually do the trade at all? What would have happened this morning if you had heard about the krona interest rate hike, and you had gone in and just written out a ticket, *saying* that you bought four billion krona at seven a.m. from, say, Warburg's?'

Mike followed the idea through. 'What would happen is that my ticket would go through to the settlements department, and they would send settlement instructions through to Warburg's, who would have no dealing ticket and they would deny that the trade had ever occurred. And they'd be right. And then settlements would come back to me, and unless I had a record of the trade on tape, then Steinberg's would have lost money on the whole trade, and then I'd be sacked, and then I'd probably go into a lunatic asylum, which is where I would deserve to be – '

'Just a minute. What if Warburg's *did* have a dealing ticket? What if they had the other side of the trade also booked at seven a.m.? What would happen then?'

Mike stared at him. 'Fitz, I must be missing something here. What you're saying is that there's a trader at Warburg's, who knows that at seven-thirty krona interest rates went to seventy-five per cent. At eight o'clock in the morning, he writes a ticket saying that he sold krona at the price they were before the rate hike, and he stamps the ticket for seven a.m.?'

'That's right.'

'What kind of a dickhead would do that?'

'The sort of dickhead who might want to make a million dollars quickly.'

'It's impossible, Fitz. That sort of fraud might be very

easy, but the two traders would have to do a bunk. They'd have to go to Venezuela and live on a beach for the rest of their lives, and as soon as they left, everyone would realise what had happened, and the banks would reverse the trade.'

'I don't think so, Mike. This is where we come back to the stock price, right? If that loss is so big, the stock price goes down, right? So Steinberg's buy a big stake in the merchant bank. And they make a lot of money – first from the trade itself, and second from the equity investment. Now, what if the Steinberg's trader was guaranteed a big slice of that profit? And let's say that he decided to give the merchant bank trader a bit of the benefit of that?'

'Who's doing the guaranteeing here, Fitz?'

'Well, me, for example.'

'Are you asking me to bribe someone to enter into a fraudulent trade with me, and then jack in my career for a million dollars?'

'Nothing so sordid, nor so dangerous.' Fitz leant forward, so that he was inches away from the trader. 'And nothing so cheap. What I'm asking you to think about is simply to say that you did a trade, persuading somebody else in another house to agree with you, and in exchange I will personally assure you of a bonus of several – I'm talking four or five, maybe more – million dollars. You can then stay in Steinberg's if you like, and see if I manage to win this little political battle we're engaged in, or you could move to another bank, with a glowing reference from me, or you could trade your own portfolio from a beach in the Caribbean. It would be your own decision. Of course, I would hope that you would stay.'

'And what about the other trader?'

'Well, I assume that he or she would be likely to lose their job. Not even English merchant banks are particularly civil to people who lose them that much money. It would be up to you how much you wanted to pay her – or him. That would be a strictly personal arrangement.'

'So no one would get caught?'

'No one at all. I wouldn't even call it a fraudulent trade, myself. You and somebody else would confirm that the trade had been done, and that would be that. Everyone would stay in the country, stay in their jobs, and you would simply be handsomely rewarded for a job well done, in an entirely above board manner. After all, I do personally approve your bonus. There's nothing irregular with that.'

'There's just one problem. We could wait a long time for another big swing like the krona swing, Fitz. There would have to be a major currency move to incur such a big profit, right? We couldn't do it on an ordinary trading day.'

'That's right. But we're both patient men, Mike. I think that if we felt we both had a way out of all this, we could afford to be patient, don't you buddy?'

Mike sat silently, thinking. He picked up the salt cellar, as if weighing it in the palm of his hand.

'There's one other big problem, Fitz. There's no one I'm really close enough to at Warburg's.'

'It ain't Warburg's, Mike. It's Hayes Goldsmith. Know anybody there?' He winked at Mike. 'Think about it.' He slapped Mike on the back, and was gone.

Teddy and Candida were the last to leave the office, as usual. Teddy was waiting for Konrad von Budingen to call back, and had also left a message for Esther. She had decided to tell Esther how things stood. Even though there was still a slim chance of getting Esther into FRG, it was very slim, and Teddy wanted to suggest broking her as a 'warm body'. This was the standard headhunting phrase for sounding out the market about somebody who wasn't exactly available, but might be persuaded to move.

As she was about to give up and call it a day, she saw a phone line flashing. Candida was on the other line, and the switchboard was deserted. Teddy picked it up.

'Aston-Redmayne?'

'Hey! That's sounds like Teddy!'

'That's correct. Who's speaking?'

'Teddy, it's your Uncle Alex. How are you, sweet thing?'

'I'm fine, thank you, Fitz. I'm afraid that Candida's on the other line.'

'Well, I'm just enjoying the sound of your voice. I had lunch with Mike today, Teddy. He talked about you a whole lot. He's really cut up, you know.'

'Oh, is he? I shouldn't shed too many tears for him, Fitz.'

'I'm not the one that's crying, Teddy. Mike is.'

'Oh yes? Well, Mike's tears dry faster than anything I've ever seen. He's a big boy. He can look after himself.'

'I'm sure he can, honey. It's you I'm worried about. Aren't you getting a bit miserable all on your lonesome?'

Teddy's nose wrinkled in distaste. That had to be one of her least favourite expressions of all time. 'No, Fitz. I keep myself too busy to do that . . .'

'Sounds exciting. Now you just let me know if you need any help keeping yourself occupied.'

'You'll be the first person I call, I promise. It's sweet of you to be so concerned. I'm afraid I have to take another call, Fitz. Do you want to hold for Candida?'

'No; just give her a message. It's an important one, so write it down carefully, there's a good girl. Just tell her that Alex has found the fool in the market, you got that?'

'The fool in the market?'

'That's right, honey. You just tell her that ol' Alex has found the fool in the market.'

'Will do. Bye.'

As Teddy left the office, she popped her head round Candida's door. 'That creep Fitzgerald called. He said to tell you he'd found the fool in the market, whatever that means.'

Candida looked puzzled for a moment, and then laughed. 'Of course! It's the old Warren Buffett line.'

'Warren Buffett? The investor?'

'Yes. He apparently said that any player unaware of the fool in the market probably *is* the fool in the market. Did he really say that, Teddy?'

'He certainly did.'

'Thank you. Thank you very much. You've just made my weekend.'

Teddy shrugged. If Candida and Alex wanted to play childish games, it was none of her business. She wasn't exactly immune to playing childish games herself.

Summer had abandoned England. As it was raining, Teddy treated herself to a taxi ride home, and as she sat in the back, she pulled out the *Financial Times* which she hadn't had a chance to read that morning, and started writing in the margin:

John Arthur Mungo Delavigne
Theodora Laura Winnington-Smythe

She quickly crossed the matching letters, and sat back, a smile spreading slowly across her face. He adored her, and she loved him. Not bad. Not bad at all. She had scribbled the names in the margin of the paper, and she now glanced down at the page. It was early September. The paper was full of how the currency markets were under strain. A cursory glance at the headlines painted a bleak picture: 'ERM hit by weak dollar and high interest rates'; 'Central banks losing the fight over the dollar'; 'Bank of England battles the fear of devaluation'; 'Obligations of European ERM members'. Teddy's mind turned to Mike. A few months ago she would have been sharing all this with him, biting her fingernails for his sake, and worrying about the ten year benchmark bond yields. Now she didn't care – except for the mean-spirited fleeting hope that Mike was on the wrong side of the market. She couldn't care less what happened to sterling or the dollar. It wasn't as if she were planning a holiday to the States. It wasn't as if she were marrying a currency trader. Her eyes turned back to the names in the margin, and she checked them again, in case she had added them up wrong. She had been right the first time. No one could see her, but she suddenly felt embarrassed, scratched through the names, and began to read the editorial. She felt a need to keep informed.

Arriving home, Teddy found a letter from Christian waiting for her, courtesy of Federal Express. She had opened it before she had even removed her coat, and stood in the hall, reading quickly.

'My darling Théodora,

I am mortified by my behaviour on the telephone last night. It was unforgivable, and my only excuse can be that I felt a sense of urgency to tell you about my wife. You will say that I should have done this long ago, and perhaps you are right. But can you find it in your heart to blame me simply for being unable to resist your many charms? Should I have told you when we first met, you and I might never have come together, and I cannot regret that we did. I have a philosophy about love, Théodora. It is a rare thing, and should be seized with both hands when one finds it. The fact of marriage does not prevent my loving other women, and I believe that it should not prevent them loving me. It only prevents my marrying them. And I do not believe that marriage is the essence of love. What we have is the essence of love – uncomplicated, and untouched by the mundane things of life. It is my earnest hope that we can continue to love in the future as we have in the past. My wife and I have known each other since we were children, and we agree on this matter. We have a sensible and understanding union. You and I have something different – my English is not good enough to describe it, and I would like to hold you in my arms when I tell you how I feel, to show you how I feel. I am sure that you will in time understand that this is for the best, and should not prevent our most special friendship. I yearn to be with you again. I await your call, and will be with you as soon as you allow.

Yours ever,
Christian.

I have spoken to Paul Driver to express my apologies. We had a pleasant talk, and I was particularly sure to tell him what an excellent headhunter he employed.

C'

Teddy crumpled the letter into a ball and hurled it across the room. She could not believe that Christian actually had the gall to think she would ever see him again. What a revolting letter. His style, which she had previously regarded as elegant and charming, now seemed artificial and smarmy. Steaming with indignation, she sat down to write a reply which listed his many failings and entirely ungentlemanly conduct, not omitting to say that this was something to which an Englishman would never stoop. The letter went on for pages, becoming far less articulate and more rambling than Christian's had been. The process of writing it all down vented much of her anger, and when she came to reread it, she realised that she wasn't actually angry any more. After all, what had Christian actually done? She had been a willing victim to his seduction, and she couldn't, hand on heart, say that she wouldn't have slept with him if she had known he was married. She hoped she wouldn't have, but she couldn't swear to it. Had he told her that he had an 'understanding' with his wife, she might just have gone ahead. And what had she lost by sleeping with Christian? Who had been hurt? Not Christian; not, at least by his account, his wife; and not, when it came to the heart of things, Teddy herself. She had enjoyed the affair. Christian had restored her confidence at a time when it was at rock bottom, and he had not betrayed her. He had not made promises, made commitments, and then broken them. The simple, undeniable fact was that she felt better now, even when she knew that he was married, than she had felt before she had started sleeping with him. In a strange way, hearing Christian say that his wife wouldn't consider a move to London had been like taking an emetic: very hard to swallow, but she felt enormously better afterwards. Teddy wasn't going to go so far as to say that she owed Christian any gratitude, but she didn't feel resentful. Her first letter joined his in a crumpled ball on the floor, and she started again.

'Dear Christian,

Thank you for writing so quickly – I can't imagine how you found the time in your busy schedule. You have no need to apologise for the manner in which you told me you were married. As I remember, I put you under a lot of pressure to tell me why you were turning down FRG.

I must say that I do not approve of the way in which you conducted interviews with my client when you had no intention of accepting an offer from them. I would advise you not to do so again – you risk acquiring a bad reputation, and I'm sure you wouldn't want to do that, would you?'

Teddy sucked the end of her biro. Perhaps she wasn't brimming over with anger, but there was no reason to let Christian get away with his morale entirely intact:

'None the less, you are quite right in what you say about Paul Driver. He seemed almost *relieved* that you turned down FRG's offer, and he and I are both confident of filling the position with a more suitable candidate.
As to the other matters you raised, I am of course flattered that you would like to see me again in London, but I am afraid that it is out of the question. My hands are very full at the moment.

With my best wishes for the future,
Teddy Winnington.

Teddy turned on the television to watch the news. Trevor MacDonald, his well-modulated voice heavy with portent, spelt out the crisis in the currency markets. Attention seemed to be focused on the Italian lira. The lira had dipped below its floor in the ERM, and the Italian central bank seemed to be pouring money into a bottomless pit in their attempt to rescue it. Devaluation looked certain. Teddy popped a chocolate into her mouth, and looked at the charts which covered the screen. The dollar, lira and sterling charts looked like the descent from Kilimanjaro; only the Deutschmark enjoyed an upward trend. Teddy mused whether or not this would affect FRG's offer to Konrad von Budingen. FRG might have to guarantee his salary in D-mark terms . . . She was interrupted by the telephone.

'Yarumph?' Her mouth was full of chocolate.

'Is that you, Teddy?' Jack asked. She swallowed hard.

'Sorry, Jack, my mouth was full.'

'Are you having dinner? Shall I call back?'

'No, I was just stuffing my face with chocolates. How are you?'

'Fine, fine. I just thought I'd call and see what you were up to.'

'Well, I'm lying on the sofa, drinking a glass of wine and working my way through a box of chocolate-covered, brandy-filled cherries . . . and listening to Trevor McDonald's obituary on the lira.'

'Sounds like a really fun time.'

'It is. Would you care to join me? I could put some cherries aside.'

'I would love to, but I'm still at the office. I don't think I'll get away for hours yet.'

'Well,' Teddy eyed the box doubtfully, 'I've only got eight left now, and I don't think I can hold out that long. You could always bring round another box,' she finished hopefully.

'Funny, you don't look like a glutton.'

'I'm not, normally. Only for chocolate-covered cherries. And a few other things. It's my shameful secret.'

'So *that's* the way to your heart!'

'Yup. I'd take Bendicks white chocolate mints, too.'

'I'll remember that.' He paused. 'What are you wearing?'

Teddy laughed in surprise. 'Jack! What's come over you? That's hardly the sort of thing you say to your headhunter! You sound like a dirty old man!'

'Believe me, I feel like a dirty old man . . .'

'Well in *that* case . . . I'm wearing a black lace negligée, stockings, high heels, suspender belt . . . how does that sound?'

'Awful. You sound like something out of an Anne Summer's shop.'

'Thanks very much. I was only trying to cheer you up.'

'Try harder. I need all the help I can get at the moment.'

'Okay.' Teddy thought for a moment. 'I'm wearing a red rubber mac, pink stilettos, and I've got my wrists chained to the bottom of the TV set, right underneath Trevor MacDonald . . .'

Jack laughed. 'Getting better, but it's still not right.'

'You're a hard man to please', Teddy said grumpily. 'To tell you the truth, I haven't changed from work, so I'm wearing a grey suit. Incredibly dull. My stockings are splattered with mud and rain, and my hair has gone funny and I look like a poodle. I have, if you must know, removed my jacket, and undone the zip of my skirt, and I've taken off my shoes, but they aren't even high-heeled.'

'Now *that's* more like it! Now I have something to fantasise about!'

Teddy chuckled. 'You're a strange man, Jack Delavigne.'

'Not at all. I'm just like most men. I like thinking about, and talking to, nice, pretty women who have good brains and a sense of humour, and who are doing perfectly normal things like stuffing themselves with chocolate-covered strawberries.'

'Cherries,' Teddy corrected him. 'What are *you* wearing, Jack?'

'I'm wearing the carpet out pacing up and down . . . I'm wearing everyone's patience . . . I'm wearing my heart on my sleeve . . .' His voice trailed away.

'Oh Jack! You sound so low! You're not wearing *my* patience . . . Are you sure you can't drop round for a drink?'

'I can't. I'm meeting some clients later, and I have a ton of paperwork to get through. I'm off to Sydney in a couple of days. I just knew it would cheer me up to talk to you, and it has. You are a real tonic, Teddy. I'm very glad that I met you.'

Teddy was touched by his comment, but made an effort to sound friendly and casual. 'Well, come round for a drink when you get back, okay? Or call me again. Call me from Sydney, if you like.' She didn't want to sound pushy.

'I might just do that. And when I come back, I'll bring you that box of cherries, okay?'

'Bring two boxes. I don't like sharing.'

Jack laughed and hung up. Teddy put the phone back carefully in its cradle, and watched the weather report. Her spirits were not dampened by forecasts of continued rain.

CHAPTER TWELVE

Jack prepared for his Australian trip with a sense of foreboding. Hayes Goldsmith's foreign currency trading position was precarious to say the least. Two of Malcolm's junior traders had been to see Jack personally to express their concern about the position, going over Malcolm's head. The combined forces of the world's central banks had been losing the fight to stop the fall of the lira against the Deutschmark, and financial pundits predicted ever more gloomy scenarios for the other currencies in the ERM. Normally wary of central bank intervention, currency dealers were testing their muscles, banking on the fact that the German central bank, the Bundesbank, was not fully committed to the support of the lira. Glory, with Malcolm's blessing, had continued to purchase sterling, which was edging ever closer to its ERM floor. Jack wanted the position closed. His instincts told him that if Glory was right, and the Treasury retaliated against dealers with a large wave of intervention, the potential profits were small, and the risk huge.

There were three factors playing on the minds of the currency traders: first, how soon and how hard would the Bank of England intervene to support sterling's slide against the mark? Second, sterling was in bed with two partners — the weak dollar, and the strong mark; what would happen to the pound in that uncomfortable *ménage à trois*? Finally, how would the French vote in the Maastricht referendum on September twentieth? The whole thing was a game of bluff, like the Mexican Sweat version of poker, and Jack didn't like the idea that Glory McWhirter would be sitting at the table holding the cards. He wanted to withdraw from the game. Glory and Malcolm told him time and time again that he was chicken, that they had judged the game correctly. Glory's case lay in the fact that the Bank of England had intervened already, albeit discreetly, and would be committed to continuing to do so. The government could not countenance a sterling devaluation, and equally the French would not countenance a franc devaluation. Sterling was strong against the dollar, and strong against the yen, and would continue to strengthen. Jack decided on one last confrontation with Glory and Malcolm. As he expected, they were both adamant.

'Jack, hun, look at what Norman Lamont said. Let me read it to you. "Devaluation would lead to a collapse in market confidence and a damaging rise in interest rates. Withdrawal from the ERM . . . would cause a huge fall in the pound and an explosion in inflation." He's ruled them out, hun. His only options are to intervene heavily, or raise rates. Either way, we're going to be looking good, and half the traders in this goddamn city are going to lose their shirts.'

Jack shook his head, unconvinced. 'He *has* to say that, Glory. What do you think he's going to say — I think we should devalue sterling or withdraw from the ERM? The market would take him to the cleaners.'

'Look at the Swedes, Jack,' Malcolm intervened. 'Rates up to seventy-five per cent, and they borrowed twenty-two billion quid to support the krona. Glory's right. Lamont isn't going to be beaten by speculators.'

'We're not the Swedes, Malcolm. It's not a parallel situation at all. Anyway, what about yesterday's rumour that the Bundesbank wanted to see the lira and sterling devalued?'

'What about Major saying last night that any realignment

or devaluation would be the soft option, and a betrayal of England's future? If Major doesn't stick to that, he's slit his throat, and the throat of the Tory party. They've got an election coming up. Shit, Jack, if you're going to believe every rumour you hear, you ought to bloody well stay out of the dealing room.' Malcolm glowered at his boss, and Glory laughed.

'Rumours like that fly around every ten minutes, Jack baby. Stay cool. Trust me.' She pouted her lips and blew him a kiss. 'The Bundesbank is gonna bring rates down some time in the next few weeks. This is the time to buy the weaker currencies – you Brits and the Eyeties are going to have to pull in public sector borrowing to meet the Maastricht criteria. That's gonna be good for sterling. Trust me. Just a couple of weeks.'

'I can't wait a couple of weeks, Glory. It's the eleventh of September now. Frankly, I'm not interested in what Major says – he's trying to talk his way out of a crisis, that's all. If the Germans keep their promise not to increase their interest rates, and if the French vote yes on the twentieth, and if the other ERM currencies stay stable till the vote, then Major might have a chance. Personally, I don't trust the Bundesbank here, and I wouldn't ever place a bet on a Frenchman to do anything. What if the French vote no, Glory? What if European Monetary Union goes for sudden death? Do you really want to put money on those ifs, Glory? *My* money?'

'*Our* money, Jack. Yeah, I do. And so does my boss.' She patted Malcolm on the thigh. 'So it's two against one, hun.'

'I have the casting vote here, Glory, and don't you forget it.' Jack's face was carved out of stone. 'I've made a decision. I'm flying to Sydney on Sunday night. I'll be back sometime on Thursday the seventeenth. If things aren't a whole hell of a lot better when I get back, you will close the position on Thursday, agreed?'

Malcolm stared at the floor, bristling with resentment. Glory stared at Jack, her eyes challenging. Neither of them spoke.

'I've told you my decision. I don't need your fucking agreement.' Jack turned on his heel and walked out of the dealing room. He was cursing them inwardly.

By the time he reached his office, he had calmed down enough to curse himself. He'd played the scene all wrong, and he knew it. If his instincts had told him that they should close the position, then he should have told Malcolm to close the position now. Malcolm and Glory would have been angry, but Hayes Goldsmith and Partners would have been safe. As things stood now, Glory and Malcolm were angry all right, but the bank wasn't safe. The bank was on the edge of a precipice, and Jack had simply asked it to stay put, teetering on the edge, until Thursday. He thought about his conversation with Teddy the previous week, and remembered how he had assured her that he didn't believe in luck, he believed in making measured decisions and taking responsibility for them. Well, this time, he'd made the decision, hadn't acted on it, and now he was going to take the responsibility anyway. He stood at the window of his office, staring out over Cannon Street, and hoped to hell that he'd been wrong about Lady Luck.

Teddy spent Saturday quietly, and left for New York early on Sunday morning. She needed to interview a few strategists for Morgan Stanley, and had squeezed in dinner with Esther on Sunday night. She wanted to sound Esther out on a couple of other potential jobs in London. Esther had instructed Teddy to meet her at Zapata's, a Mexican restaurant on East Fifty-Third Street, and had warned her not to expect a swanky business restaurant. Teddy was grateful not to have to put on formal clothes, and turned up at the restaurant in straight-leg jeans dressed up by a Myrène de Prémonville white shirt with tortoiseshell buttons. Esther was waiting, a beer in one hand and a cheroot in the other.

'Don't give me a hard time, here, Teddy. I know booze and butts are *verboten* for the baby, but my survival depends on them, so what can I do? Anyway, it's only a lite beer – you know, low alcohol. Did you have a good flight? What do you want to drink? A margarita? Frozen or on the rocks? Or a tequila shot? You look like you could use one. How's that schmuck Paul Driver? You want me to order for you? You look great – I'm never gonna squeeze into a pair of jeans again. You know what, though? You should get your hair cut while you're over here. I've got a great guy – Ramon at Davir on Fifty-Sixth. He'll sort you out. Tell him I sent you. He's a fag, of course – but then, what man isn't in this city, you know what I mean?'

Teddy had forgotten how much, and how quickly, Esther talked. She had hardly even sat down. After a couple of drinks, Esther paused to draw breath. 'So tell me, Teddy. How does my future look? Are we talking rosy, or are we talking not a dog's chance, huh? Give it to me straight.'

'As I told you on the phone, Esther, it's no go with FRG. They've picked the German, and he's almost sure to accept. We need to tweak his contract a little, but I'm sure it will go through. I'm really sorry about it.'

'Not your problem. Not your fault.' Esther spoke with her mouth full, and Teddy watched in horror as she heaped a couple of tablespoons of raw jalapeno peppers on to her chicken enchilada, and topped with it several dollops of sour cream. God only knew what it was doing to her stomach, let alone her baby.

'Hey, Teddy – don't look like that – I'm eating for two, remember. So tell me how I blew it. I need a little coaching, I guess. My interviewing style's pretty rusty.'

'There's nothing wrong with your style, Esther,' Teddy

said reassuringly. 'If you ask me, there's something wrong with your sex. Paul's excuse was being worried about your being American, but I just don't believe that. When I worked at Steinberg's, I have to say that I wasn't very aware of discrimination — I guess I was lucky, and it was an American house — and I probably wasn't very perceptive, to be honest. You get accustomed to things, and then you don't notice them any more. As a headhunter, I'm more and more aware of what an uphill fight women have.'

Esther nodded vigorously. 'Tell me about it, sweetie. I've worked for American houses all my life, and most of the time it's so uphill I'm hanging on by my fingernails! So what are we going to do about it? Roll over and die? Hell, no!' She bit savagely into the enchilada.

'I've had a few ideas. I'd like to introduce you to Marcus Drucker — '

'Nice Jewish firm.'

'You got a problem with that?' Teddy joked. 'I'd also like to approach Fletcher Fielding, and I'd like you to go see Anderson Squires when you're in London.'

'Anderson Squires?' Esther frowned.

'Yes. They're one of ARC's rivals. Headhunters.'

'No, Teddy. I'm happy sticking with you. If you can't get me a job, I'm sure no one else can.'

'That's flattering, Esther, but you're wrong. Go and see them with my blessing. They're very well connected with First Boston, and with JP Morgan, and you owe it to yourself to see them. Do it,' she urged.

'Okay, okay, I will. I'll do whatever you say, Teddy.'

'How about giving up smoking?'

'You're worse than my doctor,' Esther growled, but ground out her cigar.

After dinner, the two women walked up Lexington Avenue together. Esther had persuaded Teddy to stay at Jack's, a restaurant that kept four suites for visitors and had a lot more charm than most of New York's hotels, and wasn't far from her own apartment. The entrance to the private rooms, which were more like mini-apartments, was through the bar of the restaurant. Teddy and Esther said their goodbyes outside on the street, Teddy promising to keep Esther informed of any progress, Esther promising to cut down on the cigars. As Teddy pushed open the door of the restaurant, she came face to face with Mike. For a moment, she thought she must be mistaken – there were a lot of tall, good-looking dark men in New York – but the expression on Mike's face left her in no doubt.

'Teddy!' He jumped up from his table, leaving his two companions. 'What are you doing here?'

'Well, I haven't come here to find you. I'm staying here. I'm on a business trip.'

Mike looked her up and down. 'You don't look like you're on business . . .'

'I just flew in today,' Teddy snapped. 'Look, Mike, you'd better get back to your friends. I'm tired, and I want to go to bed. It's four o'clock in the morning my time.'

'Come on, Teddy, this is the coincidence of a lifetime! It's an act of God. You won't see me in London, you're always hanging around with your mate Charles . . . give me a break. Let me buy you a drink. Just sit down for ten minutes, okay?'

Teddy eyed the two men at Mike's table doubtfully. They peered back at her curiously, craning their necks for a closer look.

'Don't worry about them. They're just a couple of guys from Steinberg's. Come and sit over here.' He took her by the elbow and drew her towards a little table in the window. 'Would you like some champagne?'

'No, Mike. All I'd like is to go to bed.' Teddy didn't allow him a chance to offer her any assistance. 'Alone. I'll have a glass of wine. House red. Just one, and then I'm leaving, do you understand?'

'Sure, sure.' He pulled out her seat and hung up her jacket. Mike was all eagerness, very much on his best behaviour, showing Teddy a degree of charm that she hadn't seen for a long time. Charm didn't come naturally to Mike; he had learnt it as one learns a foreign language, and although he had mastered the vocabulary, his accent betrayed him as a foreigner.

'So what are you up to in New York, Mike?'

'Just seeing the troops, really. I'm running the book from here for a few days.'

'How is the New York desk coping without Glory? Or should I say, how are you coping without Glory?'

Mike's face reddened. 'Don't tease, Ted. How many times do I have to tell you that it was an accident?'

'How many times do I have to tell you that it wasn't an accident, Mike? An accident, if I have my definition correct, is walking under a bus, or falling under a train, or breaking your neck. An accident is *not* screwing a female colleague. And accidents tend not to be repeated; they only happen once.' She spoke sarcastically, her resentment surfacing in her voice.

'You're right. It wasn't an accident. It was a mistake. A big mistake.'

Teddy didn't comment. Mike lowered his voice, speaking quickly and intensely. 'Doesn't it matter to you that I'm desperate without you? Doesn't it make any difference that I'm really sorry? Why do you want to throw everything away because I fucked up once – '

Teddy raised one eyebrow at Mike's choice of words.

'Okay, okay, more than once. I just fucked up, okay? But I won't do it again. It taught me a lot, Teddy. It taught me that I need you. I do. I really need you. Since we broke up, I can't sleep properly, I can't concentrate on work, I feel like

I've lost my taste for everything. I can only think about what a jerk I've been.'

'How unfortunate.' Teddy looked over his head at the lights twinkling on the street outside. The faces of Mike's colleagues were reflected in the window, and she could see them laughing and pointing towards her, straining to hear what Mike was saying.

'Teddy, will you listen to me? Will you give me another chance? Will you marry me?'

Teddy acted as if she hadn't heard. 'Mike, will you give me a cigarette?'

He looked confused. 'You don't smoke.'

'I want a cigarette. Will you give me one, or shall I get my own?'

He shook out a Marlboro, lit it and passed it to her.

'What were you saying, Mike?'

'I asked you to marry me.'

Teddy inhaled deeply on the cigarette, relishing the sensation of smoke hitting the back of her throat. 'Why?'

'Why should you marry me? Because I need you. Because I love you more than anything else.'

She exhaled slowly. 'Don't you want to know how *I* feel?'

'Of course I do! It's all that matters to me!' He grabbed her free hand, holding it tightly.

'I don't want to marry you. I no longer love you, but if it's any comfort, I no longer hate you either. I don't really want to spend time with you, not for a while at least. I don't regret that you slept with Glory – however many times you did it – because it showed me that however much you may love me, or *need* me, it's not the way I want to be loved.'

'I know that, Ted. I've learnt how to love you, it wouldn't happen again.'

'That doesn't matter. If I loved you, I don't think it would bother me if it did happen again. But I don't love you. You're like a child, Mike. You act without thinking; you are so much the centre of your own world that you can't even predict how other people will be affected by your actions. If you *were* my child, I might make the effort to understand, and make allowances for your lack of emotional development. I could at least feel that you were moving forward, progressing towards some sort of sensitivity and maturity. But you're not a child. I don't see any signs of change, I don't see any signs of progress. I don't want to be pompous, Mike. It's just that, frankly, I've had enough of it all.' Mike listened to her in silence, still gripping her hand. 'You are childish in that you always have only one thing in your mind. If you need sex, and Glory's there, you'll have her. If you're hungry, you'll eat. If you need me, you can't think about anything else except getting me. I don't think you are capable of thinking about more than one thing at the same time. So do yourself a favour. Concentrate on what matters. Think about your job. Think about trading. I'm surprised you're not, seeing how shaky the markets are. Put me out of your mind. I assure you that you won't find it very difficult.' She stubbed out her cigarette, and stood up. 'You just worry about your positions, and I'm sure that if you need sex, you'll find someone to satisfy that. Now I'm going to bed. Good-night.'

She walked across the restaurant, looking coldly at Mike's colleagues, who nudged each other in the ribs as she approached them. She halted as she reached their table, and addressed them politely, in her clearest and most British tone. 'Would you two fine young gentlemen be very kind and help my friend over there? He will be able to fill you in on any snippets of our conversation that you might have missed.'

When Teddy climbed, exhausted, into bed, she didn't

bother to turn on the television in her room. Had she done so, she would have learned that Mr Helmut Schlesinger, the Bundesbank president, Mr Carlo Ciampi, the Italian central bank governor, Mr Theo Weigel, the German finance minister, Mr Jean-Claude Trichet, director of the French Treasury, Mr Norman Lamont, the UK Chancellor, and finally, Mr Robin Leigh-Pemberton, the Governor of the Bank of England, had spent a busy weekend on the telephone. They had agreed to a seven per cent devaluation of the Italian lira to be followed by cuts in German interest rates. Later that Sunday night, Norman Lamont issued a press statement:

'The UK government has repeatedly made clear that there is no question of any change in the central parity of the pound against the Deutschmark, and that we will take whatever action is necessary to secure that. Sterling's central rate therefore remains at DM 2.95.'

The *Daily Express* heralded the weekend's activity as a stunning coup by Mr Norman Lamont.

Had the devaluation of the lira left the pound in the firing line, or would sterling be saved by the reduction in German interest rates? It was anybody's guess. When Glory heard the announcement, she leapt into a high-five slam with Malcolm Fairchild. Jack Delavigne, arriving in Sydney, was told of the immediate surge of the dollar and sterling against the German currency on the Australian and New Zealand exchanges. He breathed a sigh of relief. Mike Miccinelli didn't hear the announcement. He sat in Jack's Bar three floors below Teddy's bedroom and downed his fourth bourbon.

Jack phoned into the office to speak to Malcolm first thing on Monday morning. Malcolm was smug, his voice dripping with satisfaction.

'I'm not going to say I told you so, Jack.'

'Aren't you, Malcolm? You surprise me.'

'I'd just like it understood that from now on you don't interfere with our trading decisions. We know what we're doing.'

'I think the jury's still out on that, Malcolm. Let's see how things look when I get back in on Thursday.'

'For God's sake, Jack, nothing's going to happen between now and the French referendum. It's going to be quiet till next Monday morning, I guarantee it.'

'As I said, we'll review the situation on Thursday. Keep me posted if there are any new developments, okay? I want to be informed.'

'Tell you what, Jack; we'll let you know if Lamont so much as takes a crap, okay? We've got our fingers on the pulse here.'

On Tuesday morning, September fifteenth, Glory came into work late. She had made the most of Mike's absence in New York by persuading Malcolm to take her to Annabel's the night before. Glory looked as though she had gone to bed at eight o'clock with a mug of hot chocolate. She could see Malcolm Fairchild at his desk, the telephone pressed to his ear. Malcolm looked as though he had not been to bed at all; his eyes were red-rimmed, his face was puffy. He was unshaven; he looked fifty, and felt twice that. Glory knocked on the glass wall that separated his office from the rest of the dealing floor, and when she had attracted his attention she pouted her lips and pressed them to the glass, leaving a scarlet smear. Malcolm waved nervously, and Glory walked slowly to her position on the trading desk, swaying her hips deliberately. She flicked on her dealing screens, and surveyed the currency markets. As she expected, they were quiet. She put her feet up on the desk, exposing nearly thirty-eight inches of leg – seventy-six, if you counted both of them – and relaxed. It looked like she was going to make a profit on sterling, which was fine and dandy. What was even dandier was that Mike had told her point blank that she would lose. In a couple of hours, she would be able to call him and gloat.

'Hey, Glory, did you see the news flash?' Mark, one of Hayes' principal traders, work her from her daydream.

'Don't tell me, the Deutschmark's been devalued,' Glory drawled.

'Nope. Honest John Major has just announced that he's cancelled his trip to Seville for Expo' 92.'

Glory sat forward and stared at the Topic screen. Mark wasn't lying; the Prime Minister had cancelled his trip, 'to deal with business on his diary'.

'Stupid *asshole*!' Glory hissed.

The implication that the Prime Minister had got slightly behind schedule, which seemed like an innocent and deeply boring news item to most people, was enough to send those working in the Square Mile into a state of apoplexy. Whatever Downing Street said, whatever pat excuse they provided, there could be only one conclusion: John Major felt sufficiently uncomfortable about the health of the British pound to cancel his trip. The Prime Minister was going to stay by the sickbed. Shortly before lunchtime, currency dealers around the world renewed their assault on the Italian lira, and the volume of trading in the pound against the D-mark began to gather pace ominously. As the trades ticked across the screens, it was apparent that the pound was heading in only one direction: down. By the afternoon, the pound had hit 2.80 D-marks, despite the fact that the Bank of England had intervened in the markets, and was rumoured to have spent three billion pounds defending the currency. It didn't take a mastermind to realise what had happened. Dealers had made a killing on the lira. They had been able to buy it cheap, knowing full well they could sell it back to the Bank of Italy for a guaranteed profit. It was the central banks against the rest of the world. It was no contest. Now it seemed that dealers had developed a taste for blood; they wanted a re-enactment of the lira devaluation, and had picked a new, and somewhat diffident, co-star: the Bank of England.

The air in Malcolm Fairchild's glass office was thick with smoke. Glory reclined in an armchair, a couple of other currency traders leant against the edge of Malcolm's desk, peering over to watch the screens, whilst Malcolm paced up and down.

'What the fuck is going on?' Malcolm asked nobody in particular. 'Why the fuck is sterling crapping out?'

'Chill out, Malc. It's perfectly clear what's happening – to me, anyway.' Glory examined her nails, intent on pushing back the cuticles to form perfectly matching half moons.

'Do you think you could enlighten the rest of us poor fools, Glory?'

'Sure, it's like this. There are rumours hitting the market every five minutes. Whenever that happens, you get crazy movements. The pound has been jittering around 2.80 down to 2.78. Its absolute floor in the ERM, as I'm sure you clever big boys all know, is 2.7780. As the pound nears its floor, all the central banks will have to intervene. Either intervention will work – '

'Or it won't,' said Mark glumly. Mark Mitchells was known as Eeyore in the market; he could be relied upon to take the most pessimistic view of any situation.

'Or it won't,' Glory repeated slowly. 'In which case, Lamont will raise interest rates sharply, we will make a lot of money, and everyone will go home and call it a day.'

'And the country will be plunged into ever deeper recession.'

'Who gives a fuck about the country? We're not paid to give a fuck about the country, we're paid to make money, and that's exactly what I'm going to do.'

'How high do you think rates will go, Glory?'

'I'd say that Lamont would be prepared to take them up to fifteen per cent,' she drawled.

'Fifteen fucking per cent! That would take a five per cent hike! He can't do that!'

'I don't think he'll have to. If he took them up to twelve per cent or thirteen per cent that'd do the trick. His credibility is on the line, for Christ's sake. He said that the probability of realignment within the ERM is zero. So far, they've tried to talk themselves out of trouble. It hasn't worked. Traders are banking on what you've just said, Malc. They're betting on the fact that Lamont won't have the guts to raise rates. What I'm saying is, he does have the guts. He's going to have to find them. And I'll be behind him all the way,' she finished smugly.

Malcolm resumed his pacing. He wanted to believe Glory. It was Malcolm's nature to believe whoever put their case most strongly. His staff thought of him as 'the sponge'; he absorbed whatever was swilling around the dealing room, and at the faintest hint of pressure, the merest squeeze, it all dribbled out again.

'So what do you think we should do?' He sounded almost like a little boy asking his mother for guidance.

Glory smiled at him. 'It all depends on the size of your balls, hun. We had a rule on the desk at Steinberg's: no position is ever a hold. If you think something's goin' down, then you sell more of it; if you think it's goin' up . . .' she paused, looking at each of the three men in turn, 'you buy more.'

Malcolm stared at her, his eyeballs nearly out of their sockets. 'Glory, at the moment you are sitting on a long position of nearly a billion pounds. Are you honestly suggesting that we go into the markets now and buy more?'

Glory smiled, but didn't look at him. She resumed her manicure. 'Like I told you, hun, it all depends on whether you've got the balls.'

Malcolm chewed his own nails, his eyes darting nervously from Glory, to Mark, to Dick Rogers, and back again to Glory. 'I'm going to have to phone Delavigne. I'll have to tell him what's going on. I can't sanction buying more. I'll call Sydney.'

Glory stood up and smoothed her microscopic skirt over her bottom. 'Don't do that, hun. We *know* he hasn't got the balls. The question is, do you?'

When trading wound down at a little after five p.m., sterling had touched its lowest possible level of 2.7780 Deutschmarks, its lowest point since Britain had joined the ERM in October 1990. The Italian lira and the Spanish peseta had also fallen dramatically.

From the artificial safety of his glass box, Malcolm Fairchild watched his traders leaving the floor; Glory defiant, Mark hangdog, the rest of them showing every emotion on the scale except detachment. Turmoil on the currency markets played strange tricks on the psyche of traders; it was like alcohol. It made some traders aggressive, some excited, and others comatose. On a few, a very few, it seemed to have no discernible effect at all. Years of trading had given them an immunity. Malcolm reached into the bottom drawer of his desk, shuffled under a pile of papers, and withdrew a fifth of Scotch whisky. He poured a large splash into his coffee cup, took a couple of swigs, and stared morosely at the Reuters screen, its sickly green light reflecting in the pallor of his face.

In Regent's Park, Mr Ray Seitz, the US Ambassador to the Court of St James, was hosting a dinner party. Amongst the great and the good in attendance were the Chancellor of the Exchequer, Norman Lamont, and his wife, Rosemary. Their fellow guests barely noticed Mr Lamont twice leaving the table to talk to Treasury officials at Whitehall.

In Threadneedle Street, Robin Leigh-Pemberton, the Governor of the Bank of England, was also on the telephone. He placed two calls to a house near Frankfurt, the home of Bundesbank president, Helmut Schlesinger.

On Primrose Hill, Candida Redmayne stood in her state-of-the-art kitchen and instructed her caterer on the arrangements for dinner. She had ordered a cold cucumber and mint soup, to be served with tiny *empanadas* of spiced lamb, followed by *boeuf en croûte*, followed by a selection of French cheeses. Satisfied that the correct procedure would be followed, she returned to her solitary guest in the smaller drawing room.

At Heathrow's Terminal Three, Teddy Winnington waited impatiently for her bag. She had made the mistake of checking it in, and was now paying the price. Her return flight from New York had been delayed for six hours owing to suspected terrorist activity at JFK airport, and the fact that she had been deemed SFU, or suitable for upgrade, by American Airlines, and had therefore flown back first class, had done little to appease her. She longed to get home and soak in a hot bath. She seemed to be spending her whole life in airports.

At the very centre of the forty thousand square foot dealing room that was the heart of Steinberg's New York head office, Mike Miccinelli watched the screens in silence. There were early reports from one of the news wire services that in an interview with the *Wall Street Journal* and the

Handelsblatt, a German newspaper, Helmut Schlesinger had clearly implied that a sterling devaluation could not be ruled out. Mike drew a slip of paper from his jacket pocket, and dialled the number of a mobile phone in London.

In Sydney, it was two minutes past six in the morning. The plushly carpeted corridors of the Sydney Regency were being vacuumed by an army of cleaning staff. The machines worked swiftly and silently, so as to avoid disturbing the hotel's guests. On the seventeenth floor, Jack Delavigne woke from a short and restless sleep. He phoned Malcolm Fairchild, but was told that he had left the office. He phoned Malcolm at home, but there was no reply.

In the calm, discreet offices of the Federal Reserve Bank of New York, and the Bank of Japan in Tokyo, two teams of dealers bought the pound sterling throughout the night.

CHAPTER THIRTEEN

There were few people working in or near the Square Mile of the City of London, few people in Whitehall, Parliament Square or Downing Street, perhaps few people in England at all, who would forget where they were on Wednesday, September sixteenth and what they were doing. In weeks to come, people would speak of their experiences on that day in hushed tones. It would take on the significance – temporarily – of November twenty-second, 1963, the day President Kennedy was assassinated. The assassination that occurred on that wet Wednesday in September was of no one so important, no one so charismatic. It was the assassination of the British pound, and it wasn't just the currency that was devalued; it was the national identity of the country.

Glory got up and dressed to kill. She had told Malcolm that she intended to make a killing, and although she was not as confident as she had led him to believe, she was smart enough to know that appearances mattered. It wasn't so much what you knew, it was that you looked as if you knew that counted. She wore a lime green short skirt, a white shirt of a gauzy, translucent fabric, her lime green sports bra clearly visible, and a screaming yellow box jacket. Her heels added a good three inches to her height, taking her well over six foot. She drove to the office, took her normal quick route around Trafalgar Square – the one reserved for taxis only – and marched into the office at five past seven a.m. She greeted her colleagues and her boss breezily, and asked Malcolm to get her a cup of coffee. He did so obediently.

'So, Malc. Did you make your mind up? Can I go in and buy the hell out of the little sucker?'

'I can't let you do it, Glory. It's not that I don't trust you – I do, I really do – but the exposure's too large as it is.' His voice was edgy, his eyes pleaded with her not to expose him. 'Let's run with it as it stands, okay? I'm behind you all the way.'

'I know you are, hun; and that's a kinda nice place to be, if I say so myself . . .' Despite the early hour, and despite the tension that hung over the dealing room, Glory's suggestiveness was as powerful as ever. Malcolm felt an ache in his groin.

As the markets opened, six men hovered around Glory's chair, watching the all-telling screens.

'There he goes – there goes Hard Eddie . . .' muttered Mark Mitchells.

'Hard Eddie – who's hard Eddie?' Malcolm simply didn't have a clue.

'Eddie George – deputy governor of the Bank of England; he's in charge of market operations. You can see the Bank intervening in the markets – they're buying heavy.'

'Sure they are! They know a good buy when they see one. Shop till you drop, Eddie baby, shop till you drop, as we say in the good ol' US of A.' Glory actually seemed to be enjoying herself.

They watched the prices flicker on and off the screen, keeping an eye on the volume of trades done to indicate how the central banks were reacting.

'We are talking two, maybe three billion so far – '

'Chicken shit. You're gonna see a whole lot more than that – the pound and Deutschmark are two of the most traded currencies. If they want to beat the speculators, it's going to cost them a lot more than three bill – '

'Fuck me sideways! I haven't seen anything like this in all my born days.'

Only Malcolm was silent. He chewed on an unlit cigarette, too frightened to resume a habit that had taken him a painful year to quit, and too nervous not to have something in his mouth. He knew damn well he should call Jack. He had a slew of messages from him, culminating in a fax ordering him to phone Sydney, but he didn't want to call. He didn't want to speak to Jack. Jack would order him to close out the position at a loss, and Malcolm was depending on the hope that Glory was right. If she was, this would be the biggest killing of his career, and he desperately wanted to be able to tell Jack to stick it up his arse and for once hold his head up high. Malcolm had never felt that he was regarded as a good trader. This was his chance, and he didn't want to blow it. He didn't want Glory to think he had no balls. He didn't want to take orders from Jack. What he *did* want to do was slip off to the Gents and have a couple of swallows of whisky, but maybe he'd get a chance later . . .

Harry Howell slipped on his white jacket, grabbed his pad and screamed along with the best of them on the floor of the London stock options exchange. He was a big man, not overweight, but somehow gave the impression of looking slightly seedy and unfit. He was under thirty, and yet he looked jowly, pasty-faced with tinges of red high in his cheeks, around his eyes and on his nose. His physical decline had been dramatic in the past four years. Up until then he had played rugby for Swansea, and had done well until a spot of trouble in the scrum had ended up taking three quarters of his right ear clean off his head. He'd decided to call it a day, and although his hair was thinning, it was long enough to sweep over his mangled ear. He had two passions in life, rugby and bridge, and when retirement from rugby had been forced upon him, a careers consultant had drawn the perfectly natural conclusion that his skills suited him for only one place: the London options exchange. His prowess on the rugby pitch had made him an immediate hero amongst his fellow option traders, and his experiences in the scrum stood him in good stead on the floor of the exchange. The two battle grounds had a lot in common.

This morning, the atmosphere wasn't just chaotic – it was demented. Harry pushed himself to the forefront of the crowd, delivering a well-aimed elbow shaft here, and mid-shin kick there. There was no referee on the exchange. It was a free for all, and that was why he liked it. When Harry arrived there four years earlier, he thought that options were to do with whether you preferred salt and vinegar or cheese and onion, smoky bacon or barbeque beef . . . there were endless options. Boy, was he ever wrong. There were only two kinds of options: a *call* option, which meant that you could buy a certain stock – or share – in a company at a certain price, and a *put* option, which meant that you could sell it. At a certain price, of course. Harry dealt in options. His special stamping ground was options on financial stocks, meaning banks, brokers, whatever other shit the market wanted to trade. If one of his clients – one of his mates, as he called them – thought they might like to buy some shares in a company, but didn't want to put a whole shit-load of money up front, they called Harry and bought a call option or two from him. If the stock went up, they could buy it at the previously agreed price, and hold on to it or sell it for a lot of money. If the stock went down, they lost their money, but only a fraction of what they might have lost if they had bought the underlying stock itself. Now, if another mate thought a stock was heading south – heading down, in layman's terms – then they could buy a put option on the stock from him. If the stock went down, they had a guaranteed price at which they could sell it, and they'd make a lot of money. If the stock went up – well, they lost their money of course, and it was their own lookout. People made and lost fortunes in the options market, particularly on a day like today. It was a game for real professionals, and if Harry had been an amateur at rugby, he was a real pro on the options exchange. When it came down to the bare bones of the business, options were fun; options were dangerous; options were the life blood of the City. Being an options trader was like playing against the All Blacks and the British Lions rolled into one. It made life worth living.

Harry looked around the room, and caught sight of a shambolic figure scurrying across the floor. It was Hugh Kent, a *Financial Times* journalist who had been assigned to cover the equity options market for the paper. Harry was fond of the journo, mainly because Hugh was different from the rest of the people on the floor; he spoke thirteen languages and could hold a conversation in Latin, for God's sake – not that he found many traders able to converse with him. Harry called him over on the pretext of giving him an insight into what was going on, and took the opportunity to slap him soundly on the back several times. Hugh scribbled in his notebook, thanked Harry and scurried away. For the rest of the day, Hugh couldn't understand why the mad men on the floor laughed at him even harder than usual. It was only when he returned home and removed his jacket that he found the sign Harry had stuck there: 'Kick Me.' To Hugh, the atmosphere on the options floor was his worst nightmare; it was like being assigned to report on the activities of a zoo in hell. To Harry, it was his idea of heaven.

Harry's mobile phone, which was as important to him as an artificial limb, buzzed at him. He held it up to his good ear: 'Harry Howell, trader to the stars, trader by royal appointment to Her Majesty – '

'Harry, this is Alex Fitzgerald at Steinberg Roth.'

Harry was surprised. He knew Alex, of course; everybody knew Alex. But Alex rarely placed orders himself. He had a team of stock and options traders to do it for him.

'Fitz, my old mate! What can I do you for?' His years in rugby had taught him never to be intimidated by anyone; Harry treated everyone the same, be they a heavy hitter like Alex Fitzgerald, or his Auntie Gladys in Cardiff. None the less, he was curious to see what Alex was doing. Steinberg tended to be big traders in the options market.

'Harry, I want you to start buying October '92 put options at 260 on Hayes Goldsmith. I want you to buy gradually and discreetly, you hear me? I want you to buy up to twenty-five thousand contracts, but I want a minimum of twenty thousand, and buy in small lots, okay? I'm giving you the whole order, so work it carefully. It shouldn't be too hard. Do it at best – I'm not too bothered about the price.'

'Let me make sure I heard you right, Fitz. Up to twenty-five thousand contracts, October '92s, 260, on Hayes Goldsmith?' Harry was aghast.

'You got it. But the important thing is that you buy carefully, gradually, discreetly, quietly. You understand me, Harry? Do this well, and there could be a lot of business coming your way. It's for the account of Steinberg's principal book.'

'Got it, Fitz. No sooner said then done. I'll get on to it right away – '

'– and Harry? Buy five thousand contracts for my personal account, okay?'

'Got you. Twenty-five thousand for Steinberg's, and five thousand for Mr Fitzgerald PA.'

Harry shoved the phone into his breast pocket and

thought hard. What Alex had told him to do was to buy twenty-five thousand contracts: each contract was worth one thousand shares, so that meant twenty-five million shares – a fucking enormous order, and over ten per cent of the total shares outstanding – that would entitle Alex to sell Hayes Goldsmith stock at 2.60 a share at any point between now, September sixteenth and October thirty-first. Hayes Goldsmith's stock was currently trading at 3.98. Alex Fitzgerald, or Steinberg Roth, clearly had some reason to believe that the stock price of Hayes Goldsmith was going to fall by well over thirty per cent before October was out. He whistled. Well, bugger me, he thought. If the story was good enough for Alex Fitzgerald, and good enough for Steinberg Roth, it was certainly good enough for Harry Howell. He'd buy another five thousand contracts for himself. Personal account: PA. This kind of order was the dog's bollocks. It merited something special – some sort of celebration. It was a quarter past ten in the morning. Harry trotted off to the Gents, settled himself comfortably in a cubicle, and took a slim envelope of paper from his inside pocket. He balanced the sheet of paper carefully on his knee, unfolded it, dug around in another pocket for what looked like a silver straw, and inserted it up his nostril. Moments later, he flushed the loo briskly and stepped out to the washbasins. He peered into the mirror. A thin trickle of blood emerged from his nostril, taking a path along the edge of his lip. He wiped it away with the back of his hand.

'Another billion dollar deal, me old china,' he muttered, smiling at his own reflection. 'Another fucking billion dollar deal.'

Shortly before eleven o'clock in the morning, a team of Treasury and Bank of England experts gathered around a Reuters screen in a small office in Threadneedle Street.

They were waiting for the news report. Moments later, a two per cent increase in interest rates was announced, taking the UK base rate to twelve per cent. Eight pairs of eyes were glued to the small, blinking screen, waiting for the sterling price to tick up on the back of the news. Silently, they watched the pound stay glued to the bottom of the ERM grid at 2.7780. More than one person in that room knew then that it was all over, bar the shouting. The battle, a short, furious *blitzkrieg*, had already been lost.

It was a little after six in the morning that Mike Miccinelli heard the news of the UK base rate hike. He went into the office early, and took the only course of action open to him. Two hours later, when the US foreign exchange markets officially opened, Mike, and thousands of other American forex dealers, money managers, pension funds and corporates began to sell the hell out of sterling. Billions of pounds poured out of markets like water running out of a tap. The central banks of the world tried desperately to lap it up; to lap up a puddle the size of the Atlantic Ocean.

Malcolm Fairchild ran to the Gents, his stomach muscles in spasm. His fear erupted in an explosive bout of diarrhoea. He flushed it out with whisky.

Glory's eyes narrowed to two yellow, tigerish glints as she looked at the screen. The fuckers hadn't raised the rates enough. Three per cent, four per cent would have done it. Two per cent was a case of too little, too late. Her nails drummed the hard top of her desk. She couldn't pull out now. Their only hope was another hike – there would have to be a further increase in base rates. When Malcolm emerged from the bathroom, she glared at him, her eyes flashing dangerously, daring him to challenge her. They didn't exchange a word. Malcolm opened his mouth a couple of times, but nothing came

out. He retreated to his office. His pretty secretary – every
woman in Malcolm's department was pretty – popped her
head round the door.

'Malcolm? Jack just called from Sydney airport. He's
catching the last flight out from Sydney.'

'How long does the flight take?'

'Well, if it's direct, it's usually about twenty-four hours
– so he'll be in around lunchtime tomorrow.'

Malcolm swallowed. 'Open the window, could you,
Jane? And clear those fucking pigeons off the ledge. I have
a feeling I'm going to need it.'

His bowels twisted again.

At two fifteen p.m., the Bank of England fired its best
shot, straight at the broadside of the currency markets. Base
rates were raised to fifteen per cent, effective immediately.
The shot missed by a mile. The pound stayed wedged at the
bottom of the grid on 2.7780, and God only knew where it
would go when the official market closed.

Glory sat alone at her desk. Her fellows traders had left
her to manage the sterling book, whilst they frantically
sold the peseta, the lira and the Danish krone. They sold
anything they could spell. Malcolm hovered at Glory's
shoulder. He cleared his throat.

'Glory, I want you to close your sterling position. Sell
it.'

She turned on him. 'You amaze me, Malcolm. You're not
just a budgie-brain, you're a fucking moron. I *can't* sell the
sterling position. It's a billion fuckin' pounds. Where the
hell am I going to get a price to sell that? We'll drive sterling
down to 2.70 if I try to unload that in these markets. You're
going to have to sit it out, Malc.'

Malcolm's shoulders slumped.

'And Malc? It's not *my* position, babe; it's *our* position.
And don't you forget it.'

'Then we're finished. We're fucking finished.'

Glory shrugged. 'Look at it this way, babe. What have we got to lose by holding on for a couple of days till things settle? It's only money.'

Only money. They stood to lose thirty to forty million pounds, if Malcolm had done his sums properly, and he wasn't even sure he'd done that. Glory was right about one thing. They couldn't do anything else about it today. The central banks were obliged to stop their intervention at four p.m. After that, the markets would be thin. They were forced to wait for Thursday to see if there would be a little more volume. Maybe people would sleep on it, absorb the interest rate hikes and the pound could even trade up a little on Thursday. He decided to leave a skeleton staff on night duty, just in case. The rest of them might as well pack up and go home. God only knew if they'd have jobs to come back to. Malcolm decided he would sleep in the office. Jack would expect it, after all.

At six p.m. Glory, Malcolm and a handful of traders sat around the dealing room, drinking whisky and telling jokes. Malcolm was getting steadily drunk. He didn't like the jokes – it seemed like graveyard humour to him.

'How many people does it take to collapse the price of sterling?' This was Dick Rogers.

'How many?' they chorused, except for Malcolm.

'Just two; Norman Lamont and Glory McWhirter.'

They all shrieked with laughter, the laughter of desperation. Malcolm shivered. It wasn't even funny. He cleared his throat.

'Look, guys. There's no point everyone hanging around. I'm going to stay here tonight – I only need a couple of people to man the phones – '

'I always say three's a crowd, Malc: how about if just you and me man the desk together? After all, you're my main man . . .'

Malcolm blushed. He hadn't slept with Glory – yet – although everyone on the desk had received the clear impression that they were bonking each other stupid. Glory didn't know the meaning of the word discretion.

'All right Glory, that sounds fine to me.' He tried to assume a brisk, professional manner, but his voice trembled. 'The rest of you can leave. Glory, I'll, ah, be in my office if you need me.' He strutted away, but not fast enough to miss Dick Rogers' comment:

'He means he'll be in the men's room, Glory, tossing his cookies with terror!'

Malcolm continued walking to his office, accompanied by guffaws of laughter.

In New York, Mike was feeling good. He may have lost money on the krone, but he had just about made it back by selling sterling. He slightly regretted that he wasn't in London – it would have been fun to be on the desk, in the centre of things – but he could control his position perfectly well from New York. And besides, Alex Fitzgerald had given him strict instructions to stay in New York until summoned home. Suddenly, all ten lines on his phone lit up green and started blinking. He ignored them. He leant close to the screen, and read the news flash. He read it again, more slowly. There was no mistake. It was official.

At seven thirty-six p.m. London time, Norman Lamont had emerged from the Treasury office into the circular courtyard and told the world press that Britain had suspended it's membership of the ERM.

'Michael! I've got Fitzgerald holding for you on line five!'

Mike hit the button. 'Yo! This is Mike Miccinelli.' Mike sat up. It looked like he was being called home. 'You want me in London, Fitz?'

'Like hell I do. I want you right where you are.'

'Big news, hey, Fitz? What happens now? Lamont resigns, sterling goes – my bet's around 2.60, no? What a day, boss man, what a day. You saw the Swedes took rates to five hundred per cent? Can you fucking believe it?'

'Michael, I want you to leave the desk.'

'You're kidding me.'

'No. Leave the desk, and go to Lombardi's office on the sixth floor. It's empty. He's sitting outside my office now. Go there and call me back immediately on my private line. You got it? Do it immediately.'

Mike shook his head, hung up, walked across the dealing floor and waited for the elevator. He got off on six, and strolled to Lombardi's corner office. His secretary was not in sight. Mike went in, shut the door, and called Fitz back.

'Michael. This is the chance. This is the market move we've been waiting for.'

'I don't know what you're talking about, Fitz.'

'So listen hard. I'm only going to say this once. You're not going to make partner Mike; not this year, not next year, not before the year two thousand. We want to buy Hayes Goldsmith. You want to make a lot of money. I do too. We have the same needs. All you have to do is to call Glory McWhirter. Call the bitch, and tell her to confirm that you did a trade at four p.m. today London time. You sold her one billion pounds at 2.7780 D-marks – that was the London close – at four p.m. today. You write out a ticket to confirm the trade, she writes out a ticket. You get a five million pound bonus on the thirty-first of December. You hear me? Five million *pounds*. You decide what to give to Glory. You and Glory get to do whatever the hell you like. You want to stay, you stay. You want to fuck off and do your own thing, I'll back you.'

There was a silence.

'Fitz, I don't feel good about this.'

'Trust me, Mike. You're gonna feel real good about it. I'm gonna do whatever it takes to make you feel fuckin' fantastic about it.'

'What about the tapes, Mike? All dealing calls are taped.'

'Not this one, Mike. Listen to me. When do you get out the tapes and listen to them?'

'When a trade is disputed.'

'Right. Well, this trade ain't gonna be disputed, is it? You're gonna book the trade, and when it clears through Hayes Goldsmith tomorrow morning, Glory's gonna accept the trade, isn't she?'

'Someone will insist on listening to the tapes.'

'No one's going to listen to the tapes, Mike. The only guy who would isn't in the fuckin' country. By the time he gets back to London, it's gonna all be over. The tapes get wiped, lost, I don't give a shit.'

Mike was shaking. 'I don't feel right about it, Fitz. What if somebody finds out?'

'There are only gonna be three people who *ever* know about this, Miccinelli. You, me, and the lovely lady. You think I'm gonna tell anyone? You think Glory's gonna go along to her boss and say, hey, buddy, guess what I did, I lost you a fucking fortune legitimately, and then doubled the loss in a fraudulent trade? Are *you* gonna tell anyone, Mike? I don't think so. Now the longer you leave this, the harder it's gonna get. So tell me one thing, Mike.'

'What?'

'Did you trade with Glory McWhirter today?'

Mike paused. He couldn't even think. He had butterflies in his stomach, his head was pounding, he knew this was the big decision of his life. What did he want? Five million pounds, and a hold on Alex Fitzgerald for life? Five million quid and the chance to do whatever he wanted?

Five million quid and his freedom? Or fucking zero and his integrity?

'As a matter of fact, I did trade with Glory today.' He spoke slowly.

'That's nice, Mike. What did you trade?'

'I sold Glory a billion pounds. Sterling. Against the D-mark.'

'At what rate?'

'2.7780 D-marks. That was the London close.'

'And when did you trade it?'

'Fifty-seven minutes past three p.m. Fitz. Three fifty-seven.'

'Good man, Miccinelli. Now you have a good time in the Big Apple, okay? You have a real good time tonight. Find yourself a lady – not too much of a lady – and show her a real good time. On me. And you hurry on back to London. Not too fast, say you fly back Friday, okay? So we better say goodbye, Mike. You've got a call to make, and you better make it on Lombardi's line, you read me?'

'Yes I do. It's been good talking to you, Fitz.'

'Likewise. I always like talking to a rich man. See you, Miccinelli, my friend.'

Alex Fitzgerald hung up the phone. He called Candida.

'It's me. We're on. We're doing it on the withdrawal from the ERM. You've got to do your stuff now, Candida. That kid is all lined up. Get Malcolm Fairchild out of the office now, and keep him out until tomorrow morning. Do whatever you have to do. Around nine a.m. tomorrow, you call Joanna French at *The Times* and tell her what's going down. She'll spread it for us.'

'Right, I'll handle it.'

'We've arrived, Candida. It may have taken eight years, but we've done it. Together.'

Candida hung up. She had no sense of togetherness. She felt alone, and was happy to be alone. She had work to do.

When Mike hung up the phone, his eyes were smarting with tears. He would have given anything in the world – maybe not five million pounds, but anything else – to have somebody to call and discuss this with. If he was still with Teddy, he would have talked to her about it. Who else could he talk to? Not his parents – he hadn't spoken to them in over a year. He hadn't even told them that his engagement was off. And anyway, they wouldn't understand a situation like this. Who else could he call? A fellow trader? No way. One of his old male chums? He didn't really have any. There were guys he played poker with, guys he played football with, guys he drank with, even; but there weren't any guys he really talked to. There was only one person he trusted, and that was Alex Fitzgerald. There was only one person he could call now, and that was Glory McWhirter. He pushed his hair off his forehead. He was sweating like a pig. He dialled her direct line. The phone rang and rang. There had to be somebody in Hayes Goldsmith, for fuck's sake – it was only eight p.m., on the most dramatic trading day of all time. They must have left somebody on the desk.

'Yeah?' Glory sounded breathless.

'Glory, it's Mike.'

'Well, wha'd'y'know . . . How are you, Miccinelli?'

'I'm doing fine, Glory. I wanted to know what you were up to.'

'Well, my boss and me are holding down the fort. We were having a little drink to celebrate – '

'*Celebrate*? Glory, you must have been wiped out. What the fuck are you celebrating?'

'My boss is celebrating the profits he thinks he's gonna make tomorrow. He's so fuckin' drunk, he thinks we're gonna come out of this smelling like roses. I don't have the heart to tell him he's gonna be R-E-D-U-N-D-A-N-T.' She spelled out the word as if she were talking in front of a child. 'I'm just celebrating getting drunk.'

'So you think it's all over, Glory?' Mike was speaking carefully. He knew this conversation was being recorded on the Hayes Goldsmith dealing room tapes, and he watched every word he uttered.

'Yup. It's all over. We're up the Swanee. I should never have left Steinberg's, Miccinelli. That was my big mistake.'

'That was it? Not what happened at four o'clock?'

'Four o'clock?' Glory sounded confused. 'Yeah, I guess.' Was that when the bastards decided to pull out of the ERM? She couldn't remember what had happened when, or what Mike was referring to.

'Glory, have you got your mobile phone with you?'

'Sure.'

'Switch it on, okay? I'll talk to you in a minute.'

Glory was clearly going to be some time on the phone. Malcolm watched her through the glass wall, and did his flies up. It was ironic that the day had ended like this. He had expected it to be his day of triumph, and instead, it had been a disaster. There was no doubt in his mind that somewhere around lunchtime tomorrow he would be sacked. Ironic that on this day of all days he should receive the best blow-job of his life. It had blown his mind. Ironic that it should come from the woman who had cost him his job, and what little credibility he had managed to retain. His phone rang.

'Malcolm Fairchild?'

'Darling, it's me.'

Malcolm sat bolt upright. 'Candida!' She never called him at the office. She hardly ever called him at all.

'Darling, it's been such an awful day – God knows I've found it a strain and I'm not nearly so involved or so important as you. How are you bearing up?'

'It's a nightmare.'

'Look, I thought you might need a little . . . sustenance. I'm at home. I'm cooking dinner. I have some champagne on ice. Get in a taxi and come round.'

'Candida, darling, I'd love to, but I can't tonight. I have to watch what happens – I'm responsible for the desk . . .'

'Malcolm, you need to eat. You need to relax. You'll be able to handle things better if you have a little R and R. And I know just how to give it to you. You won't be away from the office long. We'll have a quiet dinner, then you have a long hot soak in the tub, and I'll give you a back rub. Then you can go back to the office refreshed. You'll be at your best. I promise. Malcolm? Please let me help you. You've helped me so much . . .'

Malcolm couldn't resist it. He saw Glory pick up another call on her mobile line and slipped out of the office. He left his jacket on the back of his chair and his briefcase open on the desk, so that if anyone came in they would think he was still somewhere in the building. It was an old trick, but it usually worked.

Mike smoked a cigarette quickly. So far, so good. If anybody listened to the tape, all they would think was that Glory had done the trade with him at four o'clock and then got drunk. It was credible, all right. He dialled the number of Glory's mobile.

'Glory, I've thought of a way out of this. You're going to lose your job, right?'

'You bet I am. Are you making me an offer?'

'In a way. I want to make a suggestion.'

'You don't have to suggest anything, sweet thing. Just get your sweet ass over here, and Glory will take care of the rest . . .' Her voice was slurred.

'Glory, I want you to write out a dealing ticket. Say you bought one billion pounds from Steinberg Roth New York at three fifty-seven p.m. – before the announcement – at an exchange rate of 2.7780.'

'Miccinelli, you're forgetting something. I've already got a billion pounds on my book at an average price of 2.8085.'

'I'm not forgetting it, Glory. That's precisely why I'm saying this. You've got nothing to lose. You're out the door already. Even if you clear out your position at 2.70, which I doubt, you'd still be taking a loss of thirty-eight million quid. I see pink slips from Wall Street to Liverpool Street. Tomorrow morning, you say you did the deal at four, just before the central banks pulled out of the market, because you firmly believed that interest rates were going to be hiked again tomorrow morning. How could you have predicted that Lamont would withdraw from the ERM? You just decided to double your position to bring your average cost down. So you were wrong. So Hayes are exposed two billion, not one billion. So big deal. You're fired, but you're going to be fired anyway. You do it my way, and I'll write you a cheque for a million pounds – or take cash, if you'd rather – the day they sack you. Like tomorrow. You don't do it my way, and you'll walk out the door with an empty pocket and a pink slip in your hand. I doubt your boss is gonna give you a glowing reference. What do you say, Glory?'

'I like what I hear, Miccinelli. Tell me more.'

'There's nothing more to tell. You've got nothing to lose. You just write out the ticket, and then tomorrow you go shopping. No questions asked. We never mention it again. I'll just hand you the cheque.'

Glory pulled a pad of dealing slips towards her, and picked up a pen.

'All you've got to do, my sweet,' Mike was still trying to persuade her, 'is fill out a tiny little dealing slip. One billion sterling, bought from Steinberg Roth New York, at three fifty-seven p.m. London time, on the sixteenth of September, for 2.7780 D-marks. It couldn't be easier.'

'You're right, Miccinelli. I've already done it. It didn't take a minute.'

'So walk it along to the settlements room, my darling, and leave it in the pile for them to process tomorrow. Then you go out and buy yourself something to wear. I'm taking you out on Saturday night.'

'I'd rather buy nothing to wear, and stay in.'

'It's your call, Glory.'

'Hey, Miccinelli? Why are you doing this for me?'

'I wanted to help you out of a spot Glory. I'm a nice guy, and I like you.'

'You're full of shit, but I don't give a fuck.'

Two tickets were written. At the cost of three phone calls, and two small scraps of paper, Hayes Goldsmith was likely to lose over one hundred million pounds, and nearly half of it was owed to Steinberg Roth.

Candida was wide awake, waiting. Next to her, Malcolm slept, snoring lightly. She had managed to persuade him to come to bed – which had been a cinch – and to make love to her – which had been slightly more difficult, owing to the amount of alcohol Malcolm had consumed – and to get some sleep, which had been the easiest thing of all. Malcolm always fell asleep post-coitally. Sometimes he fell asleep pre-coitally. Candida waited for the phone to ring. She knew he would call her first, and her hand lay draped over the receiver, ready to pick it up instantly so that it wouldn't disturb Malcolm's barely earned rest. It rang.

'Hello?' She spoke softly.

'It's me. It's done. Like clockwork. All your worries are over, baby. You just lie back, and do whatever comes into your pretty head. I want to thank you for your help Candida. From the bottom of my heart.'

'It's been a pleasure doing business with you, Fitz.'

'Yeah? Well, there's plenty more coming your way, baby.'

'That's what I like to hear.'

'D'you think maybe I should come visit and celebrate?'

'It might be a bit of a crowd. I'm not alone . . .'

'Don't tell me that shithead is still there! You go beyond the call of duty, honey. You are a one hundred per cent professional. I mean it.'

'Well, I thought we should be on the safe side. I didn't want him wandering back to the office.'

'I just hope it wasn't a complete waste of your time, baby. I hope you got something out of it, you know what I mean?' Candida could imagine his face as she listened to him; she could just see it cracking into a lascivious grin.

'No, Fitz. I didn't get anything out of it.' She spoke crisply. 'I was never in this thing for kicks, and I certainly wasn't in it for sex. You know that.'

'So keep it for me, baby. Keep it warm for me.'

'I'll do that.' She hung up, and relaxed against the pillows, staring into the darkness of her bedroom, a crisp white Porthault sheet pulled tight over her breasts.

Of course she hadn't had an orgasm with Malcolm. She'd never had an orgasm with Fitz, either, although he didn't realise it. She couldn't remember when she last had had an orgasm. The problem with men – at least with the men she knew – was that their dicks weren't attached to any other decent part of them . . . not to their hearts, and more significantly, not to their brains. It disgusted her that Fitz didn't use his brain when he made love. He was a clever man, after all. Somehow, it bothered her less making love with Malcolm. She suspected he didn't even have a brain, so she couldn't complain about the faulty connection.

She looked at him now, peaceful, quiet, smiling, even. For the first time, she wondered what all this would really mean to Malcolm. Looking at things rationally, it was likely that he would be ruined. He might never work again. Candida bore Malcolm no grudges; she didn't want him to suffer, but she hadn't seen a way to avoid it. So be it. He had stopped snoring. Candida was on the point of kicking him out of bed. He had served his purpose, and could no longer do anything to upset her carefully laid plans. She thought through the next stages in the plan, guessing what Jack would do. By the time he returned from Australia, not only Malcolm, but also the market would know that Hayes Goldsmith had suffered a ruinous loss. The stock price would collapse. Alex Fitzgerald would be sitting on a huge profit – partly profit from the foreign exchange position, and partly from gains on his option position. He would use the proceeds to acquire stock in Hayes Goldsmith. Basically, because he owned so many put options, he would be in control of the stock price of the merchant bank, at least for a little while, and would be able to build a stake at the level he chose. Alex had told her it would be a matter of days rather than weeks before Jack Delavigne was calling him 'boss'. The thought made her smile. She glanced at Malcolm again. She felt in a good mood, and wanted to make a benevolent gesture. She'd let him sleep in. It might be the last trouble-free sleep he had for a long time. Maybe she'd even stretch to making him a cup of coffee in the morning.

CHAPTER FOURTEEN

Glory sat on Malcolm's desk, swinging her heels, her lips set in a sulky pout.

Malcolm was shaking. 'I can't believe you did that Glory. Tell me you didn't do it. You're teasing me, right?'

'No. I told you, Malcolm. I did the trade just before four o'clock with Mike Miccinelli at Steinberg's.'

Malcolm shook his head in disbelief. 'But I remember when we talked about it yesterday afternoon, we discussed a sterling position of a billion. Now you're telling me we were running two billion? It's unbelievable. I know you are just trying to wind me up.'

'Now, why should I want to do that, hun? This isn't exactly a joke for either of us. When we talked about it yesterday, I *was* running a billion. At four o'clock, I just got the feeling that rates were going to be pushed right up after the markets closed. The way I looked at it was that intervention clearly wasn't working, and that Major and Lamont had given their 'absolute commitment' to the ERM. So I bought another billion. I thought a short overnight profit on that would level off our losses. I was wrong, I admit it. I didn't guess that they could possibly renege so far on their commitments as to pull out of the ERM. I made an error of judgement – '

Malcolm nearly choked at the word.

'– a *big* error of judgement. But don't get pissed off with me. You should be pissed off with Major and Lamont. They are a real team, those two. An awesome duo.'

Malcolm sat down. He couldn't control his trembling. 'But why didn't you tell me', Glory?'

'To tell the truth, Malc, I *did* tell you. I distinctly remember telling you. My mouth was wrapped around your, ah, *member*,' she said the word with her distinctive accent, pronouncing it mem-bah, 'and I took my lips off for just a moment to update you on our position. I have to say, hun, as I remember, you looked mighty pleased, but maybe you hadn't heard what I was sayin'. . .' She looked at him from the corners of her eyes. Malcolm held his head in his hands, his fingers pressed against his eyeballs. He couldn't remember. He could remember the blow-job, but he couldn't remember any conversation. By the time he had reached Candida's house he had been pretty legless, and by the time he had finished dinner, he hadn't been able to remember his last name. He felt Glory's hand on the back of his neck.

'Maybe you don't want to tell Big Jack that I did tell you about it. Maybe it's better if we don't mention what happened here last night.' Her foot kicked the waste-paper basket. 'Maybe you wanna remove that bottle of whisky from the trash.' Malcolm groaned. 'Maybe I should start closing the position now. Wha'd'ya think, boss?'

'Yes. Yes, you're right. Just close the position. Sell it out. Dump the whole fucking thing before it gets any worse. What's the rate now?'

Glory leant across him to look at the screen. Even in his disturbed state, Malcolm felt aroused by the warm, slightly salty scent of her.

'It's around 2.65, but it's a very thin market. I don't think we're gonna be able to dump the whole load. It looks like all the activity is in the krona, the franc and the dear little Irish punt. They're all heading south.'

Malcolm's head sank back into his hands. 'Do what you

can, Glory. Just sell what you can. I've got to think about
what to tell Jack.'

Malcolm was amazed that Glory was taking it all so
calmly. He knew, and she almost certainly knew, that she
was about to lose her job, and yet she was behaving like
she'd lost a game of Trivial Pursuit. Shit. He didn't have
time to worry about Glory. She could look after herself.
He had to worry about his own neck.

It seemed only moments later that Jack paced into his
office. Malcolm looked at Jack's white, pinched face and
tried a nervous smile. He regretted it instantly.

'Malcolm. Somebody on the dealing floor has just told
me that we currently own two billion sterling, bought
at an average price of 2.793. I nearly sacked him on
the spot. On the grounds of an execrable sense of humour.'
Jack spoke very quietly, his tone far more menacing
than angry. 'Would you be kind enough to tell me why
we have such ludicrous rumours flying around our own
dealing floor?'

Malcolm couldn't meet Jack's eyes. 'It's true, Jack,' he
blurted out. 'I'm afraid it's true.'

'You must be absolutely mad. How could it be true?'

Malcolm shuffled some papers on his desk. 'We, ah,
were running a position long the pound, as you know,
somewhere around the one billion level.'

'Continue.'

'Well, yesterday afternoon, we — well, Glory, that is —
decided to double up.'

'Glory decided to *double up*?' Jack repeated the words
slowly, carefully enunciating each syllable.

'That's right. She felt there would be a major rate hike
this morning.'

There was silence in the room.

'Only there wasn't.' Malcolm said lamely.

'But Malcolm, I assume that when the announcement of

withdrawal from the ERM was broadcast, you instructed Glory to sell the position in New York?'

Malcolm didn't reply.

'Malcolm, look at me please.' When Jack saw Malcolm's red-rimmed eyes and pleading expression, he knew the truth.

'You *did* sell the position, Malcolm?'

'Well, not exactly. Not quite. Not yet, that is.'

Jack leant his hands on Malcolm's desk, his long body leaning over it until his face was inches from Malcolm's own.

'Why not?' It was a straightforward, simple question.

'I wasn't here. I didn't hear about it until this morning.'

Jack swung away from the desk. He wanted to hit Malcolm, wanted to punch him harder than he'd ever wanted to hit anyone.

'I see.' Jack stared out of the window into Cannon Street. 'Malcolm, would you be kind enough to get me the trading reports, all yesterday's dealing tickets, and ask Glory to join us? I don't suppose you've listened to the tapes yet?'

'The tapes?' Malcolm looked confused. 'No, it didn't occur to me. There's nothing dodgy about this, Jack. Glory confirmed the trade. It was properly booked and settled.'

'I'd like to see the records now, Malcolm.' Jack's tone was icy with contempt.

Jack studied the dealing report before speaking to Glory or Malcolm. It looked perfectly in order. The ticket was clearly written at three fifty-seven p.m., the amount was for one billion pounds, and the rate was at 2.7780, the pound's absolute floor in the ERM. The facts supported Malcolm's story. One of Jack's eyebrows snaked upwards as he saw that the counterparty was Steinberg's, but it wasn't all that surprising. They were very big players in the market, one of the few houses able to deal in that sort of size, and of course, Glory had friends there from her days on the desk. There were only two things he couldn't believe. He couldn't believe that Malcolm had left the office early on Black Wednesday, as the papers were calling it, and he couldn't believe that Glory had been so confident in her judgement that she had backed it with a second billion. She had taken an enormous risk for what would have been a relatively small profit even if she had been right. And she had been hideously wrong.

'Glory, did you clear this trade with Malcolm before you dealt?'

Glory sneaked a sideways look at her boss, and winked quickly. 'No. I guess I should have, right?'

'You should have, right.'

'So does that mean the trade isn't legit? Does that mean we can renege on it?'

'Unfortunately not. The trade stands. You did the trade, whether you had the authority to do so or not, and Hayes Goldsmith is not a house that reneges on trades. I could of course approach Steinberg Roth and argue that they should have realised that a trade this size would be out of your limit, but they would quite reasonably argue that they had assumed it had the approval of the head of trading. Not an unreasonable assumption.' He looked darkly at Malcolm. 'I could also order an investigation, on the basis that I believe this to be a fraudulent transaction, and I'm not sure that that isn't the best route to go. None the less, we would still have to settle with Steinberg's, and then attempt to reclaim from our insurers. I suspect we would have a very tough fight to get any money back. We don't have a policy protecting us from insanity or idiocy on the part of our traders. What is the current position? How much have you sold?'

'Oh, round about four hundred million.'

'I see. So we are still long over one and a half billion pounds, correct?'

'Give or take a pound or two.' Glory seemed almost complacent.

'All right. Malcolm, I would like you to instruct Mark Mitchells to take over Glory's position and close it. Sell at any price. Glory, I would like you to leave the office now.'

'Are you giving me the sack?' She looked at him boldly, and Jack met her gaze head-on.

'No. At the moment I am suspending you temporarily for unauthorised trading.' He turned to Malcolm. 'That's correct, isn't it, Fairchild? The trade *was* unauthorised?'

'Oh, yes, yes. Absolutely. Yes.' Malcolm spluttered hurriedly, avoiding looking at the woman.

Jack slowly turned back to Glory, and caught the look of absolute contempt she gave Malcolm. It could only mean that Malcolm *had* approved the trade, and was now trying to use Glory as a scapegoat. The man disgusted him.

'So as of now, Glory, you are suspended. I most probably will terminate your employment contract, but I need to look into the technicalities first. Could you leave a contact number with my secretary, and I will call you in the next few days.'

'It would be a pleasure, Jack.'

Glory sauntered out of the room, followed shortly by Malcolm, shuffling nervously. He caught her up near the lifts.

'Glory? Glory, wait.'

She turned, and blessed him with her widest and most natural smile. 'Yes, hun?'

'I just wanted to say – I just wanted to say – ' He took her hand in his. 'I just wanted to say that if there is anything I can do for you – *anything at all* – you only have to say the word.'

'Gee, that's real sweet of you, Malc.' She looked thoughtful. 'You know, hun, as a matter of fact, there *is* a little something – '

'Say it. Anything. Really.'

'You could kiss my ass.' She flashed her perfect teeth at him, and stepped into the lift.

Teddy had gone through von Budingen's contract with a fine-tooth comb, anticipating any quibbles the German might raise. She wanted to tie this up. She felt a little sad today that she had opted out of the hustle and bustle of investment banking. She could well imagine the thrill of being on the dealing floor during these frantic markets, and briefly regretted stepping on to the sidelines of the game as a headhunter. But, as Candida had said, they were going to end up as the umpires. This sort of market crisis generally provoked a wave of City reorganisations, and that meant hirings and firings, and that meant more business for headhunters, and ARC were poised on the edge of the battlefield. Teddy didn't quite agree that headhunters were like umpires in the game; she thought they were more like vultures, picking away at the rotting corpses. Anyway, it added a little spice to life. She strolled down to Candida's office to ask a couple of quick questions about pension rights.

Candida, as ever, was on the telephone. 'Joanna? It's Candida.' She waved Teddy to a seat.

'I heard something this morning that I thought you might be interested in.' She chuckled. 'Yes, I think it *is* a good one.' 'It's about Black Wednesday all right.' 'Well, a certain little bird told me that late yesterday afternoon a trader – who shall be nameless – at a certain bank in Cannon Street bought over a billion pounds, shortly before Lamont's announcement.' 'Yes, it would happen to be number twenty-two Cannon Street.' 'Well, I'd say the loss is a *very* sizable per cent of their capital, yes.' Candida laughed. 'You've got to do your own verifying, Jo, I can't do it all for you, but I am certain of it, yes.

You might also like to mention the fact that neither of the two senior directors – Fairchild and Delavigne, it's up to you if you want to name them – were available during the crisis.' 'No, I don't know where they were, how could I know that?' 'I thought you'd like it.' 'You don't have to give me anything for this one. It's a freebie.' 'Okay, lunch would be nice. Are you going to the Guild lunch?' 'Yes, I stupidly agreed to talk to the sixth form about careers for women in the City.' 'See you then.'

Candida beamed at Teddy. 'That was Joanna French on *The Times* Diary. She and I were at school together.'

'Oh really? Were you talking about Hayes Goldsmith?'

'I certainly was. From what I hear, Teddy, you don't want to touch that stock with a bargepole. In fact, now that I think of it, let's pull a list of every Hayes employee off the database – quite a few of them are going to be looking for jobs, and we might as well strike whilst the iron is hot.'

'What's happened?'

'They were caught wrong-footed on the pound yesterday. Your friend Glory McWhirter. I always said she was stupid. God knows why they hired her. Let's you and I go through the list this afternoon, and then we can make a few discreet approaches. It's the early bird – '

'That catches the worm.' Teddy completed the cliché for her, before raising the pension provision questions.

When Teddy left Candida's office, she felt troubled. She respected her boss, admired her even, and yet she felt that Candida's obvious elation over what could only be a disaster for Hayes Goldsmith was pretty sick. Of course Candida hated Jack, and despite the fact that Teddy liked him – rather a lot – she didn't find it hard to understand why. Tommy's death had been the sort of tragedy that women frequently didn't recover from, and if Candida's way of coping was to hate Jack, then she was entitled to feel that way. Jack clearly accepted it, so why shouldn't Teddy? None the less, she felt uncomfortable. She knew that part of her discomfort arose from the fact that she hadn't told Candida about her own blossoming friendship with Jack. She was embarrassed to mention it, and yet felt that she was nursing a dirty secret from a woman who was at the least her boss, and she hoped her friend. And then there was something else. She could accept that Candida hated Jack, but why did she seem to pursue him? Why had she been so insistent to get Glory hired by Hayes? Why did she leak bad news about Hayes Goldsmith to the press? And how the hell had she heard about it so quickly? Questions chased each other round in Teddy's mind as she settled down to print off the list of 'potentially mobile' or 'warm' bodies at Hayes Goldsmith. Teddy could justify pulling off the list, but if there was poaching to be done, then Candida could damn well do it herself. She found she could no longer take Candida's side. If Jack was having a hard time, Teddy certainly wasn't going to make life any harder for him. She faxed through a provisional contract to Paul Driver, and to Konrad von Budingen's home fax. Konrad was likely to sign it in the next couple of days, and then ARC would have something to celebrate. It didn't cheer Teddy up. Her spirits sank lower and lower as she worked. She needed to talk to a friend. She needed to talk to Charlie. It seemed like weeks since she'd seen him.

'Bartholomew? This is your conscience talking.'

'Teddy, you old cow! How splendid to hear you! I was just about to unplug the phone because I'm so pissed off listening to snivelling little fund managers whining about how much money they've lost. I came in this morning to find a pile of messages from them on my desk, and I dumped each and every one into the bin. Every time one of the little creeps calls up and starts blubbering about their bond portfolios I want to punch the air and say, "Yes! Another one bites the dust!"'

'Charles, you take such pleasure in people's suffering I think you ought to change jobs. I think you ought to be a wheel clamper. That's what would really fulfill you.'

Charles laughed. 'Good idea. I'd make a hell of a lot more money than I'm likely to do here, anyway. And it would be more fun.'

'So, what have you been up to, Charles? You haven't called round, you haven't phoned, you haven't asked me to dinner . . . I miss you.'

'That's sweet, Teddy. Warms my heart. What's happened to all your lovers? You must be desperate if you're calling me for a date.'

'Is there something wrong with wanting to keep in touch with an old friend?'

'Nope, but if it's money you want, I haven't got any, and if you want to borrow my mobile phone again, the answer's no. You failed to keep your side of the trade last time.'

'I simply want to know how you are!'

'Well, it just so happens that I'm very well. Very well indeed. I have some news for you. I think I'm about to get married.'

'Teddy sat bolt upright. 'Charles! How extraordinary! Who is she? Do I know her? When did this happen? Is she pregnant?' She didn't believe he was serious.

'You revolt me, Theodora. Every time I think I have plumbed the bottom of your sordid little psyche, you sink to new depths.'

Teddy laughed. 'So when do I get to meet her? Before the wedding, I hope? Can I be your best woman?'

'You can be the senior bridesmaid if you like. Except that you are really too old to be a bridesmaid. When is somebody going to pick you off the shelf and dust you off, Winnington?'

'Fuck off, Bartholomew. Now let's make a date. Dinner at my place. You, me and . . . what's her name?'

'Gertrude. Gertie to her friends.'

'You're kidding me.'

'Yes, I am. Her name is Melissa, but it doesn't matter, because you are not going to meet her. Not now, not next week, not at the wedding, not ever.'

'Charles! Why not? I'm your best friend!'

'And that's precisely why you are not going to meet her. The truth is, I'm ashamed of you, Ted. She might not want to marry me if she met you.'

'Oh, I won't let you down! I won't tell her about your bad habits, and I *promise* I won't mention that night in Naples . . .'

'What night in Naples?'

'The night you got completely smashed, and so angry with all of us that you came downstairs wearing my black bra and pants and fell over the stereo . . .'

'Oh. *That* night in Naples. As a matter of fact, Ted, I had forgotten about that. Anyway, the real reason I don't want you to meet her is nothing to do with you. It's to do with her.'

'What's wrong with her?'

'Well, for starters, she's a lot older than me. She's fifty-four. And she's ugly. And boy do I mean *ugly*. In a contest between her and a potato, the potato would win hands down. I'm marrying her for her money. I'm tired of scrambling around, struggling to make ends meet. I want to live in luxury, and I don't want to sit in this shithole talking to fund managers who couldn't manage a piss-up in a brewery. That's the truth, Ted. She's old, she's ugly, but she's rich. Who was that guy? The rich guy?'

'Jimmy Goldsmith? Donald Trump?'

'No – richer. Croesus. That's the bloke. She's as rich as Croesus.'

'Listen, Charles. Tomorrow night I'm going down to Matty's for the weekend. She told me to bring a couple of friends – '

'Boy, that's going to be a tough one for you! You're going to have to trawl the old address book – '

'– so why don't you and old moneybags come down to Wiltshire and join me?'

'I'll think about it. It's not such a bad idea. Maybe Melissa and Matty could talk about what it was like during the blitz – you know, swap stories about coupons and things. I'll ask her.'

'Good. Come down around dinner time, Friday.'

'Gotta dash, Ted. I've got Fidelity holding on the line, and *this* guy is one of my favourites!'

'Why is that? Is he that rare thing, an intelligent fund manager?'

'Hell, no! He's *so* stupid . . .'

'How stupid is he?' Teddy played the straight man obligingly.

'He's *so* stupid, he still thinks securities have something to do with burglar alarms . . .'

Teddy felt much better after her conversation with Charles. She still didn't believe he was really going to get married; he probably just had a new girlfriend, and the affair would run its average couple of months. If he was really getting married, Teddy wouldn't have been quite so happy about it. It was one thing not marrying a man yourself, but it was quite another handing him on a platter to some other woman. If this was serious, she was going to find it pretty hard to be happy for him. Things seemed normal again. She wanted to call Jack, and make sure he was all right, but each time she called his secretary said he was 'in conference' and couldn't be disturbed. Teddy declined to leave a message.

Jack had spent most of Thursday talking to his fellow

directors. He would remember it for a long time as one of the worst days of his life. He had nothing to pin on Glory, other than the fact that she was a godawful trader. He had nothing to pin on Malcolm, other than the fact that he had hired Glory, and left the desk without making sure the position was controlled. Things were deteriorating fast. Mark Mitchells had struggled valiantly, and dumped most of the pound position in New York, a market where liquidity had been a little higher than in London. Now Jack stood by his side. So far, Hayes Goldsmith were showing a loss of around ninety-eight million pounds, and there was more to come.

'What a fuckin' nightmare, Jack. What a day. The lira's been withdrawn from the ERM, the peseta has been devalued by five per cent, and the fuckin' Bundesbank are sitting on their arses refusing to bring down rates. It's World War fuckin' Three.'

'What's Lamont saying?'

'He ain't sayin' nuffin'. There's a nice little comment from Downing Street that all his Cabinet colleagues are right behind him; if you ask me, that's the worst fuckin' place they could be. He's not even gonna know which one threw the knife when it lands between his shoulder blades.'

'What about the pound?'

'Don't call it the pound, mate. It's not worthy of the name. Call it The Turd. The Turd Sterling. It's a bucket of shit, and I've been up to me elbows in it all day.'

Jack patted him on the back. 'Keep it up, Eeyore. I'll make sure you are rewarded for this.'

Mark looked at him seriously. 'You can't fool me, Jack. I haven't sat in this dealing room for fifteen years and not learnt that this is going to make our Christmas bonuses look like chicken shit. Don't worry about rewarding me, mate. This one's for you.'

'Thank you, my friend.'

Jack returned to his office. Hayes Goldsmith shares had taken a bath – down ten per cent – but that was in common with the financial sector as a whole. Once the news leaked out about this loss, they were going to fall a lot harder and a lot faster. Hayes were now in breach of every Stock Exchange and Bank of England capital requirement in the book. Jack had already addressed all the staff, telling them that this was vitally confidential, and that no one should discuss it with anyone outside the firm. He had guaranteed them their jobs – with Dick Belton-Smith's blessing – but he didn't think that would count for much when the future of the firm was clearly at stake. They had to find more capital to restore the equity of the firm, and his desperate bid was to do that before the news of the foreign exchange loss hit the press. That was why he hadn't sacked Glory on the spot. So long as she was under contract – even if she was suspended – she couldn't talk about the firm's trading positions. Both Jack and Mark slept in the office on Thursday night, Jack in his chair and Mark stretched out on the plush beige carpeting of the dealing room.

On Friday morning, the pound continued to fall. Selling pressure on all the ERM currencies against the D-mark was intense, and Mark closed out Hayes Goldsmith's position at 2.615. After asking Jack's permission, Mark left the office at lunchtime to spend a quiet weekend with his wife and kids. He wasn't at all sure that he'd bother to come back to the office on Monday. He felt as if the past three days had cost him ten years of his life.

Jack didn't care about the pound. He didn't even really care about whether Mark returned to the office. What he cared about was an article on page seventeen of *The Times*, an article by Joanna French, an old friend of Candida's, who had attended their wedding and innumerable dinner parties. It was a short piece, less than two hundred words, but each and every word was devastating:

'At least the Bank of England weren't entirely alone in their attempts to save the pound on Wednesday. They were nobly supported in their attempts by Hayes Goldsmith, who at the eleventh hour waded into the markets to rescue the ailing currency. Some say that Hayes' rescue attempt committed as much capital as the Bundesbank itself, and reliable sources indicate a purchase of a billion pounds shortly before the pound was withdrawn from the ERM. Senior executives Jack Delavigne and Malcolm Fairchild were yesterday unavailable for comment. Funny; neither of them were at the helm on Wednesday either. Poor old Hayes Goldsmith; a once noble institution, left rudderless on the Black Wednesday. Some City pundits, who favoured withdrawal from the ERM, are calling it *White* Wednesday. For Hayes Goldsmith, it was blacker than pitch.'

When the stock market opened, Hayes Goldsmith's share price fell immediately, like the proverbial lead balloon, to 2.50. On Wednesday, it had been trading at 3.98. Jack's worst fears were materialising. He had received three calls from friendly brokers who had told him that there was heavy selling pressure against his stock, and one of them had mentioned a rumour that somebody – unidentified – was controlling the stock through a large put option position. There was very little Jack could do except to ride out the storm. The lower the stock fell, the more likely it was that somebody – unidentified – would try to acquire a controlling stake in Hayes Goldsmith. That in itself wasn't necessarily a bad thing. The bank badly needed fresh capital, and the current shareholders were in no position to provide it. Jack's sole objectives were to safeguard the futures of his staff, and to try to salvage the reputation and existence of Hayes Goldsmith. The bank had been operating for something over three hundred years, and he was damned if it was going to be brought to its knees by the stupidity of Glory McWhirter and the incompetence of Malcolm Fairchild. He saw no route by which he could salvage his own reputation. It looked like his credibility was going the way of Norman Lamont's. He had no way of identifying who was controlling Hayes' stock price; once someone had built a position that represented five per cent of the firm's equity capital, they would have to declare their hand, but until then, Jack would be left in the dark. His intercom buzzed.

'Yes?'

'Jack, I've got Alex Fitzgerald on the line from Steinberg Roth. Do you want to take the call?'

'Yes, put him through.'

There was a short pause before Jack heard Alex's confident, ringing tones. 'Jack, old buddy! How you doing?'

'I could be better, Alex, to tell the truth.'

'Yeah, I saw the piece in *The Times* City Diary. Bum rap. Helluva time to be away on holiday, huh?'

'I wasn't on holiday, Alex. I was in Australia on business.'

'No kidding. Still a bum rap, though.'

'What can I do for you, Alex?'

'Hell, Jack, I was just calling to give you my commiserations. It could have happened to any of us, know what I mean? I just wanted to say, if there's anything I can do – *anything* – you just say the word.'

'Thank you Alex. I'll bear it in mind.'

'No problem. You know, Jack, if you're looking for a job . . .' Alex could hardly keep the glee out of his voice, and he didn't try to.

'I appreciate your concern, Alex, but I'm not looking at the moment.'

'Not at the moment, huh? Well, you take care now, old buddy. I shouldn't go jetting off anywhere if I were you.'

'No, I don't suppose I shall.'

'Well, you know where to reach me. *Ciao*.'

'Goodbye, Alex.'

Great. An offer of help from Alex Fitzgerald. Things couldn't get any worse.

'Jack? I've got Teddy Winnington on the line. Do you want to take it, or shall I put her off? I think she's a headhunter.' His secretary said the word with distaste, as if it were 'leper'.

'She is, Mary, but she's not trying to recruit me. Put her through.'

'Jack?'

'Hallo, Teddy. Good of you to call.'

'How are you?'

'I was hoping you wouldn't ask that. Frankly, I feel like I've been run over by a steam roller. I just wish another one would come along and finish the job.'

'Listen, Jack, this probably isn't the right time . . .' Teddy sounded uncharacteristically hesitant, 'but I wanted to ask you if you were free this weekend. I'm going to Wiltshire – to my grandmother's – with a couple of friends, and I thought you might like to come. If you're tied up, or you want to think about it for a bit, that's no problem . . .'

Jack didn't think about it for a moment. 'I'd love to come Teddy. How about if I drive you?'

'That would be great. Why not pick me up at home, say around six o'clock?'

'It might be a bit later, I'm not sure when I'll be able to get away. Things are a little – disorganised.'

'Whenever you like. I'll be at home from six.'

'See you later, then. And Teddy?'

'Yes?'

'Thank you.'

'Don't thank me, Jack. You don't have anything to thank me for. Bye.'

CHAPTER FIFTEEN

Jack arrived at Teddy's flat, apologetically, at seven on Friday evening, and they set off for the A303 immediately. Jack didn't seem in the mood to talk, and Teddy didn't push him. Tension sat on his face like a mask, and Teddy guessed that the best thing to do was to let him unwind quietly and in his own time. She relaxed into the soft leather seat and stared out of the window, watching Chiswick and Richmond pass by. She began to hum to herself.

Jack felt intensely grateful to Teddy for not chattering. She seemed to exude a spirit of calm, which was exactly what he needed right now. The road was clear, and he put his foot down, feeling the powerful engine of the car surge forward. For two days, he would try to forget about Hayes Goldsmith, and his problems. It began to rain. He heard Teddy humming happily, and glanced across at her. Her eyes seemed to be closed. He couldn't recognise the song. Teddy hummed out of tune. It could have been the National Anthem, or some new pop song for all he knew. The sound pleased him a great deal, and he smiled to himself.

Teddy sank further back in her seat. The rain was driving against the windscreen, which somehow increased the sense of privacy in the car. She felt as if she and Jack were alone in the world, and the small contained space of the car gave her a sense of exclusion, of intimacy and warmth. She could see Jack's hand resting on the gear stick. He held it in a strange way; most people clutched the knob of the stick tight like a ball, making a fist around it, but Jack held it gently in the tips of his long fingers, seeming to caress and nudge the stick

into place. It was a gentle manoeuvre, and yet supremely
in control. Watching through downcast eyes, so that she
could see nothing other than his left hand and forearm,
Teddy found herself thinking once again about how Jack
would make love. She nestled deeper into the seat, and
felt her body sinking heavily, pulled down and down, as
a warm glow spread from the pit of her stomach.

Jack looked at Teddy. He would have said she was asleep,
sleeping with a slight smile on her soft, full lips, except for
the strange, throaty humming. Jack suddenly realised what
he liked about the sound. It wasn't very melodic, one had to
admit. It was that Teddy wasn't afraid to do something that
she wasn't very good at – was actually very bad at. She just
did what she wanted to do, naturally and spontaneously.
Everything about her was inviting, but he forced himself to
pull away from the spell she cast, and concentrate on the
road. The minutes and miles slipped away as the rain fell
around them.

Matilda's house was a large, sprawling butter-yellow building, set in spacious gardens on the outskirts of the village
of Great Wishford. The gardens looked immaculately
maintained, the house less so: it had a much-used and
much-loved, familiar quality to it. As Jack's car came to a
halt in the driveway, an elegant, grey-haired woman came
out of the house to meet them bearing a large umbrella.

'Come in, darlings! Such terrible weather, and I was
so hoping you would all have a nice weekend! You
must have had an awful drive – come inside for a drink
at once.'

She ushered them into the house, and Jack caught the
heavy scent of late-flowering honeysuckle that embraced
the porch. It was a scent that reminded him of his own
childhood days in Dorset, a scent a million miles away from
London, two million miles away from Cannon Street.

'Granny, this is Jack Delavigne. Jack, my grandmother, Matilda Winnington-Smythe.'

'I'm delighted to meet you, Lady Winnington-Smythe, and grateful for your hospitality.'

'Call me Matty, please, Jack, and come in and warm up. Ludicrous to have a fire in mid-September, but I thought you might appreciate it. Teddy, take Jack to the small sitting room and give him a drink. Charles and his fiancée are waiting for you. I shall ask Barton to take Jack's bag to the yellow guest room; you can show him up when he's had something restorative. Now I must see Mrs B about dinner, and will join you shortly. We won't dress, as we're just family.'

The fact that Charles had told Matty that he was engaged to be married meant he was serious; he might have been flippant with Teddy, but never with her grandmother. As Teddy flung open the door of the sitting room, she saw two figures standing next to the fire pull apart suddenly and each look with intense absorption at an ornament on the mantelpiece. It was the tell-tale action of a couple caught in an embrace. Teddy went straight to the tall, willowy blonde girl who stood nervously near Charles, and kissed her.

'You must be Melissa. How lovely to meet you!' Teddy's enthusiasm was genuine and spontaneous. As soon as she had looked into Melissa's wide-spaced blue eyes and seen her shy smile, she knew she would like her. She turned to Charles with a frown. 'As for you, I'm not sure – *not at all sure* – that I've forgiven you yet. Moneybags indeed. Don't think you fooled me for a minute, Bartholomew. I've had you taped for a long time. Charles, do you remember Jack Delavigne?'

'Of course; we met in Paris, didn't we? Good to see you again, Jack. Can I introduce my fiancée, Melissa Brown?'

The foursome were soon joined by Matilda, who shepherded them into the dining room like a small flock of lambs. Dinner was pleasant and relaxed. Charles, Teddy and Jack began to discuss the sterling crisis, and the future of Lamont, until Matilda, conscious of Melissa's exclusion, changed the subject to include her. After a dinner of watercress soup, steak and kidney pie and rhubarb and gooseberry flan, Matilda asked to be excused.

'I think I'll leave you young people to your own resources, if you don't mind. I'm no longer good company after ten o'clock.' The twinkle in her eye and the spring in her step belied her excuse, but she resisted her guests' pressure to join them for a nightcap and withdrew.

As they left the dining room, Charles whispered in Teddy's ear. 'Ted, your grandmother has put us in the guest wing . . . what does that mean?'

'What do you mean, what does it mean? It means she wasn't born yesterday. It means she's telling you to sleep where you want, so long as you stick to your own wing and don't come near her. She always puts couples she likes in the guest wing.'

'So why hasn't she put you and your hunk – who, if I remember correctly, you told me that you hated – in the guest wing?'

'Because she never puts me in the guest wing,' Teddy said grumpily, 'and furthermore,' she stuck her nose in the air, 'he's not a hunk. He's just a friend. A good friend.'

'I *see*. That explains why you were watching him all through dinner.'

'I wanted to make sure he was comfortable, you arsehole. That's the way nice people treat their friends. Not that you'd know.'

Melissa and Jack had gone ahead to the sitting room, and caught none of this whispered conversation.

After an hour of whisky and chat, Charles and Melissa both claimed weariness, and said their good-nights. As they stood at the door, Teddy decided to take her small revenge on Charles.

'By the way, Melissa. Have you ever been to Naples?' She asked the question innocently, and saw Charles scowl.

'Naples? No, I don't think I have. Why? Should I go there?'

Teddy peered into her whisky glass. 'Oh yes, absolutely. You must. You must have Charles take you. He knows the city *terribly* well.'

Melissa smiled hesitantly, fully aware she had stepped into an in-joke, and turned to leave. After a flurry of V-signs at Teddy, Charles followed her. Teddy kicked off her shoes and curled up on the over-stuffed sofa, elbowing a black labrador out of the way.

'Jack, you look terribly tired. Are you sure you don't want to go up too? Don't force yourself to stay awake on my account.'

'Do you know, Teddy, for the first time in weeks I feel relaxed. I feel absolutely bloody exhausted, but I don't think I could sleep just yet. I'd just like to sit here and talk to you for a while.'

'Let me get you another drink.' As he accepted the glass from her outstretched hand, his skin brushed against hers, and Teddy felt a tingle of excitement. Charlie had been right. She couldn't stop looking at Jack, mainly because she was trying to read him, trying to see if he felt the same attraction that she did, the same magnetic pull. Teddy had always believed that she could tell if a man were attracted to her, and if she was honest, she would admit that most of the time she knew that most of the men would be. She had known it the instant she met Christian, and his desire had been a powerful motivating factor in her own attraction to him. But with Jack . . . she just couldn't tell. Maybe he was immune to her appeal, maybe he was attracted, but chose not to show it. Maybe he only had eyes for Candida.

She felt uncomfortable, restless, and couldn't settle in the room. While they talked, she moved from chair to sofa to chair, unconscious of her own movements, shifting the poor black dog every time he settled in a new spot.

'Jack, what actually happened at Hayes this week? You don't have to tell me if you don't want to, but I read the article, and then something Candida said confused me.'

'It's not a long story, Teddy, and there's no reason why you shouldn't hear it. When I left for Sydney, Glory and Malcolm were running the trading book very long of sterling. I didn't like it, but stupidly, I didn't do anything about it. I thought nothing dramatic would happen until next week, after the French referendum. By Tuesday, I realised things could move much faster and decided to fly back early. Whilst I was in the air, on Wednesday, Glory did another trade in sterling. A big trade. She bought a billion pounds shortly before the markets closed. According to Malcolm, he didn't know anything about it. I don't believe him. Not even Glory McWhirter has the balls to take on a position that size without clearing it with her boss. Anyway, the trade was done, properly and correctly. Malcolm left the office. That's another thing I'm finding hard to accept. You would think that no head of trading could have left the office on the day that interest rates were raised twice, and total central bank intervention must have been around fifteen billion pounds. Anyway, he *did* leave the office. I guess I made the mistake of expecting rational behaviour from Glory, who is clearly a lunatic, and Malcolm, who is clearly a moron. Three and a half hours later, Lamont breezed out of the Treasury and announced the withdrawal from the ERM. It cost us one hundred and eighteen million pounds. That's over a third of our shareholders' equity. That's all that happened. That, and the fact that the stock price has collapsed and Hayes is on the brink of ruin.'

'Oh God, Jack. I'm so sorry for you.'

Jack shrugged his shoulders in resignation. 'I learnt a lesson about good management. The first rule is, you hire good people to do a specific job. The second rule is, you keep out of their hair and let them do it. I followed the second rule well enough, but boy did I screw up on the first!' He smiled sadly at her, and took a long swig of Scotch. 'I should have had your advice before hiring Glory.'

'Well, you had Candida's, or at least Malcolm did, and she has far more experience than I do.'

'True. What would you have told me about Glory if I had asked?'

Teddy shrugged her shoulders noncommittally. There was no reason to tell Jack about Mike's betrayal. The fact that Glory was a screaming slag had no bearing on her abilities as a trader.

'I don't know. Mike hired her. He thought she was okay, but had a lot to learn.'

'Well, he was certainly right there! He didn't have much trouble taking advantage of her ignorance, anyway.'

'What do you mean?' Teddy asked sharply.

'Didn't I mention it? It was Steinberg Roth that Glory traded with. I think it was the New York office though, so I suppose it wasn't with Mike himself.'

Teddy stood up, and paced across the room. 'But Mike was in New York. I met him there. It could have been Mike.'

'No matter. It doesn't really make any difference now if she traded with Attila the Hun. Whoever it was quite rightly did the trade, and took her, and Hayes Goldsmith with her, to the cleaners. The only significance in it being Steinberg Roth was that I had the misfortune of receiving a gloating phone call from Alex Fitzgerald today. He actually offered me his help, but he was only calling to rub my nose in it.'

'That creep.' Teddy gulped at her whisky as if trying to wash a bad taste out of her mouth.

'I am assuming he was the one who told the press. It certainly wasn't one of my boys.'

Teddy shook her head slowly. 'Jack, I don't know if I should say this, but it wasn't Alex who told the press. It was Candida. I heard her talking to Joanna French about it.'

Jack closed his eyes, and pinched the bridge of his nose between those beautifully long fingers. Teddy wanted to hug him, but stood aimlessly in the middle of the room.

'Well, that doesn't surprise me too much. It's not nice to hear, but there's very little that surprises me about it.'

Teddy resumed her pacing. There was plenty that surprised her about it. It surprised her that Mike had happened to be in New York, when all the excitement was in London. It surprised her that Mike, whom she suspected was still sleeping with Glory, had willingly done a trade that would ruin Glory's career. It surprised her that Candida knew about the trade before anyone else did. It surprised her that Candida and Alex were in some way connected in an unholy alliance. And she remembered the memo that now lay in her desk at Stanley Gardens, the internal memo deliberately sent by someone at Steinberg's to Candida, discussing Mike's chances for partnership. Somehow this was all connected. It was on the tip of her tongue to spill out her suspicions to Jack. She looked at him. He was massaging his temples as if in pain, his eyes still closed. She decided not to say anything.

'Jack?' She shook his shoulder gently. 'We should go to bed. You need some rest.'

His cool grey eyes met hers, and he sighed. 'I suppose you are right, Teddy.'

She pulled him to his feet. 'I'll show you your room.'

It was hard for Teddy to leave Jack. She wanted to comfort him, she wanted to stroke him, but she hadn't picked up any signs, apart from that one accidental, clumsy kiss, that he thought of her as anything other than a friend. She closed the door of his room, and invited Matty's ever-willing black labrador to share her bed. It still felt empty.

Teddy spent most of Saturday getting to know Melissa. She was quite unlike any of Charlie's former girlfriends, and Teddy understood why he had been so willing to break his vow of perpetual bachelorhood. Melissa was quiet, but not really shy. Her golden hair and cornflower blue eyes had triggered a knee-jerk reaction in Teddy; any woman who looked that good and went out with Charlie had to have a head stuffed with sawdust. But Melissa was smart, and sensitive, and pretty. As she relaxed in the garden after breakfast, she talked easily to Teddy, telling her about her work at the Courtauld Institute, and the research paper she was writing on Piero della Francesca.

'How on earth did Charles ever manage to find you, Melissa?' Teddy asked. 'I know I'm being disgustingly nosey, but I've never seen him hanging out with the history of art crowd'.

'All too easily, I'm embarrassed to say. I was visiting a gallery in Dover Street where a friend of mine works. It was pouring with rain; I hailed a taxi. As I got in one side, Charles stepped in the other. We agreed to share the taxi, and by the time we got to Kensington, Charles had invited me for a drink, and I accepted. We've hardly been parted since. I'm afraid Piero has had to take a bit a back seat for the past few weeks.'

'What on earth do you see in Bartholomew?' Teddy persisted, wanting to hear her friend's praises sung.

Melissa gazed lovingly at Charles, who took her hand, nervously awaiting her answer.

'I see many things, Teddy. But the most important one is a genuinely kind and generous heart.'

Teddy turned away, pretending to be preoccupied with

pruning one of Matty's trailing roses. She felt rather humbled by Melissa'a straightforward honesty. Melissa was not embarrassed to be thought naïve or sentimental. She said what she thought, and Teddy was inclined to agree with her that Charlie's best quality, his seriously distinguishing feature, was that he was a kind man. For all his insults, and banter, and bravado, Charles *was* kind, and good and loyal, all those silly unfashionable traits which he tried so mightily to hide. She saw the couple together now, Melissa resting her pretty head on Charlie's shoulder, and Charles' arm placed firmly and securely around her waist. Much as Teddy loved Charles, much as she wanted him to be happy, the sight was too painful. She simply felt too jealous to bear it. It wasn't just that she realised that Charles would no longer be hers exclusively, it was that she so wanted the happiness that he and Melissa so visibly shared. God, what an awful stage to have reached – the point where you felt envious of your best friend's happiness!

The rest of the day was spent in idle chatter, the five adults drifting into natural groups of twos and threes. Sometimes the two men talked business; and sometimes Matty, Charles and Teddy argued about their prognostications for the stock market, Matty showing a degree of investor sophistication that no longer surprised Charles and her granddaughter. Charles listened so intently to Matty's analysis of the UK economy, he might as well have been taking notes. Teddy eavesdropped on Melissa and Jack; they were comparing the relative merits of Piero della Francesca and Fra Angelico. Not for the first time, Teddy thought how little she knew about Jack Delavigne; she could have written it on the back of a postage stamp, even in her large, expansive script. Jack was the managing director of Hayes Goldsmith; thirty-eight years old; divorced; no children . . . that was it, really. In some ways, she knew less about him than she knew about most of the men and women on ARC's database. She didn't know him at all, and yet she *felt* that she knew him so well.

Towards the late afternoon, Matty excused herself, saying that she had to go down to the village church to arrange the flowers for Sunday's services. Teddy offered to help, but Matty declined, saying that she needed to leave Teddy in her place as hostess to look after the needs of her guests. The four young people decided to play a game of croquet. It could have looked like an idyllic, English late summer scene – two handsome young couples, dressed in whites, slapping a ball on a perfectly manicured green lawn in the late afternoon sunshine, calling, 'Nice shot, old man!' to each other in encouragement, and sipping tall glasses of Pimms. It could have looked like a scene from a movie. But it didn't. The sky was grey, laden with ominous rain clouds. Charles and Jack were dressed almost identically, in ancient cords, so old that their original colour was indistinguishable, and frayed, viyella checked shirts. Melissa was dressed in blue-stocking fashion – a long, shapeless grey skirt, thick black tights, a black, polo-neck sweater, and Charles' oldest tweed jacket to ward off the cold wind that swept across the croquet lawn. Teddy thought that Melissa looked somehow elegant, whereas she herself looked like a mess. She wore an old pair of straight-leg jeans, which she kept at Matty's house for occasions such as this, and a yellow cashmere sweater that her grandfather must have bought at least twenty years ago. Teddy liked old clothes, but she had to admit that this particular sweater was old enough to have been condemned even by the moths. The jeans were actually very fashionable, although Teddy wasn't aware of it. They were ripped across each knee, and were of such a pale, faded blue that they were white in places. They made an odd picture, the four of them. They weren't drinking Pimms – they were drinking mugs of steaming coffee, thoughtfully delivered by Mrs B, who had added a splash of whisky to Charles and Jack's, but had not obliged for the ladies. And they weren't saying, 'Nice shot, old chap!' The two girls were playing together against the two men, and each time Charles hit Teddy's ball out of the arena, or Teddy's ball knocked Charles' a mile away, they would scream, 'You bastard!' or, 'You rotten old cow!' at each other. So much for English gentility. Gradually, the spirit of competition affected them all, and when the two girls won, they threw their arms around each other, hugging and whooping like a couple of West Ham forwards after a goal. Jack and Charles retired, disgusted, claiming foul play and muttering about the fact that women were in general getting too big for their boots. By the time that Matty returned from church, it was after seven o'clock. Teddy and her guests were ensconced in the little sitting room in front of the fire, still arguing about whether or not Melissa's shot at the final hoop had been legitimate. Matty stood in the doorway, shaking her head, a smile on her lips.

'I never thought I would say this, but the younger generation has gone to the dogs,' she said, with mock sincerity. 'It's nearly time for dinner, and I've never seen a more ragamuffin collection of people!'

Jack and Melissa rose nervously to their feet. It was their first visit to Great Wishford, and they were not yet accustomed to when Matilda Winnington-Smythe was serious, and when she was playing games. Charles and Teddy, who knew the old lady well, were more relaxed.

'Granny, darling, would you like us to dress for dinner?' Teddy asked, her be-jeaned, slim leg thrown casually over the arm of the chair, and her bare foot swinging.

'I most certainly would!' Matty replied fiercely, and then continued with a smile to Jack and Melissa, 'It's not for my sake, you understand, it's for Mrs B. She takes her cooking very seriously, and feels that we should all dress accordingly.'

Teddy poured half a bottle of Mary Chess stephanotis oil into her bath. She loved staying at her grandmother's. She loved the fact that the guest bathrooms were full of strange, old-fashioned bottles of *stuff* – there was no other word for them – full of oils and unguents and skin tonics, large crystal bowls full of mysterious bath salts and white lilac talcum powder. The medicine cabinets had no Anadin Extra, no Hedex – they were full of things like calamine lotion and tiger balm cream, remedies that had served Matilda in India, and continued to serve her in Wiltshire. On the window ledge, hand-painted porcelain bowls lay heaped with pot-pourri so old that it had lost its scent, but Teddy knew it was home-made with the petals from Matilda's own garden. Matilda had made only three concessions to modern life: the Manor had the latest in central heating, and was never cold; the towels piled in each bathroom were the plushest thick pile white cotton, and not the old, thin, scratchy cotton rags that she had grown up with; and she took the *Financial Times* every day, faithfully, and scorned the *Telegraph*. Her husband Nathaniel had read the *FT* every morning over a breakfast of kedgeree, and when he died, Matilda had been unable to cancel the subscription. Now, Teddy knew, she read it avidly. Teddy relaxed her head against the end of the bath and soaked in the steamy, scented water, humming something. Even she didn't know what it was.

Matilda came downstairs first, and instructed Barton to serve drinks in the drawing room. She stood at the large bay window, surveying the climbing roses on her trellis while she waited for her granddaughter and her friends. Matilda was curious about Jack Delavigne. Teddy had called on Thursday to ask if Charles and his girlfriend could come for the weekend, and had then called again on Friday afternoon to ask if she could bring a guest herself. There had been no mention of the exotic Frenchman. Matty didn't know anything about Jack. Teddy had never mentioned him before, and had not offered any explanation about him. But Matilda was watching Teddy and Jack, and she watched the way they looked at each other – particularly the way they looked at each other when the other one wasn't looking. She heard someone clear his throat behind her, and turned to find that Jack had come into the room. He had a drink in his hand, and asked if he could get her one.

'Thank you, Jack. I'd like a pink gin, please.'

Jack splashed the angostura bitters on to ice cubes, and added gin and soda. He liked the old lady. He liked the fact that within her experienced, weather-beaten face he could recognise Teddy's intelligent eyes, that he could see the same challenge, the same spark of curiosity in the older woman that he saw in the younger. It was apparent to him that Matilda Winnington-Smythe was evaluating him, and it was apparent that she hadn't yet reached a conclusion. He liked that. She was a woman who reserved judgement until she was sure, and he felt that Teddy would be the same. Of course, Teddy was impetuous. Of course, Teddy was, as she had made clear to him, occasionally rash. But there was a wisdom in those green eyes that was ageless, and he saw it in Teddy's as he saw it in her grandmother's.

'You are a good friend of Theodora's.' Matilda spoke the words factually, as if she were not asking for confirmation.

'We're not old friends, but we are good friends, I believe.'

'Jack, I hope you will excuse my directness. I have slipped into the habit saying what I mean. I believe that age entitles one to certain liberties that youth does not. Are you and my granddaughter just friends, or are you more than friends?'

Jack looked away. He wasn't a coy man, and he wasn't offended by the question. None the less, it was a difficult question for him to answer, and he knew he could neither lie, nor fob this woman off with a pat response. If he was honest with himself, he had to admit that it was not a question he had allowed himself to think about very much. He knew perfectly well how much he was attracted to Teddy. He knew in every inch of his body how much he wanted to take Teddy to bed. But that didn't necessarily say anything about whether they were just friends or not.

'Are you asking me whether my intentions are honourable?' He asked with a smile.

'No,' Matty said, rather crossly. 'I'm not Teddy's father, and I'm not nearly such an old-fashioned, silly old woman as you seem to think. I asked you, quite simply, if you were friends, or more than friends. You are quite entitled to tell me that I shouldn't ask such an impudent question, and that it's none of my business. Nevertheless, I ask it.'

'I suppose I do think that it isn't any of your business, but that isn't why I can't answer. I simply don't know the answer. Perhaps you could ask Teddy.'

'Perhaps I shall.'

'Well, if you do, I should be grateful if you would tell me what she says . . .'

Matilda saw the earnest, wistful look in his eye, and smiled at him. 'Why don't you ask her yourself?' she said encouragingly.

'Ask her what?' Teddy sashayed into the room, her right arm linked through Melissa's and her left arm linked through Charles'. 'Ask me what, Granny? What should Jack ask me?'

'How many times have I told you that people who eavesdrop never hear well of themselves?' Matty waved to Barton, who hovered in the doorway, indicating that he should bring the newcomers drinks.

Jack stared at Teddy. He had seen her dressed up before, at the AIBD dinner, and he had seen her dressed for work, but the transformation between the worn jeans and bedraggled sweater and what he saw now took his breath away. Teddy wore a black dress that fitted her body closely. Over the silk sheath of the dress, folds of glinting greeny gold chiffon draped in loose pleats across her stomach and hips, gathering at the sides. It was a mirage of a dress – at one moment, you looked at her and it seemed like a figure-hugging, simple dress, at another, she moved, and the chiffon glimmered as each curve of her body caught the light. The neckline skimmed her shoulders, allowing her golden skin to rise from the shimmering fabric. She wore her hair up, but no jewellery other than a pair of large, square emeralds at her ears. She needed no further adornment, smiling, laughing, turning this way and that, glowing in her loveliness. For a second Jack closed his eyes, and opened them to find Charles at his side, looking at him knowingly.

'She scrubs up well, doesn't she?'

Charles was a master of understatement.

Teddy's high spirits continued throughout dinner, and were infectious. They all adopted a party mood – it might have been New Year's Eve – but it was an ordinary September night. Sometimes dinner parties are like that. Sometimes, for no apparent reason, people become intoxicated by something far stronger than a burgundy *grand cru*, something that hangs heavy in the air, and is absorbed through the skin. Matilda knew what it was. She had seen it too many times not to recognise it instantly. She took coffee, and even indulged in a small cognac with the younger people in the drawing room, and then she withdrew. There was something about the air, something about the atmosphere, that was almost too strong for her. In some ways she would have liked to stay as an observer, but she knew it wasn't her place to observe, and anyway, she knew what was going to happen, whether she was there to witness it or not. As Matilda rose from her chair to go to bed, and as Jack and Charles politely rose from their seats, Teddy flung herself into her grandmother's arms, a whirl of glinting gold and green and black.

'Thank you, Granny. Thank you for a *wonderful* dinner.'

Matilda held Teddy's face between her hands, and kissed her cheek softly. 'My dearest girl. Good-night.'

Once Matilda had left the drawing room, the atmosphere changed, slightly but unmistakably. Teddy put on a record, an old collection of the blues, and the husky voice of Ella Fitzgerald crept into the corners of the room. Charles and Melissa sat close to each other on a little sofa, their faces almost touching as they whispered to each other, oblivious to Jack and Teddy, even to Ella Fitzgerald. Teddy watched them, so clearly in love, so clearly united, and Jack watched Teddy. She seemed in a strange mood, at one moment excited and sociable, the next strangely aloof and distant, preoccupied with her own thoughts. She moved around the room constantly, humming along with Ella, making casual observations – to no one in particular – about the music, about the moon, about the magnolia outside the drawing room window, ghostly in the moonlight. Jack watched her; he sat with the ends of his fingers and thumbs pressed together in an arc, the tips of his index fingers pressed against his mouth, his grey eyes fixed, unblinking, on Teddy. He sensed Teddy's discomfort, but couldn't yet tell if she was uncomfortable because of him, or because she was witnessing the intense intimacy between Charles and Melissa. He waited for her to give him a sign. She didn't seem nervous, exactly, but there was a visible tension in the way she carried her head and in her movements, which were normally so graceful, and tonight seemed jerky and coltish. She moved behind him. Jack could hear her soft humming right behind his chair moments before he felt her hands come to rest hesitantly, light as feathers, on his shoulders. His stomach flipped over – once, twice – and he closed his eyes, letting his head spin.

Teddy turned on her heel, and strode across the room to Charles and Melissa.

'Right, you two. That's enough. Off to bed. Matty will expect us all at church tomorrow, and you two should definitely come to practise plighting your troths, or whatever it is you intend to do.'

Had Charles not been quite so absorbed in Melissa, had he been able to take his eyes away from her face for just a moment, he would have seen something in Teddy's face that would have stopped him leaving the room. Her eyes were lit with a dangerous light. Her chin was raised in the stubborn, adamant stance he had seen her adopt when she was determined to have her own way. But Charles couldn't stop looking at Melissa, and welcomed the chance to be alone with her.

Once they had left, Teddy turned to Jack. 'Jack, will you dance with me?' She held her hands out to him invitingly.

Jack Delavigne caught his breath. It wasn't the first time a beautiful young woman had asked him to dance, when her eyes were asking him to bed. It *was* the first time – since Candida – that he had really wanted to accept. He looked at Teddy, her chest heaving slightly, the swell of her breasts just visible above the neckline of her dress, her nipped-in waist, the sensuous curve of her hips, the slim line of her calves, and neat ankles. His eyes returned to her face, and he saw her lips slightly open, slightly moist, her chin pulled down a little towards her chest, a bold, direct challenge flashing in her green eyes.

'Will you dance with me, Jack Delavigne?' She shifted her weight to her front foot, her hips tilting forward provocatively.

Was this a point of no return? It wasn't that Jack was a celibate. It wasn't as if he hadn't made love to a woman since Candida. He'd loved many women, for a night, for a couple of weeks, even for a few months. Yet there was something about Teddy that made him stop in his tracks. Something was wrong. Something was also very right. He wanted to feel how her hips lay against his own, how his hand fitted into the hollow of her back, how her breasts felt pressed against his chest, how her hair felt against his lips. After all, they had kissed before, and had managed to pretend it hadn't happened. It hadn't damaged their friendship. He knew he couldn't go to bed with her. If he and Teddy were to have any hope of a relationship, it would have to take time. She couldn't throw herself from Mike, to the Frenchman, to Jack in such a whirlwind. And he feared that if he *did* allow it time, Teddy would go back to Miccinelli. But what real harm could there be in a dance? If he closed his eyes, he would be able to imagine how their bodies would fit together, he would imagine the texture of her skin. Yet a dance meant nothing; no promise, no commitment, no risk. A dance was safe.

'For the third time, will you dance with me? I won't ask again,' Teddy spoke huskily, her hands on her hips.

Jack rose slowly to his feet, loosened the tie at his neck, and undid a couple of buttons before pulling Teddy into his arms.

Jack Delavigne was an intelligent man. He was mature, experienced, and perceptive. He had an unusual degree of self-knowledge. He knew all about women, the dangers from them and the dangers to them. He was, above all, a good man. He was also a fool. He thought a dance was safe.

They danced – slowly – for twenty minutes or so. Neither of them was watching the clock. Neither of them was a 'good' dancer, but that didn't matter; neither of them was actually interested in the dancing. Teddy was interested in being held by Jack, and fortunately for her, Jack was interested only in holding her. His instincts had been right. She fit his body as if she had been designed to be there; her hip bone felt firm against the top of his muscular thigh, her slightly rounded stomach pressed closely against his groin, her head rested against his chest, just under his chin. They swayed slightly, their feet moving only a few inches at a time. Jack felt the warmth of her body through the thin fabric of her dress. Teddy felt that strange, tickling ache in the pit of her stomach, and lifted her head, standing on tiptoe to brush her lips across Jack's jawbone. His hands, resting on her bottom, pulled her closer to him, so that one of her legs was held between his own. Teddy felt a swirling dizziness, a rush of certainty and conviction, and she put her hands behind her back, taking Jack's hands in her own.

'Jack?' she whispered.

'Hmm?' The noise rasped in his throat.

'Jack, will you come to bed with me?' She spoke a little hesitantly, but her passion was evident in her hands, gripping Jack's, her nails biting into his skin.

Jack groaned, an animal noise wrenched out from somewhere inside him. Teddy knew at last that Jack wanted her as much as she wanted him.

'Jack, would you come to bed with me now?' She spoke more strongly, growing in confidence, her voice hungry with desire.

'Teddy, come and sit down next to me for a minute.' His arms dropped from her waist, and he almost pushed her away.

'Why? We'll be much more comfortable upstairs . . .' She tugged at his hand.

'No, Teddy. I don't want to go to bed with you.' He ran his hand across his eyes, rubbing them briefly, and then pinched the bridge of his nose in the characteristic gesture that Teddy had learnt to recognise as a sign of tension. He sat down heavily on the sofa, an expression of dread on his face. Teddy refused the place next to him, and remained standing, her feet planted slightly apart, her jaw clenched tight.

'Why not, Jack? Why the hell not?'

'I can't really answer that, Teddy. I just can't, that's all. It wouldn't be right.'

'Why wouldn't it? What's *wrong* with me, goddamn it?' Her eyes were flashing again – with desire, with anger, with confusion, and with pride.

'Nothing's wrong with you, Teddy, everything's right with you – '

'I see. Well, Jack, you don't have to say any more. I'm sorry. I made a mistake. I misjudged things.'

'No, you didn't, Teddy. It was my mistake.'

Teddy walked rapidly to the door.

'Teddy, please! Let me try to explain what I feel. I didn't want this to happen – '

'No, I can see that. It isn't exactly the way I planned things either. Believe me, Jack, I understand everything. Really. I do.' Her tone of voice was flat, neutral.

'No you don't, Goddamn it! Could you just listen to me for one minute before letting your heart take over your head – '

'You are quite wrong, Jack. I didn't let my heart rule my head this time – I let my body rule my head, and that's even worse. Now listen to *me* for a minute. There's something I want to say.' She drew a deep breath and exhaled, speaking calmly and seriously, her voice controlled, her eyes fixed on a painting above the fire, avoiding looking at Jack. 'I am sorry I embarrassed you. There's no reason for you to feel uncomfortable about this. I don't want you to leave, or have your weekend ruined, or anything so silly, simply because I threw myself at you. It won't happen again, I promise you.'

She turned on her heel, and walked across the hall slowly.

Jack called out to her, but her footsteps didn't falter, and he stayed sitting on the sofa, listening to the sound of her heels clicking along the corridor above his head, and the sound of her bedroom door closing.

Jack, as has been said before, was a fool.

Teddy closed the door of her bedroom, undressed, and had climbed into bed before she realised that the black dog was lying on the bed next to her.

'Fuck off, Arthur. There's nothing you can do for me. Just fuck off.' She aimed a vicious kick at his side, but the labrador inched further up the bed, wriggling his whole body to get closer to her, brown eyes pleading.

'Oh, Arthur! He still loves her – I know he does, I always knew it. Oh, Arthur, I can't bear it any longer!'

She pulled the dog into her arms, and wept into his shining black fur.

CHAPTER SIXTEEN

At church the next morning Teddy did her best to act as if things were normal, but Matilda noticed how her granddaughter avoided looking at Jack, and jumped away if his hand accidentally brushed hers as if his touch had scalded her. Charles and Melissa were far too engrossed in the hymn book to notice anything odd. They sat close together discussing which hymns they should select for their wedding. They all recognised the self-absorption of the newly engaged; Matilda found it enchanting, Teddy less so. After the service, and a quick drink with a neighbourhood Brigadier-General, they returned home and decided to watch *Walden* before lunch. It was expected to be a momentous interview. Norman Lamont had been scheduled to be grilled about the currency crisis by Brian Walden, but had cancelled at the last moment, and Kenneth Clarke had stepped into his place.

'Clarke's going to be the next Chancellor – I'd put money on it. Whether Lamont goes next week or next year, Fatty's going to be the one to step into his shoes. Probably going to be the next PM, too. Mark my words,' Charles grunted as Kenneth Clarke struggled to defend the government's actions on Black Wednesday. It was a botched job, but at least he had the guts to face the television cameras.

After lunch, Jack said that he had to make an early start for London, but hoped that Teddy could get a lift back with Charles and Melissa.

'No, I'll come back with you, thanks,' Teddy said calmly. 'I have an awful lot of work to catch up on, and it would suit me to have some time at home. There's something I really need to do tonight.'

'As you wish. I'd be happy to drive you.'

They were overly polite to each other. Jack loaded Teddy's bag into his car, thanked Matilda and congratulated Charles and Melissa once again. He stood aside whilst Teddy kissed Charles and Melissa fleetingly, embraced her grandmother, and squatted down to give Arthur a huge hug. Moments later, they pulled away down the drive.

Jack placed his hand carefully on Teddy's leg. 'Teddy, I would really like to talk about what happened last night . . .'

She turned to him, her eyes wide and clear. 'Please don't, Jack. If you want to do me any favours, then please don't ever mention last night. I'm not angry, and I'm not upset, and I don't want you to be embarrassed about it. But I really don't want to discuss it. Ever.' Jack heard the entreaty in her voice, and sighed. It was just possible that he had blown his chances with her for ever. Not another word was said until they pulled up in Stanley Gardens.

'Teddy. May I come in for a moment?'

'I'd love you to, Jack, but I really *am* busy. It wasn't just an excuse to get away. Why don't we get together tomorrow, or in a couple of days? I just need to be alone at the moment.'

'All right, I'll call you tomorrow. Thank you. It was a wonderful weekend. Every bit of it. I mean that.'

'Good.' Teddy swung her legs out of the car, not wanting to say another word in case her voice broke.

Behind her back, Jack caught her hand, and raised it to his lips. 'Goodbye, Teddy.'

She nodded briskly a couple of times, her throat clenched tight as if she were being choked, and ran up the stairs to her front door without looking back, one hand raised in a wave.

Once inside, Teddy went straight to the telephone. She had decided, that morning in church, that she could resurrect something from the ruins of her relationship with Jack. She knew instinctively that there had been some sort of foul play on Black Wednesday. Whether Jack wanted to investigate it or not, whether Jack was in love with Candida or not, whether Jack wanted anything to do with her or not – and she was pretty sure she knew the answers to all those questions – she could still do something to help him, something to put the record straight. She was fed up with watching the bad guys win.

She phoned the office. As she expected, there was no one at ARC on a Sunday afternoon. She dumped her bag and drove there immediately. She unlocked the door, switched off the burglar alarm, and went straight to the printer room. Nothing. The shredder box was empty. Either Candida had had nothing to shred on Friday, or Julie had been particularly diligent. Teddy moved to Candida's office. No one was watching her, but she felt the colour flood her cheeks as she began to sift gingerly through the files on Candida's desk. She felt like a thief. Candida had clearly been working on the Hayes Goldsmith file when she had left for the weekend. The list of names that Teddy had pulled off the database were on the top of Candida's desk. Some of the names had a line drawn through them, some had other banks' names written beside them, with question marks. Candida was clearly considering who to approach in her planned raid on the struggling firm. Teddy was fascinated by the list. Lots of her friends outside the City had knee-jerk, negative reactions to people in finance jobs. They talked with disdain about corporate raiders, asset strippers and the like. Here was asset stripping at its finest and purest. What were the assets of an investment bank, after all? Nothing but its reputation, and the collective skills of its staff. Once the reputation had gone, it didn't take much to peel off the assets, one by one, and put them to work in new companies, leaving the old bank as a worthless shell. There was nothing wrong – nothing exactly unethical – about Candida exploiting a professional opportunity like the downfall of Hayes Goldsmith. There was nothing strictly wrong with it, so long as Candida herself wasn't in any way responsible for the downfall of Hayes Goldsmith.

Teddy slumped into Candida's chair. She didn't even know what she was looking for. She wasn't at all sure that she wanted to find anything. It would almost be a relief if she didn't. Teddy respected Candida. She also felt that the woman had had an extremely tough time, and if she had come up not exactly smiling she'd come up none the less. Teddy pulled another file – unlabelled – towards her. In it were four CVs, the résumés of Jack Delavigne, Mike Miccinelli, Glory McWhirter and Malcolm Fairchild. Teddy wasn't surprised to see three of them: they tied in with Hayes' staff list, but she couldn't understand why Candida had filed Mike's CV along with the other three. It could even have been an accident. Only Glory's CV had an account reference number typed on it. That made sense; Glory was the only one of the four that ARC had placed. Teddy jotted down the reference number on a scrap of paper. There was very little else on Candida's desk. A file on Spanish management consulting firms, some interview notes that Candida had just transferred on to the database, an address book . . . Teddy opened it. Most of the numbers seemed to be business contacts. She looked under 'D'; there was nothing for any Delavigne. She flipped to the 'F' section, and saw five numbers for Alex Fitzgerald – two London office numbers, a mobile number, a home number, and a New York number. She replaced the address book carefully and tried Candida's desk drawers. None of them were locked and most contained office stationery, spare notepads and pens, standard contract forms . . . nothing of any interest. In the bottom left hand drawer, Teddy saw a sheath of what appeared to be bank statements. She shut the drawer quickly. She had no need, and no desire, to pry into Candida's personal finances.

She crossed the office and went into the little administration room where Julie prepared all the client billing records. She pulled up one of the swivel chairs and switched on the computer. She had never had any reason to check a fee billed to a client before, so it took her a while to get into the system. The computer asked her for a reference number, and she typed in the code she had taken off Glory's CV. Numbers and dates whirled before her eyes on the screen. As Teddy saw Glory's basic salary – three hundred and twenty thousand pounds per annum – she was so surprised that she forgot what she was actually looking for. No wonder Jack felt so sick. It was bad enough to have a trader lose a hundred million pounds, but when you were paying them one of the highest salaries in the City to do so, it must really stick in the throat. Hayes Goldsmith had been billed ARC's standard fee of thirty-three per cent of salary and estimated bonus, and had coughed up £158,000 for the pleasure of hiring Glory. A lot less than it was going to cost them to get rid of her. There was a second account under the Hayes Goldsmith entry. A second statement, also for £158,000, had been billed to Steinberg Roth and Partners. It had been sent for the personal attention of Alex Fitzgerald, and marked, 'For outplacement services'. Julie had entered the date that ARC had received payment. Now *that* was unusual; it was more than unusual – it was unheard of. ARC had collected a double fee for placing Glory at Hayes. Occasionally – very occasionally – a headhunter might collect a fee from two different houses when an employee changed jobs, but the rule was that the two firms split the fee – they didn't each pay up in full. Teddy instructed the computer to print off a copy of both accounts. She had an awful, sickening feeling that Candida was cheating someone. Either she was ripping off Steinberg Roth, by billing them for outplacement when she had already collected the fee from Hayes, or she was ripping off ARC. Perhaps the Steinberg payment had gone directly into Candida's own account? Teddy didn't stop to think why Candida would choose to steal from her own company. She acted as if she were on automatic pilot. She returned to Candida's office, mechanically pulled open the bottom left drawer, and removed the stack of bank account statements. She leafed through them until she came to the statements for May, which would tie in with the date of the fees billed to Hayes and Steinberg's. There was nothing. No irregularly large deposits, no major transfers, nothing that related to £158,000. Teddy's hands were shaking, partly from relief, partly from fear, and partly from the horror of what she was doing. Her eyes ran down the columns of figures right up to the most recent statement, but there was nothing. At the bottom of the pile of statements were some contract notes and investment statements. Nothing odd about that; everyone Candida knew played the market to some extent. Teddy glanced at the final sheet of paper. It documented an options trade. Candida had bought put options – not a large amount, only a thousand – on Hayes Goldsmith. Teddy looked at the contract note again. Candida had bought them on Wednesday the sixteenth of September. Teddy began to tremble from head to foot. She walked unsteadily to the photocopier, and made a copy of the contract note; then she shuffled the pile of statements into a neat block and replaced them in the drawer. She put the three pieces of paper into her handbag, turned on the burglar alarm, fully conscious that it had not served it's designated purpose, and locked the door behind her.

She sat in her car, shaking uncontrollably for a full

twenty minutes before driving home. It was only seven p.m.

The phone was ringing when Teddy opened her front door. She couldn't answer it. She walked straight to the kitchen and poured a large measure of gin into a glass, splashed in some tonic, and drank. She badly needed to steady her nerves. She heard a familiar drawl on the answering machine.

'Hey, Teddy, it's Glory here . . . I was kinda hopin' to catch you at home. You may have heard through the grapevine that I'm in the market for a new job,' Teddy heard Glory laughing, 'but I'm in no big rush, y'know what I mean? Anyway, hun, I thought I could bring some business your way, bein' my friendly headhunter and all, so give me a call. I'm in New York. At The Mark. Just came over to do a bit of shopping. Call me. Bye.'

So Glory, who should have been sweating her guts out worrying about where she was going to get the money to pay next month's rent, was staying at one of New York's most expensive hotels enjoying a shopping spree. Glory, who should have had the sensitivity to realise that Teddy would rather she go to hell and stay there than find her another job, was actually phoning Teddy for help and advice. Glory, who should have been eating humble pie like it was the special of the day, was acting like nothing had ever happened; like she'd never had an affair with Teddy's fiancé, like she'd never lost Hayes Goldsmith over a hundred million pounds, like she'd never brought one of England's most prestigious merchant banks to its knees. And Teddy, who should have been trying to work out what the hell was going on, was shakily pouring herself another gin.

On Monday morning, Louise Britcham arrived at her desk slightly late. The Northern line was never reliable, so Louise normally left at least half an hour early to make sure she would reach the office on time. But the tube had beaten her today, and she had spent over forty-five minutes sitting in a darkened train at Hampstead. She removed her coat and waited to be sacked for at least the tenth time by her boss, Alex Fitzgerald. She hung her head in shame as he came out of his office.

'Louise! You're looking lovely today. Pretty as a picture. Do me a favour and get Jack Delavigne on the line, would you?' Alex said breezily. He strolled back into his office, whistling. His secretary recognised the song: 'Every little breeze, seems to whisper "Louise" . . .' Louise felt as if she were about to faint.

'Jack? Good to hear you. Did you have a good weekend?'

'Yes, thank you, Alex.'

'Good, good.'

There was an uncomfortable pause. 'Was there a reason why you were calling, Alex?'

'As a matter of fact, now you mention it, yes, there was.' Alex relaxed back into his chair. He wished they'd installed video phones all over the City. He would have given ten years of his life to see Jack Delavigne's face for the next few minutes. 'Jack, old chap, I thought it would be common courtesy to let you in on a little bit of information I've just received.'

'What would that be, Alex?'

'I've just had a call from my senior equity trader over here. It seems that we at Steinberg's have built up a position in your stock, and it comes to a little over five per cent of your capital, so we will be informing the Stock Exchange of that. I just thought it might be the gentlemanly thing to let you know at the same time. You seem to be having a little trouble keeping abreast of what's going on inside your own house at the moment.'

Much to Alex's irritation, Jack's voice betrayed nothing. He replied in his characteristic even tone. 'I see. I appreciate your telling me, Alex. May I take it that you intend to continue buying?'

'Aw, you know I can't tell you that, Jack! Some things you're gonna have to work out for yourself, old buddy! Let's just say that if what I hear from my trading floor about this option position is true, I don't think there are gonna be many other buyers out there. It makes the market a little, kinda, nervous, you read me, Jack?'

'Alex, I'm well aware that Steinberg's are holding the option position, and I'm well aware that this allows you to manipulate our stock price whilst you are accumulating it. Are you prepared to tell me your intentions?'

Alex Fitzgerald laughed unpleasantly. 'My intentions? It's not like we're fucking each other, or something, Jack. It's not like I'm asking your dad if I can take you on a date.'

'Do you think this might be a good time to talk about the situation, face to face, Alex?'

'Yeah, this is a real good time, Jack. You come on over. I'll be waiting.'

'I'll see you this afternoon, Alex. I have a full schedule this morning.'

'Well, don't take too long, Jack old buddy, or I'll have bought your friggin' bank before you even get here.'

Jack was not surprised by the call from Fitzgerald. For years, analysts had speculated on Steinberg Roth's need for an acquisition in the UK that would give them a better grip on the European market. Hayes Goldsmith had been mentioned as a possible jewel in Steinberg's crown, if the Americans were able to acquire Hayes without paying too high a premium. And now, of course, they had been given the opportunity to take a stake in the bank at a fraction of its real worth. He had realised that Steinberg's held the option position after he had received a nervous call from Harry Howell, who was trying to wheedle out of Jack what was going on at Hayes. Jack had given nothing away, but had wheedled out of Harry just who was holding the put options. There was no way now that Jack could avoid the confrontation with Fitzgerald, much as he dreaded it. If he could negotiate a decent price for Hayes, that would be in the best interests of both Hayes staff and its current shareholders. He had no cards up his sleeve, no paddle, no lifeboat, and worst of all . . . no excuses. Before he met Alex, he had to talk to a few people and tie up some loose ends. His first call was to Mark Mitchells, who had indeed returned to his post, and confirmed that the trading desk now had a flat book – the whole sterling exposure had been sold off.

'Be thankful for small mercies, boss. If the fuckin' frogs had voted no, the pound would have been even lower today. As it was we cleared out over 2.60. Just.'

'So the total sterling loss was . . .?'

'One hundred and eighteen mill, six hundred and eighty thousand smackers. We made a bit back on the other ERM currencies on Wednesday, but it didn't make much of a dent in the loss.'

'Okay. Thank you, Mark.'

'What's going down now, boss?'

'I really don't know. I'll let you know as soon as I do.'

Jack then called Dick Belton-Smith, and explained the situation with Steinberg's. Dick agreed they had nothing to lose by opening negotiations, and discussed what sort of terms and structure might work out best. Jack made courtesy calls to a couple of Hayes' major shareholders to sound them out. They all gave their blessing to preparatory talks with Steinberg's. They didn't have any other option. The bank was effectively bust. Finally, Jack called Teddy.

She was busy interviewing, so Jack left a message that he would call later, and took a taxi to St Paul's. He toyed with the idea of nipping into the cathedral for a quick prayer before meeting Alex, but decided against mixing God and Mammon.

Alex looked delighted to see him, and was almost solicitous, urging Jack to take a more comfortable chair, pressing coffee on him, and inquiring after his health. Jack took a seat, and waited calmly for Alex to begin.

'Well, now, Jack. I think you know that for some time now we at Steinberg's have been considering an acquisition of a UK merchant bank. We've researched the market pretty carefully to find one that would be complementary for Steinberg's. You understand that an acquisition would only be of interest to us if it didn't duplicate our existing strengths . . .' Jack nodded, 'and that ain't easy to find, because between you and me, we already do most things better than any of you Brits.' Jack was expressionless. 'Now, before we start talking seriously, I have got to tell you that Hayes Goldsmith wasn't our first choice. It wasn't even in our top three.'

'You surprise me. If you really weren't considering an acquisition, then your purchase of put options last Wednesday was uncannily fortuitous.'

'So you know about that, do you?' Jack inclined his head. 'We just had bad vibes about your stock price. Your reputation has been slipping for a couple of years now, and we have a helluva lot of questions – doubts – about managerial ability for instance . . .'

'That shouldn't be a major concern, Alex. You will be able to reorganise the bank, and its management, as you see fit, provided that you have a controlling interest, and provided that the acquisition goes through.'

'Perhaps. None the less, we have to question what the bank's really worth.'

'Of course. That would appear to be the basis for acquiring anything, Alex. I'm sure you'll agree with me that the beauty of a liquid stock market is that provided the market knows all the information about a stock, it sets a fair price on its value. Now, for whatever reason – from whatever *source* – the market certainly appears to have a great deal of information about Hayes Goldsmith. So I assume you will agree that we can take the current stock price as an opening guideline, and then place a value on goodwill – '

'Sure, but when it's a kind of rescue – when that company would go belly up if someone didn't come in and bid for it – that affects the value too.'

'I believe it all comes down to a question of terms, Alex. You haven't yet told me if you are interested in taking a minority stake in Hayes Goldsmith, or a controlling interest, or if you intend to bid for the entire company. Are you looking at our foreign subsidiaries, or are you only interested in the London operation? You haven't said if you would require current management to continue under contract after the purchase. You haven't mentioned your plans for our staff. Are you only interested in an amicable agreement, or are you also considering a hostile takeover? We will need to know all these things before we can evaluate your offer. They will all affect our decision. And we will also, of course, need to know your offer price.'

'I don't give a shit about the terms, Delavigne. The fuckin' lawyers can work that out. I'm interested in only one thing: do you realise what you've fuckin' done? Do you realise that through your own fuckin' incompetence, you've handed your precious bank to me on a platter? Are you aware of what you have lost, and where your fuckin' arrogance has led you? You're finished, Delavigne. Are you aware of that?'

Jack moved slightly in his chair, and crossed one elegant

leg over the other. 'May I assume then that, should you be successful in your full or partial acquisition of Hayes Goldsmith, you won't be requiring my services?' he drawled.

'Don't assume anything. Delavigne. I ain't decided anythin' yet. Maybe we'll have you sacked and disgraced as a condition of contract. Maybe we'll put you to work in the mailroom. I don't know what else you're good for. Maybe not even the mailroom.'

Jack sighed. 'Alex, I don't feel this is a productive or professional discussion. I'm sure it would be best if you and your partners discussed your proposed method of valuation, and suggested terms, and we can meet with our lawyers and with our colleagues and see if we can arrive at something mutually acceptable.'

Alex Fitzgerald stared at Jack. His anger seemed to have dissipated. He looked at Jack almost with curiosity, but the coldness in his eyes was far more menacing than his rage.

'You are a superior bastard, Delavigne. Even now, even now when you have ruined your bank, when you've lost the whole fuckin' war, you still think you're better than me, don't you?'

'Alex, I have never thought that I'm better than you. To be honest, until this moment the question has never crossed my mind. Nor was I ever aware that we were engaged in a war, fucking or otherwise. As to whether I am personally responsible for the "ruin", as you call it, of Hayes Goldsmith, that's not for me to judge, nor does it seem particularly relevant to our negotiations. My sole responsibility is to my staff and to my share-holders.'

Alex leant across the table, his face inches away from Jack's own.

'Oh, very noble!' he hissed. 'You make me want to puke, Delavigne. I'm going to take over your bank, and I'm going to run it a helluva lot better than you and that asshole Belton-Smith ever did.'

'If that's the case,' Jack said calmly, 'then both my staff and my shareholders will be delighted. It would be ironic if the outcome of all this were to be the acclamation of my strategic vision, wouldn't it, Alex?'

'*Your strategic vision?*' Alex spat out the words. 'You're already dead in the water. You're finished, Delavigne. Your career is finished.'

Jack flicked an invisible speck of dust off his lapel. The gesture was sudden enough to make Fitzgerald pull back, as if Jack had threatened to hit him.

'That may be true,' Jack acknowledged. 'What is strange, Alex, is that it seems so very much more important to you than it does to me.' He stood up, and held out his hand. 'Now, if you'll excuse me, Alex, I have some other affairs to attend to. Doubtless we shall meet before long.'

Fitzgerald ignored the outstretched hand, and Jack left the offices of Steinberg Roth and walked back to Cannon Street.

Had Alex Fitzgerald been able to apply one-tenth of his cunning to the perception of human nature, he would have been a happy man. Had he been able to develop even a preliminary skill in intuition, he would have been able to see just how disturbed Jack Delavigne had been during their conversation. Jack believed in being the 'lord and owner' of his face, and had given few indications of how close Alex had come to provoking him. None the less, he had been deeply angered and humiliated, not exactly by Alex, but by the knowledge that Alex was right. It was indeed his fault that Hayes Goldsmith was now to be sold to the highest bidder. The events of the past week had gone a long way towards destroying Jack's self-respect, and if Alex Fitzgerald had known that, it would have made him happy. But Alex didn't know it. All Alex knew was that everything had gone like clockwork, everything was going his way, and Jack was still able to make him feel like a small-time hick.

Teddy phoned Glory in New York. She had no desire to talk to her, even less to help her find another job, but she thought that Glory might shed some light on the events of the previous week. The hope that Glory might let something slip through her big mouth about Hayes Goldsmith was irresistible. She waited whilst the call was put through to Glory's room.

'Glory? This is Teddy Winnington. I'm returning your call.'

'Hey, Teddy! Great to hear you! Just hold a minute, hun. A real nice lookin' boy's just brought my breakfast and I want to open the champagne before we settle down to a nice long chat.'

'Breakfast, with champagne, in your room? You must be celebrating, Glory.'

'Not in my room, sweet thing. In my *suite*.' Teddy could hear the pop of a champagne cork, and heard Glory saying, 'You just help yourself to something from my bag over there, hun. Take a twenty.' Then Glory purred down the phone again. 'You ever stayed at the Mark, Teddy? You ever had a suite at The Mark?'

'Can't say I have, no.'

'Well, you really have to try it.'

'Maybe I will. Maybe next time I get sacked, I'll slip along to the Mark straight away and book myself into the best suite they have. Remind me, will you?'

Glory laughed loud and long. 'Oh, that English sense of humour. You kill me, Teddy. I mean, really.'

'Listen Glory, I'm glad you're having a good time, but I need to get back to work, so if you don't mind . . .'

'Sure. Well, for starters, Teddy, I haven't been sacked.

Jack Delavigne's all in a lather about it, and he might yet sack me, but he hasn't so far. And I'm not sure that I wouldn't have a mighty fine case for wrongful dismissal if he did try to sack me.'

'Really? That's curious. I would have thought that taking such an enormous position that goes so wrong would have been pretty good grounds for dismissal.'

'Well, it went wrong for some, but not for everyone . . .' Glory laughed again. 'Frankly, I have to say that it may have been one of the best things I've ever done. Anyway, Teddy, enough about Hayes. So, are you gonna find me a cushy new job?'

Teddy spoke sternly. 'Glory, you don't seem to realise the seriousness of the situation. Everyone in the City is gossiping about Hayes Goldsmith's losses. I don't think it will be all that easy to find you a job on a decent trading desk.'

'Hun, I don't give a damn if it's decent or not! I'm not too sure I even care about having another job . . . I may decide to become a lady of leisure . . . kind of like Jackie Onassis, or Ivana Trump or something.'

'Are you planning to get married, Glory?' Teddy's dry question was met with another peal of laughter.

'Hell, no! I don't need a *man* to lead a life of leisure! I've kinda come into a windfall . . .'

'I'm sorry. Did somebody die?'

'Not die, exactly. I just got lucky.'

'Well, I'm very happy for you. But just remember, Glory; easy come, easy go.'

'Easy come is right! You're not the first person who's said that to me, hun.' Again that awful braying laugh. 'Listen Teddy. I've been in this business long enough to know what it's all about. It's all about greed and fear. That's why everything moves up and down – people get greedy, and then they get frightened. My motto is to stay greedy, and leave the fear to someone else.'

'That certainly seems to have worked for you.'

'Oh, it has, honey; it has. You take care now. Let me know if you come up with anything.'

'Goodbye, Glory.'

Teddy knew without a shadow of a doubt that there was more to Glory's story than greed and fear. There was also corruption. There had been a pay off – and a big one – and she was damned well going to find out why. It was obvious that Glory and Mike Miccinelli were involved, and possibly Candida and Alex Fitzgerald. It crossed her mind that Jack himself might know more about the situation than he had let on; she didn't think that he was involved in anything illegal or underhand, but he might be covering up. It was perfectly obvious that he was still in love with Candida. What other reason could he possibly have had for rejecting her advances? Teddy winced as she realised the vanity of her assumptions. He could have plenty of other reasons for resisting her: like not fancying her; like thinking she was a stupid little fool. Okay, she wouldn't think about that. But he could still be looking after Candida. If he knew that Candida had been insider trading, he would clearly try to protect her. Teddy drew a sheaf of papers from her briefcase. She carried them with her wherever she went. She closed her office door, and then spread the papers out on her desk: Candida's contract note showing the purchase of Hayes Goldsmith options; the invoice to Steinberg Roth for the outplacement of Glory McWhirter; and finally, the memo about the Steinberg Roth partnership elections, with Mike's name circled and the handwritten note: 'Watch this space, Candida. You and I have other plans for this guy; let's make him really hungry, right? And when he's foaming at the mouth, we'll let him loose on JO.'

Teddy studied the papers. She felt more and more certain that the memo had indeed come from Alex Fitzgerald. She wouldn't put it past him to try to double-cross Mike; she wouldn't put it past him to double-cross his own mother. But what did JO mean? She searched her memory. Joint Office? Jersey Operation? It didn't make any sense to her but there were three people to whom it probably would make sense: Candida, Alex and Mike. Or possibly Tom Pitt-Rivers, but she couldn't really justify involving him. She was going to have to talk to one of them if she wanted to get to the bottom of the story. A small voice inside her asked the plaintive question: *why* do you want to get to the bottom of the story? It's none of your business; it's nothing to do with you. Teddy silenced it. She had chosen the path, she was already well on the road, and retracing her steps, forgetting everything she had already discovered, would be far more difficult than seeing it through to the bitter end. And maybe – just maybe – it would help Jack. But who should she talk to? Who could she trust? Certainly not Alex Fitzgerald. As she considered the idea of discussing the whole thing with Candida, she realised that she would have to confess not only to conducting a secret – albeit platonic – relationship with Jack, but also that she had riffled through her boss's personal financial statements. The very thought filled her with horror.

Her office door opened suddenly and Candida came into the room. Teddy shuffled the three pieces of paper under a file and felt as if she were a fourteen-year-old caught smoking behind the bike shed.

'Teddy? Are you okay? I saw your door was closed, and I knew you didn't have an interview scheduled.'

'I'm fine – really, I'm fine. I just picked up a bit of a bug this weekend. Must have been something I ate.'

'You do look awfully pale. You haven't seemed yourself for a while. I was coming to see you to ask if you wanted to have dinner with me tonight ... I want to talk to you about the possibility of our opening a Paris office. Maybe it's not such a good idea if you're not feeling well?'

'I'll have to pass, today, Candida. I couldn't eat a thing. Maybe tomorrow?'

'Let's see how you feel, then. How's the Morgan Stanley search going?'

'Very well. We've got two offers out, and some good back ups.'

'Excellent.' Candida rubbed her hands together. 'Everything's really coming up roses, isn't it, Teddy?'

'Oh yes. Yes, I suppose so.'

Candida turned to leave, and then swung back to look at Teddy. 'I'm so glad you joined us at ARC, Teddy. I can't tell you enough what an enormous contribution you have made already.'

Teddy made an effort to smile. Thank God Candida hadn't kissed her. Candida sure as hell wasn't Jesus, but Teddy was beginning to feel more and more like Judas.

She was left with no real choice. The only person she could talk to was Mike, but she had to clear things with Jack first. If Jack *did* know all about it – if he was sheltering Candida – then Teddy would wash her hands of the whole thing. She'd go to Cornwall and become a beachcomber. Her first call was to Mike. He was surprised, but delighted, to hear her, and even more delighted when she asked him to have dinner with her that very night. He agreed immediately, and offered to book a table.

'Oh, Mike. Come round to my house at eight. I'd rather talk privately.'

'Sounds great. I got the impression in New York that you never wanted to lay eyes on me again.'

'I've done a lot of thinking since I saw you in New York. I'd like to talk.'

'My God, so would I, Teddy,' Mike said fervently.

Next, Teddy dialled Jack's number, and was put straight through to him.

'Teddy! Thanks for calling back. I wanted to ask you to have dinner with me tonight.'

'I'm sorry, I can't do that. But I'd like to come and see you now, if that's right.'

'You mean in the office? Right now?'

'Yes. There's something important I have to tell you.'

'Teddy, if it's about what happened on Saturday, I'd like to talk to you very much, but the office is hardly the place – '

'It's not about Saturday. It's more important. I'll be there in twenty minutes, okay?'

She hung up, and stopped at Jamie's office on her way out. 'Jamie, if anyone's looking for me, I'm going over to Morgan Stanley to leave some papers. I may be about an hour.'

'Hey, Teddy, let your fingers do the walking! What do you think all those hunky men sitting on motorbikes are for? Are you trying to put them out of business?'

'I just need to pick up some stuff, and talk to a couple of people. I need some fresh air, anyway.'

'Are you all right?'

Teddy turned angrily. 'I'd be bloody fine if everyone would just stop asking me if I'm bloody all right!' she snapped.

Jamie stared after her back.

Teddy wasted no time exchanging pleasantries with Jack. She stepped up to his desk and laid out the three pieces of paper.

'Jack, I think you should have a look at these. I didn't mention it at the weekend, because my suspicions were based on conversations I had overheard and nothing really tangible, but I am now relatively certain that the trade that

Glory and Mike did last Wednesday was fraudulent. I don't know how it was done, and I don't know if you'd ever have enough evidence to prove it, but I know that Alex Fitzgerald and Candida were involved, and I know that somehow, Glory at least was rewarded for her part in it.'

Jack stared at the three photocopies intently. 'Teddy, I don't understand. None of these relate to the trade at all. Who, or what, is JO?'

'That I don't know. But it doesn't matter. Listen, I've thought about nothing else for the past twenty-four hours. Why did Candida buy put options on Hayes Goldsmith if she didn't know the stock would crap out the next day? Why did she know the details of the trade on Thursday morning – probably before you did – and why did she leak it to the press?'

Jack shook his head, bewildered. 'I'd really like to believe you, Teddy – '

'Why did Alex Fitzgerald pay a full thirty-three per cent fee to get rid of Glory? Not just anywhere, but to Hayes Goldsmith?'

'Maybe he didn't know – maybe he just asked Candida to place her. Maybe he didn't know we were paying the fee as well . . .'

'My ass he didn't know! Maybe he's just a nice guy and wanted to do everyone a favour . . . or maybe he just wanted to have somebody on the inside at Hayes who would do as she was told. Tell me another thing, Jack. Why would Alex send Candida a memo about the Steinberg partnerships? What plans did Alex and Candida have for Mike Miccinelli?'

'Teddy, hold on; you're going too fast. You're jumping to conclusions. You don't even know this memo came from Fitzgerald.'

'Yes, I do know it! And so do you! You're just avoiding the facts, and they're as clear as day!'

'They're as clear as mud! If you are right, Teddy, and I mean *if*, do you have any idea how serious this is? Steinberg Roth are about to make some sort of offer for Hayes. It was Steinberg's who bought the large option position. That I know. I didn't know about Candida's position. We don't have any way of proving a conspiracy – *if* it occurred. You are talking about a scandal of far-reaching proportions concerning two of the major financial institutions in the City. I just don't want you going off half-cocked. Let's sit down and think about this calmly. If there's even a grain of truth in what you say, I would still have to be able to prove it, and I'm not sure that I would want to. Do you realise what sort of harm this could do to people if it were exposed? *If* you could prove it, that is.'

'I can prove it, and I know exactly what sort of harm it will do to people if it *isn't* exposed.'

'How can you prove it?' Jack asked quietly. He felt he knew her response, and dreaded hearing it.

'Because Mike will tell me the truth. Because I know Mike, and I know he will tell me.' Jack looked at Teddy who stood with her hands on her hips, her green eyes flashing with righteous indignation, a woman on a mission, a woman intent on justice being done.

'Okay, Teddy. Let's say that you are right. I admit that there were a lot of things about the trade that struck me as odd, and I can see plenty of motivation as far as Fitzgerald is concerned. But I don't think you should get involved any further. It isn't safe, and it doesn't really concern you. There's simply no reason for it.'

'There's plenty of reason! It does concern me. Deeply!'

'You realise this could mean getting involved with Mike again?'

'Of course I realise that.'

'I thought you didn't want even to see him again?'

'That's hardly your business, is it, Jack?' Their eyes

met, before Jack looked away, unable to bear her accusatory stare.

'I suppose not. Look, I am extremely grateful for what you've done. This could change everything, but I'm just worried about you. I can handle things from here.'

'No you can't. Mike won't tell you anything.'

'All right. Go and see Mike, if you must. But I don't want you going near Fitzgerald. And don't say a word to Candida. And don't say a word to anyone about Candida's purchase of the put options. That's an entirely different story, and nothing to do with the trade.'

'Is it a story you happened to know about, Jack?'

'I just told you I didn't. What the hell are you implying?'

'I'm just surprised that you seem to be condoning a spot of insider trading . . . however, as your wife is involved, I suppose it's understandable . . .'

'My ex-wife. I'm not condoning anything, you silly fool. I'm trying to protect you – '

'I don't need protecting. And if you think long and hard about it, Jack, I think you'll find you are trying to protect someone else.'

Teddy scooped up the papers off the desk and snapped her briefcase shut. Jack followed her to the door and grabbed her arm as she tried to leave.

'Why, in God's name, are you so angry with me, Teddy?' He spoke quietly, but the words were clipped by the tension in his voice. Teddy stared at her feet.

'I'm not. Yes, I am. I don't know why. I can't explain. Let's just get on with this, Jack. I want it finished. I want to go back to my old life.'

For a moment they looked at each other without saying a word. Jack knew what Teddy couldn't explain. She didn't want to tell him that he had been a whim, as Christian had been, and that her heart still belonged to Mike. She didn't want to tell him that Mike was the old life she wanted back, and that she wanted to avenge the wrong that she thought had been done to Mike. Teddy looked at Jack and knew that she couldn't explain to him how much it hurt to know that he still loved Candida; that no matter if she threw herself at him, or did her best to save his bank, he would still, and always, put Candida first.

CHAPTER SEVENTEEN

Even to Teddy's cynical eyes, Mike looked wonderful. He seemed older, and slightly thinner, more muscular. His eyes lit up when Teddy opened the door to him, and he presented her with a bouquet of flowers, not very different from the one he had brought to Heathrow, which now seemed like years ago.

'May I come in?'

'Of course.' Teddy flung open the door and took the flowers. She went into the kitchen to arrange them, and heard Mike prowling around her drawing room. 'Help yourself to a drink', she shouted, and couldn't resist adding, 'D'you remember where they are?' She came back into the room with an ice bucket. 'Sorry, Mike, would you rather have a beer? There may be some in the fridge if you want me to look.'

'No, a whisky'll be fine. I thought about bringing some champagne, but I didn't know if we were celebrating or not.'

'One thing at a time, all right? Let's take things slowly.'

'It's up to you, Teddy; everything's up to you.'

It seemed so strange to be sitting in this room, where they had sat so often together, having a drink with the man that she had expected to spend the rest of her life with until four months ago, and to look at him as if he were a stranger. He was so familiar – the crooked smile, the sweep of black hair that fell over his right eye, the way he flicked it back unconsciously – and yet the atmosphere was stilted, slightly formal, punctuated with short silences that they each tried to break and then ended up speaking at once. Their mutual nervousness couldn't help but amuse Teddy, and her laughter relaxed them both.

'So how are you, Miccinelli?'

'The truth?'

She nodded.

'Bad. Pretty bad, Teddy. The only good thing that's happened was your call today. You look good.'

'Thank you.'

'I mean you look really good. Each time I've seen you – since we broke up, I mean – you've looked better and better. At the bond dealers' dinner, and then in New York ... and now. Now you look best of all.'

'I haven't even changed since I got back from work!'

'You don't need to. You don't need to change at all. You look fantastic.'

'Thank you.' Teddy meant it sincerely. Since the weekend she had been feeling so demoralised that she would have been grateful if Jeremy Beadle had told her she looked fantastic. 'Did you hear that Charlie Bartholomew is getting married?'

'Really?' Mike raised his eyebrows. 'Give him my congratulations.'

'Now I know you're trying too hard, Mike!' Teddy chuckled. 'If you were being honest, you would have said, "What, that bastard? Must be a silly cow that's getting hitched to him."'

Mike laughed too. 'Maybe you're right. I never liked him. I guess he always made me feel jealous. He always made me feel like he knew you better than I did.'

'He did. He does. Anyway, we all get jealous from time to time, Mike.'

'Ted, I want to talk about that. I want to say I'm sorry, really sorry, about Glory. I don't have any excuses – I don't know why I did it. I think I kind of went crazy there for a minute – '

'A minute? Poor Glory.' Teddy teased good-humouredly.

'Seriously, Ted. It was a big mistake, and I know it, and I just want to have a second chance. I've learnt a lesson – a lot of lessons – '

Teddy stood up and took Mike's glass for a refill. She had guessed that Mike would lose no time in trying to restore their relationship, and she didn't want to trick him or deceive him. Not unless she had to.

'Mike, wait a minute. I don't want to talk about all that just now. I don't know how I feel about you. I mean that honestly. It doesn't hurt me any longer to see you – in a way, it feels very nice – but I don't want to talk about the future – our future – and that isn't why I asked you to come here. I have something to tell you. Most of all, I have something to ask you. Before we go any further, let me ask you one question.'

He spread his arms wide. 'I'm all yours. Fire away.'

'Was the billion pound trade that you did with Glory McWhirter on Black Wednesday a legitimate trade?'

Mike stared at her, his dark eyes wide in surprise. He didn't reply.

'Was it a legitimate trade?'

'How do you mean, legitimate?' he stalled.

'I think you know what I mean. Was it a normal, regular, legal trade between two counterparties, or was it a set-up?'

Mike shook his head, inhaled deeply through his teeth as if he were about to reply, but then said nothing.

'Mike? Would you tell me please?'

'God, Teddy,' he scratched his head, 'I didn't think you wanted me to come round to interrogate me! Let's not talk about work, okay? I had a hell of a week, last week, everyone did. I can't even remember every trade I did. It was a madhouse, you know? I want to forget about the whole week. It's a miracle we survived it. Let's not waste time talking about it.'

'I think you can remember this one, Mike. It was a pretty big trade, and very well timed.'

Mike drew the air in again over his teeth. Teddy could see the strain he was under, and judged that she shouldn't push him. She shrugged her shoulders as if nothing could be less important, and waited for Mike to speak.

'Why do you want to know about it, Teddy? Why do you know about it at all?'

'Oh, come off it Mike! It's been spread all over the papers!' As the words left Teddy's mouth, she realised that no press comment had named Steinberg Roth as the counterparty. 'It doesn't matter, I just heard about it. I thought you must have made a lot of money for Steinberg's, I wondered if it had improved your chances of partnership . . . I still take an interest in you Mike, you know that.'

'Do I? I'd like to believe that, Teddy. Very much. But I don't want to talk about partnership, and I don't want to talk about any goddamn sterling trades.'

'Okay. It doesn't matter.' Teddy decided to take the bull by the horns. 'Let me tell you something instead. Or rather, let me show you something that's been puzzling me.' She unfolded the Steinberg Roth memo and passed it over to Mike. He looked at it, his brow deeply furrowed. When he looked up at her, his face was white.

'Where did you get this?'

'That doesn't matter. Let's just say I know it's genuine. Do you know who it's from?'

'Of course I do! It's from Fitzgerald! Son of a bitch!' Mike shouted, and screwed the memo into a ball in his fist and hurled it across the room.

Teddy retrieved it immediately, and spread it out flat on her lap. 'How do you know it's from Fitz?'

Mike's finger stabbed at the now crumpled piece of paper.

'Because it's got his fuckin' handwriting all over it! Fuckin' arsehole!'

'Sit down, Mike. Have another Scotch. Tell me what this memo means.'

'It means the sonofabitch lied to me. That's Norman Bell's list of recommendations for partnership. See that NB in the corner? That's not *nota* fuckin' *bene*, that's Norman Bell. Fitzgerald told me that Norm wasn't putting me up for partnership. He told me that Norm had blackballed me. All the time it was that motherfuckin' piece of arsewipe who was blackballing me!'

'What does the rest of it mean, Mike? How did he make you hungry?'

'He just led me by the nose all the way! By the fuckin' nose!' Mike pounded the arm of the chair with his fist, sending his glass flying. 'Son of a bitch!'

'What's JO?'

'JO? I don't know. Let me see it again.' He glanced at the paper and tossed it back to Teddy. 'It's not JO. It's JD. I know Fitz's writing. God knows what the fucker meant.'

He slumped in the chair.

'Jack Delavigne,' Teddy whispered.

'What?'

'Jack Delavigne. He wanted to turn you loose on Jack Delavigne.'

'I don't even know who the bastard is.'

'He's the managing director of Hayes Goldsmith.'

Mike began to swing his head from side to side again. He was shaking with anger. Teddy reached out and laid her hand gently on his arm.

'Mike? Tell me now about the trade.'

His eyes were dull and cloudy, and for a moment Teddy thought he was about to burst into tears, but he didn't.

Mike hadn't cried for a long time, and it was too late to start now.

'Mike? Please tell me. You need to talk to someone. I can feel how much you need to talk. I won't let you down. Have I ever let you down? I care about you, Mike.' Teddy's voice was soft but insistent. 'Trust me, please.'

Mike took one look at her sweet, caring face, and gave up. He spoke in a monotone. 'Fitz set it up. He told me he couldn't get me partnership. Not this year, probably not ever. Told me it was Norm's fault – and the Board's. He told me Steinberg's wanted a stake in Hayes. Didn't say a lot about it. After sterling was withdrawn from the ERM, he called me in New York. Told me to call Glory, trade a billion quid with her, and that we should both back-date the trade to around four p.m., before the market closed. He guaranteed me a bonus of five million quid for doing it.'

'And so you did it?'

'Yep.' He stared into space.

'Wasn't it hard to persuade Glory?'

'Nope. She had already lost enough to know she was going to lose her job. She had nothing to lose. I said I'd give her a million if she did it. She agreed.'

Teddy was tempted to say that it served Mike right. If he had any innate sense of justice, he would at least have split the pay-off fifty-fifty with his partner in crime. Maybe Glory was right. Maybe the only two emotions that really played a part in human life were greed and fear. She didn't say anything. Mike looked like he'd been destroyed, and Teddy had never been one to kick a dog when he was down.

'What are you going to do now, Mike?'

'I'm going to go round to Fitzgerald's house and kick his fuckin' head in!'

'D'you want to go to prison, Mike – for murder? It's

not a white-collar crime . . . you wouldn't get a TV set or a mobile phone . . .'

'It wouldn't be murder, Teddy. I'd get a medal for it. Anyway, it looks like I might go to prison anyway.'

'I don't know about that.'

'What are *you* going to do? Are you going to tell this Delavigne guy?'

'Yes. Yes I am. But Mike, don't you do anything. Just go into work like nothing's happened tomorrow. It will be okay. Somehow. Trust me. I'm afraid I have to leave now. There's someone else I have to see.'

Mike struggled to his feet, and Teddy led him to the door.

'Michael, don't worry. I'm sure there's some way we can make this all right.'

'Can you make *us* all right Teddy? That's all I really want. I wouldn't have done the fuckin' trade if I hadn't lost you, if I'd been able to talk to you about it . . .' Teddy opened her mouth to correct him, but Mike laid his finger gently across her lips, caressing the outline of her mouth. 'Shhh. Don't say it. I know. I know. I wouldn't have lost you if I hadn't screwed Glory. Just desserts, eh, Teddy? I just hope one day you understand how sorry I am, and how much I love you. I'd do anything to prove that to you. Go to prison. Anything.'

Teddy hustled him through the doorway. 'Don't do anything just yet, Mike. Just lay low, and keep your mouth shut, and keep a poker face. I'll talk to you in a couple of days, and tell you what I want.'

He nodded.

'And Mike? I'm sorry I didn't give you dinner. Next time, okay?'

'Another wasted effort, huh, Teddy? Did you spend a long time cooking it?' He asked the question with a wistful smile.

'Uh-uh. Harrods Food Hall.' Teddy shut the door gently. There had been too many slammed doors between her and Mike.

Teddy tried to speak to Jack that evening, but got his answering machine. This meant that instead of discussing things over with him, she was forced to rely on her own judgement and proceed with her plans. She was relieved.

'Jack, this is Teddy. I have spoken to Mike, and everything is as I expected. I have to go out of town for twenty-four hours. Don't do anything at all, and don't let on that you know. I suggest you proceed with the acquisition talks as if nothing had changed. I'll talk to you sometime tomorrow.'

She made three other calls. She phoned Jamie and asked him to say that her tummy bug had become acute, and that she would be spending the day in bed with the phone switched off.

'I'll be right over now to nurse you, Théodora! I've still got a nurse's uniform hanging around from when I was a wee little boy, if I can just lay my hands on it . . .'

'You probably wore it last week, Jamie, if I know anything about you. I'm not really sick, you moron, I just need a day off.'

'Playing hooky, are we? Or is it one of those feminine problems? I thought you were a little bit tetchy, I must say . . .'

'It is not a feminine problem! Anyway, I thought you kept a chart on all our menstrual cycles so you would know when not to talk to us . . .'

'Now, now, Teddy, that's only for Candida, and when I told you about it, I swore you to secrecy, so remember – mum's the word.'

'Okay, Jamie. Mum's the word.'

'Teddy? I've just been struck by a terrible thought. You're not pregnant, are you?'

'No, Jamie, I am *not* pregnant. I just have to do something.'

'And a woman's got to do . . .'

'What a woman's got to do. Now be a good boy, cover for me and get off the phone. I have some calls to make.'

Teddy called British Airways next, and then the Hotel Crillon in Paris. She didn't feel like staying at the Hotel Saint Simon.

Jack Delavigne and Dick Belton-Smith received an initial proposal from Steinberg Roth first thing Tuesday morning. The Americans were proposing to buy one hundred per cent of Hayes Goldsmith and Partners at a slight premium to the current stock price. Hayes' shares had steadied at 2.53, and the offer was based on a price of 2.68, or around five per cent above the market level. Steinberg's lawyers were adamant that this was a generous offer; the fact that Hayes stock had been trading at 3.98 exactly a week earlier was irrelevant. Steinberg Roth would assume full strategic control of Hayes Goldsmith. Current management would be obliged under contract to stay for twelve months, but not necessarily in their current positions. There was no com- mitment that Steinberg's would continue to employ them after that point. All staff at Hayes Goldsmith, management or otherwise, would have to relinquish their shares in the merchant bank, at the same price as the public offering of 2.68. Steinberg's didn't believe in staff holding equity stakes in the company unless they were at partnership level, and they were not about to offer partnership to anyone currently at Hayes Goldsmith. Steinberg's would appoint a new managing director from the board of the US bank. Steinberg's would accept that none of the current staff should be made redundant, with the exception of Glory McWhirter. They were insistent that she go. Jack and Dick listened silently to Mitchell Freeman, one of the senior partners of Steinberg Roth and the man in charge of corporate acquisitions, and to the three lawyers Mitchell had brought to the meeting. Alex Fitzgerald was also present, representing the sales and trading arm of the bank, but he never opened his mouth throughout the two hour session. He sat with a large grin on his face, drinking in the atmosphere.

Jack and Dick withdrew for a private consultation.

'My God, Jack, after all these years, to have come to this! A fire sale to a bunch of jumped up New York bankers in braces!' Belton-Smith shook his grey head sadly.

'Mitchell's not so bad, Dick. But I know what you mean. It's my fault. I don't know what to say to you.'

'Not at all, old chap.' Dick patted him on the back. 'It was a cock-up, and if anyone was responsible for that ass Malcolm Fairchild it was me.' He shuddered. 'Awful to think that the same blood runs in our veins!'

'What will this mean to you, Dick?'

'Well; I lost quite a lot on the currency side last week. Mary and I also have some rather unpleasant exposure in one of our Lloyds syndicates. I must say I was rather counting on the Hayes stake to fund my retirement, and that is now somewhat – diminished. All I really ask is that they do *let* me retire. I don't fancy reporting to that bunch at my time of life . . . Don't expect they'd want me to stick around, though, do you?'

'I'm sure we can make that a condition of sale, Dick, and I'm sure we can improve the terms of the offer. I can't tell you how bad I feel. I've let you down, after all you've done for me.'

'Not another word, my dear fellow. You've always been like a son to me, Jack, and never done anything that I wouldn't have done in your shoes. I simply hope you will be all right when the smoke clears.'

'I rather suspect I shall be working for Fitzgerald in the mailroom of Steinberg's,' Jack said with a grim smile.

'Perish the thought! Go back in and tell those jokers we'll come back to them with a counter-proposal in thirty-six hours.'

Teddy spent the morning drinking endless cups of coffee in various bars around the Champs-Elysées. She arrived early for her lunch appointment, and allowed the maitre d' at the restaurant, Au Petit Montmorency, to show her to her table. She accepted a kir, and waited for her guest.

She knew he had arrived the moment he entered the restaurant. A loud voice boomed, 'Theodora Winnington! What a delightful treat!' and Philip Redmayne wedged his large frame on to the little banquette next to her, delivering a smacking kiss to her cheek.

'There I was, pootling away at my desk, and thinking what a frightfully dull day it was going to be, when in came your call asking me to lunch. Now it's not often young ladies invite me to lunch, and it's not often that they are such delightful young ladies – '

'I hope it didn't inconvenience you, Philip; I realise it was very short notice.'

'Not a bit of it! Delighted you're here! And delighted you don't have that frightful Frog with you this time! He isn't skulking under the table, is he?' He lifted the edge of the tablecloth and peered underneath. 'Grandcourt, you lily-livered, spineless, slimy amphibian! Show yourself!'

Teddy smiled. 'Actually, I haven't seen Christian for some time.'

Philip slathered butter on a roll, and stuffed it into his mouth. 'Found out about his wife, did you?' he inquired lightly.

Teddy brushed off a few crumbs that had mysteriously landed on her lapel, and nodded. 'As a matter of fact,

I did. I wished you'd told me he was married when I met you.'

'I'm sorry. Thought you knew. Everyone else does. Delightful man, Christian. Truly delightful. Lovely wife, too. Marguerite. One of the grandest ladies in Paris. And pretty as a picture. They're devoted to each other of course, but Christian has always had a way with the ladies and likes to keep his hand in. So to speak.' Philip guffawed with laughter. 'Seems to amuse Marguerite. I think it's a damn good system myself, but I could never persuade Bertine to give it a whirl. Sad, that.' His eyes, the same blue as Candida's, but watered down, twinkled mischievously. 'Now, let's order, get some of the old plonk, and then we can have a nice talk, and I can tell you which of the Frogs are safe and which are dangerous. The safe ones', he ate another roll in a single mouthful, 'are the married ones. The last thing we want to have is any form of interbreeding.'

They had nearly finished their main course before Teddy had a chance to speak. She wished she had been able to meet Philip for a purely social lunch, as she had proposed on the phone, but she hadn't. She had questions to ask, and she believed that he was the only person who knew the answers and would tell her the truth. 'Philip, I did have an ulterior motive in suggesting we meet for lunch. The thing is, I'm rather worried about Candida.'

Philip put down his knife and fork and looked at her gravely. 'Is it anything particular? I haven't talked to her for a while – maybe not for a month. Are there problems with the business? Are Anderson Squires poaching your clients? Is ARC losing market share, or something?'

'No, no. ARC's flourishing.'

'Well, then, there's nothing wrong with Candida.' He resumed his meal. 'You see, Theodora, if ARC is doing well, then Candida is doing well. You can't divide them. It's her life blood. Her baby, if you like.'

'It's just that she seems very much on edge. Nervous. As if she's very fired up about something.'

'My God, if she's really feeling fired up, she must be hell to work for! I pity you all!'

'No, it isn't like that. I can't really explain it,' Teddy finished lamely. This was going to be much more difficult than she had anticipated. She tried again.

'I get the feeling that she isn't really satisfied, that she's looking for something . . . maybe for love. I don't know. What do you think?'

'Doesn't sound like the little sister I know and love, but you may be right. I would have said that Candida had had all the love she could stand.'

'You mean with Jack Delavigne?'

'That's right.'

'Well, I think that's what I'm trying to get at. I think that in their hearts, they both want to try again. I know how much you and Bertine think of Jack. I thought there might be a way we could bring them back together.'

Philip stared at her in absolute shock. It was as if she had suddenly developed a second head. 'Did you say, you'd like to bring Candida and Jack back together?'

'Yes. I believe they still love each other.'

He chuckled. 'You've lost me there, Theodora. I can tell you one thing. If there's something wrong with my sister, it hasn't been caused by missing Jack Delavigne. She hates the man.'

'I know that. I mean, I know she *thinks* she hates him, but I'm sure that in the bottom of her heart she needs him, and she still loves him. And Jack loves her, I know it.'

Philip leant well back on the bench, although his stomach still touched the table. 'My God! Christian must have had a field day with you! Must have been like shooting fish in a barrel!'

'I realise you think that I'm a silly, romantic fool – '

'A *lovely* romantic fool: lovely, without a doubt; romantic, certainly, and yes, an absolute fool.'

'But I'm not. I happen to know Jack Delavigne quite well, and he has told me directly that he loves Candida.'

'Ah, well. Yes. Now you are talking about something altogether different. If you're saying that Jack loves Candida, then perhaps that's true. If it is, I would say he needs his head examined, but it's possible. No, my dear, what I objected to was your strange notion that Candida loves Jack. She hates him. She hates him very deeply.'

'Poor Jack.' Teddy could feel tears welling in her eyes.

'Yes, absolutely. Poor Jack. No, as I told you before, Candida loves ARC. She loves to work. Must have had a different gene strain than Jessie and I did. I work very hard to avoid working, and Jessie – well, Jessie's never lifted a finger in her life. Never will, I suspect. But for Candida, work is everything. That's her life. That's her baby.'

'You mean, it replaced her baby?' Teddy asked the question gently. She found it difficult even to refer to the baby's death.

'In a way, yes. But Candida was devoted to her job before she ever had Tommy. I think she found it very hard to stop working.'

'Well, it was an awful tragedy. I can quite see why she threw herself into work after that. And I can quite see why she hates Jack.'

'Yes, well. Maybe women understand some things better than men do. I have never been able to understand why Candida hates Jack Delavigne. He's the salt of the earth. A veritable rock. Never harmed a hair of her head, and stood by her, too. He belongs to that very rare breed of gentlemen. I fear they are going the way of the dinosaurs. But then I'm not one of those headcase fellows, you know, the psychiatric johnnies, so I suppose I might not see things

from Candida's point of view. Jack has always blamed
himself, you know.'

'Yes, I do know. It must be very hard for him to live
with that degree of guilt.'

'Certainly is. I've told him a hundred times – it wasn't
your fault. Don't punish yourself all your life this way.'

'But I suppose he can't get over the idea that it *was*
his fault. I suppose that's what Candida can't forget, or
forgive.'

'Jack's always had more forgetting and forgiving to do
then Candida has. And he's much better at it than she is.
Not that I want to say anything bad about my own flesh
and blood.' He lifted a spoonful of *îles flottantes* to his
mouth, and left a ring of white foam around his lips.

'What do you mean, Philip? How can a mother forget
and forgive the man who let her baby drown, even if he
is her husband?'

For the second time, Philip Redmayne stared at Teddy
as if she had turned an unusual shade of green before his
eyes. 'Don't you know, Teddy? Don't you know what
happened? Candida was looking after Tommy. Jack was
upstairs in their bedroom. Candida fell asleep and Tommy
drowned.'

OAXACA, OCTOBER 4TH, 1983

*Candida flung open the doors that led to the balcony from
their room, and filled her lungs with the sweet morning
air. The guide books were right for once. Oaxaca really
was one of the loveliest places in the world, a little gem
of a city, perched in the valley of Mexico's Sierra Madre
del Sur. Nothing seemed to have changed since Candida
and Jack had honeymooned here in 1979. Nothing, that*

*is, except for the fact that four years ago they had taken
the bridal suite of the Hotel Presidente, and this time they
had taken a suite of interconnecting rooms, in the smaller
of which their two-year-old son Tommy was still sleeping
blissfully.*

*Candida crept over to the bed, and leapt on top of the
supine body of her husband.*

*'Rise and shine, darling, it's the most heavenly morning,
and I'm not going to let you waste it.'*

*Jack grunted and pulled the finely embroidered bedcover
over his head, but his wife would not accept no for an
answer. Climbing under the linen sheet herself, she began
to trace elaborate patterns on Jack's torso with her long
nails, circling ever nearer to his most vulnerably ticklish
spot. With a roar, Jack sprung from the bed and wrapped
Candida in a bear hug. She lay nestled in his arms.*

'What were you dreaming about?'

'You. My happy dreams are always about you.'

'Liar.'

*'You're right. I was actually dreaming about Ramon
Monsonis. You know, the Spaniard we're doing that
equity issue for. I dreamt that he and Belton-Smith were
mud-wrestling in the middle of Broadgate. It was rather an
ominous dream. Monsonis was winning.'*

*Candida giggled. 'I thought you weren't going to think
about, let alone dream about, work for a good two weeks.
You promised.'*

*'D'you really think mud-wrestling counts as work?' He
buried his face in the sweet-smelling cloud of her hair,
nuzzling her neck with ever more insistent little nips.
Visions of his boss and Ramon Monsonis began to fade
rapidly. He began to fantasise about what Candida would
look like were she to go in for mud-wrestling ... His
reverie was interrupted by a meaningful nudge from his
wife, and Jack looked up to see Tommy, his blond hair*

tousled from sleep, rubbing his eyes in the doorway of their bedroom.

With a sigh, Jack lifted the edge of the sheet. 'In you hop, old chap.'

The little family lay tumbled together, arguing about their plans for the day. Jack advocated spending the entire day in bed; Candida opted for a trip to the ruined city of Monte Alban, the former Zapotec city that was perched on a mountain top overlooking Oaxaca. Tommy argued for a day spent by the pool, and in the manner of most two-year-olds, pressed his case most forcibly. Too devoted to deny him, and certainly too mellow to put up with the tears and tantrums that would result from denial, Jack and Candida gave in with good grace.

They had spent a week at the Presidente, during which Tommy had persuaded all the good-natured, black-eyed Mexican staff of the hotel into a state of voluntary servitude. Whereas Jack and Candida's requests were met with courtesy and impeccable efficiency, Tommy's every whim was granted with slavish devotion. The proud parents relaxed on the terrace beside the swimming pool after lunch, and watched the three gardeners who maintained the idyllic grounds of the hotel vie with each other to lift Tommy ever higher into the citrus trees that lined the courtyard.

'What a monkey he is! He's got the entire staff of this place at his beck and call,' Jack said, the criticism ringing with pride and devotion. He filled Candida's glass with wine and ordered a brandy for himself. For the first time in years he felt able to forget about the pressures of work, and to enjoy the company of his beautiful wife and handsome child. He surveyed Candida. The hot sun had turned her alabaster skin golden, a week's rest had removed the shadows from under her eyes and turned them soft and seductive. She now sat with her eyes closed, her face

_tilted up towards the sun, her long, tanned legs emerging
from a pair of white shorts. Jack watched a tiny trickle of
sweat run slowly down from her hairline, skimming past
her ear, along the jaw line and down her neck into the
cleavage exposed by her bikini top. Unable to resist, he
leant forward to run one finger along the damp path the
bead had left. Candida kept her eyes shut, but a contented
smile spread slowly over her face, and lifted one corner of
her lovely mouth._

_'Is it time for a siesta?' Jack asked huskily, desire
roughening his voice. Candida opened her clear, aquamarine eyes, and brushed her fingers over her husband's
lips._

_'You have forgotten, darling, that we're no longer on
honeymoon, and we're no longer alone. You go up, sweetheart. You're the one that's been working so frantically.
I've hardly lifted a finger for two years. Tommy and I will
have a swim, and I'll see if Conchita will have him in the
kitchens for a little, and then I'll come and join you.'_

_When Jack awoke, a beam of the late afternoon sun had
broken through a chink in the curtains, splashing a pool of
light on to the rose and blue tiles that decorated the floor
of their suite. He had slept for two hours. He had not
intended to sleep, wanting to wait for Candida to return
from her swim, but drowsiness had overcome him. As he
walked to the bathroom he stretched luxuriously, and ran
his fingers through his hair. Candida had probably come
to their room, found him asleep, and decided to leave him
undisturbed, he thought ruefully. Sure enough, as he drew
back the curtains and stepped on to the balcony, he could
see his wife reclining on one of the loungers. Tommy was no
doubt causing havoc in the kitchens. His desire for Candida
surged once again as he looked at her. Still in a somnolent
state, he returned to the bathroom, dimly aware of a sense
of unease, something strange in the absolute silence of the_

afternoon, something that stabbed his conscious mind, urging him to wake up. He rubbed his eyes again, and splashed cold water on his face. An awful sense of dread thudded hard into the centre of his chest. For a moment he stood transfixed, staring into his own reflection, and seeing the face of his son. Willing his frozen muscles into action, he raced to the balcony. His eyes skimmed the terrace of the bar, and came to rest inevitably on the pretty, mosaicked swimming pool. A small body floated face down in the crystal clear water, arms stretched out, clothes billowing in the eddies of water that slapped against the sides of the pool. Jack's knuckles were white as they gripped the wooden rail of the balcony. His anguished shout rent the silence of the former convent.

'Tommmmm-eeeee!'

'You must be wrong, Philip,' Teddy whispered. 'Everyone has told me about the accident, and everyone – including Candida – said that *Jack* fell asleep and the little boy drowned.'

Philip shook his head slowly. 'I've heard that version, too; we all have. But it's not the truth. When they came back from Mexico, right up until the funeral, Candida said that she had been babysitting, and that she had let Tommy drown. Understand me, Theodora, I'm not blaming my own sister. I care for her very much, and at the time of Tommy's death, it damned near broke my heart to see them both. "Let Tommy drown" is an unfortunate use of words. Nobody let Tommy drown. It was simply an awful accident, and Candida happened to be the person who was meant to be in charge. It could have been either of them. It could have been both of them. It could', he swirled the wine in his glass, looking at it contemplatively, 'have been any of us. But by the grace of God, it happened to them.' He drained his glass. 'After the funeral, Candida had some sort of breakdown. For a long time she couldn't, or wouldn't talk. She didn't seem to accept that Tommy had died. When she came through that, she believed that Jack had been the one looking after Tommy. Jack let her say it, over and over again. He made all of us promise never to challenge her about it. He said she simply could not deal with the reality of what had happened. I don't go in for this psychology lark myself. Seems to me that a lot of people pay a great deal of money to some stranger in order to talk about what they ought to be saying to their families or friends. Anyway, the way Jack explained it was that he thought Candida had never wanted to have a baby. That she always resented the fact that having Tommy somehow meant she couldn't do what she wanted to do. So when he died, she felt that she hadn't just fallen asleep, and that his drowning had been an accident; she somehow felt that she had deliberately wished it on him. Well, no one's mind could stand that sort of strain. In time, maybe a few months, I don't really remember, Candida turned against Jack. She started blaming him for everything. She stopped talking about Tommy. She was extremely disturbed. My sister Jess told me that one time when she was helping Jack pack away Tommy's things, Candida tried to stab Jack with a carving knife. Jess believes that Candida would have killed him, if she could. Jack went to see some shrink, who told him to go along with Candida for the time being, until she was, you know, strong enough to cope with what had happened. Candida moved out of the house. I believe she went to see a shrink herself, although she'd never talk about it. I don't have the foggiest what went on there, behind closed doors if you see what I mean. After several months of seeing this Harley Street johnny, Candida came to me, said she was starting a new business, and that she wanted me to talk to Jack about giving her a divorce. She wouldn't talk to him herself. Wouldn't see him. Poor dear Jack. He even ended up putting up the money for her to start ARC, although she always thought the last bit came from our mother. It came from Jack. Strictly, Jack probably still owns about twenty per cent of ARC, although Candida doesn't know it, and he'd never tell her. For a while he tried to see her. Then I suppose he just gave up. It was a terrible time for Candida. It was a terrible time for Jack. An awful business. It might have brought them together – they might have been able to help each other through it – but it didn't work like that.'

Teddy had a thousand questions, but she couldn't bring herself to speak. The sadness of Philip's story left her feeling empty and pointless. She had wanted to know what possible motive Candida could have for wanting to destroy Jack. She couldn't believe that Candida could still harbour such hatred for Jack because he had fallen asleep when their son was swimming – enough hatred to want to destroy everything Jack had. Now, she felt she could understand, just a little, about how deeply the tragedy had affected each of them. Enough to make Candida cling to a lie for the rest of her life as her only way of survival, hating Jack because he knew the truth; and enough to make Jack support her in that lie, and bury the truth with his son.

Teddy's objectives had been accomplished. She now knew that Candida had worked hand-in-hand with Fitzgerald specifically to exact revenge on Jack and punish him for what she needed to believe he had done. And she knew something else: that Jack was still in love with Candida; that he always would be; that there was a bond between them that could not be broken. It would not be possible for Teddy to restore Jack's son, or his wife, but she now saw a way to give him back his company. It wasn't exactly compensation, but it was the best she could do.

CHAPTER EIGHTEEN

Teddy called Jack from Charles de Gaulle airport and asked him to meet her at her house almost as soon as she returned to London. He wanted to take her out to dinner, but again she refused, asking him instead to come for a drink so that she could simply tell him what she knew. She wanted to spend the absolute minimum of necessary time with him. She had decided not to tell him about her meeting with Philip Redmayne. Doubtless, Philip would tell Jack about it himself one of these days, but by that stage Teddy would have been long gone, her mission would have been accomplished and she and Jack would no longer be fighting a common cause. As she waited for Jack to arrive at Stanley Gardens, Teddy thought about how the past four months had changed her. She was no longer the woman who had driven Mike's car on to the pavement and dropped the keys down the grate. She was no longer the woman who had danced to Georges Moustaki and so willingly allowed herself to be seduced by Christian de Clement-Grandcourt. She was no longer the woman who had asked Jack Delavigne to bed. She was no longer the woman who believed that you fell in love, and rode off into the sunset on a white stallion with the man of your dreams. She felt much older, and maybe just a little wiser. It was as if all the things that she knew, knew in her heart to be absolute, undeniable facts, had shifted into a shady world of questions and possibilities. Her only conviction was that Candida and Alex Fitzgerald should not be allowed to get away with manipulating the lives of innocent people. That was the only thing she could find the energy to fight for.

When she let Jack into the house, her heart was wrenched as she saw him with new eyes. She could hardly look at him without wanting to hold him in her arms and say that she finally understood what he had gone through, yet she knew that she could never look at him and think of him as hers.

'So tell me what happened with Mike.' He seemed uncomfortable, cautious of her. They sat down at the kitchen table.

'It was very easy, really. I asked him about the trade, and he wouldn't give me a straight answer. The poor man probably thought I was recording everything for the benefit of the SFO. He had visions of prison sentences dancing in his head. Then I showed him the memo from Steinberg's. He confirmed that it came from Fitz, and went absolutely mad. He just couldn't get over the fact that Fitz had betrayed him. He also said that what we thought was JO was actually JD. You. So then he told me everything. He and Glory – under Fitz's instructions – did the trade shortly after Lamont announced the withdrawal from the ERM. They agreed to time stamp the tickets to four p.m. That was it.' She stood up to get a bottle of wine and a couple of glasses. Without saying a word, Jack took the bottle and corkscrew from her and opened it. Teddy continued. 'Fitz promised Mike five million pounds as a bonus. Mike paid Glory one million. What I can't get over, Jack, is that it was all so simple and so easy. Mike even said that as far as the tapes were concerned, he didn't think anything could be proven against them, because although the four o'clock trade wouldn't be on record, he made sure that the later call, in which he referred to the phoney trade, was taped.'

'Yes, I heard that. So there's still no evidence? Nothing hard?'

'That won't be a problem. Mike will confirm it all, in writing, if I ask him to.'

'What else happened?'

'Nothing. I've told you everything.'

'I mean . . . what happened between you and Mike?'

Teddy shrugged. 'Well, you know . . . we just talked things over a little. It was okay.'

'You don't seem very happy about it.'

Teddy sat up straight and forced a smile. 'Oh, I am. Everything will be fine now, I'm sure.'

Jack pinched the bridge of his nose. 'I suppose you are worried about Mike – I mean what this will do to him.'

'Well, of course I am. It's not going to be easy for him, is it?'

'Teddy, since I got your message last night, I've felt like a new man. I can't tell you what a relief it's been. Now I've been thinking about this. Today we had another series of meetings with Steinberg's about the acquisition. It seemed very strange. I was sitting there listening to the offer, and thinking, My God, this is surreal . . . tomorrow this could be all over the papers, all these people will be dragged down into a ghastly scandal, Hayes Goldsmith's shares will be suspended, it could take months – years even – to sort out.' Teddy nodded. 'I thought there might be a way we could sort it all out without dragging people through the mud.'

'How do you see that?'

'If I went to Steinberg's – if I met with the board, which I am scheduled to do on Thursday morning at ten, I could just tell them what has happened. Tell them everything. We could still go through with the takeover, but under better terms. Whatever happens, Hayes Goldsmith still needs to be recapitalised. It isn't, in principle, such a bad partnership to link up with Steinberg's. It isn't in our interests, and it certainly isn't in Steinberg's interests, for this all to come out into the public arena. I don't want an investigation by the SEC, or by the Serious Fraud Office, any more than Mitchell Freeman does. Or than Miccinelli does.'

'So you want to sweep it all under the carpet? Just kiss and make up, and let the bad guys get away with it? You have a funny sense of justice, Jack.'

Jack grabbed her hand across the table. 'No, Teddy. I *don't* want to let the bad guys get away with it. But it seems to me that the only really bad guy is Fitzgerald. He won't be able to stay once I tell the board what he did. He will pay his dues. But I don't really think any one else should suffer. I thought you'd like the idea. Mike – even Glory – were just pawns. They were being used by Fitzgerald to get what he wanted. Should they suffer? He never gave a shit about them, or about anyone else. He manipulated them. In a word, he corrupted them. Don't you see, this is the only way that Mike can be in the clear?' Jack was surprised by Teddy's lack of reaction. He had expected to see relief wash over her face, but she looked at him blankly. 'I thought that's what you wanted,' he finished lamely.

Teddy tugged her hand away and stood up, so that she could move further away from Jack. 'And what about Candida?'

'I don't see that she has to be involved at all.'

'I thought you might say that,' Teddy prowled around the kitchen, picking things up and putting them down aimlessly. 'Listen, Jack. You do whatever you like. I've found out what I wanted to find out. I've told you everything. As you've made perfectly clear before – painstakingly – this is really none of my business. It's nothing to do with me. You have enough information to blow the whole thing sky high, or keep it quiet. I'm going to do one more thing for you. I'm going to get Mike to give me a written testimonial detailing the trade. Then I'm finished with it. I'm fed up with the whole thing. It's dirty, and wrong, and sordid. You protect who you like. I've had enough.'

Jack stared at her, confused. She seemed so angry – so bitter – and he had expected her to throw herself into his plan with her habitual gusto. He had grown accustomed to discussing things with her, hearing her opinion and using her as a sounding board. He had expected her to be delighted about a scheme that allowed the guilty to be punished, and Mike to be saved.

'Theodora. Come here, please.'

'Why the hell should I? This is my house. I'll do what I like in my own house, thank you very much, and I'd be grateful if you didn't talk to me like a child!'

'Then stop behaving like a fretful child! What has possessed you? You are the one who is at the *heart* of this whole thing! You're the one who has been so persistent, so convinced – you've been waving a personal banner ever since it happened, and now you're saying you don't care what happens? I don't understand you. I don't understand women at all.'

'Oh, spare me your clichés, for God's sake! You understand some women perfectly well, it seems to me. You've understood enough about Candida to protect her every step of the way, and you are going to carry on doing it!'

Jack stood up, and in two strides was next to her, his hands gripping her shoulders, nearly shaking her. 'That's enough! Stop it right now! You don't know what you're saying. You don't know what you are talking about! Now sit down,' he pushed her into a chair, 'and let's talk about this rationally.' He refilled her glass and shoved it into her hand. 'What is your beef about Candida?'

'I just don't see how you can say that Candida isn't involved. I don't see how you can say that she is a victim of Fitzgerald's. She set up the whole thing, for Christ's sake!'

Jack had recovered his self control. 'What the *evidence* tells us, Teddy, is that Candida was guilty of charging a double fee for the hiring of Glory McWhirter. We also know that she took an option position against Hayes stock. That may have been insider trading, on a small scale, but it could be considered as a well-judged punt. I'm not prepared to destroy her for those two petty sins.'

'She was perfectly prepared to destroy you,' Teddy muttered, glaring at him.

'That's right, so it should be up to me to decide what to do about it. I'm the one she tried to hurt, not you.' Teddy didn't comment, but her lips were set in a pout, and her fingers drummed the tabletop.

'Are we agreed, then?' Jack asked softly. 'Is that all right with you?'

'Oh, it's fine. Just fine.'

Jack bit his tongue. If there was one thing that made him feel that there was a genuine division between the sexes, if there was one thing that made him sympathetic to misogynists, it was the way women used the word 'fine'. 'So what are you going to do now?'

'I'm going to see Mike. Get him to write everything down. Then I'm going to go to bed.'

The word hung heavily in the air between them.

'With Mike?'

'Maybe. I haven't decided. It depends how I feel. I suppose that's okay with you? I suppose I don't have to ask your permission?'

Jack's jaw tightened, and he shook his head almost imperceptibly.

'Excuse me, Jack? I didn't hear that. *Do* I need your permission?'

'You know the answer to that perfectly well. Just don't push me, Teddy. Don't push me.'

All Teddy wanted to do was push him. She felt driven to

provoke him, to make him lose his temper. At that moment, she hated Jack's control more than she hated anything in the world. She walked to the telephone and dialled Mike's number.

'Michael?' she said softly, but just loud enough to be sure that Jack would hear. 'I'm back home. I still have that dinner in the fridge. Would you like to come over? You would, huh?' She listened, and then smiled. 'Okay, then. Give me half an hour. I want to have a shower and get ready.' She laughed again, a warm, husky laugh. 'See you soon.' She hung up the receiver. Jack hadn't moved from the kitchen table. His knuckles were white as he gripped his wine glass. Teddy refilled her own, and stood next to him, waiting.

'I don't want to leave like this, Teddy. I simply don't understand what you are doing.'

'Then we're in the same boat, Jack. I don't understand what you are doing.'

'For God's sake, Teddy! What do you *want*?' He almost groaned on the last word.

'I want to have a shower. If you don't want to leave, you can stay down here or you can come up. You can sit on the bed whilst I get ready, if you want, but I don't think I have much more to say to you. Do what the hell you like.'

Jack followed her upstairs, and had the bathroom door slammmed in his face. He sat on her bed, his head in his hands, wondering how he could make Teddy understand what he felt about Candida. Teddy emerged from the shower, wrapped in a towel, with another towel, turban-like, around her hair. She acted as if she were surprised to see him still sitting there.

'I have to get dressed now,' she said matter-of-factly.

'Do you want me to leave?'

'No. We're just good friends, aren't we, Jack? Just turn your back, would you?'

Teddy sounded as calm and relaxed as if she were talking to Charles Bartholomew, and Jack felt a sudden surge of anger as he wondered how often Charles had watched Teddy get dressed. Mike, Charles, Christian, now Mike again . . . Jack felt a surge of jealousy and anger. Teddy was using him. Teddy waited until Jack turned his back, and then dropped the towel. Her skin was steamy and glowing from the shower, but she felt cold and was shivering. She pulled on a pair of jeans, and shook out a white cotton shirt.

'Okay, Jack. You can turn round now.' As Jack turned, he saw the outline of her breasts, high and firm, as she slipped the shirt on. She hadn't bothered with a bra. She was vigorously rubbing her hair.

'As you're not doing anything, Jack, would you be a sweetheart and rub my hair for me? I love having people dry my hair.'

'I bet you do,' he said grimly.

Teddy passed him the towel and sat close to him on the bed. He reluctantly took her head between his hands, and began to rub, starting at the base of her neck. Teddy arched her neck like a cat, and leant into him. She smelt warm and sweet, her body slumped against him as limp as a rag doll. She knew exactly what she was doing. He had rejected her once, and she had behaved impeccably. Now she was angry with him, and looking for a reason to lose her temper. Jack pushed her away suddenly.

'Teddy, don't do this to me. What do you think I am? I'm not made of steel.' The words caught at his throat.

Teddy jumped up and marched indignantly across the room, shaking her wet hair out of her face. 'No, you *are* made of steel! When it comes to me, you are! If it's a question of Candida, you're as soft as butter! You'd do anything for *Candida*, wouldn't you, Jack? How can you still be in love with her? How can you be so besotted after all she's done to you? What do you think is going to happen tomorrow? D'you think she's going to leap into your arms, and it's going to be happy ever after? Do you think she's going to suddenly see the light, and say, "Oh, Jack! My saviour!"' Teddy spoke mockingly, her hands pressed together, her eyes raised to heaven in false supplication. Jack stared at her. Water trickled off her hair and down the front of her shirt, making the thin white cotton clinging and partially transparent, so that Jack could see her breasts rising and falling clearly as they brushed against the fabric.

'You must be crazy,' he whispered. 'You cannot believe that I am still in love with Candida.'

'Oh yes I can! I do! And I'm right! You may not understand women, Jack Delavigne, but I understand men, and I can certainly tell whether a man's in love or not!'

In one smooth, swift motion, Jack rose and crossed the room to take Teddy by the shoulders. She could feel his fingers digging into her flesh.

'What do I have to do to prove to you that I am not in love with my ex-wife? What ridiculous forfeit do I have to perform to convince you?'

Teddy stared up at him, her green eyes flashing defiance, meeting his furious look and answering his question bluntly. He held her slightly away from his body, and looked at her from head to toe and back again, his eyes coming to rest on her mouth. They were both breathing heavily. Jack's fingers moved down to the buttons of her shirt. As he slowly undid them, one by one, Teddy's breathing quickened. His hands caressed her breasts, now fully exposed, and ran firmly down her ribcage. There was nothing hesitant about his movements. His hands were slow and deliberate, and came to rest on the waistband of her jeans, easily undoing the top clasp and pressing down the zip with the heel of his hand so that the warm palm of his hand trailed across her stomach. Teddy leant against him, her cheek against his chest.

'Don't stop, Jack. I couldn't bear it if you stopped now.'

'What about your boyfriend?' Jack's voice said huskily in her ear. 'I'm not interested in threesomes.'

'I don't have a boyfriend.'

'Miccinelli. He's due here in about ten minutes.'

'Oh him. Well, you'd better hurry up then. We haven't got all night.'

Jack picked her up in his arms and deposited her, none too gently, on the bed. She raised her hips high to help him remove her jeans, and watched as he quickly stripped. Everything about him seemed clean and strong, long-limbed, broad-chested, upright. A soft line of golden hair ran from his chest down to the triangle at his groin. In less than a minute, he lowered himself over her and kissed her gently on the mouth.

'Teddy, I love you. I love you very much. I feel over-whelmed by you. You are the most extraordinary, mys-tifying, infuriating and confusing woman I have ever met.' The sound of his voice alone made Teddy's muscles contract and ache.

'But you don't fancy me, right?'

Jack grunted and shifted his weight slightly. Teddy felt his large hand between her legs, his long fingers inside her, and she reached down to guide him into her. She felt him pull back fractionally, and she shook her head, bringing him closer and smiling into his steady, serious gaze.

'I'm ready, Jack, more than ready. Please.'

Despite the urgency of their union, and the speed of his climax, Teddy felt intensely satisfied. It had simply been right. Perfectly natural and perfectly relaxed, as if they had been making love to each other for years, and knew each other's bodies inside out. There had been none of the modern, 'liberated' sexual correctness; she hadn't told him where she liked to be touched, hadn't felt the need to introduce him formally to her body. He had neither embarrassed her by saying, 'Does that feel good? And that? What about that?' like a game of twenty questions. He had listened to her body with an acute ear, and the sounds that they had made, if not verbal, were at least as expressive as words. She had often felt that a woman couldn't possess a man's body the way a man could possess a woman's. How can you possess something that you don't really enter? But she did feel that she had possessed Jack, then, right there, and after he had withdrawn, and she lay beside him, with her head resting on his chest, she felt that she possessed him still.

'It shouldn't be like this, darling girl. It shouldn't be so rushed. I want to make love to you all night. I don't think I could have waited another day. I don't know that I could have waited another ten minutes. Damn Miccinelli. I don't care about the billion pounds, but I don't think I'm going to forgive him for this. I've changed my mind. Let's make the bastard go to prison. Damn him for being at home.'

'He wasn't,' Teddy said simply.

'What?'

'He wasn't at home. When I heard his machine, I just held down the button on the phone. So there's no hurry.'

With a roar, Jack rolled her over and pulled her on top of him. Her hair cascaded over his face, enveloping him like a cloud, and her nipples rubbed against the hair of his chest. After a moment, she wriggled away. Jack grabbed a slender ankle.

'Where do you think you're going?'

'I'm going to get some dinner. As I told Mike, it's in the fridge.'

Jack groaned, and pulled a pillow over his face. 'How the

hell do you stay so slim, Teddy? You never stop thinking about food! Even at the most intimate moments . . .'

'I simply believe in sustenance. Feeding the appetites. You know, *mens sana in corpore sano*, and all that crap. Besides, I'm hungry. And you've got a long day ahead of you. You've got to keep your strength up.'

'We've got a long night ahead of us, you mean.' He aimed a pillow at her departing rear end. 'And don't you dare talk to me about keeping anything up!'

Hours later, before they went to sleep, they had only two irreconcilable differences. Jack insisted he should be the one to approach Mike about giving a written testimonial. Teddy stubbornly refused.

'He won't do it for you. He'll only do it for me.'

'That's precisely what I'm afraid of.'

'You know, I can be very persuasive when I want to be.'

'As I said, that's precisely what I'm afraid of.'

The other bone of contention was about whether or not Teddy would accompany Jack to the meeting with the board of Steinberg Roth.

'That is out of the question.'

'It makes perfect sense. I'm a headhunter for both Hayes and Steinberg's. If your arrangement concerns employee contracts, it isn't at all odd that I should be there. Anyway, I worked for Steinberg's. I know Mitchell Freeman, better than you do. I know all the partners.' Teddy was now sitting astride Jack, and as she made each point, she thumped his chest. 'I've even worked in mergers and acquisitions. So you can stop treating me like your floozie. You need me. And you owe it to me. You owe it to me to let me see that shit Fitzgerald's face. You don't have any choice.'

'I have every choice, and my choice is no. My choice is that you should stay at home, patiently, and have dinner ready for my return. My choice is that if I'm going to have a floozie, she should behave like a floozie. While you're waiting, you could do some needlework or something.'

'That won't work.'

'Why not?'

'Because if I'm not there, you won't have any evidence to show them. I won't give it to you.'

'Where is it?'

'I'm not telling. And if you push me, I'm going to eat it.'

'You can't *possibly* eat any more!'

'It's a promise.'

'And what if I tell you that I order you to stay at home?'

'I'll tell you to screw yourself.'

The argument was long and protracted, interrupted by frequent ceasefires. By the time they fell asleep, Jack was confident that Teddy would not attend the confrontation with Steinberg Roth. Teddy looked forward to the meeting with keen anticipation.

Bright and early the next morning, the battle lines were drawn afresh. Somehow, being dressed and sitting at the kitchen table made the topic of the previous night's discussion far more serious. Jack didn't want Teddy to go into the office at all; he feared that she would be unable to stop herself accusing Candida of conspiracy to commit fraud. Teddy was enraged – not by the idea that she should take another day off work, but by the idea that she was incapable of keeping her mouth shut when she needed to. In Teddy's mind, the course of action for both of them was absolutely straightforward. Jack was to spend the day at the office with Dick. They had agreed, sometime between two and three a.m., that Dick should be told the whole story. As chairman of Hayes Goldsmith, he would also be present at the Steinberg's meeting, and would need to be fully abreast of the facts and strategy. As far as Teddy was concerned, she would spend a normal day at the office, trying to close the two analysts for Morgan Stanley, and would then meet Mike. Alone.

'Why don't you want me to be there?' Jack asked for the fifth time that morning.

'How would it look, Jack? What do you think I'm going to say? "Hey, Mike, I'd like to introduce you to Jack Delavigne. This is the sucker that you ripped off for something around a hundred million quid, but he's not cross with you, he just wants to be friends. Now shake hands like a good boy." How do you think Mike would react to that? No, Jack. I know what I'm doing. I know Mike. I know what matters to him.'

'What matters to him is getting you back in the sack.'

'I don't think so. But the point is, you have to trust me. Whatever I do, I'll do with my best judgement, and if you don't trust me now, I don't think you'll ever be able to.'

'God preserve me from headstrong women . . .' Jack said resignedly.

'You just thank your lucky stars I *am* headstrong, buddy. If I hadn't been so keen to get my own way, you'd probably still be drying my hair.'

As soon as Jack reached his office, he buzzed through to Dick Belton-Smith's. His old mentor had been coming into the office every day since the Black Wednesday débâcle, and Jack couldn't wait any longer to lighten the load on his shoulders.

'Dick, I have a rather peculiar story to tell you. Could you meet me in the board room in about ten minutes?'

'Of course. How did you like the *FT* article?'

'I haven't even opened the paper, to be honest.'

'My God, Jack! You're playing it very cool, I must say!

The papers are full of the mooted sale of Hayes Goldsmith, and you're not even reading them?'

'I just doubt that they have all the facts, so I'm no longer interested in their verdict.'

'Well, Jack, if you have anything to say that's going to make this picture look a little rosier, then I'm all ears.'

'Meet me in the board room, my friend. Prepare for some good news.'

Teddy was having a much harder time of it than Jack. On this of all days, Candida was bending over backwards to be at her most charming and most likeable. She was relieved to see Teddy back in the office, but concerned that she was run down and needed to take a long holiday. Both the research analysts had accepted Morgan Stanley's offer that morning, and when Candida heard the good news, she insisted on taking Teddy out to lunch to celebrate. Teddy trailed down Moorgate behind her boss, feeling like a lamb who was not only being led to the slaughter, but had actually signed up on the list for volunteers. The one thing that she and Jack had not discussed, had in fact tiptoed around, was what was going to happen at ARC following tomorrow's meeting. Teddy couldn't see Candida taking the news with good grace. Nor could she see Candida offering her a partnership at ARC when she found out about Teddy going through her drawers. *If* she found out, that is. But even if the details of Teddy's espionage never surfaced, Teddy didn't see how she could continue to work for Candida knowing what she knew, knowing what she had done, and knowing that she was madly, wildly and deliriously in love with Candida's ex-husband. She prayed that she could keep the topic of conversation to safe grounds. So long as they stuck to Morgan Stanley, and FRG, they should be okay.

No sooner had they ordered than Candida leant across the table and said, 'So did you see the *FT* today? Something of a kick in the teeth for Hayes Goldsmith, didn't you think?'

'I didn't read it.'

'Well, you were probably too wrapped up with Morgan Stanley. But have a look when we get back to the office. You have a treat in store.'

'I'll do that.' Teddy played with her napkin.

'Look, Teddy. I didn't ask you to lunch to talk shop. I really just wanted to catch up on your news. We've both been so busy recently, I feel like I've hardly had a chance to ask how everything is.'

'Everything's fine.'

'Are you back with Mike Miccinelli again?'

'Not exactly, although I think I'm seeing him tonight.'

'Well, for God's sake don't worry about that stupid woman Glory McWhirter. From what I hear, she's likely to get a one-way ticket to the States.'

'Distance has never been a problem for Mike before. But I'm not worried about Glory, I have to say.'

'Jamie mentioned something about you and your French candidate – Clement-Grandcourt . . . did anything happen there?'

Teddy blushed. She didn't care about Christian, she just desperately wanted Candida to get on to a more neutral subject. Candida caught the blush, and smiled.

'It's okay, Teddy, don't look so nervous. I don't have any hard rules about separating business and pleasure. There's nothing wrong with going to bed with a candidate – or a client, for that matter – if they take your fancy.'

'Is that what you've found, Candida?'

Candida's clear blue eyes gazed into Teddy's green ones reflectively. 'To be honest, Teddy, I can't say that *any* of them have really taken my fancy. I'm not saying that I haven't had affairs, because I have – several. But perhaps for different reasons than you. I know what I need out of life, and I have long given up pretending that I want things just to try to fit in with the norm. I am simply not particularly interested in men as *men*, if you see what I mean. I don't think they provide anything I can't achieve for myself.'

'But you did get married. You did love Jack Delavigne at some point, didn't you?' Teddy had to ask.

Candida's eyes turned the colour of glass. It wasn't that her expression was hard – it was more that her eyes were transparent, and Teddy's couldn't read, couldn't see anything behind them.

'I suppose I did at some point. I must have, but I can't remember how or why. I should never have married. As soon as I married Jack, I knew it was a mistake. At the time I thought it was the concept of marriage itself – I didn't like the label of being somebody's wife – somebody's *anything*. Afterwards . . . well, afterwards I knew that of all people, I should never have married Jack. He was too . . . too . . .' Candida seemed to be searching for the right word, and then abandoned the attempt, tossing her auburn hair over her shoulder in an impatient gesture.

'Too what?' Teddy asked bluntly.

'I don't know, Teddy. It was too long ago. I was a different woman. Jack is one of those types of men that women get *lost* in, if you see what I mean. The whole time I was married to Jack, I felt that I was lost. Maybe I was too in awe of him. Maybe not enough. I no longer had any sense of myself when I was married to him. Once he was out of my life, I knew where I was again. It's a question of freedom, really. I believe in freedom more than anything else.'

Teddy listened to Candida, and was glad that she had finally agreed with Jack to keep Candida out of the Steinberg Roth affair. She couldn't empathise with what Candida was saying, but as she looked at her boss she had a sudden sense that she had more in common with Candida than she might care to admit. Had Teddy married Mike, had she been sucked into Mike's ever-narrowing orbit, it was possible that she might have reached the same conclusions. When she had been with Mike she had felt too frightened to challenge his judgement, even when she knew he was wrong. She had gone along with him, dragging her heels, maybe, unhappy quite a lot of the time, but she had gone along with him, until he went too far. She feared that, had Jamie not intervened, she might have married Mike and lost her sense of self. She saw a random, haphazard decision that had brought Candida and Jack together, created Tommy, and then left the two adults so miserably unhappy and the little boy dead. In some ways, Jack was right. It was nobody and everybody's fault. But Jack was too close to the past and the present to apportion blame. It was clear to Teddy that it was more Candida's fault than Jack's — Candida could not be held blameless, because she had done so much to hurt and to harm innocent people — but Teddy was beginning to see the misery that Candida lived with.

'Don't look so sad, Teddy. Things could have been worse. We might have been born in a time when divorce didn't exist.' Candida's lips twisted in an ironic curve. 'And anyway, the story had a happy ending. Jack Delavigne got — or is about to get — what he deserved. And I have my freedom. I won't make the same mistakes again.'

The words rang a bell in Teddy's ears. She thought about her own mistakes and misjudgements, and she thought about how sure she had been of decisions that had turned out to be the wrong ones. How could she tell now if her instincts about Jack were right? She pushed these unpleasant doubts to the back of her mind.

'So tell me about your plans for Paris . . .'

*   *   *

Jack called the office number of De Bragga & Spittler in New York, and asked to be put through to Walter Bacher, one of the toughest attorneys on the circuit. He briefly outlined the story of the trade, without naming any names, and without involving himself directly. He could hear the lawyer chuckling throughout the narrative.

'I just wanted to get your gut feeling on this, Walt. How would the case stand up?'

'Jack, if I read you correctly, this baby's never gonna get to court, am I right?'

'My *friend* doesn't want it to get to court, that's right.'

'Okay. Here's what you do – what your *friend* does. You gotta catch them in a lie. Just any old, simple little lie. Then you've got 'em by the balls. First time one of the bastards lies, they're all done for.' Jack could almost hear him rubbing his hands together. 'I *love* lies, Jack. You see, in this business, one little lie can be very important. It contaminates the whole fuckin' story, if you see what I mean . . .'

Teddy and Mike were due to meet at Stanley Gardens at eight p.m. It was a Wednesday – fortunately late-night closing at Harrods – and this time Mike arrived with a bottle of champagne.

'So, Teddy. I'm in your hands. I've done exactly what you told me. When that bastard Fitzgerald came on to the trading floor today I kept my mouth shut, although I wanted to punch the cunt in the gob. So what's going to happen to me?'

'That depends on what you want, Mike, and how you feel about what's happened.'

'I feel as sick as a parrot. Nothing's gone right since last May. Nothing's gone right since I started listening to Fitz. I just feel terrible, Ted. I don't enjoy my job anymore. I don't know what I want anymore. I used to think it was all so straightforward.' Teddy nodded in agreement. 'Teddy, you know what I want. I want you. I want to hear you say that I'm all right, that I'm not a shit, or a fool, or a loser. Ted, would you come over here please, would you sit on my lap? Just for a minute? Just for old times' sake?'

'No, Mike. We need to talk. There are two ways this can work out.'

'So tell me about them.'

'There's no question that the trade was fraudulent, agreed?'

Mike looked hesitant.

Teddy spoke firmly. 'Look, it *was* a fraudulent trade. I'll swear to what you told me till I'm blue in the face if you don't confirm it. I've already told Jack Delavigne. By this time, I expect he's told the chairman of the bank. We're prepared to tell Steinbergs all about it tomorrow. Personally, I'm prepared to go to court.'

Mike's black eyes bored into her. 'Where does that leave me?'

'If you want to co-operate, then all you have to do is to write down on a piece of paper all the details of what happened a week ago. I don't think there will be any investigation. Jack doesn't want it, and nor will Steinberg's. All Jack wants is a fair value put on Hayes Goldsmith. As far as I can tell, you will just carry on working for Steinberg Roth as if nothing had ever happened.'

'No investigation, you say?'

'That's what we all want, but of course I can't guarantee it. What I can virtually guarantee is that there *will* be an investigation if you don't confirm what happened.'

Mike shifted restlessly. 'What about the five mill?'

'What about it?'

'Well,' he looked uncomfortable. 'Do I get to keep it?'

Teddy folded her arms over her chest and looked at him

coolly for a moment before replying. 'What do *you* think, Mike?'

'I think I don't.'

'You think right.'

'Why should anyone believe me? What if they think Glory and I just set it all up alone, and that Fitz never knew anything about it? Why should he admit he was telling us what to do?'

'Don't pretend to be more naïve than you are, Mike. You may be many things, but you are not naïve. You thought that one through when Fitz first mentioned it to you. If you and Glory set it up, then by this time,' she looked at her watch for effect, 'you and Glory would have been somewhere in South America wearing beards. You would have had to have the funds transferred to an account you could access, not Steinberg's ordinary proprietary account. And you wouldn't be sitting around waiting for the shit to fly. No. Your story is the true one, and that's why it's credible. Fitzgerald is the only person in a position to guarantee you a five million pound bonus, and money is the only motive you could have had for doing what you did.'

'So what's my motive now, Teddy? For doing what you want me to do?'

She looked at him with a calm and steady stare. 'Are you asking me for a bribe, Mike? Is that it? Do you only do things for money? No deal. I'm not going to offer you a penny. It isn't my money to offer. Just like the money Fitzgerald offered you wasn't his money. It's called theft, Mike. And corruption. Are you ready to do it all again?'

Mike put his head in his hands, and spoke to the floor. 'I don't want money, Teddy. I just want everything to be the way it was, do you understand?' When he raised his head, Teddy could see that his eyes were nearly brimming over with tears. 'I just want to be with you again. I just want to hold you, and make love to you, and touch you, and get married to you. I want to be with you. I always have. I want you to love me. Me. It's the only thing I've ever wanted – '

'That you didn't get. Isn't that right, Mike? Let's say we got back together. Let's say we even got married. How long do you think it would take for you to be in some other woman's pants? How long would it be before you were ranting about how Steinberg's didn't pay you enough, how I'd ruined your career, blocked your potential, restricted your freedom . . . stopped you from going out for a drink with your mates. How long, Mike? How long would you give it?'

Mike stood up and paced the room. 'What if I've changed, Teddy? What if I've learnt something from all this? It's not impossible, is it? Everyone else thinks I'm a bright guy. I don't think you've ever had a high opinion of me, but why the hell should you have such a low one? I'm not a shit, I'm not stupid. Okay, I fell for Fitzgerald's line. I was weak. I was vulnerable. I was – goddamnit – corruptible. I am not a model of virtue. Are you? Is anyone? At least I've learnt something. I know I didn't treat you right, but I would now. You've got to believe me, Teddy!'

Teddy shook her head sadly and slowly. 'I don't know that I can believe all that, Mike. I just don't think I can trust you. Maybe you're right. Maybe you've changed. But I've changed too, and I'm more careful about who I trust and why. I don't want to be hurt again, do you understand me? I don't think I could stand being hurt the way you hurt me.'

Mike knelt down on the floor at her feet, and put his head in her lap. Teddy was frozen in her place. Her hands hovered, not wanting to touch him, not wanting to push him away. She stared at the wall, not wanting to look down at him. She hadn't expected to feel so upset by Mike. She had expected him to press for another chance, but she hadn't realised that it would bother her, that despite all that had happened, Mike was still capable of wrenching her heart, making her remember how she had loved him.

'I wouldn't hurt you ever again, Teddy. I promise you. You *have* to believe me. You are the most precious thing in the world to me. More than my work, even.' Teddy stiffened slightly. '*Much* more than my work. I want to take care of you. I want to look after you . . .'

'That's just it, Mike. I don't want anyone to take care of me. I don't need anyone to take care of me. You say you've changed, but you're still lumping me in there with your luxury flat, and your mobile phone and your fucking Ferrari! I know what good care you take of them, and I don't want it! What about *my* life, Mike?'

She shoved his head off her lap. Mike immediately moved next to her on the sofa, and began to kiss her neck.

'Don't kiss me! For God's sake don't kiss me! That doesn't make it all better!' She pushed him away as hard as she could.

'I'm sorry, Teddy. Jeez, I'm sorry. I'm doing it again. I do care about your life. All you have to do is tell me exactly what you want. I want you to be happy. I just know that you'll be happy with me.'

'It seems to me that everybody knows a hell of a lot of things about me that I don't know myself! Just back off, Mike! Give me some space. I don't know what I think, or what I feel, or what will make me happy. I just don't know.'

'I'll do anything you want. Just tell me.'

She glared at him. 'Right. Sit down at the desk and write down what happened. Put down all the numbers, times, dates, everything. Don't leave anything out. Put down your calls with Fitz, with Glory. Everything. I'm going to get dinner ready. Then we'll talk.'

Teddy walked shakily to the kitchen, and without turning round to look, heard Mike pull out the desk chair, and the sound made by the lid of her rolltop desk opening. As she took the dishes out of the fridge her hands were trembling, and she whispered a chant to herself, 'Get a grip, Teddy; get a grip, get a grip.' She felt strangely out of control, and was unable to focus on what she was doing. She put the grill on, not the oven, and took four plates out of the cupboard. 'Get a grip, Teddy; get a grip, get a grip.' She switched off the grill, and turned on the oven. She put two plates back in the cupboard. Maybe it was to do with getting this testimony, maybe it was to do with Mike. When she had felt his hot breath on her neck, she had had that sleepy sense of slow arousal, and yet she could still smell Jack on her own skin. Candida's cynicism came back to her . . . how was she going to know who was the right man? Were either of them? Would she lose her own life to them both? Did it matter anyway?

Teddy restrained herself from looking at what Mike had written. They had dinner rather quietly. There didn't seem to be any point in discussing work. Neither of them knew where their futures were headed. Teddy told him about her conversation with Glory, and Mike visibly flinched.

'Mike, I don't want to know about your affair with Glory, past or present – '

'Past, Teddy, past. Definitely past.'

'I do want to know what makes her so irresistibly attractive. I mean, I realise she has a good body and everything, but surely that's not enough? Most men I know seem to be like moths to the flame around her. Why?'

'Ah, Teddy. Now you're probing deep into the male psyche!'

'Not that deep. It isn't that deep,' Teddy muttered. 'Is it just that she's so obviously available? Are all men irrefutably drawn to a tart?'

'No. It's not the tartiness that appeals. That's something you have to overcome. What appeals about Glory is that she makes it perfectly clear, from the very start, that she wants *you*. Men like that. There's no big philosophy about it. All you women spend your lives trying to make men say how much they want you, how much they desire you, how they can't resist you. Glory's great gift is that she treats men the way men are trained to treat women. She lays her cards on the table. She says straight out that she'll die if she can't get your body. Sometimes, that's a pretty persuasive argument for a guy. Then after a while, you realise that she feels that about pretty much everyone, and it isn't quite so flattering. But don't get Glory wrong; she may be coarse, and crude, and not a lady. Maybe she didn't fit in with all your nice friends. But there's nothing artificial about her. If she's a slut, then she's a genuine slut, and there are a hell of a lot of girls swanning down Sloane Street who are sluts pretending to be ladies.'

'What are you saying, Mike? That you can't like sex and still be a lady?'

'No, I'm not saying that. I'm only saying that Glory isn't a tease. She's a natural. She makes men feel really good and really powerful, and sometimes that counts for a lot. She's also a pain in the arse, and I wouldn't want to take her out to dinner. But you asked me a question, Ted, and that's the answer. She makes men feel really special. There aren't many women who try to do that.'

'Do you think I ever tried to do it?' Teddy asked in a small voice.

'You never needed to, darling. You made me feel so special just by deciding to be with me, that was all I needed.'

Michael's answer was profoundly unsatisfactory. When he talked about Glory, Teddy knew that he was speaking from the heart, and that what he said about Glory was true.

Even another woman could see it. It had scared the pants off Charles, for God's sake. She also was forced to admit that for most of her life, she had believed that it was a man's job to make a woman feel desirable, whether they were in bed or not. And Teddy knew that after twenty years, Mike wouldn't still be feeling special just because she had chosen to be with him.

She cleared away the dishes and edged over to the desk. Her eyes skimmed what Mike had written. It looked perfect, exactly what they needed. She left the sheet of paper on the desk, and turned to Mike.

'What would you like? A brandy or something?'

'We still haven't had the champagne.'

'Oh, okay. Why don't you open it.' Teddy sat down on an armchair, and wasn't overly surprised when Mike sat on the arm of it. His hands trailed through her hair, twisting strands around his fingers. His lips brushed the top of her head, then her cheekbone, and then fleetingly her lips.

'Mike, I think it's getting late. I have to be up early tomorrow.'

'Is that right?' Mike didn't seem to be aware of what she was saying. One of his hands rubbed the nape of her neck, the other cradled her face.

'Mike, I really do think you should go now.'

'Shhh, Teddy. Just drink your champagne. Let's relax for a minute. Just for old times' sake.'

Teddy waited a minute, but she didn't relax. She felt as if her entire body was hooked up to an electric cable ready to put four hundred volts through her at any moment. When she felt Mike's lips on her collar bone, she leapt out of the chair.

'Mike, please leave. I'm not ready for this. Not at all.'

He followed her as she retreated backwards across the room. He stalked her.

'Mike, I really don't think I want this — I mean it.'

'You don't know what you want. Relax. Stop talking. Stop thinking.'

He held her in his arms, her back pressed against the front door. She felt his hands move down to her buttocks, pulling her hips hard against his pelvis. She inhaled deeply, and steadied her voice.

'Mike. Stop this at once. If you ever want to see me again, you have to leave now.'

His black eyes burned into her as he held her rigid body against his own.

'Michael. Please. Give me time.' His grip was tight. His hands ran down and across her body, as if familiarising himself with the shape of her curves, and then suddenly he let her go.

'Okay. I just wanted you to know I'm serious. But I guess you don't want it, right?'

Teddy hung her head. Mike roughly took her chin and tilted her face up to his.

'I always knew it was just a dream, Teddy. You've never given me much credit for smarts, but I always knew you were just a dream.' He kissed her on the lips, moved her aside and left the house.

Teddy picked up the testimonial and slipped it into her briefcase. Underneath it, there was another piece of paper with Mike's writing on it. She held it up, and began to read.

'Darling Teddy,

If you're reading this, then I know it's all over between us. It doesn't surprise me. I didn't deserve you.

You never let me have the last word. So I wanted to write it down so you couldn't say anything afterwards. I do love you. I've made a lot of mistakes, and I've behaved like a cunt (I know you won't like me writing that – that's why I've put it) but the worst thing I ever did was let you think I didn't love you.

I get the feeling you've got another bloke. That's no surprise either. You could have anyone you wanted. If he doesn't treat you right, call me, anytime. I'll come round and bash his head in.

There's one other thing I want to tell you. About Glory. I just want you to know that when we were in Tokyo, and I bought you those earrings, Glory wasn't with me. She didn't choose them. I chose them. I hope you like them. They reminded me of you.

Love,
Mike'

Teddy raised one hand to her earlobe.

CHAPTER NINETEEN

Jack Delavigne and Richard Belton-Smith sat in a small waiting room on the third floor of Steinberg Roth's offices. Jack flipped casually through the *Wall Street Journal*, whilst Dick hummed and studied a large coffee-table book emblazoned with a silver star, called *The History of Steinberg Roth and Partners, 1912–1990*. The door opened, and Teddy was shown into the room. She was wearing a Prince of Wales check suit, a white shirt, and had her hair folded into a graceful, loose knot on the nape of her neck. She had dressed for a trial.

'Good morning, Jack,' she said softly, and turned to greet the man with him. 'You must be Richard Belton-Smith.'

'And you must be Theodora ... I've heard a great deal about you, young lady, and I believe we owe you a huge debt.'

'Let's see if you still feel that after this morning's meeting.'

'Did you get it?' Jack asked.

In reply, Teddy opened her briefcase and handed him a slim, manila envelope. Jack opened it, read Mike's confession silently, transferred four sheets of paper to his own briefcase and resumed his study of the *Journal*. He seemed utterly relaxed, wearing an expression that was close to boredom. Teddy and Richard were less comfortable. To Teddy, the atmosphere reminded her of a dentist's waiting room. The odds of getting out with an absolutely clean bill of health seemed slim. None of them knew how the partners would react. It was possible, in time-honoured tradition, that they would isolate a scapegoat — Alex Fitzgerald — and offer him up for sacrifice to appease the gods. It was equally possible that they would rally together, all for one and one for all, in the hope that if they all lied together the lie would stand up as the truth.

'Mr Delavigne? The partners are waiting for you and your party in the boardroom.' The elegant receptionist turned on one patent leather high heel and led them down a long, silent corridor, and then flung open a set of double doors. Mitchell Freeman rose from the table to meet them.

'Jack; Richard. Welcome. Let me introduce you to my colleagues.'

Jack placed his hand behind Teddy's back and propelled her forward. 'Mitchell, I took the liberty of asking Theodora Winnington from the Aston-Redmayne Company to join us. She's fully informed of the situation, and I believe her input may be useful to both sides.'

'Certainly! Well, we all know Teddy. It's good to have you back under Steinberg's' roof.'

The long, rectangular table was set up for a meeting. Before each place there was a yellow notepad next to a leather folder, three pencils, a flask of water, a glass and coffee cup. Jack, Teddy and Richard took their seats on one side of the table, and surveyed the men opposite them.

'Allow me to introduce my colleagues.' Mitchell moved down the table, placing a hand on the shoulder of each man as he introduced them. 'You've met Daniel Carpenter, our in-house counsel. Brad Finch, partner for global markets, has joined us from New York. Alex Fitzgerald, partner in charge of sales and trading, I believe you all know. Morton Wise, also from New York, represents our international business. Stephen Carruthers has come over from Herbert Smith to advise us on the legal aspects of the proposal.' He turned last to a heavy set man with red hair, who sat at one end of the table. 'And John Hirsch, our senior partner in the London office.' Mitchell waved to a woman hovering at the side of the room. 'Now let's have some coffee, gentlemen – and lady – and then perhaps we can begin. Herbert Smith have prepared a provisional document as a basis of discussion. If you open your folders, perhaps we can start at the beginning.'

Teddy looked at Jack, waiting for him to call the proceedings to a halt. Jack calmly opened the leather wallet, and began to read. Teddy and Dick followed suit. Jack was clearly happy to leave the ball in Steinberg's court for the time being. Mitchell continued in his soft, mid-Atlantic drawl.

'Now, so far, we have agreed a broad outline for Steinberg's acquisition of a one hundred per cent interest in Hayes Goldsmith. This is the minimum stake we are prepared to acquire. Are we all agreed with that?'

The suits around the table nodded, with the exception of Teddy, who sat down hard on her hands to stop them trembling.

'The proposed exit price is a five per cent premium to the current stock price,' Mitchell glanced at Morton Wise, 'which this morning opened at?'

'2.69,' Belton-Smith and Morton Wise answered simultaneously.

'Thank you. I see the stock has risen slightly since we last met, no doubt on the back of speculation about our stake. Now are we all unanimous that, subject to other terms being mutually agreeable, that is a fair basis of valuation?'

Teddy held her breath. Jack said nothing.

'Good. Now if you'll turn to page two of the document, we can move on to certain other areas that require consideration. The foreign offices. Richard, Jack, we believe that whereas Hayes has a stronger established presence in continental Europe, Steinberg's is better perceived in the Far East. We would propose a merger of the Paris and Milan offices, the retention of Hayes' existing subsidiaries in Frankfurt and Madrid, which would continue to trade under the Hayes name, and the immediate closure of all Hayes' operations in the Far East.'

'Closing and redundancy costs to be met by Steinberg Roth, I assume?' Jack asked.

'Of course.'

'Right.'

Teddy kicked Jack under the table. He ignored her.

'The relevant numbers, and estimated costs, are laid out in appendix four. We can come back to the details later.' Mitchell turned the page. 'Now, if we move on to page three, we have a suggested outline for the securities divisions. There are clearly some synergies to be gained by merging the two operations. We would propose that all secondary market activity, whether sales and trading of debt or equity instruments, should be gathered under Alex Fitzgerald's umbrella. Of course, Hayes covers certain sectors which we do not follow, and I have no doubt that your research team will greatly enhance our operations. As to the proprietary trading department, we at Steinberg's believe that this is likely to represent the core of our profits for the next two or three years, and that as the risk profile of the department is so important, this should be managed entirely within Steinberg Roth.' He paused, and raised an eyebrow to allow Jack to intervene. Jack nodded.

Mitchell Freeman worked slowly and meticulously through the provisional agreement. When he reached the end, it was obvious to all of them, despite Mitchell's tact, that Steinberg's acquisition of Hayes Goldsmith would result in the virtual obliteration of Hayes through its absorption into the American house. Teddy turned from Jack, seemingly intent on the appendices, to Dick, who poured himself a

glass of water and was whistling a gay little ditty through
his teeth. If one of them didn't interject in a minute, she
thought she would burst. She scribbled a note to Jack across
the top of her pad: 'Have you gone absolutely mad? Are you
deaf and dumb? Give 'em both barrels!' Jack read the note
and smiled. He cleared his throat.

'Mitchell, I think that we all see the logic of a formal
co-operation between Hayes and your fine institution. That
is a principle we can all accept. What concerns me are
some of the figures given in the equity statements and
stock price analysis in appendix two.' They all leafed
hurriedly through the memorandum. 'There appear to
be a few miscalculations. I am moderately – not entirely
– happy with your proposed price of five per cent over
market valuation. However, I am not happy with using
the price of 2.69.'

'That's what the market says, Jack; you can't deny the
market.' This came from Fitzgerald.

'No; but in this case the market has been duped.' Jack
rose to his feet, and leant across the table, directing his
comments to the morose face of John Hirsch at the head
of the table. 'John. Gentlemen. I am afraid that I have
some rather serious allegations to make which have a great
impact on the outcome of these talks. I believe that it would
be in your interests, John, if the representative from Herbert
Smith were not present for the next few moments.'

'Jack, we cannot proceed without our legal counsel
present – '

'I said it is in your interests, Mitchell. Let me say
what I have to say, and then, if you would like his
opinion, by all means call him back and I'll say it all
again.'

'No, Jack, that is absolutely out of the question. We
cannot – '

'Carruthers?' John Hirsch spoke suddenly, cutting across

Mitchell Freeman. 'Get out. We'll call you when we need you.'

'John, I cannot recommend this. I cannot advise you on the basis of negotiations that I haven't been party to – '

'Get out.' Hirsch waited until the board room door had closed behind the lawyer.

'Okay, Delavigne. Say your piece. It had better be good.'

'Wait a minute! If this just concerns the two firms, if it's just between these four walls, then why have we got a goddamn headhunter sitting in?' This question came from Alex.

'She's here because I asked her to be. I have nothing to hide from her. Do you, Alex?' Jack smiled.

'Don't push me, buddy,' Alex snarled.

'With all due respect, Jack, it's a fair objection.' Again, Mitchell spoke in his melodic, reasonable pitch. 'If you don't think we should have a lawyer here, then I don't think we should have a headhunter, either.'

Jack looked at Teddy and shrugged. She read the message in his eyes, and reluctantly rose to her feet, making certain that the heel of her shoe drove into Jack's foot as she turned to leave. Jack winced, but she could tell he was inwardly delighted. Teddy sat on a chair outside the conference room, next to the disgruntled lawyer from Herbert Smith. She expected she'd hear something of the meeting anyway.

'I shall be brief,' Jack promised. 'We have reason to believe that the trade that occurred between Steinberg Roth and Hayes Goldsmith on the sixteenth of this month, the trade which purportedly was booked shortly before the withdrawal of the pound from the ERM, never occurred. As you all are aware, it was this trade that resulted in a ruinous loss for my own bank, and a sizeable profit for Steinberg's. Furthermore, it was the news of this apparent loss that caused the collapse of the Hayes stock price.'

The room was eerily silent. After a few moments, which seemed like an age, Alex Fitzgerald began a slow handclap.

'Nice try, Delavigne. Nice try. What is this, one last heroic gesture to save your neck? Well, it won't wash.'

Jack ignored him, speaking only to John Hirsch. 'I believe that the trader who did the trade at seven forty-three on the evening of Wednesday the sixteenth, well after Norman Lamont's announcement, agreed with one of my own traders, who used to work at this firm, to book the trade at three fifty-three, at the prices then prevailing. I believe that he was instructed to do so by senior management at this firm.'

'Shit. He's talking through his ass! I know who did that trade. It was Miccinelli. Miccinelli doesn't take instructions from anybody but me.'

'Alex, did you instruct him to enter a false trade?' Jack addressed the question directly, waiting for the denial.

'Of course I didn't!' Fitz's lie rang across the room, and could be heard clearly in the corridor outside.

'I have in my briefcase a statement by Miccinelli confirming that these allegations are true.' Jack looked at John Hirsch. 'We have sufficient information to prove it.'

'If Miccinelli has signed anything, it's because this schmuck has bribed him. You're sick, Delavigne. We don't need to hear any of this crap.' Fitzgerald stretched out in his chair so that he was almost lying prone, his arms folded across his chest, his mouth set in a disdainful sneer.

'I'm not sure that I see what you're getting at, Delavigne. If you knew that these two traders had set up a fraud, why didn't you just call the police and have them picked up? Where the hell are they now?' John Hirsch spoke gruffly.

'To the best of my knowledge, Michael Miccinelli is on

the seventh floor of this building trading his book. Glory McWhirter has been temporarily suspended from Hayes, pending our investigations, and is staying at the Mark Hotel in New York.' He looked down at his notes. 'Room number 112.'

John Hirsch looked steadily at Jack, and slowly shook his head. 'I get the feeling I'm missing something here.'

'If Miccinelli and McWhirter had conspired to perpetrate this fraud, where would the money have gone?'

'I guess into an account they had opened.'

'And where did it go?' Jack's finger stabbed at appendix eight, which showed a record of Steinberg Roth's last twelve months' proprietary trading record. 'If Miccinelli had been trying to hive off some of the funds for himself, where would Miccinelli be now? I doubt he'd be sitting at his desk trading your book.'

Fitzgerald laughed heartily.

Even muffled by the thick doors of the room, Teddy could hear how artificial his laugh was, and cursed the fact that she was left sitting outside like a turkey. She had a sudden inspiration, picked up the telephone, and dialled Mike's extension.

'Mike, this is Teddy.'

'Where are you?'

'Downstairs on the third floor.'

'What the hell are you doing there?'

'Never mind about that. I wanted to suggest that you took an early lunch break.'

'Teddy, it's only eleven o'clock!'

'Just do it, Mike. Go to lunch. Now.' She hung up.

'Miccinelli works for me. I know him. I know he wouldn't do something like this. I know my guys. They're handpicked, every one. He works for *me*, I tell you!'

'He certainly does, Alex. And you're loyal to your staff, aren't you?' Jack mused, and drew another piece of paper from his briefcase. 'You like them foaming at the mouth, I believe?'

'Let's get Miccinelli down here!' Alex jumped to his feet. 'Let the bastard speak for himself! If he did this, John, I swear I'll pull his balls off myself,' Jack watched Fitzgerald's display of bravado with something close to admiration.

'Sit down, Fitzgerald,' Hirsch ordered. 'You seem to be keeping a couple of things rather close to your chest, Delavigne. D'you think you could let me have a look?'

Jack passed the copy of Mike's statement down to John Hirsch. Alex Fitzgerald stood up, sat down, and half stood up again before a look from Hirsch put him back in his place.

'I'm telling you, John, I know this guy. I used to work for him, for fuck's sake. He doesn't play straight. You can't trust him. He's just trying to save his own neck. He'll pull anything he can to fuckin' do me down. You've gotta believe me, John, I didn't know anything about this, if anyone's behind it, it's some scam of Delavigne's – '

'Shut up, Fitzgerald. Shut up or get out.' Hirsch's voice was icily cold. He didn't look at his colleague as he read and reread Miccinelli's statement.

'Do you have anything else concerning this matter, Delavigne?' His expression was impenetrable. Belton-Smith fiddled with his watch nervously.

'Yes, I do. I took the liberty of finding out a little about the options position in Hayes stock that Steinberg's is running from the proprietary desk. I also have some evidence that Steinberg's were involved in the placement of Glory McWhirter at Hayes. I also have some information which points towards insider trading on the part of members of Steinberg Roth, but I have no intention of pursuing that.'

Hirsch laid his hands flat on the desk. 'Gentlemen, I find myself in an extraordinary position. I came in here this morning expecting to reach a decision about the terms for the acquisition of Hayes Goldsmith. I saw it as something of a rescue mission of an old and respected London firm. A lucrative one, I admit, but a rescue mission none the less. Now I find my own firm in jeopardy. Certain things that I have heard – and seen – this morning make that decision almost impossible to take. However, a decision must be taken, and taken quickly. I would like to speak to Mr Delavigne alone, but I suggest that we reconvene here,' he glanced at his watch, 'in precisely thirty minutes. When I say reconvene, I mean *all* of us,' he looked hard at Fitzgerald, 'and bring Carruthers back with you.' He sighed heavily. 'All right, Mr Delavigne, let's you and me make a deal.'

Teddy had been waiting for an explosion. She was taken aback to see Alex Fitzgerald emerge first from the room, and storm down the corridor. He looked like he was heading back to the trading floor. Shortly behind him came a stream of Steinberg executives, shaking their heads and speaking in hushed voices. Richard Belton-Smith was bringing up the rear, a huge, beatific smile spreading over his face.

'Teddy, my dear, let me take you round the corner for a swift celebratory drink. We have to be back here in half an hour, so get your skates on.'

'What on earth happened?'

'I'll tell you when we're sitting comfortably.'

'Where are Jack and John Hirsch?'

'They're cutting a deal.'

Richard Belton-Smith began to laugh, and the sound of his laughter filled the corridor.

In the privacy of the conference room, Jack Delavigne told John Hirsch the entire story. He omitted nothing. He explained Candida's involvement, although he did not discuss her motivation. He explained about Fitzgerald's personal investment alongside the option contract he had bought in Steinberg's name. He explained how Fitzgerald had led Mike to believe he would be made partner, and dashed his hopes at the last minute. He explained about the five million pounds, and the million pound advance Glory had received. He explained about the tapes – that there were no calls recorded to or from Steinberg Roth between three-fifty and four p.m. on the sixteenth, although there was an ambiguous tape on which Glory appeared to acknowledge a four o'clock trade. John Hirsch listened silently until Jack had finished.

'What do you want to do about it, Jack?'

'I want it to stay between us. I don't want any official investigation. I want to proceed with the acquisition as if nothing had happened, but I want the price to reflect the real value of Hayes Goldsmith. I also want it to be described as a merger. Let's say we fix the price at a five per cent premium to the shares on the fifteenth of September. That would be a price of 4.18 per share. Let's round it up to 4.20.'

'No deal. Even without the fraud, you would still have taken a bath on your legitimate sterling position, and the shares would still have been hit by the downgrading of the financial sector following Black Wednesday. No. My best offer would be 3.51. That's dead in the middle between our offer this morning and your price.'

Jack smiled to himself. Even in a state of major shock, John Hirsch was tough enough to keep negotiating.

'Well, there is another factor, John. Call it the goodwill factor. You see, I had an interesting talk with a lawyer of my acquaintance. An American lawyer. We just knocked a couple of ideas back and forth, you know, on a "what if" basis . . . I told him a story about a friend of mine who worked for a bank, and this sort of thing had happened to him. The lawyer liked the story. He said the interesting thing about this sort of case in the US is not the damages you can claim from the individual, but the punitive damages he would be able to claim from the firm. Of course, he's the kind of guy who doesn't really like the big Wall Street houses – he has a chip on his shoulder about something – but he was talking in the region of a quarter's earnings in punitive damages.' Jack picked up the memorandum and flipped to Appendix nine. 'Now let me see . . . on the basis of Steinberg's 1991 earnings . . . that's 798 million dollars, so let's call it 800 million dollars, that would mean average quarterly earnings of about 200 million dollars that Hayes could arguably claim from Steinberg's . . .'

'4.20 per share sounds good to me.'

'Good. I'm glad you agree. Now, as to the other details. As far as the staff of Hayes are concerned, those who want to stay, stay; those who want to go, go. If offices are closed, every member of staff is given the opportunity to relocate.'

'Agreed.'

'For a variety of reasons that I don't want to go into, I would like Miccinelli to retain his position, with an unblemished record.'

John scowled. 'I don't like hiring guys I can't trust.'

'I don't like firing guys who aren't to blame. You won't have any trouble from him in the future, I'm confident of that.'

'Okay. Done.'

'Candida Redmayne and her company are in no way implicated in any of this. You are the only person, other than Teddy Winnington and myself, and of course, Fitzgerald, who knows the extent to which Ms Redmayne was involved. I want it to stay that way.'

'I've got no problem with that.'

'Fine. I don't really have anything else that the lawyers can't sort out.'

'What about you, Delavigne? What are you going to do?'

'I don't know, John. I really haven't considered the options.'

'I'd like you to think about joining us here. As a partner. You could still run Hayes, and a lot else besides.'

'I don't know, John. I don't know that I would want to be in partnership with Alex Fitzgerald.'

'Tell me what you're saying, Jack. Spell it out.'

'Fitzgerald goes. He goes in a way that he'll never work again.'

'He doesn't work for this firm as of now. And I have ways of being sure he won't work for any other. I'll get rid of him, all right. Leave it to me. But I'd like to have you on our team, Jack.'

Jack patted a burly shoulder. 'I'll think about it. I appreciate the offer, but I have some other things to sort out before I make any decisions about the future. I need to consult a professional.' He stood up and stretched. 'I think I could use a drink.'

'Brandy okay for you?'

'Absolutely.'

The two men clinked glasses, and drank a silent toast. As the rest of the team filed into the board room, they found Jack Delavigne and John Hirsch talking about the US presidential elections as if they had bumped into each other at a cocktail party.

No one was going to prison. No one was going to be out of pocket. No one would see Alex Fitzgerald's face when he was unceremoniously told to pack his bags. No one would question the generous premium that Steinberg's were about to pay for their stake in Hayes Goldsmith. No one was ever going to know the whole story. It was the way things were done in the City, quietly and courteously and discreetly. It was a gentleman's agreement, within an ungentlemanly world.

CHAPTER TWENTY

Teddy was still sulking when they left Steinberg's offices. She was annoyed that Jack had not stood up for her right to stay in and attend the meeting, but she was point blank furious that he was being so smug about it.

'I told you from the start that it was out of the question that you should sit in on the meeting. I relented, I allowed you to come, and then the decision was taken out of my hands.'

'Liar. Bastard. The only reason you got rid of that lawyer was to get rid of me!'

'How can you suspect me of such duplicity?'

'Very easily,' Teddy grumbled. 'So where are you taking me for lunch?'

'*I'm* not taking you anywhere. Richard's going to take you to one of his favourite haunts, and has promised me to make sure that he delivers you home safely whilst you can still stand on your own legs.' They both eyed Richard Belton-Smith dubiously. He had only had two brandies, but they seemed to have gone to his head. He was trying extremely hard not to step on the cracks in the pavement. He sensed them looking at him strangely, and stopped.

'I do it for luck, old chap. You know, if I don't step on a single line for the whole day, something good will happen. Lloyds will announce record profits; Steinberg's will buy me out at a huge price.' He resumed the strange stepping. 'I've been doing it since you called me last Thursday.'

Jack hailed a taxi, and hustled Teddy and Richard into it. Teddy leant out the window.

'Where are you going, Jack?'

'I'm going to ARC.'

'To *ARC*? Oh my God! I have to come with you! I didn't even call in this morning!'

'I'll make your excuses. Go and have a nice, long lunch. I'll see you later.'

'When? Where?' The taxi began to pull away, heading for the West End.

'Heathrow. Terminal Four. Six o'clock sharp. At the BA desk for passengers without baggage.'

Jack stepped up to the receptionist at ARC's offices.

'My name's Jack Delavigne. I'd like to see Candida Redmayne, please.'

Julie fluttered a little. She knew who Jack was, of course. She hadn't expected him to be so good looking. She also hadn't expected him to walk bold as brass into Candida's offices without so much as calling for an appointment; Candida rarely saw anyone without one. She tapped on Candida's door nervously, and popped her head round. 'Candida. There's someone to see you,' she whispered.

Candida was sitting at her desk. She was working on the computer and looked irritated by the interruption. 'I don't have any appointments scheduled, Julie. Make an appointment for them to see Jamie or Teddy tomorrow, or me if they absolutely insist.'

'Candida, it's – '

'I don't care if it's God Almighty! I'm busy.'

Jack pushed past Julie, and stepped into Candida's office. 'Candida. It's Jack,' he said quietly, and closed the door behind him.

Candida leant back in her chair and continued to look at the computer screen. She leant forward and switched it off before she turned to look at him. She had waited a long time for this moment. 'You'd better sit down, Jack. Would you like anything to drink?'

'No, thank you.'

She walked across the room and sat down opposite him, in the chair she always used when conducting her interviews, with her hands in her lap.

'Is there a reason for this visit, Jack, or is it just a social call, after all these years?'

'There's a reason for it. There are some things I have to tell you.'

Candida seemed frozen. She stared at him without blinking, her eyes so pale that they were like transparent glass. Not a strand of hair moved. She looked like a beautiful, waxen image, pale, finely chiselled and utterly lifeless.

'I simply wanted to tell you that Steinberg Roth will be merging with Hayes Goldsmith. We agreed a price this morning. I don't think it is quite what you expected, but I want you to know that no harm is going to come to you.' He waited for her to react. Nothing. 'I don't think that Alex Fitzgerald will be continuing to work for Steinberg's. I don't know if that interests you.' He was talking to a stone wall. 'Look, Candida. I know what you did. What you tried to do. It doesn't matter. It's all over. Can't we just let it be finished?'

Not a word. Not a flicker of an eyelash. She confirmed and denied nothing.

'I'm going away for a little while. I don't know when I'll be back or what I'll be doing. I also have a message for you, from Teddy. She's going to come with me. For a holiday at least. She won't be in the office for a while.' No response. 'I think I'm in love with her.'

Candida blinked slowly, but said nothing.

'Look, I'd better get going. I have a plane to catch. I think you should sell your Hayes put options. They're still worth something today, but they won't be tomorrow. I hope you'll be all right. I'm sorry that you can't talk to me. I'm sorry we can't be friends. I'm so damn sorry about everything.'

'Are you sorry you married me, Jack?' Her voice was calm and clear, almost bell-like. She spoke as if she were in a trance, without any discernible emotion.

He put his head in his hands. 'Yes. Yes, I am sorry. You were never happy, were you, Candida?'

'No, not really. Will you marry Teddy?'

'I don't know. I really don't. Right now, I don't know if I'll ask her, and I have absolutely no idea what she would say if I did.'

'Are you sorry we had Tommy?'

'No. No, I'll never be sorry about that. I'll never forget him, and never stop missing him. Never. I'll never stop thinking about him, about what he'd be like now, and I'll never stop wanting him.'

'No, I suppose you won't,' Candida said in a deadpan voice. 'I never wanted him. I never wanted to have him.'

'I know.' Jack couldn't bear it any longer. He couldn't talk to this woman about his child. She wasn't the woman who had given birth to Tommy, or laughed with him, or loved him, or been demented with grief at his death. This was somebody else, somebody he pitied with all his heart, but couldn't reach.

'I killed him, you know.' Her eyes were dull with misery.

'No you didn't, Candida. He drowned. It was an accident.'

'No. I killed him, because there were times when I wished he hadn't been born. There were times when I wished he was dead.'

'You didn't kill him. You didn't wish him dead. You wanted him, and you wanted your own life. You just wanted your life back, and somehow, when he died, you confused that with Tommy's life. You didn't kill him.'

He stood up to leave. 'Candida, I brought you something as well.' He laid a small parcel gently in her lap, and left.

Candida held the little package, wrapped in brown paper, loosely in her hands for five minutes without moving. Then she unwrapped it. She looked at the small, silver-framed photograph. It was old and worn, was in black and white, and was heavily creased from when she had crumpled it and thrown it in the bin. It even had a badly repaired tear across one corner. But the frame shone brightly.

Candida didn't make a sound, but tears began to flow down her cheeks.

Jack stood at the British Airways desk shifting his weight nervously from one foot to the other. It was six o'clock. He had no idea if Teddy would come. She might have thought he was joking; she might even have gone to see Mike. At six fifteen, he checked in. At six thirty, he called her at home. The sound of her voice, even mechanised, thrilled him.

'This is Teddy. I can't take your call at the moment, but I'll be back shortly, so please leave a message.'

She hadn't changed the message. He didn't leave one.

He paced back to the desk and spoke to the clerk. 'I'm meant to be travelling with a friend. She hasn't arrived yet. She won't have any baggage. There should be time. They've called the flight for boarding, so I'm going through to the gate. Will you hold the ticket for her?'

'Certainly, sir. If you have her passport you can even check her in.'

'I don't have her passport, Goddamn it! I don't know anything about her!'

The female clerk didn't bat an eyelid. She spent her life dealing with bullies and lunatics. 'Would you happen to know what your friend looks like? Then I might be able to recognise her if she arrives late.'

'She's very pretty. Small. Well, not that small. So high.'

He indicated wildly between his waist and his shoulder.

'Is she blonde? Dark? Redhead?'

'God, I don't know! Sort of light brownish. With red bits. And fair bits.'

'Shall we say, ash-blonde? Chestnut, perhaps?'

'Yes, yes. Whatever you like. And green eyes. Big ones.'

'Fine. Would you like to give me the ticket, sir?'

Jack waited at the gate until seven fifteen, and was then shepherded on to the plane much against his will. He sank, heavy-hearted, into the soft leather seat of the first class cabin, and ordered a whisky and soda. She wasn't coming. He knew she wasn't coming, because he no longer believed in fairy tales and he didn't believe in happy endings. And she wasn't coming because she didn't like being told what to do. And she wasn't coming because she was going to miss the bloody flight.

Teddy sat down next to Jack.

'You said Terminal Three, you idiot. I've been waiting over there driving BA crazy. I couldn't even tell them what flight it was, or where we were going. It was sheer brilliance that I got here at all. I finally called your secretary. She gave me a flight number, and they told me I was in the wrong terminal.'

'I told you Terminal Four.'

'You did not.' She finished the remains of his whisky. 'Where are we going, anyway?'

'You don't know?'

'Nope. I just ran for a gate number.'

'Well, you'll just have to wait and see.'

'Fine. I honestly couldn't care less. I just wish they'd serve dinner. I'm famished.'

Teddy leant her head back into the soft chair, closed her

eyes and in minutes was breathing softly and steadily. The noise of the engines firing up failed to disturb her slumber. Jack smoothed her hair and buckled her seat belt. She murmured slightly, and her head fell to one side, resting against his shoulder.

'Teddy? Teddy?' Jack nudged her to no affect. She was dead to the world.

The well-modulated tones of the chief steward's voice came over the intercom: 'Good evening, ladies and gentlemen. On behalf of Captain Rogers and the crew I would like to welcome you aboard British Airways flight 190. Our departure from London has been a little delayed, as we had to wait for a couple of passengers, but we should be able to make up any lost time during our flight this evening. We expect to arrive on time in Bangkok at around ten twenty-five tomorrow morning, and for those of you continuing to Jakarta, you should reach your final destination at fourteen thirty-five. We will be cruising at an altitude of thirty-six thousand feet. When we have reached our desired altitude, we will switch off the seat belt signs and you will be free to move around the cabin. We hope you will have a pleasant flight, and thank you for selecting British Airways . . .'

'Teddy,' Jack whispered, although he knew she was sleeping, 'I love you.'

Teddy smiled. 'I know you do, Jack.'

Epilogue

'Teddy, open your mouth.'

'No, I don't trust you. You'll put something horrible in it.'

'Trust me.'

Teddy opened her mouth, without opening her eyes, and Jack popped in a piece of papaya sprinkled with lime juice. They were lying by the pool of their private thatched bungalow, too lazy to stroll the fifty yards to the larger, hotel pool, and far too lazy to walk the hundred yards to the private beach. In the three days since they had arrived in Bali, they had done little but talk, sleep and make love. Jack had made a couple of calls to London, just to be sure that the acquisition was going through smoothly, but other than that, nothing disturbed them. Teddy had quietly told Jack about her lunch with Philip Redmayne. They had talked a little about Candida, a little about Tommy, a little about Mike. They had a long time ahead of them to talk, and were in no hurry.

'How does it make you feel about . . . things?' Teddy sat up on the lounger, and busied herself with retying the string of her bikini. She put on her sunglasses, and picked up a bottle of suntan lotion.

'How does it make me feel about *things* . . . ? That's uncharacteristically vague for you, Theodora. Well, I feel pretty much at peace with *things* . . . and how do you feel? How do you feel about marriage, for example?" He leant forward and removed her sunglasses.

'I think it's a pretty scary thought. I think that I don't

really trust my judgement any more, and that I don't know if I believe in happy ever after. It seems so random, Jack. Two people get married, thinking they love each other, maybe even knowing they love each other, expecting to be happy, expecting they will always feel the same way, and what happens. Kapow! Everything changes. Something happens, some tiny little thing, and everything changes, and suddenly you're not happy, and you don't love him, and you don't feel like you even *know* him, and you start thinking that maybe you never loved him, maybe it was all just a bloody big mistake . . .' She shuddered. 'I don't know that I've got a very good track record in picking men. I have to say – I mean, I have to tell *you*, Jack – that much as I would like to deny it, there was a time when I really did believe that I loved Mike, and there was a time when I – this makes me so embarrassed – really did think I loved Christian. And I was wrong. So I don't know how anyone's meant to make this sort of decision with absolute certainty.'

'No one can. No one does. Teddy, my darling,' he held her hands in his own, 'I can't promise you anything with certainty. There's no guarantee that we will be happy together. I don't think marriage is about finding your one and only perfect love. I think marriage is like a rope around the waists of two people – '

'So long as it's not around their necks – '

'And that rope bears an awful lot of strain, and sometimes one end comes loose, and sometimes both ends, and sometimes it frays in the middle. The thing is, you have to look after the rope, and rebind it, and repair its vulnerable places. It's not a very romantic idea, but that's what I feel about . . . *things*.'

'So that's the best you can offer, Jack? That's it? No romance, no roses, no dinner, no music? Just an old, fraying rope?'

'Let's just hope it gets old, Teddy. At this stage, it's rather new, but very strong.'

'Hmm.' She looked unconvinced. 'No moonlight? No candlelight, even? No sunset? No dancing? No waltzes?'

He pulled her on to his lap, cradling her.

'No kisses? No passion? No tears? No bended knee? No champagne? No chocolate-covered cherries? Just a bit of papaya and an old rope? You don't really leave me much choice, Jack Delavigne. This isn't quite what I had always dreamt of . . . I mean, if you'd just let me have one little speck of romance, maybe just the moonlight! This is more like one of those game shows – you know, take the money or open the box.' She looked deep into his grey eyes. 'Well, I guess I'm going to have to open the box.'

It was midday, but as Jack kissed her, he could have sworn he smelt the moon in her hair.